The Bay At Midnight

DIANE CHAMBERLAIN

The Bay At Midnight

MIRA®

ISBN 0-7783-2146-0

THE BAY AT MIDNIGHT

www.MIRABooks.com

Printed in U.S.A.

First Printing: February 2005
10 9 8 7 6 5 4 3 2 1

ACKNOWLEDGMENTS

Do you miss some special place from your childhood and wish you could return there for a while? When I was a child, my family had a summer bungalow on the Intracoastal Waterway, also known as the Point Pleasant canal, in New Jersey. I miss those childhood summers in Bay Head Shores, so I decided to revisit the area by setting a story there—although the setting is the only autobiographical aspect of *The Bay at Midnight*. My family's easy life at the Jersey Shore was never marred by the sort of drama and mystery that befalls the Bauer family in this story.

Many people helped me add a dose of reality to this fictional world. I drew upon the memories of my siblings, Tom Lopresti, Joann Scanlon and Robert Lopresti, as well as those of my childhood fishing-and-hayride buddy, former Bay Head Shores resident Rick Neese. Lieutenant Robert J. Dikun of the Point Pleasant Beach Police Department was an invaluable source of information as I explored the aftermath of Isabel's murder. Rodney Cash gave me insight into the 1962 world of the Lewises, the African-American family who fished on the opposite side of the canal—and a world away—from the Bauer family. My ex-college roommate and Westfield native, Jody Pfeiffer, helped me with the details of her hometown. Ahrre Moros gave me information about the Coffee with Conscience concerts. I am also grateful to fellow writers Emilie Richards and Patricia McLinn, my online friends at ASA, and John Pagliuca for their various contributions and emotional support. Special thanks go to the staff at Happy Tails who provided hours of quality care for my energetic pup, Keeper, as I raced toward deadline!

Thanks to everyone at MIRA Books, where I am always encouraged to write whatever is in my heart. I am grateful to Amy Moore-Benson, the editor with whom I started *The Bay at Midnight,* and to Miranda Stecyk, who picked up where Amy left off with the same intelligence, grace and passion as her predecessor.

A special thank-you to my former agent, Virginia Barber, along with my best wishes for a glorious and fulfilling retirement!

In memory of my grandparents,
Thomas and Susan Chamberlain,
For giving us so many memorable summers
down the shore.

CHAPTER 1

Julie

All children make mistakes. Most of those errors in judgment are easily forgotten, but some of them are too enormous, too devastating to ever fully disappear from memory. The mistake I made when I was twelve still haunted me at fifty-three. Most of the time, I didn't think about it, but there were days when something happened that brought it all back to me in a rush, that filled me with the guilt of a twelve-year-old who had known better and that made me wish I could return to the summer of 1962 and live it over again. The Monday Abby Chapman Worley showed up at my front door was one of those days.

I was having a productive day as I worked on *The Broad Street Murders,* the thirty-third novel in my Granny Fran series. If I had known how successful that series would become, I would have made Fran Gallagher younger at the start. She was already seventy in the first book. Now, thirteen years later, she was eighty-three and going strong, but I wondered how long I could keep her tracking down killers.

The house was blissfully quiet. My daughter Shannon, who'd

graduated from Westfield High School the Saturday before, was giving cello lessons in a music store downtown. The June air outside my sunroom window was clear and still, and because my house was set on a curve in the road, I had an expansive view of my New Jersey neighborhood with its vibrant green lawns and manicured gardens. I would type a sentence or two, then stare out the window, enjoying the scenery as I thought about what might happen next in my story.

I'd finished Chapter Three and was just beginning Chapter Four when my doorbell rang. I leaned back in my chair, trying to decide whether to answer it or not. It was probably a friend of Shannon's, but what if it was a courier, delivering a contract or something else that might require my signature?

I peered out the front window. No trucks in sight. A white Volkswagen Beetle—a convertible with its top down—was parked in front of my house, however, and since my concentration was already broken, I decided I might as well see who it was.

I walked through the living room and opened the door and my heart sank a little. The slender young woman standing on the other side of my screen door looked too old to be a friend of Shannon's, and I worried that she might be one of my fans. Although I tried to protect my identity as much as possible, some of my most determined readers had found me over the years. I adored them and was grateful for their loyalty to my books, but I also treasured my privacy, especially when I was deep into my work.

"Yes?" I smiled.

The woman's sunny-blond hair was cut short, barely brushing the tops of her ears and she was wearing very dark sunglasses that made it difficult to see her eyes. There was a pretty sophistication about her. Her shorts were clean and creased, her mauve T-shirt tucked in with a belt. A small navy-blue pocketbook was slung over one shoulder.

"Mrs. Bauer?" she asked, confirming my suspicion. Julianne Bauer, my maiden name, was also my pseudonym. Friends and neighbors knew me as Julie Sellers.

"Yes?" I said.

"I'm sorry to just show up like this." She slipped her hands into her pockets. "My name is Abby Worley. You and my father—Ethan Chapman—were friends when you were kids."

My hand flew to my mouth. I hadn't heard Ethan's name since the summer of 1962—forty-one years earlier—yet it took me less than a second to place him. In my memory, I was transported back to Bay Head Shores, where my family's bungalow stood next to the Chapmans' and where the life-altering events of that summer erased all the good summers that had preceded it.

"You remember him?" Abby Worley asked.

"Yes, of course," I said. I pictured Ethan the way he was when I last saw him—a skinny, freckled, bespectacled twelve-year-old, a fragile-looking boy with red hair and pale legs. I saw him reeling in a giant blowfish from the canal behind our houses, then rubbing the fish's white belly to make it puff up. I saw him jumping off the bulkhead, wings made from old sheets attached to his arms as he attempted to fly. We had at one time been friends, but not in 1962. The last time I saw him, I beat him up.

"I hope you'll forgive me for just showing up like this," she said. "Dad once told me you lived in Westfield, so I asked around. The bagel store. The guy at the video-rental place. Your neighbors are not very good at guarding your privacy. And this is the sort of the thing I didn't want to write in a letter or talk about on the phone."

"What sort of thing?" I asked. The serious tone of her voice told me this was more than a visit from a fan.

She glanced toward the wicker rockers on my broad front porch.

"Could we sit down?" she asked.

"Of course," I said, pushing open the screen door and walking with her toward the rockers. "Can I get you something to drink?"

"No, I'm fine," she said, as she settled into one of the chairs. "This is nice, having a front porch."

I nodded. "Once the mosquitoes are here in full force, we don't get much use out of it, but yes, it's nice right now." I studied her, looking for some trace of Ethan in her face. Her cheekbones were high and her deep tan looked stunning on her, regardless of the health implications. Maybe it was fake. She looked like the type of woman who took good care of herself. It was hard for me to picture Ethan as her father. He hadn't been homely, but nerdishness had invaded every cell of his body.

"So," I said, "what is it that you didn't want to talk about over the phone?"

Now that we were in the shade, she slipped off her sunglasses to reveal blue eyes. "Do you remember my uncle Ned?" she asked.

I remembered Ethan's brother even better than I remembered Ethan. I'd had a crush on him, although he'd been six years older than me and quite out of my league. By the end of that summer, though, I'd despised him.

I nodded. "Sure," I said.

"Well, he died a couple of weeks ago."

"Oh, I'm sorry to hear that," I said mechanically. "He must have been—" I did the math in my head "—around fifty-nine?"

"He died the night before his fifty-ninth birthday," Abby said.

"Had he been ill?"

"He had cirrhosis of the liver," Abby said, matter-of-factly. "He drank too much. My father said he...that he started drinking right after the summer your...you know." For the first time, she seemed a little unsure of herself. "Right after your sister died," she said. "He got really depressed. I only knew him as a sad sort of person."

"I'm sorry," I said again. I couldn't picture handsome, athletic Ned Chapman as a beaten-down, fifty-nine-year-old man, but then we'd all changed after that summer.

"Dad doesn't know I've come to see you," Abby said. "And he wouldn't be happy about it, but I just had to."

I leaned forward, wishing she would get to the point. "Why are you here, Abby?" I asked.

She nodded as if readying herself to say something she'd rehearsed. "Dad and I cleaned out Uncle Ned's town house," she said. "I was going through his kitchen and I found an envelope in one of the drawers addressed to the Point Pleasant Police Department. Dad opened it and..." She reached into her pocketbook and handed me a sheet of paper. "This is just a copy."

I looked down at the short, typed missive, dated two months earlier.

To Whom it May Concern:

I have information about a murder that occurred in your juris-diction in 1962. The wrong person paid for that crime. I'm ter-minally ill and want to set the record straight. I can be contacted at the above phone number.

Sincerely, Ned Chapman

"My God." I leaned against the back of the rocker and closed my eyes. I thought my head might explode with the meaning behind the words. "He was going to confess," I said.

"We don't know that," Abby said quickly. "I mean, Dad is abso-lutely sure Uncle Ned didn't do it. I mean, he is *completely* sure. But he'd told me about you long ago. My mom and I have read all your books, and so of course he told me everything about you. He said how you suspected that Uncle Ned did it, even though no one else did, so I thought you had a right to know about the letter. I told Dad we should take it to the police. I mean, it sounds like the guy who was sent to prison might not have done it."

"Absolutely," I agreed, holding the letter in the air. "The police need to see this."

Abby bit her lip. "The only thing is, Dad doesn't want to take it to them. He said that the man who was convicted died in prison, so it doesn't really matter now."

I felt tears spring to my eyes. I knew that George Lewis had died of pneumonia five years into serving his life sentence for my sister's murder. I'd always believed that he'd been wrongly imprisoned. How cruel and unfair.

"At the very least, his name should be cleared," I said firmly.

"I think so, too," Abby agreed. "But Dad is afraid that the police will jump to the conclusion that Uncle Ned did it, just like you did. My uncle was screwed up, but he could never hurt anyone."

I pulled a tissue from my shorts' pocket and removed my glasses to blot the tears from my eyes. "Maybe he *did* hurt someone," I sug-gested gently, slipping my glasses on again. "And maybe *that's* what screwed him up."

Abby shook her head. "I know it looks that way, but Dad said Ned had an airtight alibi. That he was home when your sis—when it happened."

"It sounds like your father wants to protect his brother no matter what," I said, trying not to sound as bitter as I felt. "If your father won't take this to the police," I said, "I will." I didn't mean it to sound like a threat, but it probably did.

"I understand," Abby said. "And I agree the police need to know. But Dad..." She shook her head. "Would you consider talking to him?" she asked.

I thought of how unwelcome that conversation would be to Ethan. "It doesn't sound like he wants to talk about it," I said. "And you said he'd be angry that you came here."

"He won't be angry," Abby said. "He never really gets angry. He'll just be...upset. I'll tell him I came. But then, if you could call him, maybe you could persuade him. You have the biggest personal stake in this."

She didn't understand how the thought of revisiting the summer of 1962 made my palms sweat and my stomach burn. I thought about George Lewis's sister, Wanda, and the personal stake *she* would have in this. I thought about his cousin Salena, the woman who'd raised him. Nothing would return my sister to her family or George Lewis to his, but at the very least, we all deserved to know the truth. "Give me his number," I said.

She took the letter from me, wrote Ethan's number on a corner of it and handed it back. Slipping her sunglasses on again, she stood up.

"Thank you," she said, returning her pen to her tiny pocketbook. She looked at me. "I hope...well, I don't know what to hope, actually. I guess I just hope the truth finally comes out."

"I hope so, too, Abby," I said.

I watched her walk down the sidewalk and get into the white Beetle convertible. She waved as she pulled away from the curb and I watched her drive up my street, then turn the corner and disappear.

I sat there a long time, perfectly still, the letter and all its horrible implications lying on my lap. Chapter Four was forgotten. My body felt leaden and my heart ached, because I knew that no matter who turned out to have murdered my sister, the responsibility for her death would always rest with me.

CHAPTER 2

Julie

I was still sitting on the porch half an hour later, the letter on my lap, when I was surprised to see Shannon walking toward our house. She was a distance away, but I would have recognized her at a mile. She was five feet nine inches tall with long, thick, nearly black hair. She'd been a presence from the day she was born.

I was worried about her. When Glen and I allowed her to skip the third grade, I'd never thought ahead to how I would feel watching my seventeen-year-old daughter go off to college, moving into a world outside my protection. I liked to have at least the illusion of control over what happened to the people I love. Glen said that's why I wrote fiction: it gave me total control over every single character and every single thing that happened. He was probably right.

But there was more that worried me. Something had changed in Shannon during her senior year. She'd never been shy about her height; she'd had an almost regal carriage, a haughty confidence when she'd jerk her head to toss her hair over her shoulder. Recently, though, she seemed uncomfortable in her own skin. I was certain she'd put on weight. A few nights earlier, I'd found her in her room eating from a bowl of raw cookie dough! I'd lectured her about the possibility of getting salmonella from the raw eggs in the batter, but I'd really wanted to ask her if she had any idea how many calories she was consuming.

I would sometimes catch her staring into space, an empty look in her almond-shaped eyes, and she rarely went out with her friends anymore. She'd had one boyfriend or another—all the artsy, musical types—since she was fourteen, yet I didn't think she'd been on a date for at least six months. Her new homebody behavior made it easier for me to keep an eye on her, but I couldn't help but be concerned by her sudden transformation.

"I just want to end my senior year with a bang," she'd said, when I'd inquired into the change in her social life. "I don't want to be a slacker."

I knew Glen had talked to her about how important it was to keep her grades up during her senior year, in spite of her early acceptance into the Oberlin Conservatory of Music. No problem there. She'd ended her high-school career as senior class president with a 4.2 grade point average, but still, something seemed wrong. I wondered if she was afraid of leaving home. Or maybe she was having a delayed reaction to the divorce. It had been nearly two years and I thought she'd handled it well—aside from the fact that she seemed to blame me for it—but perhaps I'd been kidding myself.

She spotted me as she turned onto the sidewalk leading up to our house.

"Hi!" She waved. She was wearing a white-and-lime-green-print skirt today, the sort of skirt my sister Lucy liked to wear—long and flowing—and I liked the way it looked on her. That was another change: Shannon seemed to have traded in her low-rise pants for this more feminine look.

"What are you doing home?" I called from my seat on the rocker.

"I have some time before the next lesson," she said. "Thought I'd take a break."

We lived in a neighborhood of turn-of-the-century houses near Westfield's downtown. It was an easy walk for her to and from the music store, as well as to the day-care center where she spent two afternoons a week as an aide, caring for the toddlers.

She climbed the porch steps, carrying a can of Vanilla Coke.

"Love that haircut," she said as she settled into the rocker Abby Worley had vacated only a short time before.

I'd had my hair cut to my chin a few days earlier in preparation for a photo shoot for my next book jacket. My hairdresser had added blond highlights to the auburn shade I'd worn for the past decade, and Shannon commented on it every time she saw me. Even my mother had noticed, telling me the cut-and-color looked "sassy." I knew she'd meant it as a compliment.

Shannon leaned forward to get a good look at me, her own hair falling away from her face in a thick dark curtain. "I think you need some new glasses, now," she said.

I touched my rimless frames. "Do I?" I asked. I thought my glasses were stylish, but I was usually three or four years behind the trend.

"You should get some cool plastic frames," she said. "Like in a bronze color."

"I don't think I'm ready to be that cool." I was amazed at my ability to carry on such a mundane conversation when my mind was still reeling from Abby's visit.

Shannon took a long drink from her Coke. "Actually, Mom," she said, "I came home because I need to talk to you about something." She glanced at me. "I'm afraid you're going to be upset."

"Tell me," I said, wanting her to spit it out before my overactive imagination had a chance to fill the silence.

She gnawed at her lower lip. Her dimples showed when she did that. "I've decided to live at Dad's for the summer." Shannon looked at me directly then, waiting for my reaction. I tried not to show any, my gaze intent on the dogwood in our neighbors' front yard.

This is no big deal, I told myself. Glen only lived a few miles away, and it would probably be good for them to have some time together before she went away to college. So why were tears welling up in my eyes for the second time in an hour? *This is the last summer I have with you,* I wanted to say, but I kept my cool.

"Why, honey?" I asked.

"I just…you know. I've lived with you since the divorce, and I know Dad would like it if I…you know…if I stayed there this summer. I'm trying to be fair to everybody," she added, although I saw right through that. Shannon was a good kid, but she was not so noble that she'd put her needs second to someone else's.

"What's the real reason?" I asked her. "Has he been trying to persuade you to move?"

"No." She shook her head in a tired motion. "Nothing like that."

"He works long hours."

She laughed, the sound popping out of her mouth before she could stop it. "Now you get it," she said. She smoothed her hair away from her face, her Italian charm bracelet nearly full of the small rectangular charms, all related to music.

"Get what?" I asked.

"Mom, I'll be *eighteen* in three months," she said, her voice pleading with me to understand. "You still treat me like I'm ten. I have to let you know my every move. Dad treats me like I'm an adult."

So that was it. "Well," I said, "now that you're just about in college, maybe we can change the rules a bit."

"You'd have to totally revamp your rules for them to be tolerable," she said. "You don't let me *breathe*."

"Oh, Shannon, come on," I said. That was always her argument. She said that I smothered her, I gave her no freedom. I *was* overprotective—that much I'd admit to—but I was not her jailer. "You haven't even *asked* to do anything in months, so how can you say I don't let you breathe?"

She rolled her eyes. "There's no point in asking you if I can do anything, because you'll just say no," she said.

"*Shannon.* That's not true and I think you know it."

"When you go on your book tours, you still make me stay with Erika's family even though she and I haven't been friends since we were, like, twelve, just because her parents are even stricter than you and you know I can't get away with anything there. I *hate* that."

"You never asked to stay anywhere else," I said, frowning.

"And you call my cell phone constantly to check up on me," she said. "Do you know—"

"Not to check up on you," I corrected her. "I call you because I care about you. And I *don't* call you 'constantly.'" Our too-frequent arguments often had this flavor. They started off in one direction and then took a circuitous route that left my head spinning. "What is this really all about?" I asked.

She let out an exasperated sigh, as though I was too dense to possibly understand. "Nothing," she said. "It's just that soon I'll be on my own and I think it's time I got some practice, so that's why I think I should live at Dad's for the summer."

"You won't be on your own at Dad's," I countered, although I knew Glen would do all he could to please his only child. He'd greet any potential conflict between Shannon and himself with his usual passivity. I'd had to be the disciplinarian—the bad guy—with our daughter from the start.

I thought about Shannon's graduation ceremony. Glen and his sister and nephew had sat a few rows behind Mom, Lucy and me, and I'd felt as though the three of them were staring at me. I wanted to go up to Glen after the ceremony, throw my arms around him, point to Shannon and say, *Look what we did together!* But there was a wall between us, one that was probably my fault. I was still angry for what he'd done to me and to our marriage. Shannon knew nothing about any of that, and I planned to keep it that way. I would never have harmed her father in her eyes.

"I know I won't actually be on my own," she said. "That's not the point. I'm just going to do it, Mom, okay? I mean, I don't really need your permission, right? To stay with him?"

I couldn't think clearly. "Can we talk about this later?" I asked. I looked down at the letter in my lap and realized I had folded it into smaller and smaller rectangles until it could fit neatly in the palm of my hand.

"What's that?" Shannon pointed to the fat wad of paper.

I unfolded it carefully, still feeling some disbelief that Abby Worley's visit had occurred at all. "I had a visitor," I said.

"Who?"

"The daughter of Ethan Chapman. He lived next door to my family's summer bungalow when I was a kid. He was my age. His older brother, Ned, died recently and Ethan's daughter—her name is Abby—found this letter in his belongings. It was addressed to the police."

I handed the letter to her and watched lines of worry form between her eyebrows as she read it.

"Oh, *Mom*," she said, exasperation in her voice. "Like you really need this."

"I know." It came out as a whisper.

"Ned was Isabel's boyfriend, wasn't he?" She used Isabel's name more easily than anyone else in the family, perhaps because she had never known her. To Shannon, Isabel was the aunt who had died long before she was born. The one we rarely mentioned, even though Shannon looked more like her with every year. The thick dark hair and double rows of black eyelashes, the almond-shaped eyes and deep dimples. Shannon was now seventeen, the same age Isabel had been when she died. She knew what had happened the summer I was twelve and she understood that those events were the reason I held on to her so tightly: I would never let her run wild as Isabel had. Shannon knew it all, but that didn't stop her from resenting my attempts to keep her safe.

"Yes," I said. "Isabel's boyfriend."

"Your hands are shaking."

I looked down at my hands where they rested in my lap and saw that she was right.

"What are you supposed to do with this?" She handed the letter back to me.

"I'm going to talk to Ethan about taking it to the police. And if he won't take it, I'll do it myself."

She let out a long breath. "I suppose you have to," she said. "Have you talked to Lucy about it?"

"Not yet," I said, although I'd been thinking of calling my sister when Shannon had arrived. I needed to talk to someone who understood how I felt.

Shannon stood up. "Well," she said, a bit awkwardly, "I have to get back to the store. I just wanted to tell you...you know, about moving to Dad's. Sorry that my timing sucked, and that it turned into this big, like—" she waved her hands through the air "—this alter-cation or whatever."

I nodded. "When will you go?"

"In a couple of days. Okay?" She was longing for my blessing.

"Okay." What else could I say?

She handed me the empty Coke can. "Would you mind sticking that in recycling, please?" she asked.

I took the can and held it on my lap next to the letter. "Have fun at work," I said.

"Thanks." She bounced down the porch steps with an ease known only to the young.

"Shannon?" I called as she walked down our sidewalk.

"What?" She didn't bother to turn around.

"If you talk to Nana, don't say anything about this to her." It was an unwritten rule in my family never to talk to my mother about the summer of '62.

"I won't," she said, lifting her arm in a wave.

I stood up then, letter and Coke can in my hands, and walked into the house to call my sister.

CHAPTER 3

Lucy

My cell phone rang as I got out of my car in the McDonald's parking lot in Garwood. Seeing on the caller ID display that it was Julie, I answered it. "Hi, sis," had barely left my lips when she launched into the conversation she'd had with Ethan Chapman's daughter. I leaned against the car, listening, trying unsuccessfully to conjure up a cohesive image of Ethan and Ned Chapman. Ned barely existed in my memory, and Ethan was twelve and blurry around the edges. I didn't like his daughter's reason for showing up on Julie's doorstep one bit.

"You know what, Julie?" I said when she'd told me everything.

"What?"

"I grant you, the whole thing is unsettling," I said, "But I think Ethan Chapman's daughter should solve the mystery on her own. Leave you out of it. You don't need this."

"That's what Shannon said."

"I have a very smart niece," I said.

Julie didn't respond.

"What are you thinking?" I reached into my shoulder bag for my sunglasses and slipped them on. Who knew how long I'd be stand-ing out here talking with her? I couldn't walk into McDonald's while having this conversation: Our mother was in there.

"If George Lewis didn't do it," Julie said, "I can't just sit back and let the world think he did."

"Yes, you can," I said, although my zeal for justice was normally, if anything, stronger than Julie's. "Let Ethan's daughter take the let-ter to the police, then. As long as she does it, I don't see why you have to be involved at all." I was surprised at how upset I felt. My creative, sensitive sister was already clinging to the edge with Shan-non—Isabel's double—getting ready to go away to college. I didn't want anything to add to her stress and I was annoyed with Abby Chapman for dragging her into something she really had no need to be part of.

"That's just it," Julie said. "I don't think she'll do anything about it without his okay. I have to talk to him. I'm in a bind."

I could tell she'd already made up her mind. "Okay," I relented. "If you have to, you have to."

A group of kids walked past me, their laughter loud in my ear.

"Where are you?" Julie asked.

"I'm in the McDonald's parking lot."

"Don't tell Mom about this."

"Do you think I'm crazy?" I couldn't believe she thought I needed the warning.

"And I got some other good news today." Julie's voice was tinged with sarcasm.

"What's that?" I asked.

"Shannon wants to live with Glen for the summer."

"Ah," I said. Shannon had spoken with me about that possibility. She always ran things past me before she laid them on Julie. She told me things she wouldn't breathe to another adult. I was the person who'd taken her to get birth control pills when she was fifteen; Julie would kill me if she knew. This year, with Shannon the age Isabel had been when she died, Julie seemed to snap, tightening her grip on her daughter just when she should have been loosening it. So, I'd told Shannon that while it would be hard on her mother to have her live with Glen for the summer, I thought it was a good idea. It might help Julie get used to letting her go.

My lack of surprise at Julie's announcement made her suspicious. "Did you know?" she asked.

"She'd told me she was considering it," I admitted.

There was a brief silence on the line. "I wish you'd told me," she said.

"It wasn't a sure thing, and I thought it should come from her." I felt guilty. "It might be good for both of you, Julie."

Two men in their mid-thirties walked past me in the parking lot, not even glancing in my direction. I was approaching fifty, the age of invisibility for a woman, and I was more fascinated than distressed by the phenomenon. It seemed to have happened overnight. Four or five years ago, even though I'd worn my silver-streaked hair the same way I did now—in a long French braid down my back, with thick, straight bangs over my forehead—I'd still been able to turn heads. My skin was nearly as smooth and clear as it had been then, and I wore the same type of clothes, mainly long crinkly skirts and knit tank tops. Nevertheless, men my age and younger now looked right through me. Maybe I was giving off the scent of decay. I didn't mind. I was taking a long, possibly permanent, break from dating.

"She seems…distant or something," Julie was saying in my ear, and I turned my attention back to the phone call. "She's changing. Have you noticed? I think she's putting on weight and she doesn't go out anymore. I'm worried about her."

Julie was right. Shannon did seem more withdrawn lately, more reserved in our conversations, and she didn't call as often. I hadn't noticed the physical change in her until Saturday, when I saw her walk across the stage to get her diploma. There was a heaviness about her, more in her spirit than her body, but I made light of it to relieve Julie's anxiety. "She's just having a growth spurt," I said. "And as for the social life, you used to worry when she *did* go out. You need to be more careful what you wish for."

Julie sighed. "I know."

We wrapped up the conversation and I slipped my phone into my shoulder bag as I walked across the parking lot and into the restaurant. It was full of kids, Garwood's summer-school students, who were different from the kids I taught at Plainfield High School. Garwood's students were from mostly white, middle-class families, while Plainfield's public school population was ethnically diverse and economically challenged. I taught ESL—English as a Second Language—because I relished being surrounded by all those kids whose varied skin colors and languages were overshadowed by their universal yearning to belong.

I spotted my mother at the opposite end of the restaurant. She was standing next to a table in her red-and-white uniform, holding a couple of trays in her hands, talking with a young woman and her two little kids. So many of my friends my age had to visit their elderly parents in nursing homes. I got a kick out of the fact that I visited mine at McDonald's. Mom was the greeter who always had a smile for everyone, who supervised kids in the play area and who straightened the place up with as much care as she did her own home. She looked smaller to me than she had just a month ago. I used to think she was so tall, but either her spine was contracting, shrinking her, or her height had been an illusion to me. Her hair was white and very pretty. She had it done every week, and it was always soft and natural looking. Her snowy hair was set off by her caramel-colored skin, inherited from her Italian mother. People always thought she'd just returned from a cruise to the Caribbean. Isabel had looked the most like her, but I got her perfect nose and full lips and Julie got her large dark eyes. We were both very lucky to get any part of our mother's beauty at all.

I came up behind her.

"Hey, Mom," I said.

She looked delighted to see me, as I knew she would. She wrapped one arm around my waist.

"This is the daughter I was telling you about," she said to the young woman. "The bohemian one."

I laughed, and the woman smiled blankly. I was certain the twenty-something-year-old woman had no idea what *bohemian* meant, but she smiled nevertheless.

"Your mother said you just got back from Nepal," the woman said, holding a French fry in front of her little son's mouth.

"Uh-huh," I said. "It was a fantastic trip. Have you been?"

"Oh no." The woman nodded at her children. "I haven't been any-where in three years, for obvious reasons."

I hadn't been to Nepal in three years, either, but it was the trip my mother loved to drag out to impress people. To her, it sounded exotic. I wished I could take her there, but although she was remark-ably healthy for eighty-one, I was afraid the altitude and the walking would do her in.

"Do you have a minute to visit?" I asked her.

"Of course!" She excused herself from the young woman, but then noticed a mess left on one of the tables. "You take a seat and I'll join you in a minute," she said.

I bought an iced tea and sat down at a corner table. Mom was find-ing more things to do and chatting with one of her much, much younger co-workers, an Hispanic girl with a delicate tattoo on her wrist that made me want to get one myself. I *did* have a tattoo of a butterfly on my hip—a very foolish mistake made in my twenties when I didn't realize exactly how gravity would affect that part of my body in middle age. For that reason, I'd tried to talk Shannon out of getting the tattoo of a cello on the small of her back, but she'd in-sisted and, I had to admit, it was kind of pretty when she wore her low-rise pants. The tattoo was so artfully done that even Julie only freaked out for about ten seconds when she saw it.

Waiting for Mom, I thought about Julie's call. I couldn't believe that she was going to have to deal with Isabel's death again after all this time. I remembered so little of that summer that it never held the sort of pain for me that it did for my sister. I'd only been eight years old, and the images of our lives at Bay Head Shores came to me in tiny little clips, like those short videos you could make on dig-ital cameras. The picture forming in my mind as I sipped my tea was of Julie catching a huge eel. It wasn't uncommon to catch eels in the canal behind our bungalow, but that one had been particularly enor-mous.

"She reeled it in all by herself," I remembered our grandfather boasting. Julie had been his fishing partner. The two of them would spend hours in our sandy backyard, sitting on the big blue wooden chairs, holding on to their poles and talking, although I had no idea what about. I was usually huddled somewhere in the safety of the house with a book.

Most people probably tossed eels back into the water, but my mother and grandmother thought they were a delicacy. Mom came out of the house and she and Julie killed the eel—I don't recall how; I have mercifully blocked that part of the memory from my mind— and then skinned it. They were standing barefoot on the narrow platform at the bottom of our dock, Julie in a purple bathing suit, my mother in a housedress and apron. Mom held the head of the eel with a rag, while Julie tugged the skin off it like someone slipping a stocking from a leg. I was watching from behind the white picket fence at the end of the dock. I was terrified of falling in, so I never got near the edge of the dock without that fence between me and the water.

I vaguely remember Grandpop and Grandma watching from the side of the dock. There was laughter and chatter, and Ethan Chapman must have been curious because he came over from next door.

"Keen," he said, kneeling in the sand above the platform where Julie and my mother were doing their dirty work. "That is the most gigantic eel I've ever seen." Ethan was very skinny, his knees the widest part of his legs. He was entirely covered with freckles, and his hair looked brown one minute and red the next, depending on how the sun hit it. His glasses were thick.

"Why don't you come over tonight and have some?" my mother said. Then she tossed her head back with laughter at the face Ethan made. She knew the eel she cooked was safe from anyone besides my grandmother and herself.

"I don't want to eat that thing," Ethan said. "Could I have the skin, though?"

Julie had been about to throw the skin into the water, but she looked up at him, the whites of her eyes in sharp contrast to her nut-brown summer tan.

"What for?" she asked.

"It's beautiful," he said, pointing. "Look how shiny it is on the inside. Look at all the colors."

We stared down at the inside-out eel skin. I could see what he meant. The skin had a shimmery mother-of-pearl look to it.

"It's yours," Julie said, tossing the skin up to him.

Ethan reached out with one of his toothpick arms and managed to catch the slithery mess. "And can I have the guts when you clean him?" he asked.

I could see Julie wrinkle her nose. "You're gross," she said.

"Julie," my mother reprimanded her quietly. Then she looked up at Ethan. "Sure you can have them, Ethan," she said. "What will you do with them?"

"Study them," Ethan said, and I understood why Julie was no longer friends with him that summer.

Later, when my mother threw the skinned, gutted and beheaded eel into the frying pan, it still wriggled. I had nightmares about that for several nights in a row. I'd been an extraordinarily fearful child back then. After Isabel died that August, my fears gradually began to slip away. It was illogical; I should have become more fearful once my world had been shattered. But it was as though the worst had happened and I'd survived, and I knew I would be okay no matter what happened after that.

Mom finally came over to my table in the corner and sat down across from me.

"Whew!" She smiled. "Busy place today."

"All the summer-school kids," I said.

Mom was not really with me. Her eyes darted around the small restaurant, looking for customers she knew and tables in need of cleaning. She'd worked there for five years and it was her home away from home.

"That girl," she said, nodding toward the young woman she'd introduced me to earlier, "is pregnant again. Can you believe it? She's going to have three little ones under the age of four." She clucked her tongue. "The choices people make," she said.

"It's her choice, though," I said.

"Well, I'm certain her husband had something to do with it," my mother said. She pulled a napkin from her pocket and wiped at a spot on the table. "I wish you'd go to church with me Sunday," she said. "It's a special occasion."

"What's special about it?" I tried to remember when the holy days were, but drew a blank.

"It's Father Terrell's birthday."

"Ah," I said. That wasn't special enough to get me inside a Catholic church. I'd explored just about every religion possible over the course of my adult life and was probably best described as a Buddhist Quaker. I wanted peace, both inside and outside. But I watched my mother carefully fold up the napkin and put it back in her pocket. She was so cute. So devoted to her job. How could I resist her?

"I'll go," I said.

"Oh, that's wonderful, Lucy!" she said.

I got along fine with my mother, despite my lifestyle choices. I'd never been married, but had lived with three different men, eight years apiece. Eight years seemed to be my limit, for some reason.

Julie's relationship with Mom had always been a little strained, though, in spite of the fact that my sister tried to do everything right. She'd stayed Catholic, gotten married, produced a beautiful grandchild and had an enormously successful career. She was conservative and reliable, the levelheaded daughter who took Mom to her doctor's appointments and helped her with all her paperwork. Still, there was an undeniable awkwardness between my mother and Julie that I doubted would ever go away. Julie thought she still blamed her for Isabel's death. I didn't believe that for a minute, but it was impossible to know if that might be the case, because my mother wasn't the type to talk about her feelings. The topic of Isabel was always off-limits, anyway. Even *I* would have been uncomfortable bringing it up with her. Feelings kept under wraps, though, could be far more destructive than those brought out in the open. I knew that, and I was a brave woman, but I would never have been able to form the right words to speak to my mother about Isabel.

"Listen," my mother said, "I was thinking we need to have a big party before Shannon goes off to college. She'll be away for her birthday on September tenth, so it could be a combination birthday and going-away party."

"That's not for a couple of months, Mom," I said.

"But you know how time slips by," she said. "If we don't start planning it now, it might never happen."

"All right." Sometimes it was better to let my mother run with an idea than to try to stop her. "What are your thoughts?"

"We could have it here."

"At McDonald's?" I tried not to sound too horrified. "Shannon's nearly eighteen. I don't think she'd want to have a party here."

"All right, all right." My mother brushed away my comment as though she'd known it was coming. "How about at home, then?" She meant her house, the house Julie and I had grown up in.

"Good idea," I said.

She started talking about her plans for the party—who we should invite, a theme for the decorations, what sort of food we'd have—and my mind slipped back to the eel.

"Do you remember that huge eel Julie caught?" I asked suddenly.

My mother looked confused, my question so completely out of context. "What are you talking about?" she asked. "What eel? When?"

I realized I'd made a mistake starting the conversation, because I was certain the year of the eel had been 1962.

"Just…when we were kids," I answered. "She caught it in the canal. When you put it in the frying pan, it still moved."

"Oh, they always did," my mother said.

"Why?" I asked.

"Some autonomic nerve thing," she said. "They were dead as doornails. What on earth made you think of that?"

I shrugged. "I don't know," I lied. "It just popped into my head."

My mother looked dreamily into space. "What I wouldn't give for some eel right now," she said.

I leaned back and sipped my soda, feeling pleased all out of proportion to the conversation: I'd said something about the bungalow and survived.

CHAPTER 4

Julie
1962

Until my sister's death the summer I was twelve years old, I'd had a nearly idyllic childhood. The school year was spent in Westfield, a town that offered everything I could possibly need and was an easy bus ride to New York, where my parents often took my sisters and me to the zoo or the history museum or a Broadway play. My parents were smart, well educated and loving, and my overindulgent maternal grandparents, Grandma and Grandpop Foley, lived nearby. Their house was as open to us as our own.

I was a creative child—too creative, some of my teachers said— and loved making up adventures for myself and my friends. I made up stories about things going on in the neighborhood: the old lady on the corner was a witch, I had a boyfriend in another town, I was found abandoned on my parents' doorstep as an infant. I told the kids in my class that wolves had been spotted in Mindowaskin Park, close to our homes. I loved to write plays to put on in our garage and poetry to read to my classmates.

My mother was popular among my friends, because she always took our endeavors very seriously. She'd paint scenery and sew curtains for the "stage" when we put on a play, and she'd go along with the tall tales I told the neighborhood kids, as long as I wasn't scaring any of them too much.

My father was a physician with a busy schedule, but he made time for my sisters and me. Even though he walked with a limp from a World War II injury, he still managed to take us tobogganing or ice-skating or bowling. My world was safe and fun and easy.

Things started getting rocky around the time Isabel turned fifteen. She wanted to hang out with her friends instead of with the family, and she wanted to go to parties my parents didn't approve of. She was nasty to me, suddenly viewing me as a liability rather than an asset. She no longer wanted me around and barely spoke to me if she was with her friends. It was a fairly tame rebellion, in retrospect. My father still seemed to think his eldest daughter could walk on water, while my mother bore the brunt of her defiant behavior. The worst part was that, by the summer Isabel was seventeen, my parents had begun arguing about how to handle her. I had never heard a cross word pass between the two of them before, and their disagreements worried me.

All during the school year, I'd hunger for my grandparents' summer bungalow down the shore on the Point Pleasant Canal. It was in a little beach community called Bay Head Shores, only an hour from Westfield, but it seemed a world away. In 1962, we arrived at the bungalow a few days after school ended, caravanning with my grandparents, who towed our boat behind their black Studebaker. Lucy, my mother and I followed in the Chrysler, and Dad and Isabel brought up the rear in our father's flashy yellow Lark convertible. Everyone pretended that Isabel was riding with Dad in order to get a head start on her tan in the open car, but I knew it was really that she and my mother were in the middle of one of their battles and that having her ride with Dad would be more peaceful for all concerned.

Like me, Lucy, who was eight at the time, was a book lover, but she couldn't read in the car without throwing up, and her propensity to motion sickness also meant she had to sit in the front seat of the Chrysler next to Mom, which was fine with me. I lounged between suitcases and pillows in the back seat, reading Nancy Drew's *The Secret of Red Gate Farm,* which I'd read before. I'd read all the Nancy Drew books and was systematically working my way through them once again. I liked to pretend that I was Nancy Drew myself. A few months earlier, I'd started collecting things I found around my yard or my neighborhood. I'd found a glove in the gutter, a money clip on the sidewalk and—much to my mother's horror—someone's bra, discovered in the woods behind a friend's house. These items I squirreled beneath my bed in case a mystery occurred in the neighborhood and one of my finds might prove to be valuable evidence. I planned to do the same down the shore.

The small bluish-gray, black-shuttered Cape Cod was one of two bungalows at the end of a short, dead-end dirt road. My sisters and I had our shoes off before we'd even stepped out of the cars. Grandpop unlocked the front door, pretending to fumble with the key, chuckling at our impatience. The musty smell of a house closed up for ten months washed over us as we walked into the hallway, and Lucy and I raced from room to room to see that everything was exactly as we'd left it the year before.

The two bedrooms downstairs were used by the adults, while the three of us girls slept in the attic. Izzy and I loved the attic, but it terrified Lucy, who seemed to have gotten all the fear genes in the family. She and Mom had been in a car accident when Lucy was little, and she'd been pulled screaming from my mother's arms in the emergency room and taken away somewhere for the treatment of several broken ribs and a broken leg. Since that day, she'd been afraid of everything. The attic could only be reached by rickety, pull-down steps, and Lucy was always afraid those steps might somehow snap closed while she was up there and she would be trapped. The attic itself was a source of endless fascination for me. It was wide-open, its ceiling the bare wooden underbelly of the roof, and it was filled with enough beds to sleep eight people. The beds were divided by curtains strung on wires across the room, so everyone had a little bit of privacy if they wanted it. During the day, we usually drew the curtains back, though, to allow a breeze through the small windows. The attic could suffocate us with its heat.

Everyone's favorite part of the bungalow—and the reason for its very existence—was the canal that ran behind the house. Our backyard was a broad rectangle of sand shared with the Chapman family next door and sandwiched between their boat dock and ours. Our boat was just a runabout, a tiny, open thing with an outboard motor, but the Chapmans owned a big Boston Whaler fast enough to pull two skiers at once.

Anyone wanting to take the inland route from Barnegat Bay to the Manasquan River and the ocean had to pass through our canal, and some of the boaters were celebrities. My father boasted to everyone that he'd received a wave from Richard Nixon one time, as the then-vice-president's boat cruised past our house. On weekends, the water could be frightening to navigate as the canal filled with boats of all shapes and sizes. The water beneath the little Lovelandtown Bridge, well within sight of our house, grew as choppy as the ocean during a storm, and accidents were not infrequent. We all loved to watch the boats dodge the pilings on a busy weekend afternoon.

When we arrived at the bungalow that summer, though, my father did not care about going into the backyard to watch the boats or climbing down the ladder in our dock to touch the water with his toes, as my mother and I did. Instead, he went directly to the phone. He'd made sure it was already turned on for the summer, because he was on a vendetta. He was outraged by the recent Supreme Court decision forbidding school prayer, and he wanted to call every Catholic person he knew to organize a protest against the court ruling. My father was a recipient of the Purple Heart, a civic leader in our community and a well-respected member of our church, since he wrote a regular column for a Catholic magazine. Still too young to think for myself and having adopted the mores of my parents, I was as outraged as he was about the school prayer ruling. I couldn't imagine starting the school day without the Lord's Prayer. So we all gave my father the time he needed to sit near the wall phone in the living room with his pad of names, making his calls, his voice at times loud with his anger.

All four of the Chapmans were in their backyard when we arrived. My mother and sisters went over to greet them, but I walked outside the chain-link fence and sat down on the bulkhead, my book in my lap and my feet dangling a foot or so above the water. Even though I wasn't looking in his direction, I knew Ethan was probably watching me. I imagined him sitting on one of the chairs, swinging his legs, his flip-flops hanging halfway off his feet. Ethan and I had once been great summertime buddies. We'd ride our bikes to the little Bay Head Shores beach or fish together or climb trees. We'd even sleep over at each other's houses. We'd been born on the same day—March 10, 1950—and we thought that gave us a lifelong bond. But we'd started drifting apart the previous summer, as opposite-sex friends sometimes did as they grew older. It seemed mutual to me, as if we'd both received word at the same time that we should avoid each other. As far as I was concerned, he'd gotten weird. He'd developed a fascination with marine life, dissecting everything he could find—crabs, blowfish, eels, starfish and the tiny shrimp that clung to the bulkhead just below the water's surface. I was glad my mother didn't insist I go over to say hello to him.

We ate dinner—my grandmother's spaghetti and meatballs—on the screened porch that night, as we always did. There was a huge table at one end of the porch which was the hub of all activity in the house—the place for meals, card games and puzzles. After dinner, my sisters and I helped Mom clean up in the kitchen. I felt happy, two months of freedom stretching out in front of me. Lucy didn't feel that freedom, though; she felt fear.

"You'll go up to bed with me at night, won't you, Julie?" she asked as she dried the silverware. I always had to go to bed at the same time she did, some compromise hour between the two of our bedtimes, so that she wouldn't have to be in the attic alone.

I looked at my mother. "I want to stay up later this summer, Mom," I pleaded. "I'm *twelve* now."

"You'll go at the same time Lucy does," my mother said, but she drew me aside and whispered in my ear. "Go up when she does and wait until she falls asleep," she said. "Then you can come downstairs again."

"Lucy needs to grow up," Isabel said as she dried a plate. "She's never going to get over her fears if you keep coddling her."

"What would be more helpful than your criticism," our mother said, "is for you to offer to go up with Lucy sometimes so Julie doesn't always need to be the one to do it."

"Be happy to," Isabel said. "I'll tell her ghost stories."

Mom was sponging off the counter, but stopped to look at Isabel. "When did you get so mean?" she asked, and turned away. I saw the look of remorse on Isabel's face before she covered it with a smirk. My sister was not as hard as she pretended to be.

I was coming to realize that Isabel was very beautiful—and that she knew it. She could get her way with just about anyone, especially our father, using a pout of her lips or the sheen of tears in her eyes. Her dark eyes were amazing, the lashes so long and lush they looked as though they must be false. She complained about her hair all the time. It was too wavy. Too thick. Too dark. But her complaints were empty; she knew her hair was the envy of every other girl in her high-school class. She had large breasts and a tiny waist. Boys stared at her when we'd walk down the street and girls were cautious around her, afraid that their boyfriends might compare them to Isabel and decide they could do better. There was no use denying that she'd gotten the looks in the family. Lucy and I had dark hair, as well, but I had to set mine on rollers to make it wavy, and Mom had given Lucy's short hair a perm that made her look like a poodle.

The kitchen had grown very quiet. I poured the remaining tomato sauce into a Tupperware container and burped the lid, which made Lucy giggle.

Isabel lifted the colander from the dish drainer and began to dry it. "Ned asked me to a party tonight," she said. "I can go, can't I?"

My mother continued cleaning the countertop with the sponge. "Not tonight," she said. "You need to unpack and—"

"I've already unpacked and I helped Julie and Lucy unpack, too," Izzy said. "And the beds are made upstairs and I swept the floor up there and cleaned the toilet and sink and everything."

I honestly wasn't sure if all she was saying was true or not. I knew I had unpacked my things quite capably on my own, but I said nothing.

"And we're practically done in here, aren't we?" Isabel asked.

"Yes, we are." My mother turned on the faucet to rinse the sponge. "But I don't want you gone our first night here."

Isabel smacked her dish towel down on the counter. "That makes absolutely no sense," she said.

My mother looked up from the sink, wringing the sponge between her hands. "I said no," she said.

Isabel rolled her eyes and picked up the towel again. I could hear the aggravation in her breathing as she dried one of the saucepans. She didn't say another word, and neither did my mother. There was tension in the room, and I grew quiet myself. I didn't know the appropriate rules of behavior when the ice suddenly grew that thin.

Later, my mother and I were cleaning the deep drawers beneath the kitchen cabinets. Lucy stood nearby, brushing ancient crumbs from the old toaster. She'd refused to help us with the drawers because we had found mouse droppings in one of them and a spider in another. Daddy came into the room and poured himself a glass of ginger ale from the bottle in the refrigerator. He was wearing his summer uniform: baggy shorts that showed off his pale, scarred legs and one of his short-sleeved plaid shirts.

"Charles." My mother looked up from the task. "Would you find Isabel and ask her to sweep and organize the hall closet, please?"

"She's gone out," he said. He'd taken the ice tray from the freezer and although the ice had barely had time to form yet, he cracked the tray open and dropped a couple of delicate cubes into his glass.

My mother straightened up. "Gone where?" she said.

"To a party with Ned Chapman."

My mother put her hands on her hips. "I told her she couldn't go," she said.

My father looked surprised, his eyes, the same light brown as his hair, wide-open. "She didn't tell me she asked you," he said.

I watched a blotch of red form on my mother's throat. "I'm going to ground her for the rest of the week," she said.

"That's a little harsh, Maria, don't you think?" my father asked, swirling the ice and liquid around in his glass. "It's her first night down the shore and she's known Ned all her life. His father may be one of the biggest fools on earth, but you can't hold that against Ned. I don't see the harm in her going to a party with him."

"Yes, she's known him all her life, but she's *seventeen* this summer," she said, as if that explained everything. "And it's her first night here. I think she should have stayed in. Help clean up a little. Get acclimated."

Daddy laughed. "Acclimated?" he asked. I was not sure what the word meant, and I realized I had left my dictionary in Westfield. I didn't like to hear my parents argue, and I buried my head deeper in the drawer I was cleaning, brushing mouse droppings into a dustpan with a small broom. I glanced at Lucy, who looked as uncomfortable as I felt. She was concentrating hard on every crevice of the old toaster.

Daddy put his arm around my mother and kissed her cheek. "We raised her right," he said. "She's got a good head on her shoulders."

My mother looked wounded. "How can you say that when she just lied to you about—"

"She didn't lie to me," Daddy said, letting go of her and heading for the door to the hallway. "She omitted a small fact."

"She has you wrapped around her little finger," my mother said.

"She'll be fine," Daddy said. He walked out of the room, turning in the direction of the front door. I knew he was working in the garage with Grandpop this evening, organizing the fishing gear and slapping a fresh coat of blue paint on the Adirondack chairs.

My mother returned to her cleaning with a vengeance, and I could see the tight line of her lips. I knew my sister lied often to our parents. When we would go to confession on Saturday evenings, I was always amazed at how short her sessions in the confessional were. I knew she couldn't possibly be owning up to every lie she'd told. I learned from watching her. Instead of enumerating everything I did wrong, I now gave the priest the abbreviated version. "I lied five times," I'd say. I refused to count "pretending" as "lying." If I counted pretending, I would be in the confessional all night. "I disobeyed my mother once," I'd continue, "and I was mean to my little sister twice." It was a relief to do it that way, instead of spilling all the details of my sins, and the priest didn't seem to care.

I put my arm around my mother's waist, feeling very adult. "She'll be okay, Mom," I said.

My mother didn't respond. Her eyes were glassy, as though she might cry, and I felt confused by her tears. I thought she needed to be alone, so I said I would sweep the hall closet myself, and I took Lucy's hand and dragged her out of the kitchen with me.

At nine o'clock that evening, I climbed the creaky steps into the attic, Lucy following behind me. I clung to the railing myself. The stairs seemed more wobbly every year and if I'd had a smidgen of fear in my makeup, I probably would have dreaded climbing them, too. In recent years, Lucy and I had slept in the twin beds in the quadrant of the room closest to the stairs. This year, though, I wanted more privacy. I wanted to be able to leave the reading lamp on as long as I liked and to simply daydream in my own little curtained space without Lucy's incessant chatter. So, earlier in the day, we'd made up our beds in separate corners of the room, while Isabel made the double bed in the far corner behind the chimney for herself. Lucy had seemed fine with the arrangement then, but now that she climbed under her sheet in the hot attic, she was not so pleased.

"Leave the curtain open so I can see you," she pleaded. She was lying on her side, facing my bed, the white sheet up to her shoulders.

"I'm going to have the light on so I can read," I said, busying myself fluffing my pillows and turning down the covers. "It'll keep you awake." I wanted her to fall asleep quickly so I could go downstairs and play canasta with my mother and grandmother. During the school year, my evenings were filled with homework and television—*The Andy Griffith Show* or *Wagon Train* or *Ed Sullivan*. But in the summer, evenings were the time for card games and jigsaw puzzles.

"Please," she wailed.

"You'll be able to see my shadow," I said, glad that I had made the bed closest to the curtain rather than the one against the wall. "Watch." I walked over to the small table between the twin beds in my corner and lit the lamp. Then I pulled the curtain closed. It was tight against my bed, and once I'd climbed in, still dressed in my shorts and sleeveless top, I knew how I would look to Lucy. I'd been watching the silhouettes of my sister, my cousins, my aunts and uncles through those curtains for years. "See?" I said. "You can see me perfectly, right?"

"Okay," Lucy said, her voice small.

I heard her settle down in the bed and pictured her lying there on her side, eyes wide-open, watching my shadow as I dove back into Nancy Drew.

I read one chapter and the beginning of another. Then I pulled back the edge of the curtain closest to the head of my bed. Lucy's eyes were closed, her thumb stuck in her mouth as if she were a three-year-old. Her ratty old teddy bear was tucked beneath her arm. Quietly I slipped from my bed. Pulling the spread from the other bed, I bunched it up under my covers, propping the book up near the pillow, then walked into the central part of the attic to see how the shadows would look from Lucy's perspective in case she woke up. Quite convincing.

It was impossible to descend the stairs without causing them to creak, but I did the best I could.

My mother smiled at me when I walked onto the porch. She had reached some sort of internal peace about Izzy being at a party, and her smile was a relief to me.

"She's asleep?" She was sitting across the big table from my grandmother, smoking a cigarette and playing double solitaire on the vinyl, floral-patterned tablecloth. They both wore cotton housedresses, my mother's a pale yellow stripe and my grandmother's, baby-blue.

I nodded, plunking myself down into one of the rockers. Like the table, all the chairs on the long porch were painted red, the paint always a little sticky from the humidity and so thick you could dent it with a fingernail. There was also a bed at one end of the porch for anyone who wanted to sleep with the sounds of water lapping against the bulkhead and crickets singing in the wooded lot next door.

"We'll end this game and then you can join us for canasta," Grandma said, lifting her cup of instant coffee to her lips. When she shifted her legs beneath the table, I could see that her stockings were rolled down to just below her knees. Her English was perfect, but her Italian accent was still thick some sixty years after her arrival in the United States. I loved the music in her voice. I was ten before I realized that not everyone had a Grandma who spoke that way, turning her "th's" into "t's" and adding the hint of a vowel to every word that ended in a consonant.

I rocked for a while, the concrete floor smooth and cool beneath my feet. I could see the light of a boat moving slowly along the canal toward the bay, its engine a soft and steady hum, a backdrop for the slapping of cards against the table. Tomorrow, Grandpop would get our own boat in the water, and I couldn't wait. I'd piloted that boat myself for the past two summers, although always with an adult or Isabel on board. This summer, Daddy promised me I could go out in it alone if I wore a life preserver and stayed in our end of the canal, between my house and the place where the canal opened into the bay. It was not much territory, but I was excited at having that freedom nevertheless.

Someone was in the Chapmans' backyard. It was too dark to see who it was, but the person was fishing. I saw the burning tips of a couple of mosquito-repellant coils, and the faint moonlight glinted against the fisherman's white shirt. I guessed it was Ethan, trying to catch something he could cut up. I watched the shirt move as he swung the pole behind him, then batted the air with it, the sound of the line sailing out into the canal unmistakable. I felt my own fingers itching to hold a fishing pole.

"Are you ready to beat us at canasta?" my grandmother asked me.

I walked over to the table and sat down as she began to deal. My mother stubbed out her cigarette in the clamshell ashtray and was pulling another one from her package of Kents when the most hideous scream suddenly cut through the air. She was out of her seat before I even realized the sounds were coming from the attic. The screams continued, Lucy barely stopping for breath between each one. I followed my mother up the stairs.

"Baby!" My mother flicked on the overhead light and raced to Lucy's bed. Lucy was huddled against the iron headboard, her teddy clutched in her arms and her poodle hair matted on one side of her head. Our mother sat next to her. "What's the matter?"

"There!" Lucy pointed toward the ceiling near the center of the attic.

I walked over to where she was pointing and looked up. "Where?" I said.

"There," Lucy said again, this time a little sheepishness creeping into her voice. I looked up to see an old rag wedged against the ceiling beneath the elaborate network of wires used for the curtains. That rag had been there for as long as I could remember, probably to stop a leak before the new roof was put on the house.

"It's a rag," I said. Lucy was such a baby.

"It looked like a head," Lucy said. "I thought it was a head and then I looked over and saw you weren't in bed and I was up here alone!" She sounded indignant. I glanced at the curtain surrounding my little cubicle. The bunched-up bedspread seemed to have collapsed. It was obvious I was no longer there.

My mother stood and turned out the light and the three of us looked at the rag.

"See?" Lucy said.

"It looks like a rag," I said.

Mom sat down next to her again. "All you had to do was turn on your light and you would have seen it was just a rag," she said. "It's not fair to Julie to have to stay up here with you, Lucy. You're eight years old now. You have to learn there's nothing to be afraid of up here. You know we're all right downstairs if you need anything. Now lie down." She reached for the sheet and drew it over her youngest daughter.

"Can we leave the light on?"

"You'll never fall asleep that way."

"Yes, I will," she said, her gaze darting to the rag again.

"All right." My mother got to her feet with a sigh, smoothing the skirt of her housedress and offering me a conspiratorial look of exasperation that made me feel very mature and brave. She hit the wall switch for the single bare bulb that hung from the ceiling. "Good night, dear."

"Night, Luce," I said, following my mother down the stairs.

I awakened at five-thirty the following morning to the crowing of a rooster. I lay in bed, smiling to myself. Early-morning pink sunshine flowed through the window in my little curtained "room," and the sense of summer freedom washed over me again.

I moved to the other bed in my small cubicle, crawling down to the footboard so I could look out the window. I knew where the rooster lived. I'd forgotten all about him and his early-morning wake-up call. Across the canal, kitty-corner from our bungalow, was a small wooden shack, gone nearly black with age, its roof sagging and its yard home to shoulder-high grasses and cattails. It was the only house, if it could even be called that, on that side of the canal and I couldn't remember ever seeing a soul around it, but someone had to live there to feed the rooster. A dock was cut into the land near the house. I could zip over there in the runabout, dock the boat and climb up into the tall weeds surrounding the house without being seen. I mentally added "exploration of the shack" to my agenda for the day.

I got out of bed, knowing no one else would yet be up. The curtains were pulled around Isabel's double bed. I didn't know what time she'd gotten home the night before and I wondered what sort of punishment my parents had agreed on for her. I hoped it was harsh. I hated that she could lie and get away with it.

I put on one of my bathing suits and pulled my capris over it, then walked across the linoleum-covered floor. We'd been at the shore less than twenty-four hours and already I could feel the gritty sand beneath my bare feet. I tiptoed as I passed Lucy's bed. Her curtains had not been pulled shut, and I didn't want to wake her. I was nearly to the stairs when I heard Isabel's voice.

"Julie?"

I turned to see her pull back part of the curtain around her bed. Her long, dark hair was a tangled mess, but she looked beautiful in the pink sunlight.

I tiptoed over to her bed. She took my arm and pulled me behind the curtain.

"I need you to do me a favor," she said. Her shoulders were bare above the sheet and I felt shock when I realized that she had slept naked. I didn't know anyone who actually did that.

I sat down on her bed. This close, I could see that her eyes were red. "What did Mom and Dad say?" I said. "You shouldn't have gone to Daddy after—"

"Shh!" she said. "That's none of your business." She fumbled among the covers on her bed and picked up a small plastic giraffe, about the size of her fist. "Give this to Ned Chapman, okay?" she asked, although I knew it was more of a demand than a request.

I looked down at the red-and-purple giraffe nestled in my hands. "Why?" I asked. I knew she couldn't tell me it was none of my business if she wanted my cooperation.

"It's his," she said. "I forgot to give it to him last night."

"What would an eighteen-year-old boy want this for?" I asked. The giraffe looked like something even a toddler would get bored playing with after a minute or two.

"Don't ask so many questions," Isabel said. "Just do it. Please. I'm not allowed to leave the house all day."

"That's all?" I thought Mom was right—she should be grounded for a week.

"That's enough," Isabel said. She flopped back onto her pillow. "I'm going back to sleep."

"You're welcome," I said, annoyed at her ingratitude.

No one was up when I got downstairs. I went outside where the warm, damp morning air filled my lungs. I stuck the giraffe under one of the Adirondack chairs to keep it safe until I saw Ned. I grabbed my bucket and the crab net from where it leaned against the tree and began making the crabbing rounds, standing at the edge of our dock, peering into the water, looking for crabs that rested against the bulkhead below the water's surface. I found three in our dock, then I walked outside the fence, balancing myself on the top of the wooden planks of the bulkhead as I checked the canal for crabs. The current was pulling strongly toward the river and I watched a paper cup sweep past me in the water, followed a moment later by a crab. I put my net into the water in the crab's path and drew him up and into the bucket. It was almost too easy. A giant tangle of seaweed floated past me, and then a little ball, which I scooped out with my net and examined. It was nothing special, just a dented Ping-Pong ball, but I would put it under my bed to kick off my Bay Head Shores clue collection.

I glanced across the canal, looking toward the rooster shack, and my gaze was drawn to the tall reeds directly across the canal from my house. Fishermen were arriving. They walked along a path cut through the reeds and began setting up their gear and their folding chairs behind the fence. Every one of them was colored, and they weren't all men, either. It was hard to tell the women from the men at that distance, but I could tell for certain that a couple of them were children.

"Crabbing, huh?"

The voice came from behind me, surprising me so much that I had to grab the fence to keep my balance. I turned to see Ned Chapman walking toward me, grinning widely. Something happened to me in that moment. I don't know if it was the way his blue eyes shone in the sunlight, or the triangle of tanned chest clearly visible beneath the collar of his open shirt, or the way he held his cigarette between his thumb and index finger, but I thought I might keel over and fall into the canal. I'd gotten my period for the first time in the early spring, and ever since then, I felt my stomach turn inside-out at the sight of a cute boy. And Ned was definitely *cute*. His hair was thick, the color of sunshine. He looked a little like Troy Donahue.

"Hi, Ned," I managed to say, and only when I said his name out loud did I realize that he had the same name as Nancy Drew's steady boyfriend. "Hi, Ned," I repeated, this time to myself, just to feel his name on my tongue again.

He'd reached the opposite side of the fence from where I was standing and leaned over, his elbows resting on the metal bar at the top of the chain link. "You're an early bird," he said.

"You, too."

"How many did you get?" He leaned farther over the fence to try to look in the bucket.

"Five, so far."

"You like them?"

"To eat, you mean?"

He took a drag on his cigarette and let the smoke out in a long stream. "What else?" he asked.

"Actually, no." I giggled and was annoyed with myself for sounding like a kid. "Grandma loves them, though. And I love catching them, so it works out okay."

"So." He rubbed his hand across his chin as though checking if he needed a shave. It was a sexy gesture. "Did Izzy get in trouble last night?"

I nodded. "She can't go out all day. She asked me to give you something, though."

I balanced carefully as I walked back along the bulkhead, trying to impress him by not holding on to the fence. In my yard, I put down the bucket and the net, then grabbed the giraffe from beneath the chair and carried it over to him. "She asked me to give you this," I said.

He smiled, taking the giraffe from my hand. I felt embarrassed for Isabel that she wanted to give him something so dumb. I didn't believe her when she'd said it was actually his.

"That's nice of you to do that for her," he said, looking right at me, and I stood as tall as I could, wondering how my small, barely there breasts looked in the childish one-piece bathing suit I was wearing. I needed to get a two-piece this summer, if Mom would let me.

"She said it belonged to you," I said.

"Yeah, it does, actually," he said. "Thanks for bringing it over. Tell her everything's copacetic."

Why, oh why, hadn't I remembered to bring my dictionary? I heard sounds coming from his screened porch and didn't want to be in the Chapmans' yard when goofy Ethan came outside, so I said goodbye to Ned and went back to our dock to see if any new crabs had appeared along the bulkhead.

Right after lunch, Grandpop, Daddy and I towed the boat down to the marina. We gassed it up, Grandpop hopping onto the pier like a young man happy to be alive. I knew how he felt. Just the smell of the gasoline mixing with the salty scent of the water filled me up with joy. I thought to myself, *I take after him.* Grandpop loved everything about the shore—the water, fishing, boating, the smells, the night sky—everything, just as I did. We looked nothing alike: he was nearly bald, with a sad sort of face that always reminded me of a basset hound, but in many other ways, we were the same.

He and I went for a spin on the bay before taking the boat through the canal and into our dock. Grandpop let me pilot it myself part of the time, even allowing me to maneuver it into our dock, and he told me I did a terrific job. Our boat had no steering wheel, just a tiller handle attached to the motor, and I felt good that I was getting the hang of it so quickly. I nearly fell when I tried to get from the boat to the bulkhead, though, but Grandpop said I would have it mastered in a few days. I tied the boat to the hooks at the sides of the dock, loving the wet, rough feel of the rope beneath my fingers. I felt sorry for Izzy. Here it was, her first full day at the shore, and she wasn't even allowed out of the house.

I sat with her and Lucy on the porch for a while, reading. Lucy and I were in the rockers, and Isabel was stretched out on the bed at the end of the porch, as close to the Chapmans' house as she could get. I noticed that she wasn't turning the pages of her book. She gazed in the direction of the Chapmans' yard, probably waiting for a glimpse of Ned. He and Mr. Chapman were working on their boat, and I doubted she could see their dock from her place on the bed, but when Ned walked through their yard to get something from their house, I could nearly hear Izzy's heartbeat quicken. I understood how she felt. He was having the same effect on me.

Before dinner, I took the boat out by myself. Mom was nervous about it, but Daddy talked her into letting me as long as I wore the hideous orange life preserver. It was a Monday and the weekend congestion on the canal had vanished overnight. I took the boat right to the mouth of the bay. The water stretched in front of me wide and inviting and I longed to go out into it, just a little way, but I didn't dare. Instead I turned around in a broad arc and headed for the dock between the colored fishermen and the rooster house.

Once inside the unfamiliar dock, I cut the motor. There was a short ladder on my left and I tied my boat to a rung, took off the life preserver, then climbed up. The colored fishermen made me nervous. I didn't look directly at them, but I could feel their eyes following me as I walked between the cattails and the fence, heading away from them in the direction of the shack. I finally found a narrow path cut through the tall grass, and I followed it right to the front porch of the ramshackle little cottage.

"Who are you?"

I jumped at the sound of a man's voice, disembodied because I couldn't see through the screens of his porch.

"I was just coming to see where the rooster lives," I said.

The screen door creaked open a few inches and a man stood in the doorway. He had a thick beard and a dirty old hat on his head. The early evening sunlight fell onto his face and he squinted, his eyes reduced to little beads of translucent blue, making him look a bit demonic. *The Mystery of the Warlock's Shack,* I thought to myself. I liked the title. Maybe I would try to write my own book.

"Where do you live?" he asked.

I turned and pointed to my bungalow, which was barely visible through the reeds. It looked very far away.

"You come over by boat?" he asked.

"Yes."

"By yourself?"

"Yes," I said, turning to go. "And I'd better get back."

"What were you planning to do to my rooster?" he said, as I moved away.

"Oh!" I said. "Nothing. I wouldn't hurt it. I just wanted to see where it lived."

He held the door open wider. "Right here," he said.

I looked past him onto the porch and saw the rooster and a couple of hens walking around on the floor as if they were mechanical toys. I took a step backward, wondering if the man's sneakers were caked with the droppings of his feathered pets.

"Thanks for showing me," I said.

"There are some people around here who'd like to wring my rooster's neck," he said, and I thought he sounded suspicious.

"Not me," I said. "Thanks again for letting me see him." I turned then and walked as quickly as I could through the tall grass. It probably only took me thirty seconds to reach the dock, but by that time I'd made up two or three different stories about the man. He kept children locked in closets inside the rickety old house. He'd murdered his wife and her bones were buried beneath the porch. When I was about to climb down the ladder, I spotted something shiny in the flattened grass near the head of the dock. I walked over and stared down at a pair of sunglasses, then picked them up. Maybe they belonged to the wife the old man had killed. Who knew? They would go beneath my bed to wait just in case.

That evening, Grandpop and I walked to the end of the dirt road. For as long as I could remember, he'd kept a path cleared through the tall grasses that rose a couple of feet above my head. We followed the path, and I loved the feeling of being closed in by the grass walls. Dragonflies flew along with us as we walked, but we were covered in insect repellant so the mosquitoes left us alone. We emerged from the path in a swampy area of still water that was connected to the canal by a narrow opening in the bulkhead. As he always did, Grandpop had set his bait trap in the shallow water here, tying it to a stake in the soft, sandy earth among the grasses. I pulled in the trap. It was full of green-gray killies, flapping on the wire mesh. Grandpop opened the trap and spilled the bait into his bucket. While he was doing that, I spied something in the water a few feet from where we stood. A baby shoe! I rolled up my capris as high as I could, waded into the water to my knees, and reached out to grab the little white leather shoe, a real prize in the world of clues.

"What do you do with all that stuff you collect?" Grandpop asked me as he closed the trap again.

"I keep them under my bed," I said. "They might be clues to something that happened. Like, what if a baby got kidnapped or something? I could take this shoe to the police and tell them where I found it and maybe they could solve the mystery."

"I think you need a better place than under your bed," Grandpop said. "Your mother could clean up there and toss out all that old stuff you found."

I loved my grandfather so much right then. He always took me seriously.

"Where else could I put it?" I studied the tiny shoe in my hands.

"I have an idea," he said. He put his hand on the back of my neck as we walked, his fingers a little rough and damp against my skin. "When we get back to the house, you gather up your clues and I'll show you where you can keep them."

Once home, I did as I was told. I only had three paltry clues so far: the baby shoe, the sunglasses and the silly Ping-Pong ball, but that seemed pretty good for two days worth of sleuthing. I carried them out to the backyard. Grandpop was digging a hole near the corner of the house closest to the woods. Next to him was an old tin bread box with a removable red top.

He grinned at me, his sweet basset hound face lighting up for a moment. "What do you think, Nancy Drew?" he asked. "We'll bury this bread box in this hole, cover it with a little sand and no one will ever know your clues are here."

I helped him lower the bread box into the hole. I put my clues inside, then slipped on the lid and covered it with a couple of inches of sand. I loved my new hiding place. No one would ever know the clues were there.

Or so I thought.

CHAPTER 5

Julie

The sunburned waitress poured more iced tea into my glass, and I interpreted the look she gave me as sympathetic. *This is why I don't date,* I thought. It was the waiting, the wondering, the analyzing. Why was Ethan late? Was he stuck in traffic? Had he forgotten we were to meet for lunch? Or had he simply been annoyed that I'd twisted his arm to talk with me? I wanted to explain to the waitress that, although I *was* meeting a man here, he was not a date. Not a romantic interest. But then I realized that the waitress probably saw me as too old to be dating, anyway. She was in her mid-twenties; most likely I reminded her of her mother.

The Spring Lake restaurant was barely ten miles from Bay Head Shores, and that was closer than I'd been to our former summer home since I was twelve. When I'd gotten out of my car, I could smell the salt from the ocean a few blocks away. I was surprised that the scent elicited not only the discomfort I'd expected, but also a longing, as though a tiny piece of me was still able to remember the good times I'd had down the shore in spite of all that had been taken from my family there.

The waitress stopped by my table again on her way to another. "Can I get you a roll or something to munch on while you wait, hon?" she asked. It felt so strange to be called "hon" by someone half my age. Better, though, than *ma'am*.

"No, thanks." I smiled at her. "I'm fine."

It was warm in the restaurant, or at least *I* was warm. I had on cropped black pants and a sleeveless red top cut high on my shoulders, but I noticed other women in the restaurant were pulling on their sweaters. I didn't even bother carrying a sweater since menopause hit me a year ago.

I'd taken a table at the front of the restaurant so I would be able to see Ethan when he walked in. I wasn't sure I'd recognize him. Through the window, I studied the men walking by, searching for lanky academic types. I watched people entering and leaving the little shops on the other side of the street. A young man stood directly across the street from me, rubbing lotion on a woman's back. I watched the two of them until a pack of bicyclers sped by, blocking my view.

I looked at my watch. Twenty minutes late. Maybe he wasn't going to show up. He certainly had not welcomed my call.

"I'm sorry Abby disturbed you with this," he'd said, once I'd identified myself. He had a soft voice, exactly the sort of voice I would have imagined him having, and he did not sound irritated or angry. Just tired.

"She had to." I was on the phone in my office, staring at the words *Chapter Four* on my computer screen. The rest of the page was still blank. "She was right to," I said. "And she and I agreed that the situation needed looking into."

He was quiet. "I'm not sure that *I* agree," he said finally.

"We're talking about a serious injustice," I said. "A man served time in prison for something he didn't do. And we're talking about my *sister*." Along with the old sense of loss I felt at the mention of Isabel came the suddenly realization of my insensitivity. "I'm sorry, Ethan," I said quickly. "I didn't even offer you condolences. I'm very sorry. I know what it's like to lose a sibling."

I heard him sigh. "Thanks," he said. "Ned…I don't know what happened to him. He had some sort of breakdown in his late teens and early twenties. He became...I don't know how to describe it. He was just existing. Not really living."

Don't you think that suggests he was carrying a guilty secret? I wanted to ask but decided against it. This wasn't the time.

"How bad was it?" I asked. "Was he able to work?"

"Oh, yeah," Ethan said. "He wasn't *that* bad off. He spent time in Vietnam, which didn't help his condition, and he was eventually discharged for a sleep problem. Then he got his degree in accounting and worked for a plumbing company, doing their books. He never got married. He dated a little, but never anything serious."

"Abby said...or rather, implied, that he had a drinking problem."

"Yes, he did," Ethan said, "but he wasn't a sloppy drunk. It didn't get in the way of his work or anything. Just kept him numb. We tried to get him help, but he would never admit to having a problem. You can't change someone who doesn't want to change."

I had many more questions but felt anxious about asking them over the phone. I was afraid if I probed too deeply, he would hang up on me.

"Can we meet?" I asked. "I'd like to talk to you in person about this. About the letter."

There was a silence so deep and long I had to ask him if he was still on the line.

"I'm here," he replied in that soft, soft voice. "And yes, I'll meet you. Where are you living?"

"Westfield," I said. "How about you?"

"On the canal," he said, and I doubted that he knew how those three words stopped my breath. "We winterized the summer house years ago," he added.

"Do you live there with..." I wasn't sure who else might be living in the Chapman's old house with him. His parents? His wife?

"Alone," he said. "My wife and Abby used to live here, too, but I was divorced five years ago and Abby's out on her own now, of course. She has a daughter. My granddaughter. Did she tell you that?" There was pride in his voice. I could hear the smile.

"No," I said. "That's wonderful."

"Do you want to come here?"

"No," I said, nearly choking on the word in my rush to get it out. There was no way I was going to Bay Head Shores. "Maybe we could meet halfway."

"Well," he said. "I have to be in Spring Lake Friday. If you want to meet me there for lunch, we can do that."

It was more than halfway, but that was all right. I needed to see him face-to-face to persuade him to take Ned's letter to the police.

A man carrying a soft-sided briefcase walked through the door of the restaurant and I looked up expectantly, but the red hair and glasses were missing and I gazed out the window again.

"Julie?" I turned to see the man standing next to my table.

"Ethan?" I queried back.

He nodded, his smile subdued, and held out his hand. "Sorry I'm late," he said. "I got stuck in beach traffic."

"That's okay." I shook his hand, and he sat down across from me.

"I would never have recognized you," I said, then wondered if that sounded rude. The truth was, age had done him many favors. His red hair was now a gray-tinged auburn, thin at his temples. He wore no glasses. The freckled skin of his youth had weathered into something kinder and he'd put on weight in the form of muscle. He was wearing a cobalt-blue short-sleeved shirt and his arms were lean and tight. The nerdiness from his childhood was gone. Completely. "You look great," I added.

"And you look wonderful," he said. "I would have recognized you anywhere. But of course, your face used to be all over our house on the back of your books."

"Used to be?" I asked.

"We both read them, but my wife got custody of the books," he said. He glanced down at my bare ring finger. "You're married, right?" he asked. "I recall something like 'the author lives with her husband in New Jersey' or something like that from one of your book jackets."

The waitress appeared at our table, pad at the ready. "How're you two doing?" she asked.

I looked up at her sunburned face. "He hasn't had a chance to look at the menu," I said.

Ethan handed the waitress his unopened menu. "Just a burger, medium well," he said. "And lemonade, please."

I ordered the shrimp salad, then returned my attention to Ethan. "I'm divorced," I said. "Two years."

"Children?"

"A daughter. Shannon. She's seventeen. She just graduated high school."

"College plans?"

"The Oberlin Conservatory of Music," I said. "She's a cellist."

He looked impressed. "Wow," he said.

"What kind of work do you do?" I asked, then held up my hand. "Wait. Let me guess," I said. "You teach marine biology."

He laughed. "I'm a carpenter," he said.

"Oh." I nodded. That was not what I'd expected. If anyone had told me skinny little Ethan Chapman would end up working with his hands instead of his head, I never would have believed it. I thought of his ambitious father, Rosswell Chapman III or whatever he had been. The summer I was twelve, he was chief justice on the New Jersey Supreme Court and he later ran unsuccessfully for governor. I wondered if he'd been disappointed to see his sons turn out to be an accountant and a carpenter rather than follow him into law or politics.

"I wasn't the least bit surprised you turned out to be a writer," Ethan said.

"No?"

"Your family was so artsy. Your mother painted, right?"

"That's right. She was a teacher, but she painted as a hobby." I'd almost forgotten how my mother loved to set up her easel on the bungalow porch.

"And your father was a doctor, but wasn't he a writer, too?"

"A columnist for a magazine," I said.

"You've got a daughter who plays the cello," he continued. "And your little sister, Lucy, used to play that plastic violin."

"What?" I laughed. "I don't remember that at all, but you're probably right because she does play the violin now. She's in a band called the ZydaChicks."

He smiled. "There you go," he said.

I took a sip of my iced tea, wondering if Isabel would have shown any special talent if she'd been given the chance to grow up.

Ethan was still smiling at me, his head cocked to one side.

"What?" I asked.

"You really, really look terrific," he said.

I felt myself blush. "Thanks," I said.

"I mean it," he said, then leaned back in his chair with a sigh. "Well, I guess we'd better talk about what we came here to talk about." He lifted the briefcase from the floor and pulled out an envelope. "Abby told me she showed you a copy of the letter," he said, handing it to me.

I studied the envelope. Unlike the typed letter, the address of the police department was handwritten, printed in precise, slanted letters.

"Why haven't you taken it to the police?" I asked, shifting my focus from the envelope to his eyes. They were a clear, deep blue. I'd never noticed their color behind the Coke-bottle glasses he used to wear. "I mean, it's obvious that Ned wanted them to have it."

"No, he obviously had second thoughts," Ethan corrected me. His voice might have been gentle, but the words carried their own force and, although I didn't agree with him, I liked how he stood up for himself. Glen always allowed people to steamroll right over him. "The letter was dated a couple of months before he died," Ethan added.

"But he didn't throw it away," I said.

Ethan sighed. "Julie, if I take it to the police, they're going to assume Ned did it. They're going to start asking questions. I don't care what they ask me, but my father is elderly. I don't want his last years to be spent thinking that his son murdered someone. I have a buddy at the police department and I ran this by him, in a hypothetical sort of way. He said they'd open the case up again. They didn't do much with forensics back then, so they'd be looking at the evidence from a new perspective now. But they'd almost certainly want to talk with my father. I don't want to put him through it."

I saw genuine concern in his face and couldn't help but be touched by his reasoning. I hoped I could protect my mother from ever knowing anything at all about the letter, no matter what the outcome. I wasn't sure I would be able to, though. I knew from the sort of books

I wrote that Ethan's friend at the police department was right. It didn't matter how old the case was, the police would reopen it. Start fresh. I just prayed they could leave my mother out of it. Ross Chapman, though, would certainly be questioned, since he was the person who'd confirmed Ned's alibi.

"Is your mother also still alive?" I asked.

The waitress arrived with our food before he could answer, and we fell into small talk with her about her sunburn. She'd fallen asleep on the beach, she said, pressing her hands to her crimson cheeks once she'd set our plates on the table.

"I'm in *agony*," she said, with a flair for drama.

Ethan reached into his briefcase again and pulled out a tube of lotion. "Here," he said, handing it to her. "Put this on the burn. It takes the sting away instantly."

She looked surprised. "Thank you," she said.

"You can keep it," Ethan added.

"That's so nice of you," she said, slipping the tube into her apron pocket. "Don't worry about a tip."

Once she'd left our table, I turned to him. "Do you always carry sunburn cream with you?" I asked. I liked that he'd talked so easily to the waitress. Glen would have looked right through her. Why did I keep comparing him to Glen?

Ethan shrugged. "I love being outdoors," he said, "but two minutes in the sun and I'm burned. I have to work up to it gradually."

I smiled. I could still see the delicate little kid in him, hiding behind a much manlier facade. I watched the muscles in his forearms shift as he lifted the hamburger to his mouth. The triangle of skin in the open collar of his shirt was the same ruddy tan as the rest of him, and for a moment, I got lost in the shallow valley at the base of his throat. The muscles low in my belly suddenly contracted. It had been so long since I'd experienced that sensation that it took me a moment to recognize it as desire.

Oh, I thought, *this is very strange.*

"I was asking about your mother," I said, returning to the relative safety of our conversation.

"Right," he said, swallowing a bite of his hamburger. "She died last year. And that's part of why I'm concerned about my father. He was broken up about Mom, and Ned's death really hit him hard. I'm trying to get him to see a counselor, someone who works with the elderly, but he won't accept help any more than Ned would." He lifted a French fry to his mouth, then set it down again. "I actually think he wants to die at this point."

"Is he ill?" I asked.

"Not ill. Just old. Just old and very sad. He lives in an independent-living residence in Lakewood. I mentioned that I was having lunch with you today, just to test his reaction. He seemed surprised, but that was all. It's like he didn't really get it. Didn't understand who you were." He ate the French fry. "Are your parents still living?" he asked.

"My father died of a heart attack two years after Isabel was killed," I said. I didn't need to add that the stress of losing his favorite daughter had taken a terrible toll on my father. "My mother still lives alone and is doing very well. She works at McDonald's."

He managed a laugh. "She always was a pistol," he said.

I nibbled at my shrimp salad. "I think," I said slowly, "that in addition to your father and my mother, we also need to consider George Lewis's family, don't you?"

He pressed his napkin to his lips. "Of course," he said. "And I don't feel good about that. But Lewis is dead and—"

"That makes me so unbelievably sad," I interrupted him, shaking my head. "I always knew he was innocent and there wasn't a thing I could do about it."

Ethan fell silent. Slowly he lifted his hamburger and took another bite.

"Did Ned ever say anything to you that might make you think he knew more than he was letting on?" I asked.

Ethan shook his head as he swallowed. "We never talked about it. Early on, I remember my parents attributing the change in him to what had happened to Isabel, but he and I never spoke about it at all." He moved the straw from one side of his lemonade glass to the other. His fingernails were clean and short, his hands nicely shaped. "Ned and I were really different," he continued. "Our interests were different, and...our philosophies on life. I tend to see the glass as half-full, while Ned was usually pretty down."

"How about your father?" I asked. "Did he ever change his story on where Ned was that night?"

Ethan leaned back in his chair again, narrowing his eyes at me. "Julie, please don't play Nancy Drew with this," he said. "Don't think about this as a plot in one of your books. This is real life. You're talking about my father and my brother."

His words took me by surprise and I felt anger rise up in me. "What about *my* family?" I asked, trying to keep my voice as calm as his. I recognized the power in his quiet demeanor. "I don't want to deal with this either, Ethan. Do you think I want to relive Isabel's death all over again? I don't. The idea terrifies me. But we need to know what really happened. All of us. And if you don't take the letter to the police, I have no choice but to send them the copy Abby gave me."

Other diners were staring at me, forks halfway to their mouths, and I knew my voice had not been as quiet as I'd thought.

"I'm sorry," he said. "You're right. Both our families are mired in this mess. And you're also right that the authorities need to know about this. But would waiting a bit longer matter that much? Please."

"I don't want to wait, Ethan," I said. "Your father could live another decade." I felt cruel, but my family had lived with Isabel's loss for forty-one years. George Lewis and his family had endured his unjust imprisonment. I hated to think that he might still be alive if he hadn't served time for a murder he didn't commit. If a terrible mistake had been made, it needed to be set right.

"You think Ned did it," Ethan said.

Slowly I nodded.

Ethan closed his eyes and let out his breath. "All right," he said, opening his eyes again. He looked out the window instead of at me. "I'll take the letter to the police."

"Why?" I asked, mystified by his change of heart.

"Because," he said, looking me squarely in the face, "I need to know that you're wrong."

CHAPTER 6

Lucy

I lived in Plainfield, a ten-minute drive from my hometown of Westfield and only two blocks from the high school, so I always walked to and from my teaching job. Today, the air-conditioning in the school broke down during the first ten minutes of my summer-school class. I had a hard time focusing on my lesson plan, and the kids, never happy to be there in the first place, wanted to be anywhere but cooped up in that building. There we sat, twenty grumpy kids and me. I was as glad as they were when the bell rang.

Walking home, I wondered how Julie's lunch with Ethan was going. As much as I'd tried to talk her out of it, I knew she was right to want the police to know about the letter. I just hated for her to have to go through something so emotionally taxing, and I wished she'd at least waited to meet Ethan until a day I could go with her. She'd been anxious about it. I called her during my break to give her moral support. She was on the parkway headed for Spring Lake and wouldn't talk to me on her cell phone while she was driving. That was Julie. Always, always careful. Always afraid of making a mistake.

I lived in one of Plainfield's painted ladies, the huge, beautifully restored Victorians on West Eighth Street. The house was divided into three spacious apartments, and mine was on the top floor, where I used the turret as my sunny music room. My neighbors were the gay couple who'd renovated the house and an African-American couple who also taught at the high school. Sometimes, in the evening, the five of us would sit on the porch and exchange stories. Everyone was tolerant of my violin practice, which was fortunate. I loved living there.

I knew Shannon was in my apartment even before I reached the house, spotting her in the turret window. Most likely, she'd been watching for me. I waved and she waved back, and I wondered what was wrong. Shannon had a key to my apartment and could come and go as she pleased, but she hadn't stopped by unannounced in months.

I crossed the marble-floored foyer, and had started climbing the broad, circular staircase when I heard her voice from above.

"How was school?" she called down to me.

I tipped my head back to see her leaning over the railing of the top level, high above me.

"Hot," I said. "Air conditioner broke."

"Ugh," Shannon said. "You poor thing."

"And aren't you supposed to be working?" I asked once I reached the landing. I gave her a hug.

"I'm going in late," she said. "I have to talk to you." She had the most beautiful brown eyes. I imagined guys melting into puddles at her feet. Were her eyes a bit bloodshot today, though? I tried not to stare.

I put my arm around her as we walked into the apartment. "What's the problem, kiddo?" I asked.

She circled my waist with her own arm. "Only everything," she said.

I dropped my briefcase on the dining-room chair. "Do you want something to drink?" I lifted the hem of my green tank top and waved it back and forth with my hands, trying to let some cool air reach my damp skin. "Soda? Iced tea."

She shook her head. "I helped myself," she said, pointing to the coffee table in the living room. I saw a glass of iced tea on a coaster. It was nearly empty; she'd been there awhile.

"It's mango," I said. "Good, isn't it?"

She nodded. "Uh-huh."

"Let me get some and then we'll talk, okay?"

She sat on my old floral camelback sofa in the living room, looking like a model, her white shirt and capris in stark contrast to the mauve and cranberry tones of the upholstery. I poured my iced tea in the kitchen, planning my end of the conversation in my mind. Certainly, she was here to talk about Julie's reaction to her living with Glen for the summer. I'd told her I would support her in that, and I would.

She shifted to the very edge of the sofa when I came back into the room, as if preparing for a job interview. I sat down sideways in my favorite overstuffed chair and threw my legs over one of the arms, kicking off my sandals and letting them fall to the floor.

"I know your mom didn't react well to you wanting to move in with your dad," I said, lifting the glass to my lips.

She shook her head, dropping her gaze quickly to her hands where they were knotted in her lap. "No," she said. "But that's not why I'm here."

"No?" I prompted.

She looked at me. Her eyes *were* red.

"I'm pregnant," she said, catching me completely off guard. My jaw dropped open, but no words came out.

"I'm sorry," she said, as though she'd hurt me.

"But you're on the pill," I said.

"I missed one." She played with the fringe of the beige afghan lying over the arm of the sofa. "But I took it the next day, the second I remembered. I guess I was too late with it or something."

"How far along are you?" I asked.

"Sixteen weeks," she said. "Almost exactly."

"Sixteen weeks!" I looked at her belly, masked by the loose white top she was wearing. Suddenly it made sense. Her weight gain, her deadened spirit, the lack of life in her face.

"I'm due December twentieth," she said.

"Due?" I asked. "You mean...you plan to have this baby?"

She nodded. "The baby's father and I talked about it and we decided to have it."

"Who the hell is the baby's father?" I asked, not angrily. Not with much emotion other than confusion. "Your mother said you haven't even been out on a date in months."

"She's right," she said. "I haven't, because I'm totally in love with…the baby's father and he lives in Colorado. His name is Tanner Stroh."

"How do you know him?" Thoughts were zipping through my mind faster than I could capture them: how Julie would react to this news, my mother becoming a great-grandmother, Shannon's music career. She was supposed to enter Oberlin in the fall!

"I met him online when I was researching a paper on the Civil War," she said. "He has a Web site that I went to. We started e-mailing. And we talk a lot on the phone."

I used to teach American history, and in spite of myself, I liked the fact that this guy from Colorado, of all places, had a Web site about the Civil War. I managed to stop myself from asking if the site was biased in favor of the North or South.

"And apparently you've met in person," I said, motioning toward her midriff.

"He came here over his spring break," she said, tugging one of the pieces of fringe completely free of the afghan. She grimaced, looked at me. "Sorry," she said.

"It's okay." I moved my hand in a circular motion to keep her talking. "Where did he stay?"

"He has some friends in Montclair." Her lower lip suddenly began to tremble. "He's awesome, Lucy," she said, shaking her head as if she couldn't believe her good fortune in meeting him. "You would love him," she said. "I know you would."

I wasn't at all sure about that. I wished she had told me earlier. *Much* earlier, so we could have had a reasonable conversation about her options. I felt a little betrayed by her. Shannon had always confided in me. I thought I knew everything about her.

"Why didn't you ever tell me about this guy?" I asked, thinking of all the lunches and dinners we'd shared during the past six months or so when she'd obviously had this Tanner person on her mind and yet had said nothing.

"I didn't want to hear you say I was being stupid," she said.

"When have I ever told you you were being stupid?" I asked. "And why would I start now?"

"You know…" She played with the loose piece of fringe in her hands. "Because he lives so far away and I met him on the Internet and everything."

I felt suspicious. "What's the everything part?" I asked.

"He's twenty-seven," she said, and stopped playing with the fringe as she waited for my reaction.

I tried not to let the shock show on my face. There were a hundred things I wanted to say, but none of them would be helpful to her.

"And what do you know about him?" I managed to keep my voice steady as I asked the question.

She smiled for the first time since I'd arrived home, one of her dimples showing, and her eyes got the faraway look of a woman smitten.

"He's so amazing," she said. "He's in graduate school to get his Ph.D. in history. The Civil War was his undergraduate project. Now he's working on something about the Holocaust. He's totally gorgeous and brilliant. He wants to be a college professor," she said, trying to win my heart. She knew I had a soft spot for anyone who teaches.

"What did he say when you told him you were pregnant?" I didn't trust this totally gorgeous, practically middle-aged future professor one bit. He lived two thousand miles away. He could be some sleaze-ball fabricating his credentials. But he did have that Web site. I would be sure to check it out.

"He was really upset," she said, "but mostly for me. I mean, he said he didn't really want me to have an abortion, but he understood how having a baby would screw up my plans for college and everything, and he said that if that's what I wanted, that's what I should do."

"And what—"

"I can't *do* it, Lucy." There was a plea in her voice, begging me to understand. "If it happened last year, I would have had an abortion. If it had happened before I was done with high school. But now…it would feel selfish of me to do it now. This is my *baby*." She rested her hands over her barely there belly.

"Oh, sweetie," I said, aching for her. I thought of how hard the past few months must have been for her, keeping this secret from the people who cared most about her. I thought of her 4.2 grade point average and her responsibilities as president of her class. How on earth had she held it together so well? She was pretty amazing herself.

"He'll support me and the baby," she said. "He wants me to move to Colorado and we'll both get jobs and he'll go to school part-time. Then, after the baby's a little older, I can go to college."

Tears burned my eyes. We'd all thought Shannon's future was so neatly mapped out for her. She'd gotten into a prestigious and competitive music program. She was talented enough to have a wonderful career ahead of her with a good symphony orchestra. Now I pictured her living a marginal existence in Colorado with a man she barely knew and a baby to take care of.

"You're majorly upset with me," she said.

"I'm upset, you're right. It's too much too quick for me to absorb."

"I know," she said. "I should have told you about him long ago."

"You knew I'd give you flak."

She nodded.

"Only because I love you and worry about you."

She nodded again, swallowing hard, the tremor returning to her lower lip.

I sat upright on the chair, pressing my palms together in the lap of my long skirt. My braid fell over my shoulder as I leaned toward her. "I'm trying to absorb what this means for you," I said. "For your future."

"You know how much I love kids," she said. "I'd planned to be a cellist first and a mom later. I'm just going to reverse the order. I mean, if I had to, like, choose between the two things, I would choose being a mother."

Was that true? Shannon had wanted to be a cellist in a symphony orchestra ever since Julie and Glen took her to her first New York Philharmonic concert when she was five years old. Had the adults in her life, anxious to encourage that dream, ignored her more ordinary ambitions, or was Shannon just kidding herself?

"You always said you had a *calling* to play the cello," I said.

"I still love it," she said. "I still want to play and I still want to go to school...eventually. I just can't do it now. You didn't go to college right away. Is that so terrible?"

"Of course not," I said. I wanted to ask if this Tanner guy planned to marry her. I wanted to ask how she planned to take care of a baby and "eventually" go to school. But those questions would not be helpful. Not yet. Instead, I continued listening to her, trying to be as nonjudgmental as possible. She would get enough of that elsewhere.

"How long do you think you can keep this from your mother?" I asked. "Is that why you want to live with your dad? You think he won't notice?"

"I don't know what to do, exactly." She stretched the piece of fringe taut between her hands, then dropped it in her lap. "Tanner really can't have me move in with him until September, because he's living with some other people right now and there wouldn't be room for me."

I hated him. Selfish bastard. I wondered if one of the "other people" was his wife, but I kept my mouth carefully sealed shut.

"So..." She looked at me helplessly. "What should I do? I thought maybe I should live with you, since you know about it, and I just wouldn't—"

"Uh-uh." I shook my head back and forth. "You have to tell your parents, Shannon. You *have* to. You know that, don't you?"

"Mom will go totally ballistic."

"Yes, she will." Julie would have a fit. A baby out of wedlock. Thwarted college plans after she'd driven Shannon all over the eastern half of the country to audition at the schools she'd wanted to attend. A promising future now in doubt. And above all, the worry that something might go wrong. Julie had been waiting seventeen years for something terrible to happen to Shannon. Perhaps this was it.

"Yes, she will," I repeated. "But you still have to tell her."

CHAPTER 7

Julie
1962

I thought that getting my period on our third full day at the shore was the worst thing that could happen to me. We were getting ready to go to our local beach, sometimes known as the "Baby Beach" because it was on the bay rather than the ocean and the water was gentle enough for toddlers. I loved swimming in the bay. I was hoping I could find some kids my age there to play with. I was already feeling lonely and had to admit that I missed the friendship Ethan used to provide. There were no other kids my age on our street. Lucy was useless because she was so afraid of everything and Isabel wanted nothing to do with me. In front of her friends, she treated me as though I was an embarrassment to her.

Lucy was in the living room, watching *The Edge of Night* with Grandma while she blew up her Flintstones tube. Isabel was getting the beach umbrella from the garage and I was gathering towels from different corners of the house, when I suddenly got that ache low in my belly that had become all too familiar to me in just a few months' time. I went upstairs to the attic and into the tiny curtained bathroom, pulled down my bathing suit and saw the spot. I wanted to cry, but I tried to be stoic. These were the days before slender plastic-encased tampons or stick-on pads. I pulled out the sanitary belt I had quickly come to loathe and affixed the bulky napkin to it, all the while cursing the fact that I'd been born female. Then I put on my shorts and a top, did my duty gathering the towels, marched downstairs and stood in the middle of the kitchen, the towels, some folded, some not, a bundle in my arms.

My mother was wrapping the last of the bologna sandwiches in waxed paper when she looked at me.

"Why did you change out of your bathing suit?" she asked.

"I'm not going," I said. "I got my stupid friend."

For a moment, she looked confused. Then she understood. "Oh, honey, I'm sorry." She walked over to hug me, but she was smiling, which made me doubt her sympathy. "Come to the beach anyway."

"Everyone will ask why I'm not in my bathing suit," I whined.

She shrugged as if that was no big deal. "If they do, just say you don't feel like swimming today," she said.

Isabel came into the room at that moment, bopping her head to the Four Seasons singing "Sherry" on the transistor radio she was carrying.

"Umbrella's in the car," she said to our mother.

"Turn that down, please," Mom said.

I nearly cringed, expecting Isabel to balk at the request. She and Mom were arguing night and day, usually about curfew and the clothes Isabel wanted to wear, and I was getting tired of it. But Isabel just flicked the little round dial on her radio, lowering the volume, and she never stopped moving to the music. I liked watching her. I knew she was sexy. I knew that was the word boys used to describe her. She was wearing a hot-pink two-piece bathing suit, the bottom barely covering her navel. Her skin was a soft olive tone that would darken to a rich tan in just a few days on the beach. I couldn't wait to be her age.

Isabel suddenly stopped bouncing around the kitchen and stared at me. "Why aren't you ready to go, Jules?" she asked.

"I *am* ready to go," I said.

"Oh." Isabel nodded. She looked genuinely sympathetic. "You got the curse."

"It's so embarrassing."

"I know," she said. "I'm sorry for you. I'll teach you how to use a tampon."

"No, you won't." Mom opened the cupboard and took out the little plastic badges we needed to wear on our bathing suits in order to use the private beach. "She's too young."

It didn't matter whether Isabel taught me to use a tampon or not. The fact that she'd given me her attention and had made the offer were all that mattered.

"That's *my* towel," Isabel said, abruptly pulling one of the towels from the bundle in my arm, making several others fall out of the pile.

"What's the big deal?" I said, frustrated as I picked up the towels from the floor.

"No big deal," she said, sending me a signal with her eyes that said *Shut up!*

I thought I understood. The towel she'd taken was one I'd never seen before. It was very soft and huge and it had a giraffe on it. I was sure it was a gift from Ned.

We piled into the hot car for the two-minute drive to our beach. Lucy had to put a towel beneath her legs because she thought the car seat might burn her. She already had her tube around her waist, as if she was afraid she might drown in the heat, and I helped her pin her badge to the strap of her bathing suit.

Given that it was the middle of the week, our beach was not at all crowded, and that disappointed me. We walked from the crushed-shell parking lot across the hot sand toward the water, and I didn't see another kid who looked like she—or he—was my age. Then I finally spotted one. He was lying on his stomach at the water's edge near the sea grass, poking at a pile of seaweed with a stick. Ethan. *What a spaz,* I thought. How had I ever been friends with him?

We reached a spot on the sand that my mother declared to be perfect. Isabel set down her radio and giraffe towel and pushed the umbrella stand into the sand, then opened it. Mom and I spread one of our two blankets out on the sand beneath it, not far from where the bay water lapped softly at the beach, and Lucy instantly sat down on it, the tube still glued to her body. She sat cross-legged, opened her book and began to read.

"You can lay that blanket down right next to this one," Mom said to Isabel.

Isabel looked toward the lifeguard stand and I followed her gaze. It took me only a moment to realize that Ned Chapman was the lifeguard. No wonder he was already so tan. He wore sunglasses and had white zinc oxide on his nose. His blond hair looked even lighter than it had a couple of days ago. The hairs on his bare legs glittered in the sunlight, and I felt that new belly-tightening sensation I would get each time I saw him. I'd feel that way for twenty minutes or so, then lose myself in the comfort of Nancy Drew and her safe and improbable mysteries. The unfamiliar desire that was mounting in me, in combination with my impetuous nature and need for excitement, scared the daylights out of me, and Nancy offered great relief.

As if he knew I was thinking about him, Ned looked over at us and waved. I waved back, even though I knew it was not me he was greeting.

"Can I go over to where Mitzi and Pam are?" Isabel asked.

"May I please," Mom said.

"May I please?"

"Of course. Do you want a glass of lemonade before you go?"

"No, thanks." Isabel was already on her way, her radio and towel in her arms, and I wondered if our mother realized Ned was over there. I watched my sister's long legs as she strode through the sand to where the throng of teenagers were tanning themselves, radios blaring, around the lifeguard stand. God, I wanted to be Isabel! I wanted to know how to use a tampon and have those long legs and fully formed breasts. I wanted boys' heads to turn when I walked past them, the way their heads were turning toward Isabel now. I watched the group of kids greet her. Pamela Durant sat up, tugging at a strap of her bathing suit top that had slipped down her shoulder. She grinned at Isabel, patting the blanket next to her, and Isabel sat down. It was an attractive group of teenagers. There were about ten of them, all long limbs and breasts and bare chests, wavy hair shining in the sunlight and bodies glistening with iodine-tinted baby oil. Most of them were smoking, but I didn't think Izzy had ever had a cigarette.

I knew a few of Isabel's friends because she'd belonged to this group for the past couple of years. Mitzi Caruso was the nicest of the girls, but also the shyest and the least attractive. She had black hair that stayed frizzy all summer long and she was on the chubby side. Pamela Durant was gorgeous, maybe even prettier than my sister. She wore her light blond hair in a long ponytail on the side of her head, and she reminded me of Cricket, that character Connie Stevens played on *Hawaiian Eye.* The only other boy I knew was Bruno Walker, Ned's best friend. His real name was Bruce, but only the adults called him that, and he wore his black hair in a ducktail. He had green eyes and pouty lips and his body was big and muscular. I'd heard Isabel and Pam talking one time about how he looked like Elvis Presley. They said he was wild: He rode on the hood of some kid's car once and he drank too much. He was good-looking, but he didn't interest me the way Ned did.

I saw Ned glance in our direction from his perch on the lifeguard stand, then jump down to the sand and walk the few steps to where Isabel was sitting. He put his hand on her shoulder, and my belly started turning flip-flops again as he leaned down to whisper something in her ear. She laughed, reaching up to give a playful tug on the black whistle hanging around his neck.

You're supposed to be guarding the water, I said to myself. I lay down on the blanket on my stomach, turning my head away from them and closing my eyes. I was jealous, pure and simple.

I knew something about Isabel and Ned no one else did, something I could hold over my sister if I ever had that need. The day before, she and I had been reading on the porch while Mom sketched something at her easel. It looked as if she was getting ready to paint the rooster man's shack on the other side of the canal. I wondered if she knew who lived there, but I didn't dare tell her about my visit with him. Isabel suddenly looked up from her book.

"Can I go for a ride in Ned's boat today?" she asked.

I waited for Mom to come back with her usual *May I please,* but instead she simply looked across the canal as though deep in thought. Then she nodded. "If either Ethan or Julie goes with you, then yes, you can go."

I was thrilled! I couldn't wait for a ride in the Chapmans' Boston Whaler. I hoped we could ski. But Isabel was having none of it.

"Really, Mother," she said, closing her book and getting to her feet, "that's ridiculous."

She walked into the house and Mom called after her, "Remember, you're supposed to look for a job this summer."

Mom began working on her sketch again as though nothing had happened, and disappointed, I returned to *The Secret in the Old Attic*. Later that day, I walked to the beach by myself and as I passed the little marina at the end of the canal, I saw Isabel standing on the bulkhead staring out at the water. I called to her, but she didn't seem to hear me. Then I saw Ned pull his boat up tight against the bulkhead. He reached out a hand and Isabel climbed in.

I stopped walking, my mouth hanging open. I couldn't believe she would so completely disregard our mother's rules. I watched with envy as the boat picked up speed and raced out of the marina, and I tucked that image away for some day when I might need it.

"Come on, Lucy," Mom said now. "Let's go in the water." I opened my eyes to see that she'd arranged the sandwiches and thermos, suntan lotion and her book, all in a row along one side of the blanket. Now she was ready to swim.

"I'm reading," Lucy said. She was out of my line of sight, but I was certain she had not lifted her eyes from her book.

I saw Mom kneel down in front of her. "It's a new summer, Lucy," she said. "You're eight now. It's really silly to still be afraid of the water."

Lucy didn't respond.

"Chicken," I said, closing my eyes again.

"Shh!" Mom said to me. "That's not going to help."

"Go in the water, Lucy." I sat up, feeling guilty. I didn't want to be a nasty older sister. I knew how that felt. "Then later I'll go on the swings with you."

With a sigh too heavy for an eight-year-old, Lucy got to her feet.

My mother pulled on her own bathing cap, tucking her dark, wavy chin-length hair up inside it. Then she helped Lucy pull hers over her short permed curls, as though my sister might actually go into water deep enough to get her hair wet. I watched as the two of them walked toward the roped-off section of the water, holding hands. Mom pointed to a plane that was flying above the water, trailing a Coppertone banner behind it. As I'd figured, Lucy went in up to her knees and refused to go any farther. I couldn't hear their conversation, but I could tell that my mother spent much of it coercing and Lucy spent much of it shaking her head no. Finally giving up, my mother walked into the water by herself. I watched her dive in once she'd reached the deeper water. She swam underwater to escape from the roped area, then began swimming parallel to the shore with long, fluid strokes. She looked beautiful, like a sea creature instead of a woman. I longed to be out there with her. She'd taught me to swim when I was half Lucy's age.

I looked at my younger sister. She was still standing in the knee-high water, her yellow ruffly bathing suit dry, the pathetic Flintstones tube around her waist as she watched our mother swim. Suddenly I felt so sorry for her that I thought I might cry.

"Lucy, honey," I called, the endearment slipping from my mouth before I could stop it.

She turned to look at me.

"Come back to the blanket," I said.

She did. She trudged back to the blanket, pulled off the bathing cap, shimmied out of her tube and sat down next to me to read.

"Lay down and I'll put some suntan lotion on you," I said.

Mom had already coated her with it, but I just wanted to do something nice for her. She lay down on her stomach, and I rubbed the coconut-scented lotion on her back. I felt her shoulder blades, pointy beneath my palms. She seemed so fragile. I wanted to bend over and hug her. I wished I could give her just an ounce of my courage. I had more than I could manage.

I was putting the lid back on the tube when I realized Mr. and Mrs. Chapman were now on the beach directly behind us. They were sitting on striped, legless beach chairs, and Mrs. Chapman had her head tilted back, her eyes closed, face held toward the sun. She had pretty blond hair, cut short in a cap around her head. Mr. Chapman was reading a book, but he must have sensed me looking at him, because he took off his sunglasses and I could see him returning my gaze. He did not look happy to see me.

"Oh," he said. "Hello, Lucy."

"I'm Julie," I said.

"Julie, of course."

I looked toward the sea grass where I'd seen Ethan lying down, but he was no longer there. Then I spotted him sitting on the pier, holding one end of a string that disappeared below the water's surface. He was probably crabbing. If I could still stand him, I would have enjoyed doing that with him.

"Has Charles...has your father gone back to Westfield for the week?" Mr. Chapman asked me.

I nodded. "Don't you have to go home during the week, too?" I asked.

He shook his head. "Not since I've been on the Supreme Court," he said. "We break for the summer."

I was confused. I'd had no idea Mr. Chapman was on the Supreme Court. "Why did you outlaw school prayer?" I said, taking up my father's fight.

"What?" He looked puzzled, then he laughed. His features were softer when he laughed and I could see some of Ned's good looks in him. "That's the *United States* Supreme Court," he said. "I'm chief justice of the *New Jersey* Supreme Court."

"Oh." I felt embarrassed, as though this was something I should have known.

"I *would* have outlawed school prayer, though," he added, "had I been in the position to do so."

I suddenly understood why my father didn't seem to like Mr. Chapman. I couldn't remember ever seeing them talk to each other.

"Don't start, Ross." Mrs. Chapman didn't move her head from her sunbathing, but she smiled as she chastised her husband.

"I think there *should* be a prayer to start the day in school," I said, feeling immensely adult and grateful for my father's guidance.

Mr. Chapman leaned forward. His eyes were the color of my

mother's pewter coffeepot. "It's wonderful that you're taking a stand, Julie," he said. "It's important to get involved, no matter what side you're on. But I happen to disagree with you. In this country, we don't only have Christians. We have Jews and Muslims and atheists. Do you honestly think those children should have to say a Christian prayer in school every morning?"

I only knew one Jewish girl and I certainly didn't know any Muslims. I wasn't sure how to respond. He had a point I could not argue against, but I clung so fiercely to my father's righteousness that I couldn't back down. "Atheists are stupid," I said, my cheeks reddening instantly because I knew it was my statement that was stupid.

He laughed. "And they might say the same thing about your beliefs."

"Are you an atheist?" I asked, suddenly wondering if that was his reason for wanting to abolish school prayer.

"No, I'm Catholic. Just like you are. But even Catholics can disagree on important issues."

His wife suddenly dipped her head. She shaded her eyes to look at me, then smiled. To her husband, she said, "Stop badgering her."

"We're having a healthy debate," Mr. Chapman said, and I was glad he felt that way even after my weak comment about atheists.

"How are you, Julie, dear?" Mrs. Chapman said. "We've barely had a chance to see your family yet this summer. Where's your mother?"

I turned to the bay, pointing toward the last place I'd seen my mother swimming, but she was walking out of the water, pulling off her bathing cap, her dark hair springing into curls around her face. Like most women her age, she wore a black bathing suit with a little skirt on it, but it was clear that her long, lean thighs did not need to be hidden in any way. I felt a surge of pride. She was so pretty.

"Hello, Joan," my mother said, picking up a towel from the blanket and patting it to her face. "And Ross."

"Maria." Mr. Chapman nodded to my mother.

"How's the water?" Mrs. Chapman asked.

"Chilly," my mother said. "But very refreshing." She turned her attention to Lucy and me. "Let's have some lunch, girls, okay?" She sat down on the blanket, her back to the Chapmans, blocking my view of them and putting an end to the "healthy" debate.

We were eating our bologna on Wonder Bread sandwiches when I looked over to where Isabel had been sitting with her friends and saw that the blankets were empty. On the lifeguard stand, a boy I didn't recognize sat tossing his black whistle from one hand to another. I knew where they all were. I looked out at the water toward the platform, a heavy wooden raft anchored in the deep water and held afloat by empty oil drums. Every last one of the teenagers was crammed on top of the platform, which was really too small for all of them. I could hear them laughing from where I sat. I could hear music, too, and I wondered how they'd managed to get a radio out there in the deep water without it getting wet. My sister and another girl were standing up, dancing, moving to the music. Bruno Walker was balanced on the edge of the platform, and I watched him do a perfect dive into the water. Then he swam back to the platform, hoisting himself onto it using his muscular arms rather than climbing up the ladder. He took a seat near one of the girls I didn't know.

I chewed my sandwich slowly, watching them. I'd never been on the platform, although I longed to be. I was a good swimmer and I was certain I could even hoist myself up onto it the way Bruno had just done, but I was intimidated by the teenagers who always hung out there, Isabel included. It was clearly their territory. A twelve-year-old would not be welcome. Watching them, I had no way of knowing that my sister, who looked so vibrant and alive, would be dead before the summer was over. And I had no way of knowing how that platform would one day haunt my dreams.

CHAPTER 8

Maria

I weeded my garden every day. Although it was only late June, I could already see weeds popping up through the mulch Julie and Lucy had spread for me. Most people hated weeding, but I didn't. I loved being in the sun—the Italian portion of my blood, no doubt. Maybe I had more wrinkles than I would if I hadn't spent so much of my life outdoors, but I didn't care. It was a privilege to grow old, and not everyone got to enjoy it. I was grateful for every minute I was given.

I liked keeping the flower beds neat and orderly, scratching out the weeds from around the red begonias and pink peonies, making order out of chaos. Julie was exactly like me in that regard. Lucy was another story altogether. She was sloppy and complicated. I tried not to think of where Isabel would have fallen in that continuum of neatness to messiness. Thinking about things like that could drive you crazy.

That morning in late June, I was sitting on the little seat-on-rollers Julie had bought for me, working on the flower bed near the front steps, when a car pulled into my driveway. It was a big car with a long hood, the kind of car an old man would drive, and sure enough, I watched as a man about my age got out of the driver's side.

I set down my trowel and stood up slowly. That's one thing I'd learned—I had to take my time getting to my feet after working in the sun, or everything would go dark for a few seconds. I took off my gardening gloves and dropped them to the mulch as I watched the old man retrieve a cane from the car and begin to hobble toward me.

"Hello," I called out, taking a few steps across my lawn.

He waved at me. "Hello, Maria," he said, and my mind started the frantic racing it did when someone unfamiliar seemed to know me. My memory was not bad at all, but when I'd meet people out of context, I often couldn't place them. Did I know this man from church? From Micky D's? I shaded my eyes with my hand, trying to see him more clearly. He was tall and nearly gaunt, his white hair very thin on top. He limped when he walked toward me and I knew he needed that cane and that it wasn't just for show. He looked like a complete stranger to me.

He smiled as he neared me, and although there was something familiar in the curve of his lips, I still couldn't place him.

"You don't recognize me, do you?" he said, without reproach.

I shook my head. "I'm sorry, I don't," I said. "Do you go to Holy Trinity?"

He held his left hand toward me, his right hand leaning heavily on his cane. "I'm Ross Chapman," he said.

I had stood up slowly enough, of that I was certain, yet my head went so light I thought I might pass out. I took his hand more to steady myself than to shake it and I could not seem to find my voice.

"It's been a long, long time," he said.

I managed to nod. "Yes," I said.

"You are still a stunning woman," he said, even though I was wearing my gardening overalls and probably had dirt smeared on my face.

"Thank you." I couldn't bring myself to reciprocate. Ross Chapman had once been a very handsome man, but in the forty-one years since I'd last seen him in person, he had withered and paled. After we left the summer house for the last time in 1962, I would see his picture occasionally in the papers and on TV, since he was a prominent figure in New Jersey and had even run for governor. But he looked nothing like that robust politician now.

"Is this how you spend your days?" he asked, motioning toward the flower bed. "Working in your garden?"

"I also work at McDonald's in Garwood and I'm a volunteer at the hospital," I said.

"McDonald's?" he laughed. "That's marvelous. You always knew how to keep busy," he said, nodding with what I guessed was approval.

I wasn't sure what to do with him. We stood for a moment in an awkward silence. I didn't want to invite him in, but I saw no alternative.

"Would you like to come in?" I asked finally. "Have something to drink?"

"I'd like that," he said.

I walked up the front steps and inside the house, holding the door open for him. I could see that the four concrete steps were a bit of a struggle for him and I looked away, not wanting to embarrass him by noticing his frailty.

"Why don't you sit here?" I motioned toward the armchair in the living room, then rattled off the things I could offer him to drink.

"Just ice water," he said.

In the kitchen, I took my time getting out the glasses, filling them with ice. I wished he had not come. I could see no point to this visit. I could have quite happily lived out the rest of my days without seeing my old neighbor again.

When I returned to the living room, I saw that he had not taken a seat as I'd suggested. Instead, he was looking at the pictures on the mantel. There was one of the four of us—Charles and myself and Julie and Lucy, when the girls were fifteen and eleven. It was the last picture I had of Charles; he'd dropped dead from a heart attack in our kitchen only a few weeks after it had been taken. Then there were Julie's and Lucy's old college-graduation pictures and, next to them, Shannon's senior picture. Ross lifted that last one up and looked toward me, a smile on his lips.

"A granddaughter?" he asked.

I nodded. "Shannon," I said. "She's Julie's." I thought of telling him more about her, how she'd been accepted to Oberlin, how accomplished she was already, but I didn't want to extend my conversation with Ross any longer than I had to.

"Lovely." Then he poked a finger at Julie's picture. "That's Julie, right? She was the sharp one. The one with the brains and the spunk."

His words jolted me. Julie had brains, all right, but her spunk had gone out the window long ago. He was right, though. When he knew my girls, Julie was the one who'd had the most gumption.

"Yes," I said, to keep things short and simple. "She was always up to something."

Ross limped over to the armchair and sat down. "I have one granddaughter and a great-granddaughter," he said. He took the glass I held out for him and looked up at me. "But that's not why I'm here."

I set a coaster on the end table next to him, then sat on the hassock in front of the other armchair. "Why *are* you here?" I asked. The back of my neck ached a bit, and I rubbed it. My skin was slick with perspiration, more from anxiety than the heat.

"Do you know that my Ethan and your Julie are meeting for lunch today?" Ross asked.

"What?" I'd been about to take a sip of my water and nearly dropped the glass. "Why on earth?" As far as I knew, Julie and Ethan Chapman had had no contact since 1962.

Ross shrugged. "Ethan just said he was thinking about her and felt like getting together. They planned to meet in Spring Lake."

"Well," I said, recovering from the shock. "Good for them. They were friends when they were little."

"Anyhow," Ross said, "when Ethan told me he was going to see Julie, it started me thinking about you…about your family. About how I…" He set his glass down on the coaster and looked directly into my eyes. "I mishandled things, Maria. In every which way. I—"

"Water under the bridge, Ross," I said. "It's not necessary to rehash it."

"But I think it is," he said.

I recognized his earnest look as one he'd employed when running for governor. It was a look that made you want to trust him.

"I'm old and tired," he said. "I really doubt I'll live much longer and I just want to make amends to any people I might have hurt during my lifetime."

"What's wrong?" I asked him. I wondered if he had cancer. He was so thin. "Are you sick?"

He shook his head, brushing my question away with his hand. "I lost Joan last year," he said, then looked away from me, toward the pictures on the mantel. "And Ned...Ned died just a few weeks ago."

"Oh," I said. I understood then how his world had been altered. Ned must have been close to sixty, but that didn't matter when it came to burying your child. "I'm sorry, Ross."

"It gave me a new understanding of how you felt when Isabel died."

"Yes," I said.

"So, I wanted to talk to you about...I just wanted to apologize."

"And now you have and that's fine and enough," I said. I didn't like the sympathy I felt for this old man. He was a politician, first and foremost, capable of talking out of both sides of his mouth.

He looked at me so long and hard that I had to look away. I knew he wanted to say more, but whatever it was, I didn't want to hear it. So I stood up.

"Come on," I said, holding my hand out to help him from the chair. He'd hardly touched his water, but he had not come here for the refreshments.

He clutched my hand hard as he struggled to his feet. I let him hold on to my arm as I walked with him back down the front steps and out to his car. Neither of us spoke, although I knew there was a lot we could have said if we'd had the courage. I opened the driver's-side door of his car for him. It made me nervous to think of someone in his condition driving. I had not even asked him where he lived, how far he had to drive.

"What did Ned die from?" I asked, before closing the car door.

"Drinking," Ross said. "Drowning his sorrows. I don't think he ever got over losing Isabel."

I winced at that, then closed the door. I watched him drive away before returning to my seat in the garden. I pulled on my gloves and drew the trowel through the soil, barely able to see what I was doing for the tears. *I don't think he ever got over losing Isabel.*

"Neither have I, Ross," I said out loud. "Neither have I."

CHAPTER 9

Lucy

Shannon spent most of the afternoon with me as we talked about her dilemma. It was a strange experience for me, watching her shift between tears of anxiety and worry and joy over the new love in her life. She had always been a very grounded, sane person, even as a young child, but listening to her talk about Tanner, I had the odd feeling that she had been taken away by some cult group, brainwashed and returned to us a different person. It was the same Shannon sitting there in my living room, the same beautiful girl who'd brought such joy into her family, but words were coming out of her mouth that were decidedly un-Shannon-like. I felt as though we needed a deprogrammer.

She left about four, saying she had a cello lesson to give at the music store, and she'd been gone no more than fifteen minutes when Julie showed up at my door. I'd tried to reach her on her cell phone to see how the lunch with Ethan had gone, but was only able to get her voice mail, so I'd pulled out my violin, planning to practice for an upcoming ZydaChicks concert.

"I'm interrupting your practice," Julie said, glancing at the violin in my hand. There was a damp flush to her cheeks that made her look pretty, if uncomfortably warm. I knew she was grappling with hot flashes, something that was still in my future.

"Haven't even started," I said, taking her hand with my free one and pulling her into my apartment. "So, how did it go?" I asked, as I put my violin back in its case.

"Not bad." Julie flopped down on my sofa. The two empty glasses of lemonade were still on the coffee table and I scooped them up and carried them into the kitchen before she could ask who had been there, but she didn't even seem to notice them.

I glanced at her when I returned to the room. "Are you okay?"

She pressed her hands to her cheeks, which were nearly the color of her red shirt. "I'm just..." She smiled a sort of goofy grin. "Just freaking out, I think," she said.

"Hot flash?" I asked, although by now I'd guessed it was more than that. She'd just had a conversation about Isabel's murder. That alone would have been enough to freak her out.

"What?" she said. "Oh, maybe. I don't even know." She slipped off her sandals and stretched her legs out on the couch. "I convinced Ethan to take the letter to the police," she said.

"Oh, that's excellent." I felt relieved. I sat down in my armchair again, drawing my legs onto the seat cushion, covering them with my skirt. "Did he take a lot of convincing?"

She nodded. "It took a lot of discussing," she said. "It was hard and I felt sorry for him." Julie watched her feet as she flexed them up and down. Then she looked at me. "He just can't handle the fact that his brother could be guilty after all these years."

"Of course he can't," I said. "What do you think the cops will do with the letter?"

"That's the scary part," Julie said. "Ethan has a friend in the police department and he sort of ran it by this guy—in a hypothetical way—to get a sense of what would happen. His friend said they'll probably start fresh, which I figured they would do. But that means interviewing everyone involved again. I'm guessing that would be me, which is fine, of course. Maybe Ethan and Ned and Izzy's friends.

Mr. Chapman, which worries Ethan." She bit her lip and looked at me squarely. "And possibly Mom."

"Ugh," I said.

"Right. I hope it doesn't come to that. I'd love to keep her from knowing this is even going on. I could see them badgering her with questions and then she has a heart attack or a stroke or——"

"*Julie.*" I laughed. One reason my sister could write gripping page-turners was her skill at imagining the worst possible outcome in any situation. I dreaded the scenarios she would be able to create once she learned that Shannon was pregnant. Her ability to turn an event into a catastrophe in her mind had been one of Glen's many complaints about her. *She always worries about everything,* he'd whined to me. *She never lets herself have any fun.* Although there was some truth to the statement, it still infuriated me that he'd made it, that he never took the time to understand the origin of those worries.

"If Mom has to be interviewed, she'll be fine," I said. "She would want the truth to come out." My voice sounded strong, but I too hoped our mother wouldn't need to be involved in a new investigation.

"I just don't want her to be hurt any more than she already has been," Julie said. She pulled a tissue from the pocket of her cropped black slacks, then took off her glasses and began cleaning them.

"She'll be okay," I said. "Do you think they'd want to interview me?"

"I doubt it," she said. "What do you remember about that whole situation?" She held her glasses up to the light, then slipped them on her face again.

I shook my head. "Almost nothing," I said. "I barely remember anything about the shore at all. You know what I was like—always cowering in the background while everyone else swam or went out in the boat or whatever." It was as though I hadn't truly been there. I supposed that I'd repressed most of the memories from the worst summer my family had ever endured. "The other day, though, I remembered when you caught that giant eel and Ethan wanted its guts," I said.

Julie laughed, and the high flush came to her cheeks again. It made me suspicious. Maybe I wouldn't have recognized the subtle look of infatuation in her face if I had not just witnessed the same expression in her daughter's.

"So, what is he like these days?" I probed. "As geeky as he was back then?"

She looked away from me. "He was nice," she said, and I thought she was trying not to break into a smile. "He...he looked good. I didn't recognize him at first. He's a carpenter and he has this amazing body."

"You're kidding." I tried to picture the skinny, gawky kid of my memory with an amazing body.

"And he must have had laser eye surgery, because he wasn't wearing glasses. His eyes are really blue."

"Hey," I said, turning in the chair and putting my feet on the floor. "Are you attracted to him or what?" Julie had shown no interest whatsoever in men since the divorce.

She laughed, shaking her head. "He just looked better than I'd expected, that's all."

"If you say so," I said with a smile. I liked seeing the life and color in her face. It may have been a difficult conversation, but all in all, I thought seeing Ethan Chapman had done her good. Seeing her *daughter* would be something different altogether, and for the remainder of our conversation, I couldn't get Shannon out of my mind. I sat there with my sister, knowing a secret that was going to rock her world. It was like looking at someone's smiling picture on the obituary page. You wanted to warn them: *You don't know it, but you're going to walk in front of a truck on March 3, 2003.* I listened to my sister talk, and I hated having that secret inside me. I needed Shannon to tell Julie soon, for my sake if not for hers.

CHAPTER 10

Julie

Shannon moved to Glen's on Tuesday. She was only two miles away; I reminded myself. *Two miles.* I could walk it, although I wouldn't. She'd moved out to taste her freedom. To get away from my tight reins. What I needed to do was to back off. Sometimes I felt as though the only way I could keep her safe was to be sure she stayed in my line of sight. I wished that children came with guarantees that they would stay healthy, that they would outlive their parents.

I'd walked into her room as she was packing this morning.

"Do you need any help?" I'd asked.

She'd smiled at me, but it wasn't her real smile. "I'm fine," she said. She had taken apart her computer setup, the components on her bed, and she was wrapping towels around them.

I pointed to the only free corner of the full-size bed. "May I sit?"

She shrugged. "Sure."

I watched her carefully wrap a towel around her printer. I was in need of something I couldn't quite put my finger on. I wondered if all parents felt that way when their children were leaving. It seemed monumental. A time for a good talk. To say all the things we thought about but never said to one another. I gave it a try.

"I'll miss you," I said.

"I'll still be around, Mom." She had finished with the computer and now was working on the middle drawer of her dresser. "I'm just taking one suitcase and my CDs and computer and my cello. It's not like I'm going off to school already."

"There's something I have to ask you," I said.

She didn't respond. She folded a pair of shorts, smoothing them into her suitcase, running her hands over them as though it was important to get out every invisible crease. Her long hair swung forward, cutting me off from her face.

"We've never really talked about this," I said, readying myself for a conversation two years overdue. "But I need to know. Do you blame me for the divorce?"

She glanced up at me then, stepping back from her suitcase before reaching into her dresser again, this time for a stack of T-shirts. "Of course not," she said, dumping the shirts on her bed.

"Do you blame your dad then?"

"I think it was a mutual thing."

"What do you think happened?" I often wondered if she knew, if she had somehow put two and two together and guessed about Glen's affair.

She shrugged. "I figured it wasn't any of my business," she said.

"Honey, I just want to make sure you...you know, that you don't think it had anything to do with you. That it was your fault in any way."

"I know that," she said, some irritation creeping into her voice. "I think Dad just pissed you off and you pissed him off, that's all."

That puzzled me, because I didn't think I'd ever complained about her father to her.

"What do you think he did that upset me?" I asked.

She put her hands on her hips and looked at me in genuine annoyance. "Mom, I'm trying to pack," she said. "I have to take my stuff over to Dad's and be ready to work at the day-care center by noon."

"I'd like to understand, though," I persisted. I couldn't seem to shut up. "I want to make sure that—"

"I think Dad was a slob and that got to you," she said. "And I think you're afraid of…the world and that got to him."

"I'm not afraid of the world," I said, wounded.

"Mother, you're a hermit," she said, grabbing one of the T-shirts and stuffing it unfolded into the suitcase. "Face it. You sit in your little cubbyhole of an office all day long, hanging around with people who don't exist."

"That is really unfair." I felt both defensive and misunderstood. The only thing I truly feared, other than something terrible happening to someone I love, was water. Not water in my bathtub, or even in a swimming pool. But the thought of swimming in the open water of a bay or the ocean or a lake was enough to start my heart racing. And I had to admit, I hadn't been in a boat since the night Isabel died. But I was *not* afraid of the world.

"I fly regularly," I said to Shannon. "I go on book tours—which are stressful, to say the least—for weeks at a time. I speak in front of huge audiences. I try new foods." My voice was rising. "I walk through Westfield in the dark. I teach memoir writing at the nursing home. I do volunteer work at the hospital. So please don't tell me that I'm a hermit and that my fears are keeping me locked up in my office, or whatever it was you said."

"You're right, I'm sorry." Her tone told me she was only saying it to end the conversation.

I ran my hand over the T-shirt on the top of the pile on her bed, recognizing it as one I'd sent her from Seattle when I was touring there. "The only thing I'm really afraid of is losing you," I said, the words leaving my mouth before I could stop them.

She looked at me, a few bras hanging from her fingers. "Do you know what a burden that is?" she asked. "I feel like every single thing I do, I not only have to take my own well-being into account, but yours, too."

I stared down at the T-shirt, knowing she was right, maybe fully understanding for the first time how difficult it was to be my daughter. I was uncertain what to say next.

"I'm done packing," she said, closing the flap on her suitcase and running the zipper around it. "I'm going to carry this stuff down to my car."

"I'll help you," I said, standing up. "But I want to continue this conversation some time. Not now, though. We should probably put it on the shelf for now. I don't want you to move out with either of us angry at the other."

"I didn't want to talk about it in the first place," she said, lifting her suitcase from the bed to the floor.

"I love you," I said. "I hope it's good for you, staying with Dad for the summer."

I helped her load the computer and suitcase into her little Honda, and once she'd gone, I went into my office. It was true that I usually felt safe and secure in that room with my "people who don't really exist." But I hadn't felt happy in there for the past few days. I still had a blank white computer screen beneath the words *Chapter Four,* and I had no idea how to fill it. There were times when my characters seemed unimportant and a ridiculous waste of my time. This morning was one of them.

I had written and deleted four paragraphs when the phone rang. It was Ethan.

"I took the letter to the police department yesterday," he said.

"Oh, that's good, Ethan." I got up from my office chair and carried the phone to the love seat where I could get comfortable. I was surprised and pleased that he'd taken care of the matter so quickly. "What did they say?"

"Just what we expected," he said. "They're reopening the case. I stopped at the grocery store after I dropped off the letter, and by the time I got home, there was already a message on my voice mail telling me they want to search Ned's house."

I felt a flicker of guilt. I'd persuaded Ethan to take the letter to the police and already the Chapmans' privacy was being invaded, while I sat in a house that would never be encroached on in any way.

"What could they possibly find at Ned's house forty-some years after the fact?" I asked, although I knew the answer the moment the question left my lips: DNA.

"Who knows?" Ethan said. "A journal, maybe, though I know— or at least, I don't think—he ever kept one. Letters. Keepsakes. But the truth is, and I told them this, Abby and I already went through everything. We threw out sacks and sacks of stuff that seemed un-important and it's too late to recover any of that, I'm sure. We put anything valuable in boxes that I was just going to keep in storage along with his furniture, until I have the time to go through them and see what I want to sell and what I want to hold on to. The boxes are all there at his house, and the cops plan to take them apart and go through everything."

"I think," I said carefully, "they'll probably look for DNA."

He was quiet. "How would that help them after all this time?"

"I'm not sure," I said. "If they kept anything from the scene, maybe." I knew that, these days, they bagged victim's hands, allow-ing any DNA material that might have belonged to the suspect to fall into the bags, but I didn't know if that had been done as early as 1962.

"But Isabel was in the——" He stopped himself, I knew, for my benefit.

"In the water," I finished the sentence for him. "I know. I don't re-ally know how that would affect the collection of evidence." I didn't want to talk about this, more for his sake than my own.

"Are you upset?" I asked.

"Not with you," he said. "I know you and I are hoping for differ-ent outcomes, though, and I guess I'm...I'm just worried."

"That they'll learn it was Ned?"

"No, because I know it couldn't have been," he said, a stubborn edge to his soft voice. "I'm worried they might somehow put evi-dence together that would come—incorrectly—to that conclusion, though. I mean, I don't understand how they'd collect the suspect's DNA from your sister after all this time, but she was always with Ned, so it's certainly possible they'd find his DNA on her."

Or in her, I thought but did not say.

"And as I mentioned before, I'm worried about my father having to be dragged into this."

"I know," I said, "and I'm sorry this is so hard. But let's not bor-row trouble. One step at a time."

"Right," he said. "You know one good thing that has come out of this?"

"What's that?"

"I enjoyed seeing you again, Julie," he said. "Even though it wasn't an easy conversation, it was a treat having lunch with you."

I smiled, feeling an unexpected rush of excitement run through my body. "It was," I agreed.

"I was remembering things about you," he said. "Are you still a terrific swimmer?"

"Actually, I don't swim at all anymore," I said. "I lost interest after that summer."

"Really?" he asked. "You were so good. I was remembering the time you and I raced across the canal," he said.

I laughed. I'd forgotten. We'd only been about ten the last summer we were truly friends. We'd known enough to wait for the slack tide and we were both strong swimmers for kids our age, but we got in a lot of trouble.

"I wasn't allowed near the water for a week," I said.

"I had to vacuum the entire house," Ethan said.

"I don't think I ever swam in the canal again," I said. "I swam in our dock all the time when the boat wasn't in it, but not the canal."

"Ah, that's not true," Ethan said.

"What do you mean?"

"I remember watching you float down the canal in an inner tube."

It took me a moment to place the memory, but then it came into my mind all at once. "I'd forgotten," I said, laughing, although the memory carried with it both joy and sadness since Isabel had been so much a part of it, and though Ethan and I reminisced about several other shared experiences before getting off the phone, it was that memory which stayed with me for the rest of the day.

CHAPTER 11

Julie
1962

It was a weekday in Bay Head Shores, which meant that our father was home in Westfield. We had finished eating breakfast and Grandpop was already out in the garage working on some project, while Grandma was starting to clear the table in spite of our mother's admonishment to relax a while. I started to stand up to help Grandma, but Mom told me to stay where I was and I sat down again. She shook a cigarette from her pack of Kents and lit it, blowing a puff of smoke into the air above the cluttered table.

"I have an idea for something we could do today, girls," she said to the three of us.

"What?" Lucy sounded suspicious. Whatever it was, I could tell she was prepared to say she didn't want to do it.

"Look at the current," Mom said, and I turned my head to peer through the screen at the canal. The current was moving slowly in the direction of the bay.

"What about it?" Isabel asked. She was holding a lock of her hair in front of her face, probably scrutinizing it for split ends.

"Well," Mom said, "after we've digested our breakfast a bit, how about we take the big inner tubes and ride the current all the way from our house to the bay."

"Keen!" I said. It was an extraordinary idea.

"You've got to be kidding," Isabel said, but I knew she was intrigued. It was hard to get Isabel interested in any sort of family activity, and I was impressed that my mother had managed to come up with something exciting enough to draw in her oldest daughter.

Grandma laughed, sitting down at the table again, her chores forgotten. "I remember when you and Ross used to do that," she said to my mother. She rolled the *r* in "Ross" in a way that made the name sound very pretty. I was surprised by what she'd said, though. So was Isabel.

"You and *Mr. Chapman* floated on tubes to the bay?" she asked, incredulous.

"When we were kids," Mom said.

I always forgot that my mother had spent her childhood summers in our bungalow. Her father—our Grandpop—had built the house himself in the late twenties, and the Chapmans had moved in next door shortly after that. Mr. Chapman and our mother had been friends when they were kids, the way Ethan and I used to be.

"We were probably about fifteen," my mother continued. "Once we floated all the way to the river."

"Tsk," Grandma clucked. "Do you remember how furious I was when I realized what you did?"

Mom smiled at her, turning her head to exhale a stream of smoke over her shoulder and away from the table. "I survived," she said.

"Well, I'm not going," Lucy announced, but this was no surprise and no one paid her much attention.

"The canal was different then," Grandma said. "There was no bulkhead, so you could walk right into it from the yard. And of course there weren't so many boats."

"Gosh." I turned to look at the water again, imagining it lapping at our sandy backyard. I wished it was still like that.

"The tubes are a little soft," Isabel said.

We had four of the giant black inner tubes in the garage. Ethan and I used to float on them in the dock, our arms and legs dangling over the sides. This year, though, I hadn't even bothered with the tubes. It was no fun playing in the dock alone. My loneliness was mounting, day by day. I made up stories about the rooster man, but I had no friends to scare with those spooky tales. I didn't dare tell them to Lucy and make her more paranoid than she already was.

"Why don't you and Julie take the tubes to the gas station and fill them up?" Mom said, stubbing out her cigarette in the big clamshell ashtray on the table. "By the time you get back, the current should be perfect for our adventure."

After we helped clean up from breakfast, Isabel and I went out to the garage, gathered up the four fat tubes and loaded them in the car. Isabel turned the key in the ignition, then adjusted the dial on the radio until she found "Johnny Angel," and we both sang along with it. I liked having that bond with my sister. I watched her bare arms turn the steering wheel as we backed out of the driveway. Her skin was smooth and dark, and my arms seemed pale and flabby by comparison. Isabel thought her tan was mediocre that summer because she had to work three days a week at Abramowitz's Department Store in town and couldn't lie out on the beach every day. She was stealing from the store; I was sure of it. She would come home with new clothes once or twice a week. Yesterday, she'd brought home two new bras, and when she was out with Mitzi and Pam, I tried one of them on, stuffing the pointy cups with toilet paper to see how I would look with real breasts, only to discover that I looked kind of ridiculous. I also tried to practice using one of her tampons so I'd be ready the next time I got my "friend." The tampon in its cardboard tube was huge and had been impossible to get it in. It was like trying to push a Magic Marker against a brick wall. I felt scared, wondering if there was something wrong with me and I would never be able to go all the way with my husband or have babies.

"I've got dibs on the biggest one," Isabel said, referring to the inner tubes.

"I don't care," I said. I knew the one she meant. It was fatter and

wider and supported you so well it made you feel like you were floating on a cloud. But I wasn't going to fight her for it.

As we turned onto Rue Mirador, Isabel pulled a pack of Marlboros
from the pocketbook on her lap, shook one partway out of the package and wrapped her lips around it to pull it the rest of the way out.
She pushed the cigarette lighter into the dashboard, waiting for it to
heat up.

I was stunned. "Did Mom give you permission to smoke?" I asked.

"She smokes herself, so what can she say?" Isabel asked. She held
the pack toward me. "Want one?"

I hesitated, then took one of the cigarettes, digging it out of the
pack with my fingers in a graceless manner. I put it to my lips.

"I'm not going to light it, though," I said.

"Then why did you take it?" She laughed, pulling the lighter from
the dashboard. She held it to her cigarette, inhaling as the tip turned
a bright orange.

I shrugged. "I don't know," I said, but I did know. I just wanted to
be with her. To share something with her. To be *like* her.

"I get the porch bed tonight," she announced.

"I know," I said. She and I had been taking turns sleeping on the porch
when the weather was good. I still had to stuff my bedspread beneath
my covers to placate Lucy. I'm sure she knew what I was doing, but it
seemed to give her some comfort nevertheless. As long as I did that
and left the light on, she was doing better upstairs alone at night.

"What are you burying in the yard?" Isabel asked, turning the car
onto Bridge Avenue.

"What do you mean?" I asked, all innocence.

"I saw you bury something by the corner of the house. What was it?"

Darn. If I didn't tell her the truth, she would probably dig in the
sand by the corner of the house to satisfy her curiosity and discover
my clue box anyway.

"It's my Nancy Drew box," I said.

"Huh?" She gave me that "what are you talking about" look as she
blew smoke from her nostrils. She reminded me of a dragon.

"When I find something that might turn out to be a clue in a mystery, I put it in a box Grandpop buried there for me."

"A clue in a mystery? What mystery?"

"Well, I don't know yet," I explained. "Sometimes you can find things and later on, when a mystery happens, you realize the thing you found might be a clue that would help the police solve it."

Isabel laughed. "You're a moron, you know that? You mean you just throw any old thing you find in there, waiting for some deep, dark mystery to occur?"

"Not any old thing," I said, insulted. I thought of the Ping-Pong ball I'd found in the canal. Maybe I *was* being indiscriminate, but good clues were hard to find. I did not want her to shoot holes in my theory. Deep down, I knew the wished-for mystery would never happen, but I was having fun pretending it might. Grandpop had understood that.

"You act like such a twelve-year-old, you know it?" Isabel's voice was tinged with disgust.

"That happens to be my age," I said, folding my arms across my chest, managing to bend the unlit cigarette in the process. What did she want from me? "When you were twelve you probably did things like that, too," I said, but I didn't really think she had. Isabel had always been the sophisticated older sister. I could never catch up to her. I would probably still be reading Nancy Drew and making up wolves-are-loose-in-our-neighborhood stories when I turned seventeen.

We pulled into the gas station and carried the tires over to the air pump. I tossed my cigarette into a nearby trash can. "It's a secret," I said, watching her fit the air nozzle onto one of the tires.

"What is?" She looked up at me. I could see my twelve-year-old self reflected in her sunglasses.

"The Nancy Drew box."

She laughed. "Don't worry, Jules," she said. "I don't know of anyone who would be interested in your so-called clues."

I felt humiliated by her condescension and my throat tightened. I had to swallow hard again and again to keep from crying as we filled the tires in silence. When we got back in the car, "Sealed with a Kiss" was playing on the radio. I thought that was the world's saddest song, and my heart ached as I sang along with it, turning my face toward the window so my sister wouldn't see my tears and have another reason to make fun of me.

Once we were on the road, she reached into her pocketbook and pulled out the red-and-purple giraffe.

"I'm going to stop at the beach," she said, "and I want you to run over to the lifeguard stand and give this to Ned."

"I already gave it to Ned," I said. "What's it doing in your pocketbook?"

"He gave it back to me," she said, as if that explained everything.

I looked at the plastic giraffe. "You think *I'm* acting immature," I said. "Passing a stupid toy back and forth is really dopey."

"It's none of your business."

"It's my business if I'm the one being the messenger," I argued.

She snatched the toy from my hand. "Never mind," she said. "I'll give it to him myself."

I reconsidered, thinking of how I could get a look at Ned up on the lifeguard stand. Maybe he would accidentally touch my fingers when he took the giraffe from me. "I'll do it," I said, reaching toward her for the giraffe.

She handed it to me. "Thank you," she said.

We pulled into the parking lot next to the beach, the tires of the car crunching on the crushed shells. I hopped out and ran across the sand to the lifeguard stand. It had rained during the night and the sand was damp, flying behind me in clumps as I ran.

I spotted the usual group of teenagers lounging on their blankets around the lifeguard stand. That "Sweet Little Sheila" song was playing on their radios.

"Hey!" Bruno Walker called when I neared them. "Where's Izzy today?"

I didn't want to let him or anyone else in on our planned adventure. "She'll be over later," I said. Pam Durant was lying next to him on her stomach, eyes closed, and I was shocked to see that her bathing-suit top was unhooked, the straps low on her shoulders. It almost looked as though she was wearing nothing at all on top. I could clearly see the side of her breast. I quickly averted my eyes.

I stepped closer to the lifeguard stand and looked up at Ned.

"Hi, Ned," I said.

He lowered his head to look down at me, his eyes invisible behind his sunglasses, and broke into his gorgeous, white-toothed grin. My legs felt like they were going to give out under me.

I held up the giraffe. "Isabel wanted me to give this to you," I said.

He looked toward the parking lot, spotted our car and waved. He had white zinc oxide on his nose and a cigarette in his hand, and he looked so sexy with it. Women didn't look good with cigarettes, I thought, but a man with a cigarette in his hand was something else again.

I held the giraffe up to him and he reached low for it and maybe one of his fingers touched one of mine, but I could not be sure.

"Thanks, Julie," he said. "You're a neat kid."

"You're welcome." I wasn't ready to leave. "Why are you sending that thing back and forth?" I pointed to the giraffe.

"I don't think you'd understand," he said. He looked out at the water, then stood up, blew his whistle and waved an arm, which meant that some kids were swimming out too far and he wanted them to come in closer where he could see them. Where he could protect them. The muscles in his legs were long and lean and covered with curly gold hair that I wanted to reach up and touch.

"Yes, I would. Honest," I said, once he'd sat down again. I wondered if he would remember where we were in our conversation. He did. He'd been paying good attention.

"Do you have anything that's really special to you?" he asked me, his eyes still on the water.

I had so many things that were special to me, I didn't know where to begin. The clue box, of course. And my collection of Nancy Drew books. I also had a music box my girlfriend, Iris, had given me for my ninth birthday. It was oval shaped, and when you opened it up, a girl rode a bicycle around a little track.

"A music box," I said.

"Ah, okay, then!" He seemed pleased by my answer. "When you get older and you meet someone who's special to you, you'll feel like sharing the music box with that person."

"Oh," I said. I doubted very much I'd be passing my music box back and forth between some boy and myself, but I pretended to understand. "So, Isabel is your...uh...your special person, huh?"

"You keep that between us, okay?" he said, and I thought I saw him wink behind the sunglasses. "Your old lady would flip her wig if she knew."

I knew he meant my mother by "old lady," but it was the first time I'd heard anyone use that term.

"I saw Isabel sneak into your boat the other day," I said. The words seemed to have a life of their own; I had not even thought about speaking them.

His smile faded. He took off his sunglasses and looked down at me, blue eyes piercing through me to my heart. "You won't say anything, right?" he asked.

I shook my head. *You can trust me with your life,* I wanted to say to him, but I kept the melodramatics to myself. "I won't say anything," I promised, crossing my heart. I pictured myself inside the confessional booth, the smell of incense in the air. If I withheld information like that from my parents, did that constitute a lie? I wondered.

Ned slipped his sunglasses on again and glanced out at the water to be sure everyone was all right. "How come you and Ethan don't pal around together anymore?" he asked, then smiled at me again. "Don't answer that," he said. "He's a dufus this summer, I know."

I wanted to defend Ethan but found I couldn't. I nodded. "Yeah," I said.

"You tell Izzy I'll see her later, okay?" He looked toward the car and waved again.

"Okay," I said, knowing I'd been dismissed. It had been an incredible conversation, though. We had secrets. We'd talked almost like adults.

I walked back to the car and got in. It smelled of the hot rubber of the tubes.

"What did you talk about for so long?" Isabel sounded suspicious as she turned the key in the ignition.

"About how I saw you get into Ned's boat in the marina." I looked out the car window toward the lifeguard stand, nonchalant as you please.

Isabel didn't speak, and when I looked over at her, I saw that her knuckles had gone white on the steering wheel. "And what did he say?" she asked, her voice tight.

"He asked me not to tell anyone, and I promised I wouldn't."

Her grip on the steering wheel relaxed. "Thank you," she said. Then she held the pack of Marlboros out to me. "Have another cigarette."

My mother, Isabel and I tossed our inner tubes into the canal, then quickly jumped in after them, laughing as we struggled to climb aboard.

"I'm glad no one's taking a picture of this," Isabel said as she struggled to hoist herself onto her oversized tube. Mom and I had already managed to get into position on our tubes, our bottoms, forearms and calves in the cool water.

"Bye!" Mom lifted her arm in a wave to Grandpop, Grandma and Lucy where they stood in our backyard, calling out their wishes for a good trip. The current was swift and our journey was effortless. We used our hands as paddles, staying close to the bulkhead to avoid being run over. Some of the colored fishermen on the other side of the canal waved to us, as did people passing by in their boats. We'd rise and fall on the wakes of the yachts and motorboats. It was glorious.

When we reached the bay, we rolled onto our stomachs and began paddling for real, steering ourselves along the coastline toward our little beach. I spotted Grandpop and Lucy waiting for us on the pier, Lucy holding on tight to my grandfather's hand. I was impressed that he'd been able to get her out on the pier at all. I wished that my father had been at the shore so that he too could have floated on the tubes. Maybe, I thought, we could do it again on a weekend when he was with us. But we never did.

Lying in bed that night, I felt as though I was still floating toward the bay. What a great feeling it had been to flow with the current! An idea began to form in my head. If the current had been in the direction of the bay this morning, it would be going in that direction again tonight. What if I quietly took the boat out of our dock and let it float down to the bay? No one would know, because the current would carry me and I wouldn't need to start the motor and wake anyone up. Once I was in the bay, I could start the motor and cruise around for a while. Getting back could be a problem, because I doubted I could stay out there long enough for the current to change direction, but it was only the starting of the engine that would be noisy. Coming back, the boat would just make a gentle putt-putt sound as I pulled into the dock and no one would be any the wiser.

I couldn't believe the sheer elegance of my plan! I would be grounded for life if I was caught, but the risk seemed worth the adventure. As I climbed softly down the creaky stairs, I knew I'd have one more thing to confess on Saturday night, but just then, I didn't care.

Our little runabout had no light, so I got the flashlight from the kitchen drawer, along with a mosquito coil and a book of matches, then walked onto the porch. As I started to open the screen door, I suddenly remembered that it was Isabel's turn to sleep on the porch bed and I caught my breath. The half-moon was not very bright, but there was enough light that she could probably see me if she were awake. I peered toward the far end of the porch and saw that she was lying on her side under the covers, facing the opposite direction. I was safe.

Outside, I untethered the runabout, then descended the ladder and slipped into the boat. I used the oars to push out of the dock, cringing at the sloshing sound of the water against the bulkhead. Once in the canal, I had to use the oars to keep the boat going straight—the current kept trying to turn it sideways—and I felt the tiniest bit of panic over not being able to control it. But soon I was sailing easily with the current and within minutes, I was in the open water of the bay, by myself. I could see lights along the shore, though not too many. It was, after all, nearly midnight and most of the houses were dark. The half-moon offered a rippled, shadowy view of the water, and I felt infused with joy and a sense of peace. My plan had been to start the motor once I was in the bay, but now that I was floating comfortably, I didn't feel like disturbing the silence. I was curious to see where the current would take me.

I felt a mosquito bite my shoulder before remembering the coil. I lit it and put it near me in the bottom of the boat, and as I was lifting my head from that task, our little neighborhood beach came into view. It always looked so small and perfect from the water, a smooth, pale crescent of sand. Then I heard laughter, and my eyes were drawn to the platform in the deep water. Two figures were standing on the platform. I stared at them, using the oar to move a little closer. I saw the girl's long dark hair, the boy's broad back, and I covered my mouth with my hand.

It couldn't possibly be Ned and Isabel, I thought. I remembered seeing Isabel asleep on the porch...but I also remembered how I stuffed a bedspread beneath my covers to trick Lucy into thinking I was still in bed. Isabel had apparently tried the same ruse, because now she was most definitely on the platform with Ned Chapman. I nearly forgot to breathe as I watched them. My sister had on one of her two-piece bathing suits. From that distance, I could not tell its color. They were standing up, and I saw them come together. I couldn't tell for sure, but I imagined Ned was kissing her. When he drew away from her, he took her bathing suit top with him and I saw the faint glow of moonlight on Isabel's bare breasts.

Oh my God. My hands shook as I bent over to pull the cord to start the motor. I had to yank it three times; my hand seemed out of my control. The motor finally came to life with a metallic roar. I imagined Ned and Isabel looking out to the bay in surprise. Maybe my sister would duck down to cover herself up as I sped away from them, into the night, praying hard that they had not realized I was the person watching them.

I ran a large arc through the bay water and back into the canal. I slowed the motor to a gentle sputter as I carefully steered the runabout into our dock. I cut the motor, tossed the half-spent mosquito coil into the canal, climbed out of the boat and tied it to the dock.

I was still trembling as I opened the screen door to the porch. The fake Isabel had not moved in her porch bed and my arrival did not seem to have awakened anyone. I put the flashlight back in the kitchen and climbed the rickety stairs to the attic. Lucy's breathing was soft and regular. I tiptoed past her bed and into my curtained bedroom. I did not let myself think about what I had witnessed until I was under my covers.

One sentence kept clanging in my brain: Were Isabel and Ned going all the way? I did not even know the term "making love." I knew the basic elements of intercourse, but I did not know exactly how it was done. I let my imagination take me back to that platform, myself in Isabel's place. My breasts, somehow larger and fuller, were bare, as hers had been. Ned's hands were on them. He took off the rest of my bathing suit, then lay me down on the damp wood of the platform and kissed me tenderly. He took off his own bathing suit, and I spread my legs and invited him in, and somehow he was able to fit his penis inside me, penetrating that brick wall. That seemed an impossibility to me, but people did it somehow and Ned would know how. He would shoot sperm inside me and tell me he loved me. My body ached to be in Isabel's place on the platform, moonlight on my breasts, going all the way with my lover.

I sneaked the boat out to the bay several more times that July. I only took it out once in August, and that had been a mistake.

CHAPTER 12

Lucy

I was in the basement of the Methodist Church in Westfield getting ready for my band to perform at a Coffee with Conscience concert. I stood next to the pillar near the small stage, watching the place fill up. This would be the ZydaChicks last concert of the season, and we always liked to end the year locally, performing for our supporters in Westfield. Proceeds for the Coffee with Conscience concert would go to charity, which was the way we liked to operate. Our music was the feel-good variety, a happy fusion of zydeco, folk, and rhythm and blues, and only three of the five of us were "chicks," a fact that always required me to provide a long explanation somewhere midway through our performance.

The scent of coffee was thick in the air as I watched some of my old Westfield neighbors slip into their seats at the round tables. I saw a few of my Plainfield friends walk in, and best of all, several of my ESL students showed up. Three boys, two girls, all Hispanic. The kids spotted me standing next to the pillar and waved, grinning. It touched me to see them there. They looked out of place, a little uncomfortable, but sporting their usual "don't mess with me" bravado. Two of my former lovers were there, as well, and I was glad to see that they took seats at tables on opposite ends of the room. I made a mental note to be careful after the concert. Most of my previous boyfriends knew about each other and were cool about it, but those two had a rather hostile relationship. I would have to greet each of them individually.

Finally, just minutes before we were to go onstage, I spotted Julie and Shannon entering the room. I knew that Julie had picked Shannon up at Glen's and I wondered how that had gone. I'd gotten a ride to the church from one of my band members, and Julie was going to take me home. I was hoping the three of us could stop off someplace for dessert. I wanted to try to facilitate a discussion between mother and daughter. I knew Shannon hadn't told Julie about her pregnancy yet, and she wasn't going to get any skinnier.

Julie looked a bit tense from where I stood, but then I saw her laugh as she exchanged a few words with a woman she must have known. The laughter made her look pretty and ten years younger, and I was relieved to see it.

My gaze dropped to Shannon's midriff. She was doing an excellent job of hiding her pregnancy. She had on a loose white peasant blouse, a gift I'd given her years ago when I'd returned from a trip to Guadalajara. I'd never seen her wear it before, but it was perfect as camouflage. Loose and airy, the blouse drew the eye up to the elaborate embroidery at the neckline. Shannon was not smiling, and I wondered if she ever smiled these days. Her life had taken quite a serious turn. Maybe she smiled when she talked to her twenty-seven-year-old boyfriend, Travis. Or Taylor. Or Tanner. Whatever his name was, I did not trust him.

The house was packed and too warm by the time we took the stage, and I blocked everything but the music from my mind. I can't say that our performance was seamless. Something happened at the end of every season: We tended to get too cocky. We didn't practice enough and then we screwed up in the middle of an old song we should have been able to play in our sleep. I doubted that the audience knew or cared, though. They were drinking iced coffee, tapping their toes, and some of our most devoted fans sang along. A lot of people were on their feet and the energy in the room was high. I loved it when an audience responded that way.

Afterward I chatted with my students and some of my friends—neither ex-beau hung around, which was a blessing—and then met Julie and Shannon by the front door.

"Great concert," Julie said. She took my violin case from my hand as though she knew I'd appreciate a break from it.

"You just need a cellist," Shannon teased me. It was her contention that every band on earth could be improved through the addition of a cello.

I gave her a one-armed hug. "How about we get some ice cream?" I said, as we walked outside into the warm night air.

"I need to go straight home," Shannon said, then caught herself. "I mean, straight to Dad's." She'd been living with her father for four days, and I'd been glad that she'd agreed to go out with Julie tonight. Apparently, though, she wanted to make a short evening of it.

"Oh, come on, Shannon," I said, my arm still around her shoulders. "Just for a while."

"I'm expecting an important phone call," she said, giving me a look that told me who the important call was from, just in case I hadn't guessed.

"You can call them back," Julie said. "Lucy's probably starved."

"It's true, I am," I said. "You know I don't like to eat before a concert."

If I hadn't piped up, Shannon probably would have argued with her mother over stopping for dessert, but once I'd made my case, she gave in.

"Westfield Diner?" Julie asked as she opened her car door.

"Sure," I said. "You want the front, Shannon?" I motioned to the passenger door of the car.

"Back's fine," she muttered, barely loud enough to hear, and I knew she was either sullen or scared, expecting me to bring up her situation over ice-cream sundaes, which was indeed my plan.

We settled into one of the booths at the diner, Shannon sitting next to me, the slight swelling of her belly hidden from her mother's eyes by the table.

"How's work?" I asked her.

She nodded. "Good," she said, studiously avoiding my eyes as she checked out the dessert menu.

"Are you still playing the cello at the hospital?" I asked.

"Uh-huh," she said. "I went yesterday. I saw Nana there."

"Cool," I said. We were all hospital volunteers. I was a translator for Spanish-speaking patients, Mom worked in the gift shop, Julie visited patients, often reading to them or just keeping them company, and Shannon played the cello in the hallways outside patient rooms. We had a long culture of volunteerism in my family.

"What should I do with your mail, honey?" Julie asked. "You'll probably be getting a lot of it from Oberlin over the summer."

Here was Shannon's chance to tell her mother, I thought. I squeezed her knee beneath the table, but she pulled her leg away from my hand and I sensed her annoyance. I knew right then that the talk I wanted the two of them to have wasn't going to happen tonight.

"Just stick it in a grocery bag for me, please," Shannon said, not looking at either of us. "I'll pick it up when I come by."

"Okay." Julie turned her menu over to look at the desserts. "And if it looks important, I'll let you know. You'll probably find out who your roommate's going to be in a few weeks. I think you should try to get in touch with the girl during the summer to see what she'll be bringing to the room and all of that."

Shut up, Julie, I thought.

"Uh-huh." Shannon studied the menu as if she didn't know it by heart.

Julie and I ordered sundaes and Shannon, a small bowl of chocolate ice cream. Then Julie excused herself to go to the rest room.

I shifted away from Shannon on the bench so that I could look at her.

"How are you doing, really?" I asked.

"Fine," she said. "Everything's fine."

"Living with your dad is going okay?" I asked.

She rolled her eyes. "I might as well still be living with Mom," she said. "She calls me, like, ten times a day."

"Why don't you tell her about the baby now?" I asked. "With me here? I can help soften the blow."

"Don't *push* me, Lucy," she said. "Let me do this on my own time-table, all right?"

"What *is* your timetable?" I couldn't seem to stop myself.

"I don't know." She spoke slowly, teeth gritted.

"All right." I gave up. "Sorry."

"Thank you," she said, as if I'd been holding her down on the ground and had finally released her.

"Can you give me…what's his name? Tanner?"

She nodded and looked at me, curious to know what I was asking.

"Can you give me his Web site address?"

"*Why?*"

"So I can check it out," I said, then added, "from the perspective of a former history teacher."

"Are you going to write to him or something?" She looked suspicious.

I shook my head. "No."

She hesitated. "You swear you won't?"

"You have my word. I just want to…you know, get to know this person who's so important in your life. I mean," I added quickly, "get to know him by seeing his Web site, that's all." I thought I sounded guilty, as if I *did* have plans to try to reach him—which I did not—but Shannon tore off a piece of her napkin, pulled a pen from her pocketbook, wrote down the address and handed it to me. I slipped it in my jeans pocket.

"Thanks," I said.

"It's a cool site," she said, that glowy look coming into her face again. "He knows everything about computers."

Julie returned to the table and sat down again.

"Who knows everything about computers?" she asked. "Dad?"

"No," Shannon said. "Just a friend."

The waitress took our orders

"Any news from Ethan?" I asked.

"Who's Ethan?" Shannon asked.

"Ethan Chapman," Julie said. "Remember I told you about the visit I had from his daughter? How she—"

"That letter?" Shannon interrupted her.

"Yes," Julie said. "Ethan took it to the police. They searched

Ned's——Ethan's brother's——house, but didn't find anything. Or at least, they didn't tell Ethan that they found anything." Although what she'd said was not particularly good news, Julie was smiling. Something was going on. I swore I saw a little spark in her eyes when she said the name "Ethan." I was sure now that she had a thing for him.

"He reminded me of the time Mom and Izzy and I floated to the bay on inner tubes," Julie said to me. "Do you remember that?"

"To the bay from where?" I asked.

"From the bungalow," Julie said. "You were there when we jumped into the canal and there with Grandpop when he came to the bay to pick us up."

I shook my head. I must have been a space cadet when I was eight. I remembered so little.

"*You* floated on an inner tube?" Shannon looked at her mother in amazement.

"Yep," Julie said. She leaned back as the waitress set our ice cream in front of us.

"I totally cannot picture you doing that," Shannon said, lifting her spoon. "You're scared to death of the water."

"I wasn't then," Julie said with a shrug.

"Your mother did everything," I said. "She was adventure girl. I was the chickenshit."

"That would be cool," Shannon said. "Floating down a canal on a tube."

Shannon had never seen the canal and had only been down the shore a couple of times with friends, as far as I knew. Certainly Julie had never taken her.

"It's probably not legal to do that now," Julie said.

"It probably wasn't even legal then," I added.

We finished our ice cream, then drove to Glen's town house. He waved from the front door when Shannon got out of the car, and I waved back. I didn't know if Julie acknowledged him at all. I didn't think they talked anymore. They'd been able to communicate about Shannon, though. They'd coordinated trips to colleges and actually went together to parent-teacher conferences, but I thought their relationship was truly over now. Most——although not all——of the pain and animosity seemed to have shifted to indifference, and I was glad of that. I knew from my own broken relationships just how comforting indifference could be.

"I bet she's getting zero supervision over here," Julie said as she pulled away from the curb.

The horse was long out of the barn as far as supervision was concerned, and I ignored her comment. "So," I said, instead. "Do I detect some real interest in Ethan Chapman now?"

She might have blushed. I wasn't sure. "It was good to talk with him," she said. "He has the nicest voice."

"So, he looks great," I said. "He has an amazing body. Nice voice. Is good to talk with. What more do you want?"

"I don't *want* anything," she said. "If he weren't Ethan Chapman, I might be interested," she admitted. "But I certainly don't want someone who lives in Bay Head Shores and is almost surely the brother of my sister's murderer." She was vehement and had a good point. I decided to change the subject.

"I remembered something when you were talking about floating on the canal," I said.

"What?"

"I remembered Dad going over to the other side of the canal to get you when you were fishing with the Lewis family."

"Oh," she said, letting her breath out. "He was not pleased with me."

"He was hard on you sometimes, you know?" I said. "I learned from watching you. I learned not to make waves around him."

"He was never hard on Izzy, though," Julie said. It was not the first time she'd said something like that.

"Did that bother you?" I asked.

"Not really," she said. "I think I just had a way of doing things he couldn't tolerate. Like hanging out with the Lewises." She suddenly grew very quiet as she pulled up to the curb in front of my apartment house.

"Do you want to come in?" I asked.

She shook her head. "No. I'm tired." She smiled at me. "It was a great concert. I love watching you. You have so much fun up there."

"Thanks," I said, but I felt worried about her. "Are you okay?" I asked.

She looked at her hands where they rested on the steering wheel. "You just got me thinking about George," she said.

I touched her shoulder. "I'm sorry I brought it up," I said.

She shrugged. "It's just that...if I'd never gone over there to begin with, George would never have gone to prison."

"Oh, Julie," I said, leaning over to give her a hug. "I wish Ethan and his daughter had just dealt with that letter on their own and never let you know about it."

She smiled gamely as I pulled away from her. "I'm okay," she reassured me. "Honest."

I opened my car door, then looked back at her.

"With regard to Ethan..." I began.

She waited, eyebrows raised, to hear what I was going to say.

"Grab some joy, Julie," I said. "Grab it."

Before going to bed, I spent an hour on Tanner Stroh's Civil War Web site. It was undeniably excellent, a scholarly site overflowing with information and so little bias that I wasn't able to tell if I would agree with his politics or not. By the time I turned off the computer, I had one overriding thought in my mind: maybe Shannon had actually found herself a winner.

CHAPTER 13

Julie
1962

Grandpop and I were in competition. We stood a few yards from each other behind the fence in our backyard, the morning sun in our eyes and our fishing poles in our hands as we waited to see which of us could catch the biggest edible fish. I was wearing my purple one-piece bathing suit and after spending a few weeks in the summer sun, my skin was as dark as my grandmother's. Grandpop was still pretty pale. He never seemed to tan. He wore his usual brown pants—he must have had six pairs of them—and a white short-sleeved shirt and sandals. I'd never seen him go barefoot.

By the time we'd been out there for half an hour, I'd caught absolutely nothing, while Grandpop had reeled in two blowfish, which we considered less than nothing because they were too dangerous to eat. Their organs contained a deadly toxin, and after Grandpop tossed the second blowfish back into the canal, I came up with a plot for an intriguing mystery: The colored fishermen on the other side of the canal would begin dying, collapsing right there in the reeds, and it would turn out they'd been poisoned by the Rooster Man, who had fed them fried blowfish livers. I loved the idea and nursed the story along in my mind as we fished.

After what seemed like a very long time, I felt something good and strong tug at my line. I reeled it in, only to discover a hideous sea robin on my hook. Grandpop couldn't stop himself from laughing. There was nothing uglier in the universe than a sea robin, with its long bony fins poking out all over its body. I grimaced, watching the fish sway back and forth on my line. I was not squeamish, but the thought of holding on to that spiny creature while taking it off the hook was not pleasant.

"I bet Ethan would like that sea robin," Grandpop said, nodding toward the Chapmans' yard.

I looked over to see Ethan sitting in the sand, a huge pile of mussels in front of him. I had not even realized he was outside.

"Hey, Ethan," I called.

He looked up, the sun reflecting off his glasses so that I couldn't see his eyes.

"You want this sea robin?" I held my pole in the air, the fish flapping its tail and winglike fins.

"Keen!" Ethan said. He picked up a blue bucket from the sand and walked over to where Grandpop and I were standing.

"You have to take it off the hook," I said.

"Okay." Ethan seemed undeterred. He took the rag I'd stuck in the chain-link fence, grasped the fish with it, and extracted the hook with an ease I couldn't help but admire. He looked at me, grinning as though I'd given him a chocolate bar. "Thanks," he said. He dropped the fish in his bucket and walked back to his yard.

Grandpop and I began fishing again. We were tired of standing, though, so we pulled two of the Adirondack chairs close to the fence and sat down. I put my bare feet against the fence and slumped down into the chair, feeling very comfortable and at peace with the world.

"Looks like we're on the wrong side of the canal," Grandpop said after a while.

"What do you mean?" I followed his focus across the canal to where the colored people were fishing.

"I've seen them reel in a few keepers over there," he said.

"Oh, they're probably just catching blowfish, too," I said. "Daddy said colored people eat them 'cause they don't know any better."

My grandfather stared straight ahead, not speaking for a minute. "Charles said that, huh?" he asked finally.

I nodded. "He said they're not as smart as us. And they're poor, so they have to eat whatever they can."

There was a long silence that I didn't recognize as anything out of the ordinary until Grandpop spoke again.

"Did it ever occur to you that, if they *do* eat blowfish, which I doubt, it might be because they're actually *smarter* than we are? Maybe they know how to avoid the poisonous part. Maybe we're the stupid, wasteful ones."

There was a serious tone in his voice that was rare for my grandfather. "I don't think Daddy would agree with that," I said.

"Did you know that I lived in Mississippi until I was your age?" Grandpop asked me.

"I thought you grew up in Westfield," I said.

"I didn't move to New Jersey until I was fourteen," he said. "When I was a boy, we lived with my mother's family in Mississippi. We had a housekeeper and she had a son my age. He was my best friend. Willie was his name, and he was colored."

"Your best friend?" I said, amazed. I couldn't imagine it. I had never even spoken to a colored person.

Grandpop nodded, smiling. "Willie and I had some good times together," he said. "We lived near a lake and we'd fish and swim and explore. But he couldn't go to my school because of segregation."

I nodded. I knew what segregation was, even though it was easy not to think about it in Westfield, since every single person I knew there was white.

"His school was far inferior to mine," Grandpop said. "Willie was just as smart as me—smarter in some things—but he didn't have a chance. And here's the worst thing." He shook his head and I leaned closer to his chair, wanting to catch every word of the "worst thing."

"One time he and I went into the town near our houses. We were only eight or nine and we decided we wanted to buy some candy. But coloreds weren't allowed in the store."

"That doesn't seem fair," I said.

"Of course it's not fair," Grandpop agreed. "So I went in the store—it was a general store, I guess you'd call it. And I bought a bag of candy for a few cents and took it outside and Willie and I sat on the curb and ate it. Then he had to go to the bathroom really bad. The store had a privy behind it. An outhouse. But there was a sign on it that said No Coloreds, so Willie couldn't use it. So, I went into the store and asked the lady at the counter if she would make an exception, since he was just a kid and had to go real bad, but she wouldn't allow it. We went to another store, and they wouldn't let him use their privy either. He ended up wetting his pants."

"Oh," I said, feeling sorry for Grandpop's little friend.

"And then a man came and started smacking Willie around, calling him names, saying that's why…" Grandpop hesitated a moment and I had the feeling he was going to clean up the man's language for my ears. "He said that's why Negroes weren't allowed in nice places, because they soiled themselves and such. You can just imagine how humiliating that experience was for Willie."

It was an awful tale. I thought about how it would feel to be prohibited from entering the little corner store where I rode my bike to buy penny candy. I imagined a sign on the door that read No White Children Allowed. I imagined feeling desperate to pee and not being allowed in.

But I felt uncomfortable about the conversation, because Grandpop was telling me—not straight out, but he was telling me just the same—that my father was wrong. That he was prejudiced. My father was such a good and admirable person. It was hard for me to reconcile the man I loved and respected with a bigot.

"Dad wouldn't ever…you know, tell a little boy who needed to use the bathroom that he couldn't," I said, desperately wanting my grandfather to agree with me.

Grandpop smiled at me. "You're right about that," he said. "Your daddy's a fair man. But he's really had no experience with colored people, so he just doesn't know any better than to say what he said. People are prejudiced mostly because they don't know any better."

I felt relieved. For a minute, I'd been afraid that Grandpop didn't like my father.

"Do you know that a lot of people thought your grandmother wasn't as good as they were when she was growing up here in New Jersey?" he asked. "They thought she was stupid."

"Why?" I asked, perplexed. "She's not colored."

"She's Italian. She didn't speak perfect English. To some people, that's considered even worse than being colored."

I thought I was lucky to have an Italian grandmother. She was sweet to my friends and she cooked fantastic lasagna and made cookies at Christmastime with almond flavoring or rose water. It was hard to imagine anyone not loving her.

I suddenly got another tug on my line, this one nearly pulling the pole out of my hands. Grandpop tucked his pole beneath his chair to hold it in place and came over to help me.

"You've got a good one this time, Julie," he said.

He held the pole as steady as he could while I reeled in the biggest fluke I had ever seen come out of the canal. I was whooping and hollering, jumping up and down as the fish sprang out of the water and we pulled it over the fence and onto the sand. It flopped from its flat, brown, two-eyed side to its white side and back again, and Grandma and Mom came out of the house to see what the fuss was all about. Lucy came out, too, but hung back near the porch door, afraid of the fish or the hook or the water. It was anyone's guess.

Mom and Grandma watched as Grandpop held the fluke and I carefully extracted the hook.

"He's a beaut," my mother said.

"You win, Julie," Grandpop said, as I dropped the fish into our bucket. It was nearly too big to fit. "I'm going to go clean it right this minute." That was the loser's task, to clean the catch.

I felt satisfied with myself as I watched my grandparents and mother walk back toward the house, but all of a sudden, I sensed a presence behind me. I turned and there stood Ethan, just a few feet away from me.

"That's the most gargantuan fluke I've ever seen," he said. "Can I have its guts?"

* * *

The next morning, I was sitting on the bulkhead, using binoculars to watch the boats bobbing and weaving in the rough water beneath the Lovelandtown Bridge. Grandpop had not only cleaned what he continually referred to as the "biggest fluke ever caught in the Intercoastal Waterway," but he gave me a pair of binoculars, as well.

"I've been saving them to give you for a special occasion," he said. "But I think catching that fish was pretty special."

I guessed it was my conversation with Grandpop that made me turn the binoculars on the colored fishermen across the canal. That's when I saw the girl. She was standing close to the dock that separated the fishing area from the Rooster Man's shack, and she was bending over, doing something with her pole, baiting the hook, perhaps. How old was she? I studied her hard, turning the little dial on the binoculars to try to bring her into better focus. I couldn't see what she looked like very well, but she was my age, I felt sure of it.

I went into the garage and grabbed my fishing pole and bait knife, took one of the boxes of squid out of the refrigerator, hopped in the runabout and motored across the canal before I had a chance to think about what I was doing. I pulled into the dock near the girl. I felt nervous, but a little excited, too. Maybe she would have a sense of adventure. Maybe she could become my friend, the way Willie had been my grandfather's friend. I was so tired of being by myself.

I tied the runabout to the ladder at the side of the dock, then climbed up to the bulkhead with my pole and my bucket, the binoculars still around my neck. There were six people all together. Near me were my hoped-for future friend, an older boy, a woman—probably their mother—and a distance away, three men. Every one of them turned to stare at me. All those black faces. I felt like I'd gotten out of my boat in Africa. I had never felt so white and out of place in all my life.

I had to force my legs to take the few steps to where the girl was standing.

"Hi!" I said to her, my voice far too loud and cheery. "What's biting?"

The girl stared at me blankly as though she didn't understand English. Her skin was very dark and she had large eyes in the same deep shade of brown. Her hair had a bunch of plastic barrettes in it, all of them shaped like little bows in different colors. She was shorter than me and maybe a little younger than I'd guessed. I thought she was cute, but she sure didn't seem to have much to say and my greeting just hung there in the hot July air.

The older boy standing next to the girl narrowed his eyes at me.

"What *you* doin' over here?" he asked.

"I just wanted to fish on this side of canal for a change," I said with a nervous smile.

"We got enough trouble catchin' fish for ourselves without you taking up space," the boy said.

"Hush, George," the woman said, moving closer and resting her hand on the boy's muscular forearm. "I'm Salena," she said. "What's your name, sugar?"

"Nancy," I lied. I looked at the girl who was close to my age. "What's your name?"

"Wanda," the girl said. Her voice was high and it rose up a little on the second syllable of her name.

"How old are you?" I asked.

"Eleven," she said. I could barely *remember* being eleven, but I guessed it was close enough.

"I'm twelve," I said. "Could I fish here next to you for a while?"

"'Spose," she said.

"What you using for bait, Nancy?" Salena asked.

"Squid," I said, reaching into my bucket. I cut off a bit of bait with my knife and ran my hook through it, my hands shaking the whole time. "What do you use?" I directed my question to Wanda.

"Bloodworms," she said.

"I use them sometimes, too." I baited my hook and cast carefully, not wanting to catch the hook in any of their heads and have them madder at me than they already seemed to be. Their hair was really different from mine. Salena and Wanda had stiff-looking hair even blacker than Isabel's. Wanda's stuck out from her barrettes in little pigtails all over her head. I couldn't see the men very well because they were quite a distance from me, but George's hair was extremely wiry and tight to his head. He was wearing a white T-shirt and baggy tan pants and he looked like he played a lot of sports, every bit of him thick and shiny with perspiration.

"Can you read?" I asked Wanda.

"'Course she can read." George scowled. "You think we pick cotton all day or something?"

"Shut up," Wanda said to George. Then to me, she said, "Sure I can read."

"Have you read any Nancy Drew books?" I asked.

"Some," she said.

I wasn't sure I believed her. "Do you have a favorite?" I was testing her, unable to picture a colored girl reading Nancy Drew. I wondered what it was like to be colored and read a book entirely filled with white people. For that matter, what was it like for Wanda to read just about any book or watch any TV show? The only one I could think of with a colored person in it was Jack Benny's show with Rochester, the butler, or whatever he was.

"Ain't got no favorite," Wanda said, reeling in her line, which was tangled up in a mass of seaweed. "I like them all."

I was quite convinced she was lying now. How could she not have a favorite? "Well, my favorite is *The Clue of the Dancing Puppet*," I said. "It's new."

"I ain't read that one." Wanda set the bottom of her pole in the sand and worked the seaweed loose. "I liked the one where she joined the circus."

My mouth dropped open. *"The Ringmaster's Secret?"* I asked.

"Yeah, with that—" she pointed to her wrist "—that horse charm."

"Right," I said. She actually had read it and I felt terrible for thinking otherwise. "My name's not really Nancy," I said to her, wanting to reward her honesty with my own. "It's Julie."

"Why'd you tell me it was Nancy?"

"'Cause I like solving mysteries, just like she did."

"Ain't no mysteries here," George said. "So you can go back over your side of this here canal."

"Shut up," Wanda said to her brother again. She rolled her eyes at me. "You got any brothers?"

I shook my head, smiling.

"You lucky," she said. Her worm was still on her hook, and with a forward motion, she cast the line into the canal again.

"You got a sister, though," George said.

"I have two," I said. "Lucy and Isabel."

"Which one wears that bikini?" he asked.

"Neither," I said, but I knew he meant Isabel, even though her bathing suit was not actually a bikini, since the bottom was big enough to cover her belly button. Pam Durant was the only girl I knew who wore an actual, navel-revealing bikini.

"You lie," he said. "There's one who wears that two-piece bathing suit. She sits out on the bulkhead sometimes, talking to boys in their boats."

"That's Isabel," I said. "She's seventeen."

"She a fine-lookin' woman," George said, and the way he said it made me uncomfortable.

"Don't talk about my sister that way," I said.

"What way's that?" he asked, grinning. He had the most perfect set of white teeth I'd ever seen.

"You know what way," I said.

I thought I heard something, and I cocked my head, listening. There it was—the clucking sound of chickens. I looked over my shoulder toward the Rooster Man's shack. It was barely visible for all the grasses and reeds surrounding it.

"Have you met the Rooster Man?" I asked Wanda and George.

"Who's the Rooster Man?" Wanda asked.

There was a tug on my line. I pulled back, reeled it in a bit, but whatever had been there was gone. Most likely, my bait was gone as well, but I really didn't care about fishing. I was making new friends.

"He lives in that shack." I pointed to the ramshackle little building on the other side of the dock.

"I seen him," Wanda said. "George and me went over there to fish one time and he chased us away."

"I think he's hiding something," I said.

George laughed. "You just lookin' for trouble, ain't you, girl?" he said.

"He has a rooster and some chickens he just lets run all over his house," I said.

Salena walked over with a big bowl of raspberries and offered me some.

"Thanks," I said, taking a couple of the berries and popping them in my mouth.

"Your mama know you're over here, sugar?" Salena asked me.

I shook my head. "No, but I'm allowed to go anywhere on this end of the canal," I said, telling what I hoped was the truth. I knew I was allowed to take the *boat* anywhere on this end of the canal. No one had ever addressed my getting off the boat and visiting someone.

"Well, you ask next time, hear?" Salena said.

I nodded.

"Yeah, you say, 'Hey, Mama, can I fish with dem niggahs?'" George said.

I was shocked he used that word. He looked at my stunned face, then broke into a laugh.

"Hey, girl," he said. "I'm just razzin' ya."

Salena laughed, too, but Wanda looked at her brother with disgust. "You so retarded," she said to him. Then to me, "He turned eighteen yesterday and now he's more retarded than ever."

So, I had some new friends. They were different from anyone else I knew, but that only intrigued me. I went across the canal a couple more times that week. I liked being over there. Salena turned out to be their cousin, not their mother, as I'd originally thought. I learned that all of them—including the men, who stuck pretty much to themselves—were cousins. Wanda and George had no father and their mother was sick, so this bunch of older relatives took them in.

There was always a lot of "razzin'" going on, as George would say, and it took me a while to realize it was a sign of affection between them. I gave them any fish I caught and discovered that they, too, released the blowfish and sea robins. I shared my binoculars with them, letting them take turns looking through them. I picked a bowlful of berries from the semicircle of blueberry bushes that grew in the sandy lot across from our house and shared them with the Lewises. I brought over *The Clue of the Dancing Puppet,* sat on an overturned bucket, and read it out loud to Wanda. She never offered to do the reading, and I didn't ask her, afraid she couldn't read as well as me and might be embarrassed. I put a lot of drama into the reading, and even George and Salena listened after a while.

I took Wanda for a ride in the boat, making sure I'd brought an extra life preserver with me that day. I wanted to take her across the canal to meet my family but instinctively knew I'd better not. I'd told no one where I was spending my mornings. All they needed to do was look hard across the canal to see me, but they were so used to ignoring the colored fishermen that I guess they never did.

One day, though, I was standing next to Wanda, starting to bait my hook with a killie, when a white man suddenly emerged from the path cut through the tall grass. We all turned to look at him, and my thoughts were so removed from my family that it wasn't until I noticed his limp that I realized it was my father.

"Daddy!" I said. "What are you doing here?"

I noticed some gray in my father's brown hair as he walked toward to me. He skirted a fish bucket and gave George an even wider berth. George cut his eyes at my father, looking as though he would happily stick a knife in his side if given a chance. It was a side of George I hadn't seen before.

"You need to come home," Daddy said. His voice was very calm, but I knew the calmness masked his anger. My father was not a hitter, not even a yeller, but quiet anger could sometimes be even harder to endure.

"Why?" I asked, knowing perfectly well why. I was holding the killie in one hand, the hook in another, and both my arms felt paralyzed.

"We were looking for you," he said. "You know you're supposed to let us know where you are. Throw that killie in the canal and come with me," he said.

Feeling self-conscious, I tossed the killie over the fence. "This is Wanda Lewis, Daddy," I said. "And her brother George. And her cousin, Salena."

"You got a nice girl," Salena said. "She's welcome to fish with us anytime she like."

Daddy nodded to her. "Thank you," he said. He put his hand on my shoulder and I tried to measure the anger in his touch: Nine on a scale of one to ten. I was afraid to go with him. My hands shook as I gathered my up my gear.

"What about the boat?" I asked him.

"Grandpop can come over later to get it," he said.

"Bye," I said to the Lewises, then turned to follow my father. He was already halfway down the path on his way to the small sand lot where he'd parked the car.

He didn't speak until we were both in the car and he'd turned the key in the ignition. Then he looked at me, shaking his head slowly as though he couldn't believe I was his child.

"What in God's name do you think you're doing on this side of the canal?" he asked, a cold, hard edge to his voice.

"Fishing," I said.

"You think they've got different fish over here than on our side?"

Actually, I did, but I took a different tack.

"Grandpop said I should try to make friends with them," I said, then cringed. I was a terrible person for pinning the blame on my grandfather. Daddy didn't believe me, anyway.

"You're starting to lie way too much, Julie," he said as he drove the car from the lot onto the road. "You have a good imagination, and that's fine. But you have to remember there's a difference between making up stories that are harmless—that don't hurt anybody, including yourself—and telling lies."

"There's no girls my age near us, Daddy," I said, and I suddenly thought I was going to cry.

"You can play with Lucy," he said.

"I would, except she never wants to do anything."

Daddy suddenly looked sad. He reached across and stroked his hand over my hair, his touch gentle, the anger gone and worry in its place, which was almost worse. "Honey," he said, "I know you're lonely this summer. But don't try to mix with the Negroes. No good can come of it."

"Wanda reads Nancy Drew," I said.

"I don't care if she reads Dostoyevsky," he said, his voice remaining calm. I had no idea who Dostoyevsky was. "I don't want you to go over there again. Understood?"

"If Izzy was doing it, you wouldn't care," I said.

"If Izzy was doing it, I'd lock her in the house for a year," he said. He turned the steering wheel to take us onto the road leading to the Lovelandtown Bridge, then glanced at me. "You think I favor Isabel?" he asked.

"I *know* you do."

He said nothing as we drove over the bridge, the steel grating rumbling beneath the car's tires.

"Isabel was my first child," Daddy said quietly, once we'd crossed the bridge. "She'll always have a special place in my heart, but I love all three of you equally. I'm sorry if I ever let you think otherwise."

Although I hadn't meant to manipulate my father with my accusation, it definitely seemed to have worked to my advantage. Daddy hugged me when we got out of the car in our driveway and said he thought his lecture had been punishment enough. I cried then for real, because I loved him with all my heart—and because I knew I was incapable of being the obedient girl he wanted me to be.

That afternoon, I sat on the bulkhead, dangling my feet above the water, looking over at the Lewis family as they packed up to go home. George and Wanda waved to me, and I waved back.

"Your dad went over and got you, huh?"

I recognized the voice without even turning around.

"Flake off, Ethan," I said.

"I think it was neat that you went over there," he said.

I turned to look at him, surprised. He was leaning on the fence. He had on sunglasses that were as thick as his regular glasses.

"My father had a big fight with your father," he said.

"What are you talking about?" I swiveled on the bulkhead, drawing my legs up so that I was facing him.

"Your father was looking for you, and my father was out here and your father said, 'Have you seen Julie,' and my father said, 'She's where she is every day, on the other side of the canal, fishing.'"

"Your father finked on me?" I asked.

"Your father said he was going over to get you, and my father told him that, somehow, you ended up with an open mind and your father was trying to close it. And your father called mine a *liberal ass-hole,* and said that what happens in his family is none of my father's business." Ethan grinned. "It was pretty keen."

Pretty keen if you're not the subject of the dispute, I thought. I had to admit, though, that the argument sounded like the most excitement we'd had down the shore in weeks. I couldn't believe my father had used the word *asshole.*

I did not fish with Wanda and George for a full nine days, but then I returned. I told Salena I had Daddy's permission. I brought more blueberries and ate their raspberries and big hunks of corn bread Salena had made. I shared my binoculars with them and read to Wanda. I would only go when my father was in Westfield.

And I practiced the line I would use in confession: "I disobeyed my parents just about every single day of the week."

CHAPTER 14

Julie

I arrived at my mother's house the morning after the ZydaChicks concert and was in the process of getting my gardening gloves, sunscreen and insect repellent from the trunk of my car when Lucy pulled up behind me.

"I brought bagels," Lucy said as she got out of her car. She held up the bag for me to see.

"Oh, you're good," I said. "I didn't think of that."

"Love that hat with your haircut." Lucy walked toward me, reaching out to touch the brim of my straw gardening hat.

"Thanks," I said. "Where's yours?"

"I forgot it. Mom'll have an extra, I'm sure."

We started up the sidewalk to the white split-level that had been our childhood home. We did this several times during the year—joined forces to help our mother with the yard work. Mom was able to maintain her front yard flower beds beautifully, and she even mowed the lawn herself, much to our chagrin. She used a monster riding mower we had not yet been able to wrest away from her despite our many attempts. I'd offered to pay a service to handle the job for her, telling her I was afraid she might fall or the mower might tip over, but she waved off my concerns as ridiculous. I wondered how, when the time came, we would be able to talk her into giving up her driver's license. At least Mom had accepted our help with the vegetable garden in the backyard, and that was to be our task for the morning.

We'd reached the front door, and Lucy rang the bell. I could see our reflections in the storm door nearly as well as I would have been able to in a mirror. The only thing alike about us, I thought, was our oval-shaped sunglasses. Mine were prescription. Our features were quite different, although I was usually able to see the presence of both our parents in our faces. Lucy's hair was well on its way to being completely silver. Except for her thick bangs, her hair was pulled away from her face into the long French braid she always wore down her back, and I wondered if, beneath the dye and highlights, my own hair was now the same color as hers.

"Okay, Mom," Lucy said to the air as she rang the bell again, "we're here."

We waited another full minute. It was early, but it had to be at least eighty degrees already, and I was hot standing on the shadeless front step.

"Is the car here?" Lucy leaned away from the door and looked toward the closed garage as if she might be able to see inside it.

"I called her yesterday before the concert to tell her we'd be coming," I said, a smidgen of worry making its way into my brain. I reached into my pocketbook. "I have my key."

I pulled open the storm door, glad to see our mother had not locked it, fit my key into the lock of the main door and pushed it open.

We stepped into the relative coolness of our old home.

"Mom?" Lucy called.

No answer. I walked into the kitchen and opened the garage door to see her silver Taurus.

I was about to head upstairs when Lucy said, "There she is." She pointed through the sliding glass doors leading from the dining room onto the patio. I was relieved to see our mother sitting at the glass-topped patio table, her back to us. She was still in her light summer robe and terry-cloth slippers.

"She must have forgotten," I said.

Lucy and I slid open the door and our mother jumped at the sound. She tried to look behind her, but couldn't turn her head quite far enough to see us, and I was distressed that we'd startled her.

"It's just us, Mom," I said quickly. I bent over to kiss her cheek.

She was looking at an old photograph album, and she fumbled with it, trying to close it quickly but failing. Among the black-and-white photographs, I saw one of Isabel standing on the bulkhead dressed in a pale sundress, waving at the camera. My God, she looked like Shannon! A sailboat was on the canal behind her, heading toward the bay. I caught Izzy's dimpled smile just before my mother managed to close the cover on the book, her hands fluttering, shaking.

"Hi, girls," she said, struggling to put cheer in her voice. "What are you doing here?"

Lucy gave me a worried look over the top of our mother's head. Mom was no more forgetful than I was most of the time, but it was clear that we'd walked in on a private moment.

"We're here to work in the garden," Lucy said.

"Oh, that's right." Our mother got to her feet, lifting the photograph album to her chest. We were all going to pretend it wasn't there. That was the way we operated in our family: We were masters at ignoring the elephant in the room. If we pretended it wasn't there, it couldn't hurt us.

"Let me get dressed and I'll help you," she said. She kept her head lowered as she scooted past us, as though she knew her eyes were rimmed with red and was hoping we wouldn't notice. It was clear she wanted to get away from us to pull herself together. Seeing her self-consciousness made me ache for her. I longed to touch her. Hold her. I wished I could ask her what had her so upset, but it was clear that was not what she wanted and I let her pass.

"I brought bagels," Lucy said, most likely because she didn't have a clue what else to say.

"And there's juice in the fridge," Mom said, as she opened the sliding door.

Once she was in the house, Lucy and I looked at each other again.

"Maybe we should have called before we came over," Lucy said in a hushed tone.

"How weird that she was looking at old pictures now," I said.

"What do you mean, 'now'?" Lucy asked.

"You know," I said. "Ned's letter. Me talking with Ethan. Having to think about Isabel's death. All of that."

"A coincidence," Lucy said, then reconsidered. "But you're right. It is kind of strange." She held up the bag in her hand. "Cinnamon raisin, oat bran or plain?" she asked.

We each ate half a bagel in the kitchen, then left them on the counter for our mother. Lucy found one of Mom's old gardening hats in the hall closet and she tugged it low on her head. Then we doused ourselves with insect repellent and walked out to the toolshed in the rear of the yard.

We opened the door to the musty-smelling shed and began digging through the tools.

"Any word from Ethan?" Lucy asked, as we put a couple of hoes and weeders in the wheelbarrow.

I laughed. "It's only been…what? Ten hours since you asked me that question last night." I felt the start of a hot flash, the damp heat burning the crown of my head, then radiating downward over my cheeks and neck. I took off my hat, fanning myself with it.

Lucy laughed. "One itty-bitty mention of Ethan, and look what happens to you," she said.

I was only mildly annoyed with her. "Just you wait a few years," I said. "I'm not going to forget how unsympathetic you've been to me while I've been going through this."

I put my hat back on and we began pushing the wheelbarrow toward the garden.

"Do you think sex would be difficult?" Lucy asked.

I looked at her. "*What* are you talking about?" I asked.

"I mean…" She looked utterly guileless. "You know, with you being menopausal and all that." Lucy had a knack for bringing up the most difficult subjects with an air of innocence. "Let's say that you could get past your concerns about having a relationship with Ethan and—"

"I doubt very much that I could." I stopped pushing the wheelbarrow at the edge of the garden and lifted out the hoe. "And even if I wanted a relationship with him, I doubt he wants one with me." I started raking the hoe between the rows of tomato plants. The garden was the same oversized plot of fertile soil that Lucy and I had grown up with, but it seemed like much more work now than it had been when we were kids. "And besides," I added, "I have very little interest in sex these days, anyway." That was a half-truth. I'd gotten used to thinking of myself as asexual. I couldn't have cared less about sex during the last few years of my marriage to Glen, which might have been part of the problem between us—yet another thing that was my fault. But my reaction to seeing Ethan—even to talking with him on the phone—was forcing me to rethink my definition of myself as a sexless creature.

"I'm afraid that's happening to me, too." Lucy dropped the kneeling pad next to the lettuce.

"*You?*" I looked at her in surprise. I'd expected Lucy to have an insatiable appetite for sex until she was on her deathbed—and maybe even then.

"Sad, isn't it?" she said, lowering herself to her knees on the pad, a trowel in her hand. Her hat flopped low over her sunglasses. "I never thought I'd hear myself say that."

We heard the sliding-glass door open and turned to see our mother walking toward us. She was dressed in the gardening overalls I'd bought her a couple of years earlier and wearing green rubber shoes and a straw hat, and she looked much, much better than she had just a half hour before.

"Mom," I said, "why don't you sit and relax and let Lucy and me do this today?" I suggested.

She stopped walking toward us. "Not a bad idea," she said. "I'll just get a cup of coffee and a piece of bagel and pull a chair over so I can visit with you." She turned around and disappeared into the house again, and Lucy and I exchanged another look.

"What's going on with her?" Lucy asked. It was not like our mother to let us do the work ourselves, not that we minded in the least.

I brushed a bug from my damp forearm. "Maybe she finally realizes that gardening in this kind of heat is more than she should be doing," I said, dropping my hoe to the ground. I walked over to the patio and carried a chair back to the garden, setting it in the shade near where we were working.

"How can she drink coffee when it's this hot?" Lucy said, when Mom appeared again on the patio. She walked toward us carrying a cup of coffee and half a bagel on a napkin. She sat down on the chair, all smiles.

"I was so sorry I couldn't join you at your concert last night," she said to Lucy. "How was it?"

"A lot of fun," Lucy said.

"They were great, as usual," I said, picking up the hoe again. Mom had planned to go to the ZydaChicks concert with Shannon and me, but she'd canceled yesterday afternoon, saying she was too tired to go out. I'd thought little of it at the time, but now I wondered if whatever had tired her out last night was related to her sadness this morning. As for me, I still felt a little high from having had that quality time with my daughter the night before. I missed seeing her every day. I knew I was calling her too much, irritating her, but I was only calling once out of every ten times I thought of her.

"Did Lucy tell you I want to plan a combination birthday and going-off-to-college party for Shannon?" Mom asked me.

"No," I said, delighted. "That's a great idea."

"I thought we should have it at Micky D's," she said, "but Lucy thought it should be here."

I sneaked a smile at my sister, mouthing the words *thank you* to her.

"Here would be perfect," I said out loud.

"I think we should make it a surprise party," Mom continued, "so could you put together a list of her friends for me, Julie?"

"Sure," I said. I leaned on the hoe, thinking through the idea. "How about I take care of the invitations so you don't have to worry about that part?" I suggested. "We'll have to look at our calendars and see when would be good. She has to be at Oberlin in late August."

"I don't think a surprise party is such a great idea," Lucy said.

"How come?" I asked, scraping the hoe through the dirt and weeds again.

"I don't know," Lucy said. "I think…she might want to have some say as to who gets invited. That sort of thing. I know I would if I were in her shoes."

"Well, why don't you two talk it over and get back to me on it?" our mother said. She took a sip of her coffee. "And meanwhile…" She hesitated so long that we both looked over to see if she'd forgotten what she'd been about to say. "I have a question for Julie."

"What?" I asked.

"I was wondering when you planned to tell me you had lunch with Ethan Chapman."

Speechless, I looked at Lucy. *Did you tell her?* I asked with my eyes. Lucy looked as surprised as I felt and gave a little shake of her head.

"How did you know about that?" I asked, holding the hoe at my side.

"I have my ways," she said, tucking a strand of her white hair beneath her hat.

"Mom," I said. "How?"

"His father paid me a visit," she said.

"You're *kidding.*" I pictured Mr. Chapman as he had looked the last time I'd seen him. He'd been on TV, a slender, handsome middle-aged man, shaking hands, kissing babies and making promises as he ran for governor. It must have been in the late sixties. "Why?" I asked.

"He said Ethan told him he was going to see you and that started him thinking about our family, so he decided to pay me a visit."

"Weird," Lucy said. She, too, had stopped her weeding and was now sitting down on her kneeling pad, hugging her shins. "How did it go?"

"Oh, fine," Mom said. "He's a feeble old goat. Hasn't aged too well. He shouldn't be driving a car, if you ask me."

I suddenly thought of the photo album she'd had out that morning. No wonder. Seeing Ross Chapman must have brought back many memories of the shore for her.

"What did you talk about?" I asked.

"Not much," she said. "He was only here a few minutes. What *I'm* curious about is what you and Ethan talked about."

Could she possibly know about the letter? I reassured myself that there was no way she could, since Ethan had not even told his father.

"Sort of the same thing," I said. "He just wondered about us. You know he and I were really good friends when we were little, and I guess he started thinking about me. You know how that happens sometimes."

"Is he single?" Mom asked.

"Well, actually, yes," I said. "He's divorced."

"So, he's hunting for a new Mrs. Chapman, then, I guess," she said.

I laughed. "Oh, Mom, I don't think that's what he's after at all."

"Well, if it is, I hope you'll ignore his overtures," she said.

"Why should she ignore them?" Lucy asked.

My mother let out a heavy sigh. She took a long swallow of coffee, then brushed a bagel crumb from her lap while Lucy and I waited. "Because," she said, "the Chapmans are a reminder of times I would just as soon forget."

I could almost see the elephant tromping in our direction from the patio, plopping down in the garden on top of the tomato plants.

"So—" my mother rested her coffee cup on the arm of the chair and folded her hands in her lap "—let's decide if Shannon's party should be a surprise or not."

CHAPTER 15

Lucy
1962

I remembered something.

I'm not sure what stirred the memory. Maybe it was Mom mentioning Mr. Chapman. Maybe it was that, before she managed to close the photograph album with those fumbling, anxious fingers, I'd gotten a good look at one of the old pictures. It had been taken from the water and was of our bungalow standing next to the Chapmans', the small houses bookended by our two docks. As I pulled weeds late into the morning, the sun hot on my arms, the memory came back to me in bits and pieces until it was fully formed.

When I was a child, my mother was obsessed with me learning to swim. An excellent swimmer herself, it worried her to have any of us unsafe around the water. I *wanted* to learn how to swim. I honestly did, but there was some fear in me that just wouldn't let it happen. At the bay, I would stand shivering in knee-high water, terrified of…what? Crabs biting my toes? The sucking pull of the sand in the bottom of the bay? Drowning? I am not sure now, and I'm not sure

I could have said even then what terrified me, but I could not go in. In the winter, Mom would take me to the Y, where she would hook me up with a male teacher who was known for getting even the most recalcitrant kids into the water. But I could outlast anyone in the game of "come on in, honey," and after two years of trying, that teacher gave up on me. Everyone gave up on me, except for Mom.

One day during the summer of 1962, Mom thought up a new plan for teaching me to swim. I had just gotten my first violin—a silly, lightweight, off-white plastic thing from the five-and-dime—and all I really wanted to do was sit on our screened porch and practice playing the simple songs in the music book that came with it. But Mom was insistent.

"I have a feeling today is the day!" she said, with her usual enthusiasm. She stood in front of me in a black-and-white polka-dot, skirted bathing suit, the child-size orange life preserver in her hands. "I really do," she said. "And I asked Mr. and Mrs. Chapman if we could use their dock because it has a slope you can walk down to get into the water. Doesn't that sound perfect?"

I looked through the screen toward the Chapmans' dock. I could see the top of their motorboat jutting above the bulkhead.

"Their boat is in there," I said.

"Yes, but it's a double-wide dock," my mother said. "Plenty of room for both you and the boat."

I don't remember what prompted me to set my violin down and let her buckle me into the life preserver. I don't know if I sighed with resignation as I followed her out the porch door, or if I felt some hope that, this time, I might actually do it. I might actually learn how to swim. For whatever reason, I walked with her across our yard and the Chapmans'. I remember kind of skating with my bare feet across the sand. I had walked that way in the Chapmans' yard ever since stepping on a prickly holly leaf from one of the bushes that grew in their front yard. I was determined to swish any leaves away from my feet before they could hurt me.

The Chapmans' dock was very wide, and Ned had moved their boat to one side so that there was still plenty of room for my swimming lesson. The entire male contingent of the Chapman family was there, plus Ned's friend, Bruno. Ned and Bruno were cleaning the interior of the boat with rags and a bottle of blue detergent, and "Sherry" was playing on a transistor radio that rested on the bulkhead. Ned was as tan as his black-haired friend, and it was the first time that I realized that some blondes could tan every bit as well as people with darker hair. I liked that Ned was there, since he was a lifeguard. It made me feel a tiny bit more secure.

Skinny Ethan stood in the water to encourage me, and Mr. Chapman leaned against a tree near their dock, watching us approach the concrete incline.

"Are you ready to learn how to swim today, Lucy?" Mr. Chapman asked me.

"Maybe," I said, my eyes on the water.

My mother held my hand as we walked onto the slope. It was not what I'd expected; I could barely see the concrete for the slimy green growth covering it. I was afraid of slipping, and I clung tightly to my mother's hand.

I stepped into the water up to my ankles.

"That's good," my mother said. "It's not too cold. Isn't it nice?"

I nodded, concentrating on the dark water in the dock. You couldn't see what was below the surface. I'd watched Julie net a zillion crabs in our dock and I knew this one would be just as full of them. Through the ankle-deep water, I could see that my toes were exposed and vulnerable.

"I need to go get my flip-flops," I said.

"Why?" my mother asked.

"Because of the crabs."

"The crabs have better things to do than munch on your toes," Bruno said. He was kneeling on the bow of the boat cleaning the windshield. He was wearing his swimming trunks and nothing else, and I had never seen a body like his before. Even his muscles had muscles.

"Use my flip-flops," Ethan called from the water. He pointed to the sand behind us where his flip-flops had been carelessly kicked off, one of them resting on the other. I scrambled back up the slope and put them on. They were too big, but they would have to do.

"Look, Lucy!" Ethan said, when I'd returned to the ankle-deep water and the safety of my mother's hand. He was standing at the bottom of the slope, or so I assumed. I couldn't really see. "It's only up to my waist here." He held his arms out above the water. I could see every one of his ribs.

"Let's take one more step," my mother said. "Just one step at a time."

I wanted to give her something, and so I did it. I took a baby step down the slope and shivered as the cool water inched halfway up my calf. My teeth were starting to chatter. I could barely make out my toes now, and I kept hopping from foot to foot to keep the crabs away. The flip-flops were not enough to make me feel secure. I should have worn my sneakers.

"It's easier if you get in all at once, Lucy," Ned said. He was the expert and I knew he was right, but I just couldn't do it.

"One more," my mother said, and I held my breath and took another step forward. The water lapped at my knees, and my teeth were chattering so loudly now that I was sure everyone could hear them. My arms were covered with gooseflesh.

"That's great, Lucy!" Ethan said. "Keep coming." He was patting the surface of the water like someone might pat the cushion of a sofa to encourage a friend to sit next to them.

"Are there crabs by your feet?" I asked him.

"No!" he said. "The crabs are afraid of you. They see your feet and run away."

That did not reassure me. I wanted to hear that there were no crabs at all.

"What if they don't see my feet until it's too late? Then they'll bite me."

"You're being a big baby, Lucy," Bruno said from his perch on the bow.

"Leave her alone, Bruno," Ned said.

"How do you stay so patient with her, Maria?" Mr. Chapman asked.

My mother looked up at him. "Haven't you ever been afraid of anything, Ross?" she asked.

"Not like that," he said, and I felt like a freak in a circus.

"I don't want to do this, Mom," I said. "Can we go home?"

"Please, Lucy." My mother sounded as though she was begging me.

I wanted to please her, but I was shivering all over. I didn't think I could take another step.

"I'm sorry," I said. "I just can't,"

Finally she gave up. She looked at Ethan. "Thanks for helping, Ethan," she said.

"Sure," Ethan said. He took a couple of steps backward into the deeper water and began treading. Why could he go into water that deep and I couldn't? Why was I the only one to feel such fear?

My mother and I climbed back up the slope and I felt relieved to be on level ground again. I unbuckled the life preserver and kicked off Ethan's flip-flops.

We had taken a couple of steps in the direction of our bungalow when I suddenly felt myself being lifted up and tossed into the air, the life preserver flying off my arms. I may have screamed; I don't know. I do remember my mother shouting "Ross!" as I fell. I saw the bulkhead whip by in front of my eyes, and then I was in the deepest part of the Chapmans' dock. I shot beneath the water's surface, flailing my arms in the green, blurry, underwater world. I could hear voices, muted shouts. Then I broke through the surface of the water, gasping for breath, my mother holding me up, her dark wavy hair wet around her face.

"You're okay, darling," she said to me, her hands firm and secure on my rib cage.

I was sobbing. I pressed my head to her shoulder.

"Why'd you do that, Dad?" I heard Ethan ask.

"It's the best way to get over a fear," Mr. Chapman was saying. "Just jump right in. See, Lucy? You were in the deep end and you didn't drown. You bobbed right up to the surface." His voice was kind, but I was never going to go near him again.

My mother half carried me back to the slope, where she set me down and took my arm, walking me up the slimy green surface, and I saw then that she, too, was crying. At the top of the slope she let go of my arm, marched over to Mr. Chapman and smacked him hard on his shoulder.

"How dare you!" she said.

Mr. Chapman rubbed his arm where she'd hit him. "If you took her to a psychiatrist—which might not be a bad idea—he'd recommend you do what I just did," he said.

My mother grabbed my hand. "She's not your daughter!" she said, starting toward our house with me. I had never seen her so angry. I could feel her fury in my fingers where she was squeezing them. She called back over her shoulder, "Don't you *ever* lay a hand on one of my children again!"

At home, even *I* knew I was milking the traumatic event for all it was worth. Grandma clucked over me, helping me change out of my wet bathing suit while I bemoaned the terrible treatment I'd received at the hands of our neighbor. She rubbed me all over with talcum powder from her special pink tin of Cashmere Bouquet, then dressed me in my favorite green baby-doll pajamas. I could hear my mother complaining to my grandfather about what had happened and Grandpop's soothing voice in response. I was allowed to stay up late, playing my plastic violin, and Julie was forced to go to bed at the same time as me, so that I would be able to fall asleep without nightmares about the rag-that-looked-like-a-head stuck in the wires on the attic ceiling.

When I was nine, I jumped into my neighbor's pool and began to swim. I'd had so many lessons that I knew the mechanics by heart. All I needed was the practice—and the courage that came from surviving one of the worst things life had to offer: the death of my sister.

CHAPTER 16

Maria
1927–1939

It was funny how when you neared the end of your life, you could find yourself thinking about its beginning. I was only five when my parents and I spent our first summer at the bungalow. The canal was brand-new back then, only having been completed the year before. There were very few houses in Bay Head Shores at the time, and everyone already knew one another, so I think it was particularly difficult for my mother to make friends at first. Rosa Foley was an oddity, with her exotic dark looks and Italian accent, but my father was so very American that he was able to make inroads for us with the other families and their children and I quickly had several playmates.

When I was eight, nine-year-old Ross Chapman moved in next door and became my best friend. We'd fish together in the canal and swim together at the beach. He taught me how to play tennis when I was eleven and I taught him how dance when I was twelve. The Chapmans lived in Princeton during the rest of the year, while we lived in Westfield, so Ross and I never saw each other or even exchanged letters during those months. Come summer, though, we'd pick up right where we left off.

The summer I was fourteen, I started viewing Ross differently. He'd grown tall and lanky in a very handsome way. I'd started that adolescent yearning for a boyfriend, and although he and I were still just pals, I fantasized about him being more than that. He was on my mind even during the school year, and when talking with my Westfield girlfriends, I would refer to him as my boyfriend. My friends were envious, thinking I had a luscious summer love. I knew Ross would probably clobber me with his tennis racket if he knew how I talked about him. I was still just the girl next door to him.

When my daughters were growing up, they liked to date one steady boy at a time, but things were different when I was a young teen. My friends and I did everything as a group. "Maria's gang" was how my father referred to us. At the shore, my "gang" consisted of about twelve youngsters. Many of us had boats, and we'd cruise between the bay and the river with ease.

The summer Ross was sixteen, he showed up at the shore with a Ford Phaeton convertible. Oh, my, the fun we had with that car! Of course, it was only meant for four people, but we managed to squeeze six or seven of us into it, some of the kids standing on the running board, hanging on for dear life. We were wild—not by today's standards, of course, but we thought we were pretty crazy. Everything felt so safe back then. No one I knew ever got hurt in a car crash. No one drowned in the ocean. And certainly, no one was murdered. Our placid lives would all change in a few years, with the stock-market crash and the Second World War, but our teenage years were easy and fun filled.

Once several of us could drive, we started hanging out at Jenkinson's Pavilion on the boardwalk. We nearly lived there, dancing to live music in the evening, swimming in the huge saltwater pool during the day, and basking for hours on end in the sun. It was a wonder I never got skin cancer, but I had my mother's Mediterranean skin and I guessed that saved me.

My dark looks, however, came with a price.

The summer I was seventeen, the intensity of my attraction to

Ross had deepened to the point of obsession. Not only was he handsome, he was brilliant as well, getting straight A's in his private high school and being accepted to Princeton for the fall, where he would follow in his father's footsteps by studying law. It seemed, though, that we would never be more than friends. Ross would often give me a ride to parties and other get-togethers, and on the way home, we would talk about who we were attracted to, who we would like to go out with. *You,* I wanted to say. *It's you I want to go out with.* It was hard for me to listen to him say he liked Sally or Delores, when my longing for him was eating away at my insides. I played the game, too, though, telling him I had a crush on Fred Peters, the best-looking boy in our group. Ross only responded that he thought Fred was interested in me, too.

The change came when I was crowned queen of the Summertime Gala, an annual Point Pleasant event. It featured a small parade, and I rode on a little float pulled by a few of the boys from my gang, Ross and Fred included. I was dressed all in white from head to toe and wore a crown. My envious girlfriends treated me coolly, but my fifteen minutes of fame seemed to alter Ross's view of me.

He drove me home after the parade. He turned the car onto Shore Boulevard, but instead of continuing down the road to our houses, he pulled over and parked in front of the woods.

"What are you doing?" I asked him.

He glanced at me, then smiled almost shyly. "I want to tell you something, Maria," he said.

"What?" I asked.

"You made a very beautiful queen," he said. Ross had *never* said anything like that to me before. He'd never commented on my looks in all the years I'd known him.

"Thank you," I said.

"I hope you don't think this is silly of me," he continued, "because I know we've always just been friends, but I thought about you over the winter. I thought about how swell it was going to be seeing you again this summer."

"I thought about you, too," I whispered.

"You did?"

I nodded.

"I went out with some girls in Princeton, you know, but I was thinking of you the whole time," he said. "I'd look at pictures my parents had of you and me…you know, sailing and in our tennis clothes and…you know those pictures."

I nodded again, my heart brimming with joy and gratitude. These were the words I had longed to hear from him and had heard only in my imagination—and in the lies I told my Westfield girlfriends.

"Today, when I saw how other men looked at you…" He shook his head. "I knew I had to let you know how I feel. I couldn't take the chance of letting you get away." He took one of my hands in both of his. "I'm in love with you, Maria."

I was sure that my smile lit up the car. I let go of his hand and reached out to hug him. "I've loved you for years," I said, my lips against his ear.

He drew away from me, then leaned over to kiss me, so tenderly I barely felt it. He raised his hand to my breast, touching it through my silly white queen dress, sending a spark through my body.

"I want you." He smoothed my thick hair behind my ear.

"I want you, too," I said.

"Tonight," he said, "let's break away from the gang at Jenkinson's. We can go out on the beach under the stars." He lifted my hand and drew it to his lips, and I nodded.

"All right," I said. I knew what I was saying, what I was agreeing to, and I knew it was a sin. But I didn't care.

That night at Jenkinson's, we danced, both with other people and with each other, trying not to be too obvious. Around nine o'clock, Ross and I stepped out onto the broad porch and down the stairs to the beach. We slipped off our shoes and our feet had barely touched the sand before we were kissing. We made love beneath the Jenkinson's boardwalk, while the band played Benny Goodman and Glenn Miller songs almost directly above us. It was the first time for me, although I was sure it was not for him. I lost my virginity to Ross that night on the beach. I'd lost my heart to him years before.

Ross and I began going out separately from our gang of friends. He'd come to pick me up, and my parents, who had always liked him, were delighted at seeing us together. Of course, they had no idea how far our relationship had gone. They invited him to dinner or to play cards with us, and I felt proud of how easily he slipped into my family. Our relationship, always based in friendship, became more sexual than I ever could have imagined. It was rare that one of our evenings together did not end with lovemaking, often in the sandy lot across from our bungalows, where a crescent of blueberry bushes provided the right amount of cover. It was not the sort of tender lovemaking I'd grown up imagining, but rather a hungry, animalistic devouring of each other. During daylight hours, when I would be helping my mother around the house, the memory of being with Ross the night before would make me suck in my breath with a sudden blaze of desire.

Ross and I rarely spoke about the fall, when he would be going to Princeton and I would study teaching at the New Jersey College for Women, but we *did* talk about the future.

"I'd rather you study art than education," he said one night. I was lying in his arms, encircled by the protection of the blueberry bushes, my dress draped over my bare skin. Hanging on a chain around my neck was his high-school ring, which he'd given me the day before. I couldn't stop myself from fingering it.

"What could I do with an art degree, though?" I asked him. "I've always wanted to teach."

"That's because you've been thinking you'll have to earn a living to support yourself," he said, kissing my nose. I heard the smile in his voice.

"What are you saying?" I asked.

"Well, you know I'm not in a position to ask you to marry me now," he said, "but if you and I *do* get married one day, you won't have to work. I wouldn't *want* you to work. You would have plenty to do helping me entertain my law colleagues."

I smiled to myself, snuggling closer to him. I could see my future in front of me. *Our* future. I pictured our elegant home in Princeton, our beautiful children—a boy and a girl. I could see myself in an exquisite hostess gown, welcoming our distinguished guests.

"We'll see," I said, because although the fantasy was delightful, my parents had instilled in me the satisfaction that could be gained from having a career of my own. I knew it would take me a while to let go of that dream.

Our friends had quickly realized we were a couple, despite our initial attempt to keep our relationship to ourselves. Once we were out in the open, the girls seemed to feel less threatened by me and they became my friends again. I'd missed them and I was glad.

One night, Ross and I were at Jenkinson's with the whole gang. We were standing in line at the fresh orangeade stand, the boys telling jokes and the girls groaning in response. The orangeade vendor was Italian, his accent stronger than my mother's but very similar. James, one of the boys in our gang, gave him a dollar bill to pay for a ten-cent orangeade. I was never sure exactly what happened, but James somehow tricked the vendor into giving him two dollars in change. I watched most of the boys and some of the girls in my gang snickering as we moved away from the orangeade stand. By the time we were out of earshot of the vendor, James was nearly doubled over with laughter.

"Can you believe that imbecile?" he asked us. "Stupid wop!"

I looked quickly at Ross. He was grinning. His upturned lips, his teeth, the laugh lines at the corners of his eyes—those details would stay with me for the rest of the night. They were all I could see when I looked at him. I was half Italian. My mother was a full-blooded "wop." Why couldn't I tell him how much his mockery of the immigrant vendor hurt me? If he wondered why my lovemaking that night lacked its usual energy, he said nothing about it. I was waiting for him to ask me what was wrong. Then I would tell him about my sense of betrayal. But he never did ask, and I tried to push my sadness to someplace deep enough inside me that it would not rise up again.

A few days later, my mother found a forgotten bag of pine nuts in the pantry and she made a double batch of pignoli. She put a dozen of them on a plate and told me to take them over to the Chapmans'.

I crossed our backyards and knocked on our neighbors' porch door. I knew Ross was playing golf with his father, but his mother was home, and she pulled open the screened door for me.

"Hello, Maria," she said. "How is the queen of the gala today?"

"Fine, thank you, Mrs. Chapman," I said, stepping onto the porch. In my younger years, I'd spent plenty of time in Ross's house, but now it seemed we only got together at my house. I assumed Ross felt that my parents were warmer and more welcoming than his—which they certainly were. "Mother made an extra batch of pignoli for you," I said, holding out the plate of cookies.

"How lovely of her!" she said. "Bring them into the kitchen."

I walked into their kitchen and set the cookies on the table in the corner. When I looked up at her, she had lost her smile.

"Whose ring are you wearing?" she asked me.

My fingers flew to the ring hanging around my neck. Hadn't Ross told her?

"It's Ross's," I said.

I saw by her expression that Ross had *not* told her. She looked into my eyes, confused. "Why on earth would he give you his ring?" she asked.

What could I say except the truth? "We're going steady." I dropped my hand from the ring to my side, suddenly self-conscious.

"But...he has a girlfriend in Princeton," she said.

I knew about Veronica, the girl his parents kept pushing him to go out with.

"Veronica's not his girlfriend," I said, trying not to sound defensive. I held out the ring as proof.

She turned away from me, ostensibly to put away a cup that had been resting on the counter. "I didn't know that," she said tightly. "I thought he was still interested in her."

"Well," I said, the sense of betrayal welling up in me again, "maybe you should talk to Ross about that."

I went home, angry with Ross for not telling his parents, or at the very least, for not telling *me* that his parents didn't know. I was helping Mother with the dusting when I heard the Chapmans' car chug past our house on the dirt road. I walked out to our screened porch so that I might be able to hear their conversation if it was loud enough.

The yelling started quickly, but I couldn't make out anything that was being said. I ached for Ross, wishing I could have said something to his mother that would have eased the barrage of fury being thrown his way. If only I had known he hadn't told them about us, I could have pocketed the ring. In my naiveté, I thought they were angry that he had not told them he'd lost interest in Veronica or that he'd not told them that we were going steady. The real content of their argument was something else altogether.

Later that evening, Ross came over and asked if I would go for a walk with him. Of course, I said yes, anxious to hear what had transpired between him and his parents. He held my hand as we walked up Shore Boulevard.

"I have to break up with you," he said, the words slicing clear through my heart.

"Why?" I asked. "Is it Veronica?"

"No, no," he said quickly, then tightened his grip on my hand. "I don't care a whit about Veronica. You know that. I love *you,* Maria. I always will, and maybe someday, when we're out on our own, we can start seeing each other again, but right now I just can't."

"Why didn't you tell your parents about us?" I asked, tears welling up in the corners of my eyes.

He rubbed the back of my hand so hard my skin burned. "I don't want to hurt you," he said.

"Tell me."

He was quiet a moment. "It's because you're Italian," he said finally.

"So what?" I said defensively. "And I'm only half Italian."

"Your mother came over on the boat, and to them, that's...I don't know." He shook his head. "My parents have antiquated views about things."

"You've known all along I was Italian," I said angrily. "That hasn't stopped you from making love to me when you feel like it."

"I don't care what your background is," he said. "You know that, darling."

"Then why are you letting them dictate who you can see?" I asked.

"Dad said he won't pay for me to go to Princeton if I continue seeing you." He blurted out the words.

"That's ridiculous," I said. "He wants you to go as badly as you want to go. Do you think he would actually follow through on that threat?"

"I have no doubt at all that he would," he said grimly. "I'm so angry with him right now that I could——" He shook his head, unable or unwilling to finish the sentence.

The tears began trickling down my cheeks, and when I spoke, it was hard for me to get the words out. "But we've been friends forever," I said. "Does he expect us to stop being friends?"

"We'll always be friends, Maria," he said.

We were in front of our houses again, back where we'd started our walk. And we were in front of the lot with the blueberry bushes as well. Standing there, we looked at each other a long time, the darkness no barrier to seeing the longing in each other's eyes. He took my hand again, nodded toward the bushes.

"One last time," he whispered, as he led me onto the sandy lot.

I was certain we both knew he was lying.

CHAPTER 17

Julie

On Wednesday afternoon, I drove down the shore. I'd told Ethan I would arrive at his house around four, and although it was little more than an hour's drive, I left Westfield at one o'clock. I was afraid that once I reached Point Pleasant, it would take me a while to find the courage to drive to our old Bay Head Shores neighborhood. And I was right.

I found a parking place in the huge and crowded lot across from the Point Pleasant boardwalk, but it was a moment before I got out of my car. Even with the windows closed and the air conditioner blowing, I could smell the ocean. People, some of them sunburned or deeply tanned, walked through the parking lot in their bathing suits, carrying towels and beach chairs or pushing cranky toddlers in strollers. I looked straight ahead of me at the merry-go-round I'd ridden on dozens of times as a kid. It had been a ritual in my family to visit the boardwalk at least a few times a month during the summer. We'd go on the rides and eat sausage sandwiches at Jenkinson's and frozen custard at Kohr's. I'd lived for those family outings back then; now I was afraid to get out of my car.

Ethan had called on Monday afternoon. I was rushing in from the car, bags of groceries in my arms and dangling from my fingers when the phone rang. I saw his name on the caller ID and felt both relief and trepidation. Dropping the bags on the counter, I grabbed the receiver.

"Ethan?"

"You sound breathless," he said.

"I just got in the house," I said. "Any news?"

"A few things," he said. "They're really moving on the investigation. They interviewed me this morning."

"Oh." I sank onto one of the kitchen chairs. "What was it like?" I wondered how hard it had been for him. "What did they ask you?"

He hesitated. "They want to interview you next," he said, not answering my question.

I shut my eyes. I supposed I'd been hoping the police would somehow be able to pin Isabel's murder on Ned without the need to question me again.

"When?" I asked.

"This week, most likely," he said. "And I was going to suggest you come here. Stay at my house. I have loads of room and—"

"Next door to the *bungalow?*" I asked, as though he'd suggested I sleep in a tree.

"Is that a problem?" he asked.

I was quiet for a long time. "I haven't been down the shore since Isabel died," I said. "I've avoided it. It's painful to me to even think about being there."

It was his turn to go quiet. "Are you saying that you haven't been to the beach…to the ocean at all in forty years?"

"I've been to other beaches," I said, thinking of my honeymoon in the Caribbean. Trips to California. "Just not the Jersey Shore."

"Well," he said, "you'll have to come down here to talk with the police. Of course, you don't have to come to Bay Head Shores or spend the night at my house, but I thought it might be good for us to put our heads together. There were questions they asked me about Ned's old friends, you know, that sort of thing, that maybe we could help each other remember. You could stay in a motel somewhere and I could meet you for dinner."

That sounded like an excellent compromise. "All right," I said. "I'll wait to hear from the police, and then I'll make reservations and—"

"You'll have to go inland," he interrupted me. "The beach motels will be booked."

"All right," I said again. "I'll see what I can come up with and get back to you."

"Okay," he said. "And another thing. My friend at the department told me they've been talking to George Lewis's family."

"Wanda?" I asked.

"I don't know who, exactly," he said. "I do know that Lewis always stuck to the story that he was innocent."

"I'm sure he was," I said. "I knew he didn't do it. Have they talked to Bruno Walker?" I asked.

"My friend said they're having trouble tracking him down."

"Figures," I said. "The one person who might know what really happened and they can't find him."

We talked for a few more minutes, and I was putting the groceries away when Lieutenant Alan Meyers called from the Point Pleasant Police Department. Apparently, they were wasting no time. He asked if I could come to the station on Thursday morning. I said I could, then got on my computer to find a motel in the area and instantly felt like a fool. *Grow up,* I told myself, and I called Ethan back to accept the invitation to stay at his house.

Now, sitting in my car in the heart of Point Pleasant, I wondered if I'd made a mistake. It had been so easy to be brave from the safety of my home. I took a moment to give myself an emotional checkup before I opened the car door: I was okay. I got out, merry-go-round music and salt air surrounding me, and joined the tourists heading toward the boardwalk.

On the boardwalk, I thought I saw Isabel everywhere. She was riding the Tilt-A-Whirl, centrifugal force pressing her against the shell-like back of the carriage. She was sitting on a bench next to a blond-haired boy, facing the ocean, her long legs stretched out in front of her, her feet propped up on the railing. She was walking toward me on the boardwalk in a green bikini, her body tan and hard, her head tipped to one side as she took a bite from an ice-cream-and-waffle sandwich.

I sat on one of the benches facing the boardwalk, people-watching and letting Isabel in. How would she have fit in with Lucy and me? I wondered. Would she have helped us pull weeds in Mom's garden? Would our father still have been alive if he hadn't lost his beloved oldest daughter at such a young age? Why was I torturing myself with unanswerable questions?

"Dear God," I prayed, mumbling the words aloud, "help me get through this."

I stood up and walked resolutely back to my car. It was still early, so I drove around Point Pleasant for a while. I spotted St. Peter's, where I'd gone to church every Sunday morning during the summer and to confession every Saturday evening. I remembered one of the last times—possibly *the* last time—I'd gone to confession there. For some reason, Mom had not been in the car with us. Daddy and Isabel rode in the front seat on the way to the church, and Lucy and I were in the back, and we were talking about my upcoming confirmation. Isabel had her taken her shoes off and had her bare feet up on the dashboard, her skirt just covering her knees.

"So, Julie," she said as she studied her stubby fingernails. She was a nail biter and she'd bought all sort of products to make herself stop, but none of them worked. "Have you decided what middle name you're taking for confirmation?" Isabel had taken the name Bernadette as her confirmation name. It was a great name, long and elaborate, but I was not an elaborate person and had decided on my confirmation name a year earlier.

"Nancy," I said.

"It has to be a saint's name," Isabel said with an air of authority. "I don't think there's a Saint Nancy."

"Well," Daddy said, and I knew just by the tone of his voice that he was going to take my side for a change. "I believe the name 'Nancy' comes from the name 'Ann,' and there certainly is a Saint Ann. She was Mary's mother."

Bingo, I thought. Not only had I picked a saint's name, but a really important one at that.

"So she has to take 'Ann,' right?" Isabel asked my father. She sounded hopeful. She did *not* want me to get my way in this. "That would sound really stupid," she added. "Julianne Ann Bauer."

"I'm going to take Kathy," said Lucy. She related strongly to the baby of the family on *Father Knows Best*.

"You two are missing the boat," Isabel complained. "This is supposed to be *serious*."

"Isabel's right," Daddy said. "But we can talk to the priest about whether Julie would have to take Ann or Nancy. And Lucy, there most certainly is a Saint Katharine. The important thing is for the two of you to learn about the lives of the saints you're interested in before you decide to take their names, the way Isabel did."

If he only knew about his sweet Saint Isabel, who was probably going all the way with Ned, I thought.

Daddy parked the car on the street outside St. Peters, and I suddenly got the jitters. That entire week, I'd lived in fear of dying because I had not confessed all my sins the previous Saturday and I knew I would go straight to hell if I died. I simply had not known how to tell the priest about the fantasies I was having about Ned Chapman. But now I thought I had it figured out. Somehow I'd come up with the term "impure thoughts." I must have read it somewhere, maybe in the Catholic magazine Daddy wrote for. I also remembered reading that impure thoughts were a sin even if you didn't act on them, and that's when I realized I'd better confess them as soon as I could. I was afraid, though. I was used to confessing to my lies and my fights with Lucy and Isabel and my disobedience. This new sin had a completely different feeling to it.

I sat in the pew between Daddy and Isabel, waiting my turn. I watched Lucy go into one side of the confessional with her little eight-year-old's transgressions. A woman came out from the other side, and Isabel took her place. Then Lucy came out, and it was my turn.

I could feel my heart beating against my ribs as I knelt in the darkness. I heard the mumbling of a male voice and knew that my sister had finished her probably inadequate confession and was receiving her penance. Then, before I was ready for it, the priest slid open the window.

"Bless me, Father, for I have sinned," I said, making the sign of the cross. "It's been one week since my last confession and these are my sins. I disobeyed my mother and father three times," (the trips across the canal to fish with Wanda and George) "I lied to my little sister once," (telling her there were no crabs in the Chapmans' dock) "I had some impure thoughts, and I fought with my older sister two times." There. I'd slipped it in perfectly.

"Tell me about the impure thoughts," the priest said.

Oh, God. "I…I thought about the boy who lives next door to us," I said.

"Often?" the priest asked.

I swallowed. "Yes, Father," I admitted. *Every waking moment.*

"And have you committed the most grievous offense of masturbation?" he asked.

What was he talking about? I'd never heard the word before, but I guessed he meant intercourse. I couldn't imagine what else he might mean.

"Oh, no, Father!" I said, so loudly my family probably could hear me in the pews.

"Good," the priest said. "Be sure you never do."

Never? I wanted to ask him if it would be okay to do it when I was married, but he sounded so stern and frightening that I didn't dare.

"Yes, Father," I said.

"For your penance, say six Hail Marys and five Our Fathers and now make a good Act of Contrition."

The rote words spilled out of my mouth. All the while I was thinking that I'd gotten out of it easy. For a few extra Hail Marys, I would continue having impure thoughts about Ned. I wasn't sure I could stop them even if I wanted to.

CHAPTER 18

Julie

I lay in the double bed in the guest room in Ethan's house. The room was dark, but I remembered my impressions from when I walked into it for the first time that afternoon to deposit my overnight bag on the handsome wood chair in the corner. The walls were a spectacular blue—robin's-egg, only richer and deeper. The curtains fluttering against the open window were a bold white-and-blue stripe. The painting on the wall looked like something my mother might have created: an impressionistic view of what could either have been a body of water or a green field, depending on how you wanted to look at it. I wondered if the simple yet dramatic decor was Ethan's doing or that of his ex-wife. I didn't need to wonder who was responsible for the stunning carved headboard or the dresser. By the time I'd made it to the guest room, I already knew that Ethan was no ordinary carpenter.

Many things had changed in Bay Head Shores since 1962. As I drove through the area before heading to Ethan's house, I tried to remain in control and dispassionate, as if I were a scientist making observations instead of a woman visiting a place that haunted her. The little corner store where my sisters and I used to buy penny candy had been turned into a tiny antique shop, and now it was tucked beneath the overpass leading to the large bridge that had replaced the old Lovelandtown Bridge. There were many more houses, and the area had the feeling of a resort as opposed to the simple bayside neighborhood it once had been. The sun was brilliant against the architecturally varied houses. The yards were manicured with pebbles or sand and salt-tolerant landscaping. I drove the curved road leading to our little beach—the Baby Beach—with a tight knot in my throat.

Okay, I said to myself as the beach came into view. *Be objective. There's the little playground. Could those swings possibly be the same ones Daddy used to push us on?* I didn't think so. *There's the lifeguard stand. And loads of people. Brightly colored beach umbrellas. The shallow area's still roped off for the kids. But...* My eyes searched the water beyond the shallow area. *No platform.* I was glad to find it missing. I'd dreaded seeing it. I had seen quite enough.

Shore Boulevard, my old street, had changed more than I could have imagined. To begin with, it was no longer a dirt road. Houses sat nearly on top of one another, filling both sides of the street. The woods were gone. Two houses stood in the lot where the blueberry bushes had once flourished. I was surprised that it didn't sadden me to see how built-up it had become. Instead, it relieved me that it didn't feel like the same street at all.

I nearly stumbled upon our old bungalow. Everything seemed so different that I hadn't expected the house to suddenly appear on my right. I stopped the car abruptly, lurching forward, glad there was no one behind me on the quiet street. The house looked lovely and well cared for. It had been a grayish blue when I was growing up, with black shutters. Now it was a sunny pale yellow trimmed with white. An old anchor leaned against the tree in the front yard. The obviously custommade mailbox at the edge of the road was painted to resemble the ocean, and a model sailboat rested on top of it. Someone cared about the house my grandfather had built, and I felt gratitude to them, whoever they were.

Between the bungalow and the newer house to the right of it, I could clearly see the canal. The water had an instantaneous, visceral pull on me. The current was swift, the water that deep greenish-brown I remembered so well. I rolled down my window and let the humid air wash over me. *Here's the only thing that hasn't changed in this little corner of the world,* I thought, as I watched the canal race toward the bay. *The water, with its shifting current and its salty, weedy scent.* I stared at it, going numb, a defense against feeling anything that could shake my fragile hold on the here and now. I was amazed that, so far at least, I seemed to be surviving this homecoming.

I turned into the Chapmans' driveway, parking behind a pickup truck I guessed belonged to Ethan, and got out of my car.

"You made it!" Ethan walked from his house and across the sand to where I was standing. His feet were bare and he was wearing jeans and a blue T-shirt. His smile was filled with an ease I did not feel and he surprised me with a hug.

"Quite a trip," I said, trying to return the smile.

"Traffic?" he asked.

"No. Just…I drove around."

"Ah." He seemed to understand. "Changed a bit in forty years, hasn't it?"

The screen door opened again and it was a moment before I recognized the woman who emerged from the house as his daughter, Abby. She was carrying a sleeping infant, six months old at the most, in her arms.

"Hi, Julie," she said, walking toward us. She had a baseball cap on her short blond hair and a blue quilted diaper bag over her arm.

"Hello, Abby," I said, and I leaned down to try to get a look at her baby. The child's head rested against Abby's shoulder. It had to be a girl. Her eyes were closed, but her lashes lay long and curled on her pudgy cheeks. "And who's this?" I asked.

"My granddaughter, Clare," Ethan said. He reached up and rubbed his hand softly over the little girl's back.

"She's gorgeous," I said.

"Clare and I are just leaving." Abby smiled at me. "I'm glad I got to see you, Julie, if only for two seconds," she said.

"You, too, Abby."

Ethan put his arm around his daughter. "See you Sunday for dinner," he said.

"You got it." Abby stood on tiptoe to kiss her father's cheek. "I love you," she said, stepping away. Then she walked toward the white Beetle convertible parked in front of the house.

"Love you, too," Ethan called after her. He grinned, watching his daughter and granddaughter get settled into the little car. He looked at me. "I am one lucky dude," he said.

I nodded. "Abby's really a lovely young woman," I said, but I was thinking about Shannon, trying to remember the last time she had told me she loved me. I told her all the time. When had she started responding to those words with "okay" or the occasional cherished "you, too"?

"Hand me your bag and we can go in the house," Ethan said.

I rolled my overnight bag toward him and reached into my pocketbook for my eyeglass case. I traded my prescription sunglasses for my regular glasses, then followed him into the house. Once inside, I realized that I had very little memory of its interior. When Ethan and I had played together indoors as kids—rarely, unless it rained— it had usually been at my house. We'd play cards on the porch or board games on the linoleum living-room floor. What had definitely changed inside the Chapmans' house, though, was its furniture. The first thing that greeted me in the living room was a striking, floor-to-ceiling entertainment center in a pale wood, the craftsmanship exceptional even to my untrained eye. That was only the first of Ethan's creations I noticed. Everywhere I turned, I saw evidence of his gift. There were end tables and a coffee table. Beautiful chairs with curved backs and silky smooth arms. The kitchen cabinets were a pale maple, and even the countertops were made of a eye-catching striated wood I couldn't resist running my hand over.

"Tiger maple," Ethan said. "I love the stuff. You'll see it all over the house."

I felt chastened by reality. I'd viewed his being a carpenter in negative terms. In my mind, I'd labeled him a man who worked with his hands instead of his head. But here were the results of his labor. He'd used not only his hands and head in the creative process, but there was plenty of evidence of his heart as well.

"The humidity here is terrible for the wood," he said, smoothing his fingers over one of the cabinet doors. "But I don't see the point of making beautiful things if you aren't going to use them, so I use them." Damn, he was cute, and I found myself smiling at him. He radiated a relaxed, soft-voiced, blue-eyed charm. The goofy kid who had begged for fish guts was simply not in evidence, and the attraction I'd felt to him in the Spring Lake restaurant was back in spades.

I looked through the kitchen to a jalousied sunroom.

"You enclosed your porch!" I said. Through the open jalousies, I could see the backyard and canal. "Let's go out there." I wasn't sure if I truly wanted to be in the backyard we'd once shared or if I simply wanted to get it over with.

"Sure," he said.

As we walked onto the sunporch, I squinted my eyes toward the opposite side of the canal. The weathered wooden bulkhead was gone. In its place was a steel bulkhead the color of rust. "What happened to the bulkhead?" I asked.

"I'll tell you," Ethan said. "Come on." He led me through the porch with its white wicker love seat and chaise longue. Once outside, I saw that our two yards were now separated by a decorative wire fence, nearly the color of the sand.

"Who lives there?" I found myself whispering.

He took my elbow. "Come on," he said again. "Let's sit down and I can fill you in on the neighborhood."

There was a beautiful boat in Ethan's double-wide dock. I no longer knew a thing about boats, but I could tell this one had power and speed.

Ethan pulled two of the handmade wooden beach chairs closer together and patted the back of one, encouraging me to sit.

I sat on the chair, a few feet behind the chain-link fence that separated us from the water.

"God." I shook my head. "I can't tell you how strange this feels to be here. To see this water. I feel like I was here just last week, it's so familiar to me. And look across the canal." I pointed to the thick green reeds where George and Wanda and their cousins used to fish. No one was fishing there this afternoon. "It's still undeveloped," I said.

"Right," Ethan said. "One of the few areas on the canal."

"The Rooster Man's shack is gone, though," I said, marveling at the cluster of angular gray buildings that stood where the shack had once been.

"Condos," Ethan said. "If you've got about $800,000, you can get one with two bedrooms."

I looked at him, openmouthed. "Are you kidding?" I asked.

"You don't want to know how much your old house is worth," he said.

I winced. "You're right," I said. "I don't." The current value of the bungalow didn't matter. My grandparents would have sold it even if they'd had a crystal ball to see the future of real estate in the area.

Ethan told me about the old wooden bulkhead succumbing to erosion and being replaced by the rust-colored steel walls years earlier. He told me about the changes on our street, how quickly the houses had gone up during the seventies. We watched as a massive yacht, crowded with well-heeled revelers, sailed by in front of us, and I realized I had not even turned in the direction of my old yard. I sighed.

"It's easier for me to focus on the bulkhead or the boats—" I nodded toward the yacht "—than over there." I shifted my gaze to the right, letting myself truly look at the yard for the first time since my arrival at Ethan's.

"I know," Ethan said. "I figured you'd get around to it when you were ready."

The old painted Adirondack chairs were gone and in their place, sleek metal patio furniture sat on the sand. More of the wire fencing surrounded the dock, and nearby was a large tree, barely recognizable as the tree I used to lean my crab net against. The screened porch that had seemed so big in my childhood still ran the length of the house, but it was not nearly as deep as I remembered it. A circular, above-ground swimming pool sat in the shade of the tree, and I could see the top of a motorboat in the dock.

"Who lives there?" I asked again.

"A young couple," Ethan said. "The Kleins. Very nice. They moved in about four years ago and they have a boy about seven years old."

"Ah," I said. Now I understood the need for all the fencing. It gave them the illusion of safety. I said a little prayer that the boy would grow up to be a strong, healthy adult.

"I told them that you—someone who used to live in the house— was coming to visit me," Ethan said, "and they said you're welcome to come over and see how the house has changed, if you like."

"No," I said quickly. I didn't want to set foot in that house of memories. "Do they know…you know…what happened?"

"No." Ethan smiled, leaning forward, elbows on his knees. "Julie, you have to realize that that house has probably had—" He looked out at the water for a moment, thinking. "I don't remember, exactly. Probably eight or nine owners in the last forty-one years."

I chuckled at my foolishness. To me, what happened in that house seemed like only yesterday. I wanted to ask Ethan if he missed being able to sit out on the wooden bulkhead; the steel one offered no place to sit. I wanted to ask him if he missed the blueberry bushes and the woods we used to play in and the clanging sound of the old bridge when it swung open to let the boats through. But I realized those changes, like the eight or nine owners of our house and the Rooster Man's shack being taken over by condos, were ancient history to him. In Bay Head Shores, he lived in the present, while I was still stuck in the past.

"This is hard for you, isn't it?" he asked. "Being here?"

I nodded, staring at the water. "A tragedy occurs," I mused. "Then you move on, or at least you try to move on, and you go through the motions of living your life, but you never quite forget it. It's always there under the perfectly calm surface. And then…wham." I pounded my fist on my thigh. "Something happens—like Ned's letter—and you're forced to deal with it all over again."

"You're the one who wanted me to take it to the police," he said.

I looked at him sharply. "It's not your taking it that shook things up," I said. "The letter *existed*, whether you took it or not."

He reached over to squeeze my shoulder. "You're right," he said. "And I didn't mean to sound glib or like I'm blaming you. It was the right thing to do to take it to the cops, and they got on my case for not bringing it sooner." He stared at his hands, rubbed them together, turned them palm side up, and I saw the signs of his work on his fingers. The skin looked rough and calloused. I wanted to take one of his hands in mine. I felt bad for snapping at him. This was no easier for him than it was for me.

"I think they suspect that I wanted the time to clean out Ned's house," Ethan said. "You know, to make sure they wouldn't be able to find anything incriminating."

"I assume they didn't find anything?" I asked.

"No, and I hadn't found anything when I went through his stuff, either. No secret journals. No letters of confession. My friend who works at the department, though, told me they were able to find enough hairs and...whatever at his house to use for DNA matching."

"Well, that's good," I said, although I didn't know exactly how Ned's DNA could be used at that point. "What did they ask when they interviewed you? What are they going to ask me tomorrow?"

He sat back in his chair, hands flat now on his denim-covered thighs. "They wanted me to give them the names of everyone Ned knows. Knew," he corrected himself. "His drinking buddies. Women he dated. College friends. People he might have confided in. I couldn't come up with many. Ned kept to himself. He wasn't a social drinker. He drank to get drunk. Solo. Period."

"What sort of relationship did you have with him?" I asked.

"Very difficult," Ethan said. "He didn't want to be around me because I was always badgering him about his drinking. About getting help. He didn't want to hear it. He rarely saw Dad, either, which I know just killed my father. He still feels as though he failed Ned, that he should have been able to do something to help him."

"Oh!" I said. "I forgot to tell you something."

He looked at me, waiting.

"Did you know your father went to see my mother?"

His eyes grew wide. *"What?"*

"He did," I said. "He showed up at her house the same day you and I met in Spring Lake."

He looked as though I'd imagined it. "Why would he do that?" he asked.

"I don't know, and she wasn't very forthcoming," I said. "She said he was thinking about us and decided to visit her. Does he know about the letter?"

Ethan shook his head. "He couldn't possibly," he said. "And I've talked to him since you and I met and he never said a thing about visiting your mother. Did he drive all the way up to Westfield to see her?"

"Yes. At least, he came to her house. I assume he drove."

"Oh, brother," Ethan said. "He scares me when he drives around the corner, much less to Westfield. I'll have to talk to him about it. I don't know how long I can let him live independently. He's..." He shook his head. "Now, *this* is where Ned and I communicated," he said. "We could talk about Dad—what should be done as far as taking care of him and that sort of the thing. I'm on my own with it now."

I thought of Lucy, how glad I was to have her as my sister. How much I treasured her.

Ethan rested his head against the seat back, and a faraway look came into his eyes. "I just want..." he began. "I wish there was something I could do to keep the police from talking to my father," he said. "I know they plan to, and probably soon, since he's the only one who can support Ned's alibi. I'm afraid they're going to badger him because they probably think he used his influence to get Ned off." He shook his head. "I dread telling him about that letter."

"I know," I said. "I can't imagine telling my mother about it."

"You might have to, Julie." He looked at me, the blue in his eyes so clear I felt like diving into them.

"I know," I said again, but I was thinking, *Not if I can help it.*

"Well," Ethan said, "here's what I think you and I can do that might help the investigation," he said. "We should try to remember Ned and Isabel's friends from 1962 and anything important about them. The police might want to talk to them."

I leaned my head back against the wood of the chair. I thought about Isabel's old crowd that used to hang out on the beach. "Why can't they find Bruno?" I asked.

"He's left the area, his parents are dead, and his real name—Bruce

Walker—is pretty common," Ethan said. "But my friend assures me they're looking for him."

"Isabel had two best girlfriends here," I said. "Pamela Durant and—"

"Oh, yeah," Ethan said, a little of the lecher in his voice. "Hard to forget her. She never came back to the shore, though, after that summer, but I still remember her."

"Down, boy." I smiled. "I didn't know you had any interest in the opposite sex back then, except as something to study under a microscope."

He returned the smile. "The geeky thing was just a facade," he said.

I laughed.

"Who was the other girl Isabel hung around with?" he asked.

"Mitzi Caruso," I said. "She lived on the corner. Right down there." I pointed in the general direction of the Carusos' house.

"I vaguely remember her," Ethan said. "I think she came back a few more summers, but I couldn't really say for sure. There were a couple other guys Ned hung around with, but I'm completely blank on their names. Summer kids. Do you remember any of them?"

I shook my head. The rest of those teenagers from Izzy and Ned's crowd were as faceless to me as they were nameless.

Ethan looked at his watch, then stood up.

"Listen," he said, "it's a gorgeous evening. Let's go out in the boat, and then we can make dinner—I picked up some flounder—and talk some more."

I glanced toward his dock. "I don't do boats these days," I said.

"Really?" He looked puzzled. "When I picture you, it's in that little runabout of yours. Out there by yourself on the canal, twelve years old, zipping around like you owned the water."

It was hard to believe I'd ever been that child. "I haven't been on a boat since that summer," I said.

"Come on." He held out his hand to me. "Let's go. We can head toward the river if the bay upsets you."

He didn't understand. There would be no pleasure in it for me, only a sort of panic. "I don't want to, Ethan," I said.

He saw that I was serious and gave up. "Okay," he said. "We'll skip the boat ride and go right to dinner, then. Are you hungry?"

* * *

I helped him cook, although he was at ease in the kitchen. Watching him, I realized he was a man at ease, period. And lying here now in his handmade guest-room bed, it occurred to me that he had always been that way. Even when he was a nerdy little kid, he hadn't cared what others thought of him. He'd been comfortable in his own skin. I hadn't expected to find myself admiring him any more than I'd expected to find myself attracted to him. And yet I was both.

CHAPTER 19

Julie

Sometimes you could find yourself feeling very anxious about one thing only to discover that you should have been anxious about something entirely different. That's what happened to me the morning of my interview by the police.

I'd awakened early to the sun-washed blue of Ethan's guest room and the comforting scent of coffee. I longed to stay in that room all day. My head hurt a little and I thought of calling the police department, telling them I couldn't come in, that I was sick. I did not want to go over what had happened in 1962, detail by detail, which is what I figured they would ask me to do. How would I be able to bear it? Putting the interview off until later, though, would provide only temporary relief, so I got up, showered, dried my hair, dressed in khaki pants and my red sleeveless shirt and walked downstairs. Ethan was reading the paper at the table on his sunporch, but he hopped up when he saw me in the kitchen.

"Eggs or pancakes?" He put the newspaper down on the counter. "I can go either way."

"Toast?" I asked. "And bacon." I motioned toward the plate of bacon he'd already prepared, although I wasn't sure I'd be able to eat anything at all.

"Sit down and I'll feed you," he said.

I took a seat at the kitchen table, lifting up the tablecloth to admire what I knew would be beneath it—another of Ethan's creations.

"How are you doing this morning?" he asked, putting two slices of bread in the toaster.

"I think I'm okay," I said slowly, like someone who had just sustained an injury and was trying out the muscle to be sure it wasn't sprained.

"Do you want me to drive you?" he asked.

"Just give me directions and I'll be fine," I said with false bravado. I liked the idea of him coming with me, but I was sure he had work to do.

He jotted a phone number on a slip of paper and handed it to me. "This is my cell number," he said. "I'm stopping over at a job this morning, but let me know when you're done and I'll meet you back here."

I nodded. The toast was ready and I carried it and the bacon onto the sunporch while he followed with two cups of coffee. The jalousies were wide-open, and the reedy scent of the canal, the swift current, and the boats cutting through the water all combined to take hold of my heart and squeeze. I nibbled at the toast, my appetite gone as I tried to carry on a conversation about the job Ethan had to check on that morning. I had made it through half a slice of toast and an inch of bacon by the time I needed to leave, and as I headed out the door, I wished that I'd accepted his offer to go with me.

The room I was taken to at the Point Pleasant Police Department was small and bare, and there was nothing to look at other than the faces of my two questioners. I sat on a hard, straight-backed chair across a table from Lieutenant Michael Jaffe from the Prosecutor's Office and a very young, blond detective, Grace Engelmann, from the Police Department. They each had a notepad in front of them, and a tape recorder rested on the table between us, a thick file of papers next to it.

There was a little small talk at first, designed, I thought, to put me at ease.

"It's changed a lot since you were a kid here, huh?" Lieutenant Jaffe asked after he'd introduced himself and the detective. He was a handsome man with wavy salt-and-pepper hair and a youthful face.

"Yes," I said. "I haven't been back since my sister's death."

"*Really,*" he said, as if that surprised him. "I didn't come here until ninety-two myself, so I've only known it the way it is now. What sort of changes have you noticed?"

He had to know how the area had changed, whether he'd lived here or not, but I figured I would play along with the putting-me-at-ease game.

"Well," I said, "there were a lot of summer people back then. And far fewer houses. The bulkhead is different. That new bridge wasn't there."

He frowned. "The new bridge?"

"Over the canal," I said, and he and Detective Engelmann both laughed.

"We call that the *old* bridge now," he said. "It really *has* been a long time for you, hasn't it?"

I smiled. I could hear the tape running in the small machine resting on the table.

"You know," he said, "my wife and I love your books."

"Thank you." I was tempted, as I always was, to ask which book he liked best, but decided against it, in case he was simply making conversation and had not read them at all. The last thing I wanted to do was make *him* uncomfortable. Detective Engelmann wrote something down on her pad. What I had said to prompt her to do that, I couldn't imagine.

"How did you happen to go into mystery writing?" Lieutenant Jaffe asked.

I always got that question. I had a long answer designed for speaking engagements and a short answer designed for times like this.

"I loved Nancy Drew as a kid," I said. "And I loved writing. So it seemed a natural fit."

"Ah, yes," he said, as the detective continued writing on her pad.

"You know, I remember reading an article about you in some…I don't know, probably some magazine or newspaper, where you said that when you were a child, you entertained your friends by making up mysterious events and pretending they'd occurred in your neighborhood."

Were we still in the small-talk mode, or did I detect a subtle shift in the tone of his questioning? "That's true," I said.

"And then there was the *real* mystery…the ultimate mystery in your own family," he said.

I was confused for a moment and must have looked it.

"The murder of your sister," he said.

"Oh," I said. "Yes." I shifted in the hard, armless chair. I wanted to cut to the chase. I wanted to tell him and the so-far-silent Detective Engelmann that I'd always suspected Ned was guilty and that, in my opinion, that was what he'd been alluding to in his letter. But this was not my show, and I waited for the next question.

"What can you tell us about George Lewis?" he asked.

The thought of George brought an rueful smile to my lips.

"He was a teaser," I said. "I spent quite a bit of time with him and his sister, Wanda. I don't think he knew who his father was, and I'm not sure what happened to his mother. He and Wanda had been raised by a cousin, Salena. I think his family was very poor, but they were close to each other and there was a lot of affection between them." I remembered the look of daggers George had sent my father the day Daddy came over to drag me home. "He had a tough facade and was probably pretty streetwise." I added, "Although I'm only guessing. I never actually saw that side of him. It makes me so angry…so upset…to know that he went to prison for something he didn't do."

The lieutenant nodded. "I imagine the person who's responsible for your sister's murder carries a lot of guilt around for letting the wrong person go to prison."

I didn't miss the present tense in his sentence. "Well," I said. "It's my opinion that Ned Chapman was that person and that his guilt is what ultimately did him in." I was hoping we could get down to the nitty-gritty now, but Lieutenant Jaffe folded his hands on the table and leaned forward.

"You understand," he said, "that we have to look at every angle on this case. We have to start fresh. We have your statements from 1962, but it's important for us to look at this case with a clean slate."

I nodded, feeling uncertain. I wanted to get this over with, to review the statements I'd made as a twelve-year-old and get the recitation of those memories out of my way. That wasn't going to happen though, at least not yet.

"Tell us about Isabel," Lieutenant Jaffe said.

The question was so open-ended, I didn't know quite what to do with it.

"She was beautiful," I began. I wished the chair I was sitting in had arms. My hands felt heavy and awkward in my lap. "And she was rebellious. A typical teenager. She snuck out every night to meet Ned at the platform on the bay." I was quiet a moment, trying to figure out what else I should say about Isabel. The only sounds in the room were the quiet whirring of the tape recorder and the tip of the detective's pencil racing across her notepad. When she had finished whatever she was writing, she looked up and spoke for the first time.

"How did you know she was sneaking out every night?" she asked. She had rather amazing green eyes, the color of new grass, and I wondered if she was wearing special contacts.

"I knew because I saw her," I said. "Because I was sneaking out myself." Surely they already had this information in the old records of the case. But, as the lieutenant said, they were starting fresh.

"What was your relationship with her like?" he asked.

I looked away from him quickly, annoyed with myself for doing so. I did not want to talk about my relationship with Isabel, and I knew that my sudden inability to look at my questioners made me suspect in their eyes. *That's what this is about,* I realized. They didn't care why I thought Ned had done it. They wanted to know *my* role in Isabel's death. My anxiety took a sudden, unexpected leap.

"We were close when we were young," I said, lifting my gaze to look squarely at the lieutenant, then the detective. "But there were five years between us and we drifted apart as she got into her teens, which was only natural. We didn't have much in common anymore."

"Did you argue a lot?" Detective Engelmann asked.

"Bickered," I said with a shrug. "Typical sibling rivalry."

"And how about Ned Chapman?" the detective asked. "What was he like?"

I felt a hot flash start to prickle and burn on the top of my head. *Damn.* In two seconds, my face would be as red as my shirt. I did *not* look away this time, though. I held the woman's grass-green gaze as I answered. "He seemed nice," I said. "I mean, I'd known him all my life, since he lived next door to us during the summer. He was the lifeguard at the beach. But you can't *really* know what's going on inside a person. He was nice on the exterior, but who knows what was going on inside him."

"You had a crush on him." The lieutenant made it a statement rather than a question.

I shrugged again. "A typical preteen sort of crush," I said. I was using the word *typical* too much and wondered if they'd noticed. I could barely breathe for the heat radiating down my neck and chest. I waved my hand in front of my face, looking apologetic. "Hot flash," I said. "A nuisance."

They smiled at me as if they understood, but given Detective Engelmann's age and Lieutenant Jaffe's gender, I was certain neither of them had a clue how I was feeling. I wanted to pick up the detective's rapidly filling notepad to give myself a real fanning.

"Were you jealous of Isabel?" Lieutenant Jaffe asked.

My eyes darted away from him again. *Damn it.* What was wrong with me? I wanted to say, *Of course I was jealous of her. Weren't you jealous of your older siblings?* Instead, I steadied myself and nodded. "In some ways," I said. "I wished that I'd looked like her and that I was her age and could have the freedom she did."

"Who knew she would be on the bay at midnight on August fifth, 1962?" Detective Engelmann asked.

"I did," I said. "And Bruno—Bruce—Walker. And possibly George Lewis, although I was never sure of that. If he knew, then Wanda Lewis probably did, as well. And, of course, Ned Chapman."

"Although according to the old report—" the Lieutenant fingered the file in front of him, although he did not open it to look at the pages "—Ned Chapman had asked you to tell Isabel that he couldn't meet her that night."

"Well, yes, but he later said he might be able to."

"You were really known for your storytelling back then, weren't you?" the detective asked me.

They were jumping from topic to topic so quickly that my over-heated brain could barely keep up, and once again, I was not sure exactly what she meant.

"I read a lot," I said. "I read Nancy Drew books aloud to George and Wanda."

"But you also made things up, right?" she asked. "The way you made up stories about events in your neighborhood to excite your friends."

I stared at her, uncertain how to respond. I felt something like hatred for her building inside me. When I didn't respond to her question, the lieutenant spoke up.

"Let me try to summarize what you've told us so far," he said. "There was some sibling rivalry between you and your sister. You were jealous of her. You knew where she'd be that night. You regularly sneaked out of the house. You had a crush on—"

"*Stop it.*" I stood up, the chair scraping the floor. "I didn't come here for this," I said. "I came to help in your investigation. I came to tell you what I remember, not to be accused of murdering my sister. I didn't kill her, if that's what you're getting at. I would never have hurt her."

"Please sit down again," Lieutenant Jaffe said calmly, and against my better judgment, I did so. I sat on the edge of the chair, though, ready to make my exit.

"We have to look at everyone involved," he said. "Everyone who could have been in the same place as your sister that night. That includes you."

I held on to my anger. If I didn't, I knew I would start to cry. "I didn't kill my sister," I said, slowly and deliberately. "I had nothing to do with it."

The lieutenant suddenly looked at his watch, then stood up. "We'll be talking with everyone," he said. "And we appreciate you coming in."

Was that it? I'd been expecting the handcuffs to be produced at any second. I was thinking about my lawyer, who'd never handled a criminal case in his life. But now, free to go, my thoughts shifted to my mother.

"Are you going to need to talk with my mother?" I asked, slowly getting to my feet. Detective Engelmann was still sitting at the table, still writing. She didn't even lift her head from her work.

"Most likely, yes," Lieutenant Jaffe said. "You don't have a problem with that, do you?"

I shut my eyes, holding on to the back of the chair for balance. I felt a little dizzy, and my mind was slow and logy. If I answered yes to his question, it would look as though I was afraid of what my mother might say. If I explained that my family never talked about Isabel's death, it would look even worse. I opened my eyes and spoke the truth. "I don't want my mother to suffer any more than she has," I said. "I don't want her to endure…" I waved my hand through the air, encompassing the room, my two questioners and the entire situation. "I don't want her to have to deal with all of this," I said.

"We understand," the lieutenant said. "And we'll keep that in mind."

CHAPTER 20

Julie
1962

"How about we go to the beach today, girls?" Mom said.

All the women in the family—my sisters, grandmother, mother and myself—were relaxing around the porch table after a breakfast of fruit salad and French toast.

"Okay," Lucy said. "Just don't expect me to go swimming."

"Not if you don't want to." My mother leaned over to brush a crumb from Lucy's lip, then she sat back to admire her youngest daughter. "You're turning a nice nut-brown color," she said.

Of the three of us girls, Lucy was the least tan, since she spent most of her time indoors reading or playing cards with Grandma, but it was impossible to be at the shore and avoid the sun altogether.

"I promised Mitzi and Pam I'd go to the beach with them," Isabel said, then added quickly, "but I'll see you there." She was sitting on the side of the table closest to the house, the seat that would give her the best view of the Chapmans' backyard. Her huge, almond-shaped eyes darted in that direction every twenty seconds or so. She was so obvious I couldn't believe my mother never caught on. Did Mom think for one minute it was Mitzi Caruso and Pamela Durant that Isabel wanted to hang out with at the beach?

But I supposed I was no less skillful in masking my real intentions.

"And I want to stay around here," I said, wishing I could turn around in my seat to see if the Lewises had arrived yet across the canal.

My mother raised her eyebrows at me, obviously suspicious, and I ran my fork through the syrup on my plate to avoid her scrutiny. "Maybe I'll fish and catch something for dinner," I added, for something to say. I waited for her to admonish me not to cross the canal, knowing I could not disobey her direct command to stay in our yard, and I was relieved when she didn't give it. Instead, she turned to Grandma.

"Why don't you come with Lucy and me today, Mother?" she asked. Grandma always seemed content to stay in the house, sweeping the floors or doing the laundry, an arduous job without a washing machine.

"Well, maybe I will for a change," she said, surprising everyone.

Perfect, I thought. No one would be around to care what I did. Grandpop was on an all-day fishing trip with some of his buddies. He'd invited me to join him, but I'd gone with that group last summer and had felt like I didn't belong—which I didn't.

Everyone took off for the beach after we'd cleaned up from breakfast. I grabbed my bait bucket and walked to the end of the road. Happy in my freedom, I made up a little song about the dragonflies as I walked along the path through the tall reeds until I reached the area where Grandpop kept his killie trap. I dropped to my knees in the damp sand, tossing my binoculars over my shoulder so I didn't get them wet, and was pulling the trap from the water when someone called out, "Who's there?"

I jumped, startled, before I recognized the voice as Ethan's.

"Where are you?" I asked.

"Over here." His voice came from somewhere to my left. I had to wade into the water to circumvent the reeds and cattails and finally saw him sitting cross-legged in the shallows, the water lapping at his knees. He was wearing only his trunks, and the freckles on his bare chest seemed to have converged to give him something of a tan.

"What are you doing?" I asked.

"Come look," he said. "I found some baby eels."

I had never seen a baby eel, and I was curious. I stepped as close to the grass as I could, trying not to disturb the water. Then I knelt down next to him, so close I could smell the suntan lotion on his skin.

"There." He pointed.

I saw three squiggly black eels, thinner than a pencil, wriggling below the water's surface.

"They're so cute," I said.

"I wanted to catch one of them to dissect," Ethan said, "but I can't. They're just babies."

He was weird, but I was touched nevertheless. "Yeah," I said. "Don't do it."

He glanced in the direction of the bait trap, which he could not possibly see through the tall, thick wall of grass. "Didja get a lot of killies?" he asked.

"Haven't checked yet."

"Where's your grandfather?"

"On a fishing boat."

"So…" He pushed his thick sunglasses higher on his nose. "You going across the canal to fish today?"

"Yes," I said. "And keep your big mouth shut about it."

"I will if you take me with you."

"I'm the only one allowed over there," I said, not even sure what I meant by the statement. All I knew was that I had no desire to share my new friends with Ethan. He'd want to study Wanda and George under a microscope the way he did his sea creatures.

"I'll tell, then," he said.

"You are such a spaz."

"Takes one to know one," he replied.

"Don't you dare tell, or else," I said, without finishing the sentence. I let the implied threat hang there in the air as I walked through the water, hoping that would be enough to deter him.

There were loads of killies flapping helplessly against the wire walls of the trap as I pulled it onto the sand. I emptied the small fish into my bucket, then tossed the trap into the water again. I didn't bother calling goodbye to Ethan as I walked back along the path to the road.

Wanda waved from her side of the canal as I got into the runabout. I couldn't wait to get over there. I was bringing *The Bungalow Mystery* with me today, since I thought it fit perfectly with being down the shore. I put everything I needed in the runabout, then headed across the canal. The current was strong in the direction of the river, but I had no problem and I pulled easily into the dock between the Lewises and the Rooster Man's shack. That dock felt nearly as familiar as my own these days. I kept thinking of how Mr. Chapman had defended my being over there to my father. I had the respect of the chief justice of the New Jersey Supreme Court. I adored my father, but he was wrong about this.

George stood on the bulkhead above my boat.

"Can you carry me and Wanda to the river?" he asked. He pointed in the direction of the Manasquan River.

"What?" I wasn't sure what he meant.

"We ain't catching nothin' here," he said. "But a guy told us they biting in the river."

Wanda appeared at his side. "Salena says we can go if you can carry us," she said.

Salena's crazy, I thought. Couldn't she see how fast the current was moving? I was not allowed to take the boat to the river, which was a mile and a half north of my house through the canal. I wasn't allowed to take it north of my house, period. But what an adventure it would be! I looked toward my bungalow, barely able to see the porch because of the bulkhead being in the way. No one was there, though. No one would know.

I tipped my head back to look at George and Wanda again. "Okay," I said. I leaned over and grabbed a rung of the ladder to pull the boat close to the side of the dock. "Get in," I said. "And bring a net. I don't have one."

They grabbed their gear and climbed down the ladder into the runabout. Salena appeared above us.

"Come back by one, hear?" she said.

"Okay." I yanked the cord on the motor and inched into the canal, making sure I wasn't pulling out in front of any boats that might be close to the bulkhead.

Once in the canal, the current grabbed the boat and I held tight to the tiller handle to keep us on a steady course. As we passed my empty bungalow into the water north of it, I felt exhilarated. The low Lovelandtown Bridge was directly ahead of us, though. I'd sailed beneath it with my grandfather and others, but had never taken my boat through it by myself. The current was fast, and the too-close-together pilings of the bridge were coming up on us quickly, the water racing between them as rough as rapids.

"Girl," George said, "you know what you doin'?"

"'Course," I said, hanging on to the tiller handle for dear life. I realized there was only one life preserver in the boat, and none of us was wearing it.

A bigger boat was ahead of us and I knew its wake would only add to the turbulent water. If the current hadn't been so strong, I would have tried to stall my boat and wait for the wake to run its course, but I had no choice. My sweaty palm was getting jerked back and forth on the tiller handle as we headed beneath the bridge. A huge wave from the wake of the boat rose up in front of us, and we sailed over it, then plunged into the water on the other side as a second wave headed straight for us. I may have screamed. I surely said a quick prayer. I had just enough time to think about the sin I was in the middle of committing and how death might be a fitting punishment for it. The wave washed over the front of the little runabout, soaking us, splashing salt water into my eyes and my mouth, and for a moment I wasn't sure if we were on the surface of the water or beneath it. How I kept control of the runabout, I couldn't say, but I must have seemed very confident, because George and Wanda just whooped with the fun of it all, as though we were riding a nice, safe roller coaster.

We made it through. My heart pulsed in my ears as we met the calmer water on the other side of the bridge. The speed of the current no longer seemed so daunting after what we'd just endured. I was not looking forward to the only other bridge we had to pass beneath, but as it turned out, the water there was not nearly so rough. I had managed to put enough distance between us and the larger boat that its wake was not a problem, which I think disappointed my passengers.

The current carried us into the open water of the Manasquan River. I headed west instantly, afraid that George might suggest we travel east to the inlet and out into the ocean. I'd had enough boating adventure for one day.

We were not the only fishermen on the river, but we found a nice spot just to the side of the channel out of the way of the traffic. I turned off the motor and George lifted my anchor and tossed it overboard, handling it as if it were made of paper.

Wanda took one of the killies out of my bucket and began baiting her hook. "That another Nancy Drew book?" She nodded toward *The Bungalow Mystery,* which now rested in an inch of water in the bottom of the boat.

"Yeah," I said. I lifted it up and rested it on my knees. "I'm not sure how readable it's going to be now," I said. I felt terrible. Grandpop had given me that book for my birthday the year before.

We all cast our lines into the water, and then I found the bottle of suntan lotion floating beneath my seat. I unscrewed the cap and rubbed some of the lotion on my arms and face. George took off his shirt, and he looked so handsome that I started having some impure thoughts about *him.* I wondered what was wrong with me that even a colored boy could make me feel that way.

"Can I have some of that?" he asked, pointing to the lotion.

I must have looked surprised.

"What?" he said. "You think black people don't need no suntan lotion?"

He peeled an inch of his shorts down and I could clearly see the difference in the color of his skin. Wanda smacked his shoulder.

"We don't want to see your ugly drawers," she said.

I laughed as I handed George the bottle. He used some and passed the lotion to Wanda. Then, to my surprise, he put his shirt into the water in the bottom of the boat. He soaked up the water, wrung it out over the side, then soaked up some more. I was grateful. I hadn't known how I was going to explain an inch of water in the bottom of the boat to my grandfather.

I opened the book resting on my thighs, but the pages were clumped together, already wavy from the water. It was ruined.

"Maybe when it dries you can pick them pages apart," Wanda said. I could tell she felt sorry for me. I'd really come to like Wanda. She was quiet, except when razzin' her brother, and although she never told me everything that had happened in her life, I knew it hadn't been easy for her. One day when I complained about how my father'd dragged me home from her side of the canal, she'd responded with, "'Least you have a father," which gave me something to think about. I was glad she had Salena looking out for her.

Whoever had told George that the fish were biting in the river was right. We caught black fish and fluke and a couple of feisty snappers, reeling them in one after another. I wondered how I was going to explain my magnificent haul to my mother without telling her where I'd been. I figured I would let Wanda and George take most of my fish, just keeping a couple of fluke for myself.

"Can I borrow them binoculars?" George asked, after we'd been fishing a while.

I slipped them over my head and handed them to him. He lifted them to his eyes and started exploring the world around us, his fishing pole snug, for the moment at least, between his knees.

I was baiting my hook again when I spotted something pale bobbing in the water a few feet from the boat. I handed my pole to Wanda and reached for the object with the net.

"What's that?" Wanda asked as I lifted the net from the water.

"A doll, I think."

It *was* a doll, a baby doll, no bigger than the length of my fingers. She was naked, with plastic, painted-on brown hair and perpetually open blue eyes. I took it out of the net and picked it clean of seaweed.

"What you gonna do with that raggedy ol' thing?" Wanda asked.

I shrugged. "I don't like to see trash floating in the water," I said. Even Wanda didn't know about the Nancy Drew box.

None of us had a watch, but when the sun had passed overhead, I knew we'd better start back. George raised the anchor and I pulled the cord to start the motor. It made a sputtering sound, followed by silence. I pulled again, and it made a sound like someone blowing air through his lips. I kept yanking, the boat drifting, and I imagined all sorts of nightmarish scenes of being rescued by the Marine Police and having to explain to my parents what I was doing with the colored people I'd been forbidden to visit on the river I had no right to be in. I couldn't seem to breathe.

"What's wrong with it?" Wanda asked.

"Hey, ain't that your sister's boyfriend?" George was looking through the binoculars in the direction of the canal.

"Where?" I asked.

"In that boat." George held the binoculars steady as he pointed to our right. I turned and could see several boats in the area, but from that distance, I never would have been able to tell who was in them. "I think that's him for sure," George said, "but I got a news flash. That ain't your sister he's with."

I forgot about my drifting boat for a moment. "Let me see!" I reached for the binoculars and he pulled them over his head and handed them to me. I held them to my eyes. "Where?" I said, trying to adjust the focus from George's needs to mine.

"Well, I can't tell now," George complained. "Them boats is specks without them binoculars."

"We're gonna float clear out to the ocean, you don't get this boat runnin'," Wanda said.

She was right. I slipped the binoculars' strap over my head and pulled once more on the cord. The motor sputtered again, then went silent.

"What's wrong with it?" Wanda asked.

"I don't know," I said. Sometimes I did have to yank two or three times to get it going, but I'd never had this much trouble.

"Let me," George said.

We shifted positions in the boat so that he was near the motor. He held on to the cord and pulled it back so fast his arm was a blur. Instantly the motor came to life and I could finally breathe. As we sailed toward the canal, though, my mind returned to the boat George had seen through the binoculars.

"Are you sure it was Ned?" I asked.

"I think it was that white boy you showed me the other day," he said. "Your sister's boyfriend."

I'd pointed Ned out to George and Wanda through the binoculars.

"And who was he with?" I asked. "What did she look like?"

"I couldn't see her that good," he said, "but good enough I could tell she's easy on the eyes. A blondie with a long pigtail."

"Pam Durant?" I asked, my voice high. "Was the ponytail on the *side* of her head? Were there other people with them?"

"Girl, don't get your drawers all tight." George laughed. "Maybe they was just taking a boat ride as friends. Like we doing."

We headed back to the canal, the current nearly slack now, much to my relief, making the bridges far less difficult to negotiate. I pulled into the dock where their cousins were fishing, and Salena and one of the men came over to look down into the boat, marveling at our catch. I moved a few fish from my bucket to theirs. George looked at me quizzically, then seemed to get it.

"Tell your folks it was just a good fishin' day on the canal," he said, slipping the largest black fish back into my own bucket.

I crossed the canal and docked my boat. Climbing up the ladder with the bucket of fish, I thought that as much as I craved a good adventure, I really couldn't handle a day like this one more than once a month or so. There'd been too many close calls. My guardian angel must have been looking out for me.

I was relieved to find that no one was home yet. I got the scaler and a knife from the kitchen and went out to the cleaning table in the side yard to work on the fish. It took me a long time, and when I was finished, I looked at the pile of filets and knew there was no way I could explain them to my mother. I left six of them on the cleaning table, then put the rest onto the cutting board along with their heads and tails and guts, and I carried them to the canal and tossed them into the water.

After dinner, I went out in the yard with the little baby doll I'd found in the river. I sat at the corner of the house and smoothed a couple of inches of sand from the buried bread box. I was just starting to lift the top of the box when it suddenly flew up into the air. I shrieked, jumping quickly to my feet. Then I saw what had raised the lid: a large, coiled toy caterpillar had been pushed into the box, ready to spring out at me like a jack-in-the-box. I heard laughter, and turned to see Ned Chapman standing in his yard, hands on his hips, a look of amusement on his face.

"Did you put this here?" I yelled, getting to my feet, marching in his direction.

He held his hands up in the air. "Don't look at me," he said. He was trying not to smile.

I knew he'd done it, and I knew Isabel must have told him about the box. How else could he know?

"Don't you *ever* touch my things again!" I said, a fury in my voice that I was not truly feeling. I was secretly thrilled by his attention. I thought of asking him if he'd been out on his boat with Pam Durant, but I suddenly realized he couldn't possibly have been. He would have been lifeguarding at the Baby Beach. George had probably made the whole thing up just to tease me.

It was still light out, so I sat on the bulkhead with a book. I was there about fifteen minutes when Isabel came out into the yard. She walked beyond the fence and sat down on the bulkhead a few feet away from me. She had the giraffe towel knotted around her waist and she was staring at me, no expression on her face whatsoever.

"What?" I asked.

"I know what you're doing," she said.

"What do you mean?" I was doing so many things I wasn't supposed to be doing that I didn't know which one she was talking about.

"I mean, I know you've been going out in the boat at night," she said.

I tried to put an expression of confused disbelief on my face. "What are you talking about?" I asked.

She leaned down to scratch her calf. "I happened to go outside the other night and I noticed the boat was gone," she said. "I knew Grand-pop hadn't taken it because I could hear him snoring practically from the yard. I went upstairs and saw your bed was empty."

I dropped my attention to my book again, as if I could possibly read after hearing what she'd said. "So?" I asked.

"Where are you going in the middle of the night?"

"None of your business." She'd used that line on me so often it felt good to be able to say it back to her.

"Look, Julie," she said. "You're only twelve. I'm afraid you're going to get in big trouble."

"I can take care of myself," I said.

"Either you tell me what you're up to," Isabel used her bossiest tone, "or I'm going to have to tell Mom what you're doing."

I looked at her sharply. "Go ahead and tell her," I said. "And then I'll tell her where *you* go in the middle of the night."

She didn't budge from her seat on the bulkhead, but I could see her face blanch beneath her tan.

"How would you know where I go?" she asked, some of the bluster gone from her voice.

"I have my ways," I said. "Just…you just keep what you know about me to yourself, and I'll keep what I know about you to myself." I had the upper hand with her for the first time in my life. It was an extraordinary feeling of power. I could tell she was struggling with a response, and that pleased me. "By the way," I added, "was Ned at the beach today?"

She looked confused. "What does that matter?"

"Just, was he?"

"No," she said. "He had errands to run."

My heart twisted a bit in my chest. I'd thought it would give me pleasure to imagine Ned cheating on her, but pleasure was not what I was feeling. I was about to ask her if Pam had been at the beach that morning, but she spoke first.

"I'm so in love with him, Jules," she said. She looked out toward the water, a smile growing on her lips. "I know it's hard for you to understand, but someday you will. It's amazing to feel this way. To love someone so much and to know he loves you back."

What could I say? That I was in love with Ned, too? That I understood how that half of the equation felt?

Suddenly she moved closer and put her arm around me. I stiffened, but it felt so soft and warm that my shoulders relaxed. I couldn't remember the last time Isabel had touched me with affection. "Julie," she said, and her voice was very quiet, so quiet that I had to look at her to truly hear her. Her face was very close to mine. Her eyes were like something edible, like chocolate pudding. I could imagine how

Ned felt when he was this close to her. "Listen to me, Julie," she began again. "I'm seventeen years old. What I'm doing may not be right, but it's my business and I'm old enough to take care of myself. You're not. I'm worried about you. I don't want you to get hurt."

The surprising tenderness in her words, the love behind them, stung my eyes. "I'm okay," I said, my voice small now.

"Tell me you won't do it anymore." She squeezed my shoulders. "Whatever it is you're up to. Tell me."

"I won't," I said, although I knew I was lying. My sister and I had both turned into liars this summer.

And we would both pay.

CHAPTER 21

Julie

I hadn't intended to call Ethan after I got out of the interview. I was certain I'd cut into his work time the day before and didn't want to take up any more of it, so my plan was to drive back to his house, leave him a thank-you note, and head home. But as I pulled away from the police department, still shaken from so many unexpected questions, the memories churned in my head and I felt lonely with the weight of them. *George. Ned. Isabel.* They were all I could think about, and I hadn't said anything I'd wanted to say about them to the police. I'd screwed up the interview, letting my interrogators rattle me. I needed Ethan. I needed to talk. To vent. I swerved over to the side of Bridge Avenue, stepped on the brake and grabbed my cell phone. I had to dial three times before I managed to tap out the right number.

"Julie?" Ethan answered the phone. "How'd it go?"

I started to cry, unable to find my voice.

"Meet me at my house," he said. "Are you okay to drive?"

"Yes," I managed to say. I felt such relief at reaching him.

His truck was already in his driveway when I arrived at his house.

I walked inside without knocking and he greeted me in the hallway, pulling me into a hug as he had the day before, but this one was not a surprise and it felt natural and welcome to me. I pressed my forehead into his shoulder, my hand against his back, clutching the fabric of his shirt.

"Shh," he said, as if comforting a child in the middle of a nightmare. "It's going to be okay. It's all going to be okay." He took a step away from me. "Do you want to sit outside or on the sunporch?"

I thought of the neighbors in my old bungalow, possibly sitting on my old screened porch, watching me fall apart in Ethan's backyard. "Sunporch," I said, already walking toward the back of his house.

I sat on the white wicker love seat facing the canal, and although there were other seating options available to him, Ethan sat down next to me. He'd been working outside; the skin of his arm was hot against mine and I could smell the scent of sun and soap on him. I was glad he was there with me. We were on different teams in the investigation, wanting and expecting different outcomes, yet I knew he would understand how I felt.

"So," he said, "what got you so upset?"

"They questioned me as if I were a suspect," I said.

We were sitting so close together that I couldn't really look at him, but I felt him nodding.

"I was afraid of that from some of the questions they'd asked me about you," he said. "I'm sure they don't really suspect you, though. They just need to rule you out. They have to look at everyone who was involved at the time. They asked me some tough questions, too."

"I just never expected it," I said. "I'd never thought about the case from the authorities' perspective. I *do* look guilty. I had the motive. I knew where she'd be. I was there at the same time." I shook my head. "I understand why they'd have to look at me that way. It's just that it took me completely by surprise. And I got angry and said I had nothing to do with her murder, but of course..." My voice caught in my throat.

"Of course what?" Ethan asked.

"Of course I *did* have something to do with it."

"Julie." He took my hand and held it on his thigh. "You were only twelve. You were a child."

People had said that to me before. Friends. Therapists. But Ethan had *been* there. He'd known me. He'd known the sort of person I was. The words meant more to me coming from him.

"Thinking about everything made me remember…*caring* things about Isabel," I said. "We didn't get along that summer, but I know deep down we cared about each other. I know I loved her."

"Of course you did," Ethan said. "Ned thought I was a jerk and treated me accordingly back then, but I still know he loved me. And," he added, "I also know he loved Isabel. That's why it doesn't make sense that he'd kill her."

I watched a sailboat make its graceful way toward the bridge. A child wearing a life preserver was on board with her two parents, and it looked like her father was trying to teach her to dance.

"I'll tell you what I told the police," I said, my thoughts returning to Ethan's comment about Ned. "I told them that you can never really know another person. You don't know what was really going on inside of Ned, Ethan. No one could." Glen had provided my unhappy introduction to that theory. "I thought I knew my ex-husband as well as I knew myself," I said. "I thought he was so in love with me. I thought he was honest and honorable. But while I was thinking all those things, he was having an affair."

"Oh." Ethan rubbed the back of my hand with his thumb. "I know what that's like," he said. "So did Karen. My ex-wife."

"Really?" I wondered how similar our experiences had been. "Did it go on a long time?"

"About a year."

"Glen's, too," I said. "At least I think it was only a year, but like I said, I didn't really know him. How did you find out?"

"She told me. She was in a play with the local community theater and she came home one night and told me she was in love with the director of the play and wanted a divorce."

"Wow," I said. I tried to imagine the scene. Which room of this house had they been in when she told him? Had he slept in the guest room that night? Or had she? Glen had slept on the sofa in the family room; our guest-room bed had been covered with boxes of my books. "Were you devastated?" I asked.

"Completely," he said. "I'd never pictured myself getting a divorce. It wasn't a word in my vocabulary. My parents were married nearly sixty years, and they were excellent role models on how to run a marriage. They had good communication and a lot of love. I thought my marriage was the same way, but I was wrong."

"That's what I mean," I said. "You have this illusion of what someone is like. You assume that if the marriage is great for you, it's great for them, and unless they speak up, you don't have a clue."

"Your husband didn't speak up?"

I shook my head. "No, and guess how I found out?"

"How?"

"The woman called me. She said she knew Glen was struggling with how to tell me, so she decided to tell me herself."

Ethan laughed. "Well, you know who wore the pants in *that* relationship," he said.

"I thought it was a cruel hoax," I said. "Maybe one of Glen's coworkers was angry with him and trying to hurt him. But when Glen came home that evening and I told him about the call, he started to cry…and that was the beginning of the end." I let out my breath in a long stream. "It was so incredibly painful to imagine him with someone else."

"Oh, yeah," Ethan said, and I knew he understood. "Did he end up marrying her?" he asked.

"No," I said. "They broke up right after he and I separated." I looked down at our hands where they rested together on his thigh. His skin was a ruddy color, his beautiful fingers smooth on top, rough on the bottom where they pressed against my skin. There were tiny, nearly microscopic, lines everywhere on the back of my own olive-toned hand. My hands were turning into my mother's. "It was partly my fault," I said. "The end of our marriage. I was a workaholic."

"Are you still?"

I had to laugh. "Well, I *was,* until this whole thing with Ned's letter came up. I haven't written a word since then. At least not a word worth publishing."

"I try not to think in terms of fault," Ethan said. "I know it sounds trite, but Karen and I just drifted apart. She got very involved in her theater work and it was new and exciting for her. She got more and more into it until she said she wanted to move to New York to have a better chance at acting."

"Really! Is that where she is?"

"Uh-huh. She married her lover, but she's not acting, ironically. She's still teaching, just as she was here. I think she's happy, though."

"You don't sound angry," I marveled.

"I'm not. I've forgiven her. It wasn't easy for her, either."

Men handled the end of relationships better than women did, I thought. "I think I've forgiven Glen," I said, not sure it was the truth. "But I still get angry with him for not letting me know he was unhappy. For being so passive. It's hard to fix something if you don't know it's broken." I thought of Shannon and the toll the divorce had taken on her. "Does Abby know about her mother?" I asked.

"That she left me for another guy?" he asked, and I nodded. "Yes. It was no secret. She was furious with her for a while, but they've worked it out."

"Shannon doesn't know," I said. "I don't want her to think badly of her father."

"That's wise of you," he said.

I rested my head against the wicker back of the love seat, looking at the paneled ceiling of the porch. "My own relationship with her is going south fast, though," I said.

"How come?"

"She says I've suffocated her and I probably have," I said. "Sometimes I feel as though she hates me. When I came to your house the first time and Abby was leaving, she told you she loved you, and I realized I couldn't remember the last time Shannon said those words to me."

"You tell her, I guess?" Ethan asked.

"Of course. And either she doesn't respond, or she says something like 'uh-huh.'"

Ethan chuckled. Then he asked, "How often do you tell *your* mother you love her?"

I was taken aback. *Never,* I thought with a jolt. The last time had probably been when I was a child. Probably before Isabel's death. "I show her I love her in a lot of ways," I said.

"It's not the same, though," he said. "You want to hear those words from Shannon, but how can you expect her to say them to you when you don't even say them to your own mother?"

I was quiet, thinking. How did you express those feelings after a lifetime of holding them in? I thought of calling my mother right that moment and telling her I loved her. I couldn't do it, and I knew the reason why: I was afraid she wouldn't be able to say the same words back to me.

The topic was a sad, difficult one, and still I liked sitting there with Ethan, talking with him about everything on our minds. It was perfect, like pillow talk without the sex. What could be better? Yet there was a very small part of me that was wondering how it would feel if our hands were resting on *my* thigh instead of on his. I liked this new and improved Ethan very much.

"I'm sorry I was so cold to you when we were twelve," I said.

He laughed. "Don't be," he said. "I was in my own little world. I was an oddball, and a frustrated one, because I had a huge crush on you that summer."

"You're kidding?"

"I thought you were so cool, a tomboy but with a certain twelve-year-old feminine charm."

I laughed as well.

"But I didn't know how to talk to you anymore," he said. "You'd matured beyond my reach. I wanted to go crabbing and fishing with you, like we used to. I wanted to ask if I could go out in your boat with you, but I knew you didn't want me hanging around you anymore."

"I'm sorry," I said. "If I'd known you'd turn out this good, I would have let you tag along, believe me." The words poured out easily, and I was not sorry I'd said them.

"Thank you," he said. "That's really nice to hear."

A moment passed and again I found myself imagining his hand on my thigh, my belly tightening a bit at the thought.

"You had so much spirit," Ethan said. "You were such an adventurer."

"That girl's gone," I said with some sadness. "She died when Isabel did."

"I bet she's still in there somewhere," he said.

"I don't know," I said.

"Life is so good, Julie," he said. "And it's so short. We've got to take advantage of every minute we're given."

"Are you on antidepressants or something?"

He laughed again. "I'm just lucky," he said. "I think I got an over-abundance of serotonin when I was born. Maybe I got Ned's share." He sobered at that thought, growing quiet, and I let him have his silence. Then he spoke again. "I think I was influenced by my parents," he said. "They were very positive, can-do sort of people. I always remember something my father said in one of his speeches after he lost his bid for governor. We were all there with him. It was in Trenton, and I was standing behind him with my mother and Ned, and I was about fifteen and trying not to cry because I didn't want to look like a jerk, but I felt really sorry for my father. He'd worked so hard on his campaign and, to me, it seemed as though nothing mattered anymore. Dad did the usual sort of speech about thanking his staff and the people who'd voted for him. A reporter shouted out the question, 'What will you do now?' and my father waited a minute and then answered that he didn't believe the old adage that when a door closes, a window opens. He said he believed that when a door closed, the entire world opened up to you, and that he would find other ways of serving the people. And that's what he did. He reopened his law practice and took pro bono work. We had money, so that was never the issue. He worked quietly and tirelessly until he retired. Anyhow, his words that day stuck with me. He didn't stay mired in his sadness."

"He was a wise man," I said. I was thinking, *A man like that would be able to tolerate learning about his son's guilt. He would be able to bounce back from that revelation.*

Ethan must have been thinking along similar lines.

"You know what, Julie?" he asked.

"What?"

"We're going to have to tell our parents about Ned's letter before the cops do."

"I know," I said, resigned.

Ethan let go of my hand and put his arm around me. "And maybe an 'I love you' when you share that news with your mother might soften the blow," he said.

CHAPTER 22

Maria

At McDonald's this morning, I was chatting with a woman I knew from church when my young co-worker, Cordelia, came up behind me.

"Maria." She sang my name in my ear, her Colombian accent so pretty, and there was something teasing in the sound. "You have a visitor," she said.

"Where?" I asked, turning, and she nodded in the direction of the restaurant entrance. I think I knew who it was even before I saw him. *Ross.* He stood near the door, leaning on his cane, his face unsmiling. He nodded in a gentlemanly fashion when he saw me.

I tried to keep my face impassive in front of Cordelia.

"Thank you, dear," I said to her.

"Is he your boyfriend?" she asked, grinning.

"No way, no how," I said as I moved past her in Ross's direction.

"Hello, Ross," I said to him, my voice as neutral as I could make it. I really wanted to yell at him. I wanted to say Why are you bugging me, you old goat?

"I'd like to chat a bit," he said. "I'll get some lunch and then could you sit with me, please?"

"I don't think we have a thing in the world to chat about," I said. I picked up a dirty tray from a nearby table, emptied the wrappers into the trash bin and set the tray on top of it. I was glad to have something to do so that I didn't have to look at his face as I spoke.

"Please," he said. "I drove all the way from Lakewood."

Well, whose fault is that? I thought. But there was something so pathetic about him that I gave in. "All right," I said. "You get off your feet and I'll get you something to eat. What would you like?"

"I'll get it myself," he said, still the prideful man I'd once known.

"Fine," I said. "You get what you want and I'll sit with you for a while. I don't have long, though," I added. "I'm working, you know."

He moved toward the line, which was not long, since we were in between the breakfast and lunch crowds.

I wished that more of the tables were dirty or that there were some toddlers to watch in the little play area, but there was not much to absorb my attention as I waited for Ross to get his food. I chatted with my acquaintance from Holy Trinity again until I saw Ross leave the counter with his tray in his hands, the cane over his arm. I thought of helping him, but in spite of my distaste for the man, I didn't want to bruise his ego any more than it had already been bruised by age and circumstance.

When he reached a table in the corner, I walked over and sat down with him. I was keenly aware of my young fellow employees giggling about us behind the counter, probably imagining the budding of a romance between their grandmotherly co-worker and this old geezer.

"So," I said, "did Ethan ever say anything to you about how that lunch went with Julie?"

"Just that it was nice to see her," Ross said. He had not unwrapped his burger and seemed to have no intention of doing so, but he lifted his cup of coffee to his lips and took a sip.

"Aren't you going to eat?" I asked.

He didn't seem to hear me. "Do you look back at any of your life with regret, Maria?" he asked.

I had to laugh. "Of course I do," I said, then lowered my voice. "My relationship with you is one of my major regrets."

He looked down quickly, fingering the napkin on his tray as though it suddenly needed his attention, and I thought I'd hurt him with my words. I felt a twinge of guilt for that. He was not an evil man. Maybe not a bad man at all, although I'd certainly voted against him when he ran for governor; it doesn't pay to know too much about your politicians. I knew he'd gone on to do some very good things with his life. I knew he'd represented poor people in court. I knew he had strong values and had put his money where his mouth was on more than one occasion. As I sat there studying his too-thin face and the web of wrinkles around his pewter-gray eyes, I wondered if my regret had more to do with my own weakness than with anything he had done. I was not sure. When it came to Ross, I always ended up a little confused about my feelings.

"I don't blame you for feeling regret, Maria," he said, raising his eyes to me. "And I just want to offer you my deepest, deepest apology for ever having hurt you in any way. There are so many things I did wrong…" He looked out the window next to our table, where a couple of young boys dodged the cars in the parking lot on their skateboards. "To start with, I was a covert bigot, adopting my parents' prejudices as my own. I let them rule me. Own me. I should have stayed with you, out in the open. I was a fool for that."

Whew. Did he plan to go through his crimes against me one by one, waiting for my forgiveness after each apology? That I couldn't bear. The truth was, his words were not enough. Nothing would be enough. And I did not regret his breaking up with me when I was so young and stupid; I only regretted that I'd allowed the relationship to continue in its clandestine form. I could see, though, that the only way to get rid of him now was to accept his apology. If that eased his emotional pain, I would just have to let that happen.

"All right," I said. "Thank you for telling me that."

He looked surprised, then smiled. "You are beautiful," he said. "I mean…I'm not trying to be…to flirt."

That's good, I thought. An old man flirting was not a pretty sight.

"I mean," he said, "you're not only physically beautiful, but a beautiful person as well. You always were. And I…didn't handle your kind nature very well, did I, and—"

"Ross, no more, please." I felt the Egg McMuffin I'd had for breakfast begin to rise in my throat. I couldn't do this. "We're done with this conversation. I forgive you for any and all transgressions, imagined or real. Now please, just get on with your life. And I need to return to work."

I stood up, feeling his eyes on me as I walked through the restaurant toward the rest rooms. I needed to escape, not only from him but from the inevitable questioning I would be facing from my co-workers. I splashed water on my face, swallowing hard over and over again to get that McMuffin back where it belonged, and when I emerged from the rest room, I saw that Ross had gone, leaving his tray with its untouched burger and nearly full coffee cup for me to clean up.

1939

I was never able to tell my parents the truth about my breakup with Ross. How could I tell them that Ross's parents—our next-door neighbors—had forbidden his son to date me because I was the daughter of an Italian immigrant? How that would pain my mother! So I told them that he and I had decided we wanted to date others for a while to be sure we were right for each other. I knew my parents thought that was strange; we had seemed an ideal couple to them. On a couple of occasions, they caught me crying and questioned me, wanting to make sure the breakup was my idea and not just Ross's. I assured them I had been in agreement with him.

I returned Ross's ring to him, and when the other kids in our gang expressed surprise, we said that we'd simply realized we weren't ready for a steady relationship. My girlfriends did not quite believe that excuse, and although I would usually confide just about anything to them, I could not tell them the truth. It made Ross look weak and shallow. Still in love with him, I wanted to protect his exalted image to our group of friends.

It was painful, though, to be with him in a crowd without touching him. I'd watch him talk to the other girls and wonder how each girl's pedigree compared to mine. I'd watch his hands when he ran them through his hair or when he'd cup them around a cigarette as he lit it, and I'd ache with the yearning to have those hands on my body again.

One night at Jenkinson's, I was dancing with another boy when Ross tapped him on the shoulder to cut in. Ross put his arm around my waist, his hand pressed tight against my back. The band was playing Glenn Miller's "Moon Love." Ross was a good dancer, but it was not the dance I was thinking about. It was the nearness of him, the familiar scent of his cologne that filled me with longing.

"Maria." He pressed his lips close to my ear. "I can't stand it any longer. I have to find a way to be with you."

I closed my eyes and breathed him in. "But how?" I asked. I wanted to hear him say he would stand up to his father, that he would give up Princeton, give up college altogether if that's what it took to have me. But I knew that was hardly a fair expectation, and I wanted the best for him. Giving up all he'd worked for would not be it.

"I am going to start dating Delores," he said. "And I want you to start dating Fred."

"What?" I leaned away from him, startled. "What do you—"

"Shh," he said, pulling me close again. "Listen. We date them. Casually, of course. And we let our families and everyone know that we're involved with them. But then, you and I will meet on the sly."

"How?" I whispered.

"We'll have to work that part out," he said. "But first, I need to know if you're willing. What do you say?"

I felt weak-kneed, I wanted him so much. This was a way I could have him. Maybe we could continue the ruse through his college years until he was free of his parents' control. Then we could finally come out in the open. Be married. "Yes," I said. *"Yes."*

I took Fred by surprise when I started flirting with him and in no time at all, he'd asked me to the movies. Ross had no problem arranging a date with Delores; she'd had her eye on him for years. Ross made me promise that Fred and I would do no more than kiss, and I extracted the same promise from him with regard to Delores. Thus our cover was complete.

The first night we attempted our ruse, it did not work as planned. I was to go to the movies with Fred, while Ross went dancing with

Delores. I hated the thought of him having his arms around Delores, but reassured myself that his dancing with her was only a means to an end.

Fred was to bring me home at ten o'clock, an hour shy of my curfew. I would say good-night to him in front of my house, then slip across the street to the empty lot. Ross would drop Delores off at her house, then park on the street on the other side of the lot and meet me by the blueberry bushes. There, we would have a full hour together before we needed to go home.

I said good-night to Fred in his car and started to get out, but he was too much of a gentleman for that. He raced around the car to open my door for me and then walked with me to the front stoop of the bungalow.

"Your parents would think I was a boor if I didn't make sure you got in all right," he said.

I glanced over my shoulder at the lot, wondering if Ross was there yet. If I went into the house, I knew I would not be able to get out again without my parents asking a lot of questions.

"Well," I said, when we reached my door, "I don't want to go in right away. I think I'll just sit on the step for a while and enjoy the evening."

Stupid me!

"You're right, it's beautiful out," Fred said. He sat down next to me and put his arm around my shoulders.

I heard the closing of a car door somewhere on the opposite side of the lot and wondered how on earth I was going to get rid of Fred.

"I was so glad when you and Ross broke up," he said. He turned to kiss me, and I dropped my head so the kiss landed on my forehead. The light was on. Ross could surely see us from the lot and I couldn't bear to have him see Fred kiss me. I knew how I would feel if I had to watch him kissing Delores.

"Sorry," Fred said.

"Just…not yet," I said, feigning a prissiness that was not usually part of my character. Then I slapped my arm as if a mosquito had bitten me. "They're really biting tonight," I said. "I think I'd better go in." I thought I would slip quietly into the house, stand inside the door until I heard Fred drive away, then slip out again.

I said good-night to Fred, then opened the door and stepped into the hallway. Our tiny bathroom was right next to the front door and I froze when I heard the toilet flush. The bathroom door opened and my father walked into the hall.

He looked surprised. "Well, hello, sweetheart," he said. "I didn't expect you home this early. Did everything go all right?"

"Fine, Daddy," I said. "I didn't want to make a late night of it."

Foiled, I walked to the back porch to say good-night to my mother before going into my small bedroom. My bedroom's only window faced the Chapmans' house. I thought of removing the screen and climbing outside to meet Ross, but what if my parents discovered I was gone and worried about me? I sat on the edge of the bed, the room so small that my knees were up against the windowsill, and watched for Ross's car to pull into his driveway. I heard a noise outside and yelped when his face suddenly appeared outside my window.

"Shh!" He pressed his finger to his lips and I giggled. "What happened?" he asked.

"Fred wanted to be sure I got inside all right," I said.

"Figures," he said. "Can you get out?" He touched the edges of the screen. "Does this pop out?"

"It does, but I can't, Ross," I whispered. "I'm sorry."

Whatever anxiety compelled me to stay inside that night fell away in the nights that followed. I learned how to quickly pop out the screen and slip through the window. I eased my fear of worrying my parents by leaving a note on my pillow. It read: "I didn't want to wake you. Just felt like going for a walk." And then I would meet Ross across the street, where we'd pick blueberries in the darkness and make love with their taste on our tongues.

Ross became my summer lover. I went to the New Jersey College for Women, and he followed his father's footsteps to Princeton. We didn't communicate during the school year, but I believed we both lived for the summers, when we would date others but take every opportunity we could to be together, away from the prying eyes of his parents. It was a wonder we were never caught. Perhaps it was also a shame.

CHAPTER 23

Lucy

Shannon wasn't returning my calls. I hadn't spoken with her since the ZydaChicks concert and I could only conclude that she didn't want to listen to me lecture her again about telling Julie and Glen that she was pregnant. This afternoon, though, she finally left a message on my cell phone, sounding nonchalant, as though I hadn't been trying to get in touch with her for the past week.

"How about I bring over some subs and we just veg in front of the TV?" she suggested.

I left a message for her in return. "Excellent," I said. "See you at seven." I would take her any way I could get her.

She arrived wearing no makeup, and she was fresh faced and pretty, her long hair still damp and a little tangled from a shower. She looked only slightly more pregnant than she had at the concert, and it might even have been my imagination. She could pass as a girl who had simply put on a bit too much weight. In the next few weeks, though, that was sure to change.

"I got one turkey and one Italian," she said, dropping the bagged, foot-long subs on my kitchen counter. "Which do you want?"

"I'll eat half the Italian," I said, opening the refrigerator. "Lemonade?"

She peered around me to look at the contents of my fridge. "Diet Coke," she said.

I handed her the can and dropped a few ice cubes into a glass for her. We put the subs on plates and carried them into my living room.

"What do you want to watch?" I asked as we sat down on the couch.

"I don't care," she said. "Everything's reruns, anyway."

I clicked the buttons on the remote until we found a rerun of *Friends*. We'd both seen the episode more than once, but it didn't matter. I just needed some background noise for my inquisition.

"So," I said as we started to eat, "how are you feeling?"

"Perfect." She pulled a long sliver of onion from her sandwich and popped it into her mouth. Apparently she was not suffering from indigestion. "I saw the doctor and she says I'm doing fine," she added.

"Good," I said, instead of the five million other things on the tip of my tongue. I wanted to know who her doctor was and the exact meaning of the word "fine," but I thought I'd better mete out my questions bit by bit. I kept quiet for a while as we watched Monica and Rachel argue about something on the TV—I had no idea what. They were not my concern.

"What's the latest on you and Tanner?" I asked when I'd eaten about half my sandwich and thought enough time had passed since my last question.

"He's coming here in a week and a half," she said. "We're going to talk about our plans then." She lifted the top of her sandwich and peered inside, pulling out another piece of onion and slipping it into her mouth. "I'm craving onions," she said. "Isn't that the weirdest thing?"

"I remember when your mom was pregnant with you, she craved peanut-butter-and-potato-chip sandwiches," I said. "She ate them all the time."

"Ugh," Shannon said. "Maybe *that's* what's wrong with me. She ate crap the whole time she was pregnant with me."

I reached out and tugged at a strand of her thick hair. "There's nothing wrong with you, baby girl," I said softly. "You're perfect."

She looked at me, a smile on her lips. "I can't wait for you to meet Tanner, Luce," she said.

"I'm looking forward to it," I said, lying only a little bit. "I guess you haven't told your dad yet, huh?" I was sure she hadn't told Julie. I would have heard.

She shook her head. "It's such a relief to be living there, Luce," she said. "Really. He just lets me do what I want. I don't have to call him every two seconds to tell him where I am and that I'm alive."

She sounded so mean, but I knew that was not her intent. She just didn't understand Julie the way I did.

"I wish you knew your mother better," I said.

"What do you mean?" she asked. "Who knows her better than I do? I've lived with her my whole life."

"Yes, but you didn't live with her before you were born, and that's the time that really…that formed her. It's hard for you to understand—"

"I understand *totally*," she said. "A million years ago, when she was barely out of diapers, she thinks she screwed up with her sister and caused her death and now she's afraid of everything. Of losing people. Of losing *me*." She set her plate on the coffee table and I guessed the topic had killed her appetite. "I need *space* from her, Lucy," she said. "She suffocates me."

"That's normal," I said. "You need your independence. You're ready to leave the nest."

"Then why are you giving me a hard time?"

"Because much as you want to be free of your mother, she's still your mother and still responsible for you and you have *got* to tell her that you're pregnant."

"I'll tell her when I have to," she said.

I thought of all Julie was dealing with: Ned's letter, the interview with the cops, worrying that our mother would be dragged into the investigation, Shannon moving out. It was a lousy time to lay one more thing on her, but this particular thing couldn't wait.

Another show was on the TV now and I clicked the mute button on the remote. "I want you to know what's going on," I said.

"What do you mean?" Shannon looked worried. "What are you talking about? This isn't about that letter again, is it?"

"Yes, it is," I said. I told her that Julie had gone down the shore to be interviewed by the police and that she'd stayed in Ethan's house, next door to our old bungalow. "Both things were hard for her," I said. "Having to remember everything that happened and being someplace that reminded her of your aunt Isabel. And it looks like the police might need to interview your grandmother, so your mom's going to need to tell her about the letter and she's worried about that. About how Nana will react. So she has a lot on her plate right now."

Shannon studied my face while I spoke, then shook her head slowly. "I wish I had a magic wand to make that whole thing go away," she said. "Mom should be, like, in intensive therapy or something."

"She was in therapy when she was a kid," I said. "And she's okay," I assured her. "You don't need to worry about her. You just need to know that the next few weeks might be hard on her and your grandmother."

"And you," Shannon said.

"You know," I said, and shrugged, "I remember so little of that time that it doesn't have a big impact on me. I don't even remember Isabel very well."

Shannon drew her feet onto the sofa and turned to face me. "Okay," she began. "Now, I'm honestly not saying this to be self-serving or anything, but doesn't it seem like a really bad time for me to tell Mom I'm pregnant?"

I nodded. "Yes, it does. But I think you'll have to do it sooner rather than later." I took her wrist in my hand. "Come on, sweetie. Don't let her find out by seeing you in maternity clothes, okay?"

She sighed. She had to know I was right.

"Shannon." I tightened my hand on her wrist. "I've never said anything like this to you before, honey, but if you don't tell your mother, I'm going to have to."

She looked at me in disbelief. "All right, I'll tell her," she said. "Just not, like, tonight."

"You have a week," I said.

"All right."

We turned back to the TV and Shannon clicked the remote until she found a station with old black-and-white reruns. I didn't know what show we were watching, but it didn't matter. My niece moved closer to me on the sofa and leaned her head against my shoulder. I put my arm around her and felt my spirit fill to overflowing with love for her.

"Would you be my labor coach?" she asked.

I was touched, but I knew my answer. "No," I said. "I'm not labor coach material. You know who to ask."

She let out a long breath. "I'm scared, Lucy," she said.

I tightened my arm around her shoulders and kissed the top of her head. "Of giving birth or of telling your mother?" I asked.

"Of the rest of my life," she said.

CHAPTER 24

Julie
1962

Once upon a time, I was a hero.

On a stifling hot day during the last week of July, Lucy and I were lying on our stomachs at the Baby Beach, reading while our mother swam in the bay and Isabel hung out near the lifeguard stand with her friends. Suddenly, Lucy scrambled into a sitting position.

"Something's wrong," she said. Lucy had an uncanny way of knowing when anything out of the ordinary was occurring.

"You're imagining things," I said, but then I realized she was right. There'd been a shift in the activity on the beach. I could still hear the music from the transistor radios, but the laughter and talking had changed to whispers and shouts. Something was definitely going on.

I sat up, too, and noticed a few women standing at the water's edge, shading their eyes as they looked out at the bay, and it was a moment before I realized that my mother was one of them. I heard a woman's voice from somewhere behind me calling "Donnie! Donnie!" I glanced toward the lifeguard stand and saw Ned standing on top of it, looking toward the deep water through his binoculars.

My mother started walking toward us.

"What's going on, Mom?" I asked, getting to my feet.

"Oh, not much," she said, "but I think we should go home now. It's so hot today."

I could see right through her. Something bad had happened and she was trying to protect Lucy from knowing about it. I had no intention of leaving. I took off for the lifeguard stand at a run.

"Julie!" Mom called after me. "Where are you going? We have to go home."

"In a minute," I called over my shoulder.

Ned was still on top of the stand, but now he was crouched down on his haunches talking to a woman. It looked like a private conversation, so I walked behind the stand to where the teenagers stood huddled in a mass. I tugged on Isabel's arm.

"What's going on?" I asked.

"A little boy is missing," she said.

"What do you mean, he's missing?" I asked. "In the water?"

"If I knew where he was, he wouldn't be missing," Isabel said, and some of her friends laughed.

"A three-year-old boy disappeared from his parents' beach blanket," Mitzi Caruso explained to me. "He's got light blond hair and is wearing blue trunks."

I looked around me at the beach. Nearly everyone was standing now, talking with one another, holding fast to their children. Women had their hands to their mouths, frown lines across their foreheads as they stared at the water. From where I stood, I searched the beach for a towheaded little boy and spotted several of them, but they all appeared to have at least one parent close by. I felt sad and I prayed that the little boy had not drowned. I had to do something to ease my feeling of helplessness.

"I'm going to check the playground," I said, even though the teenagers were not paying much attention to me. I ran toward the swings, my mother's request to return to her and Lucy forgotten.

I began my search for clues in a methodical fashion, using my foot to mark off areas in the sand to examine. I found a man's watch almost immediately. It lay in the sand near one of the swings and had probably come off when a father had been pushing his child. I found a playing card—the two of clubs—along with numerous Popsicle sticks. And then I found a clue that sent a chill up my spine: a small piece of blue cloth!

I ran back to the lifeguard stand just as Ned was climbing down the ladder.

"Ned!" I called as I neared him. "Look what I found near the swings." I held the piece of cloth out to him and he took it from my hand but didn't seem to know what to do with it. His face looked grim, his mouth a straight, tight line.

"It might be from the boy's trunks," I said.

"Oh," he said. "No. His trunks are plaid, not solid." He looked distracted as he handed the cloth back to me. "But thanks for trying and for keeping your eyes open." He started toward the parking lot at a run, and Isabel walked up to me, frowning.

"Don't bug him, Jules," she said. Lifting her hair off her neck, she slipped a rubber band around it to form a sloppy ponytail. "This is an emergency. There's no time to fool around."

"I know it's an emergency," I said, and I walked away from her, annoyed.

"Come on, Julie," my mother called again. She was folding the blanket and I walked over to help her.

"I want to stay, Mom," I said, taking the hem of the blanket in my hands.

"You'll only get in the way."

"I won't," I said. "I promise."

My mother took the folded blanket into her arms and looked around us. People were still huddled together in small groups, talking. Some of the adults were racing this way and that, searching for the boy, I guessed, although the beach was so small you could nearly see all of it from where we were standing. The only areas hidden from view were the patches of tall beach grass at either end of the sandy crescent, and I watched a couple of women disappear into them, calling, "Donnnnneeeee! Donnnnneeeee!"

I heard sirens in the distance and looked toward the road. Ned and Isabel and a few other people stood in the parking lot, and Ned waved at the ambulance and the police car as they came into view.

"*Please,* Mommy." Lucy grabbed our mother's arm. "I want to go *home.*"

Lucy hated the sound of sirens. They must have reminded her of riding in the ambulance after the long-ago accident she'd been in with our mother.

"All right," Mom said. "Pick up the thermos and we'll leave. Julie, you can stay, but be sure you let the police do their job."

"I will."

"And be home by three. Not a second later, all right?"

A couple of men walked past us, one of them saying to the other that the bay might need to be dragged.

"What does that mean?" Lucy asked.

"Never mind," my mother said. She picked up her beach bag and I saw tears in her eyes. She probably thought the boy was dead.

My mother and Lucy headed for the parking lot and I looked around me, trying to figure out what to do. My gaze lit on the pier. No one was out there, and I wondered if I could get a better look at the water from the end of it. I started running in that direction as a second police car pulled into the parking lot.

By the time I reached the end of the pier, there were no children at all in the water. Adults waded in the shallow section, eyes downcast as they looked for the little boy's body. I studied the water below the pier, thinking that if the boy had made it onto the pier and then fallen in, I might see him under the water's surface. But the water was too dark and, after a while, my eyes hurt from trying to pierce it.

I walked back down the pier toward the beach, and when I reached the area where the wood of the pier met the sand, I saw small footprints. They headed away from the beach toward the parking lot and they were the only set of footprints going in that direction. I followed them to where they disappeared into the crushed shells of the parking lot. Even when I got down on my knees and looked very closely, I could see how the bleached white bits of shell had been disturbed by tiny feet. I followed the footprints across the entire width of the parking lot, heading toward the clubhouse which was a nice, woody-smelling building where the kids in the area could play bingo and other games on rainy days. I picked the footprints up again in the sand at the other end of the parking lot. It was almost too easy. The footprints led directly to the rear of the clubhouse and stopped short at the lattice that enclosed the building's crawl space. I tugged at one of the seams in the lattice and it pulled away easily. Kneeling down, I crawled inside, and there I found little Donnie Jakes, sound asleep on the cool, shaded sand.

I got a ride home a little after three from a policeman named Officer Davis, to whom I'd turned over the boy after I found him. Officer Davis walked me to my front door and told my mother that I had found Donnie Jakes, alive and well. Mom burst into tears, and it took me a while to realize it was not my role in finding him that made her cry, but rather that the child, even though he was a stranger to her, was safe.

"We'd have found him eventually," Officer Davis said to her, once she'd mopped the tears from her face with a tissue, "but Julie here saved us a lot of work." He told her I was an excellent sleuth. He told her I was a hero.

The next day, the *Ocean County Leader* ran the following headline on its front page: Boy Found Unharmed. The first sentence of the article was something like, *Twelve-year-old Julie Bauer, aka the Nancy Drew of Bay Head Shores, helped police locate three-year-old Donald P. Jakes, who had wandered off from his parents' blanket on the BHS beach.*

Within twenty-four hours, everyone knew my name. The mayor called to thank me, telling me once again that I was a hero, and Daddy came to the bungalow a day early to take us all out to dinner to celebrate. I was full of pride and self-importance, and I started thinking of myself as charmed, as though I could do no wrong. If only that had been the case.

CHAPTER 25

Julie

"I told him." Ethan's voice was a soft monotone on my speaker phone.

I was sitting at my desk, once again attempting to work on Chapter Four, and I quickly picked up the receiver.

"What did he say?" I asked. "And how are you?" I'd been waiting for his call, knowing he planned to talk to his father this morning. I had not yet gotten up the courage to call my mother.

"I'm fine," he said, "but I won't pretend it was easy."

"Did you go to his house?" I knew that had been his plan.

"Uh-huh. I told him I'd bring over some pastries for breakfast and I think he knew something was up. So, we sat in his kitchen, and first I told him about Ned's letter. He looked…God, he looked awful, Julie. Shocked. His face was all…it just crumpled in on itself. I told him I didn't think it meant that Ned had done it, and he started yelling…well not yelling, exactly, but he said how he *knew* Ned didn't do it better than anyone, because he'd been with Ned that night, just like he told the police. And then he said, 'I hope you didn't do anything with that letter. We should burn it.'"

I winced. "Oh, Ethan," I said.

"I told him that I took it to the police and that they spoke with you and me and that they've reopened the case and will probably want to talk with him." The words came out in that monotone again. He sounded tired.

"What did he say?"

Ethan sighed. "He got up and walked around the kitchen for a while. He limps. Man, it just about breaks my heart to see how fast he's aged since my mother died. He said it seems unfair that Ned's not here to defend himself. He kept asking me why I took it. 'Why did you feel the need to take it?' he kept saying. I told him I *had* to take it, that it was the only decent thing to do."

"Of course," I murmured, reassuring myself that it *had* been the right thing, even with the authorities looking in my direction for their suspect.

"I knew he'd finally see it that way," Ethan said. "He's always had this strong sense of justice. Of right and wrong. And finally he sat down again and said he wished I hadn't, but that he understood. He had tears in his eyes and I asked him why and he said he was thinking about George Lewis and his family. He looked like he was going to...I don't know. Fall apart, or something. I felt like I was killing him, Julie."

The way he said my name made me feel close to him. I wished he were sitting next to me so I could wrap my arms around him.

"He finally said I did the right thing and that he'll be glad to talk to the police because he's the only voice Ned has now. He's afraid the finger's going to end up pointing at Ned anyhow, no matter what he says."

"I'm sorry it was so hard," I said. "For both of you."

"Thanks," he said. "I feel relieved that he knows now. That he heard it from me and not the police. When do you plan to tell your mother?"

"Today," I said, knowing I couldn't put it off any longer. "I've got to get it over with."

"Do you want me to come up there?" he asked. "I could be with you when you tell her."

I smiled at his offer. It was tempting; I wanted to see him again. But I knew this was something I had to do alone.

"I'll be okay, thanks," I said. "I'll let you know how it goes."

I walked the two blocks to my mother's house as soon as I got off the phone with Ethan. I found her in the backyard where she was clipping blue hydrangea blossoms to bring into the house, and she looked up in surprise when she spotted me. I didn't often drop in unannounced.

"Julie!" she said, straightening her spine, the hydrangeas in her left hand a giant pom-pom of baby-blue. "What are you doing here?"

"I'd like to talk to you," I said, "but how about I help you with the hydrangeas first?" I reached for the blooms in her hand, but she pulled them away from me.

"Something's wrong," she said, studying my face. I knew my sunglasses were not so dark that she couldn't see my eyes, and she seemed able to read the concern in my expression. "Is it Shannon?" I thought she was holding her breath as she waited for my answer.

"No, she's fine," I reassured her. "Everyone's okay." I put my hand on her back and motioned toward the patio. "How about we sit down?" I suggested.

"Oh, it's a 'you'd better sit down' kind of thing, eh?" she asked, walking with me toward the patio. Her pace seemed much slower than mine. Was that new? I wondered. Was she having problems with the hip that sometimes bothered her? I remembered Ethan's comment about his father's aging and understood how he felt.

She laid the bouquet of hydrangea blossoms carefully on the glass-topped table along with the pruning shears, and sat down, taking off her gardening gloves.

"Well?" She looked at me.

"Remember a couple of weeks ago when I had lunch with Ethan Chapman?"

She nodded. "Of course," she said.

"And you know that his brother, Ned, died, right?" I wasn't sure if Mr. Chapman had told my mother about that or not.

She nodded again, silent now.

"Well, when Ethan and his daughter cleaned out Ned's house, they found a letter Ned had written—but never mailed—to the Point Pleasant Police."

My mother frowned. "What did it say?"

Here we go, I thought. "It said that the wrong man went to prison for Isabel's murder and that he—Ned—wanted to set the record straight."

My mother looked frozen, as though she'd had an attack of paralysis. Her eyes bored into mine, and in the silent moment while she was absorbing my words, I remembered that she had slapped me—*hard*—the day Isabel died. It was the only time either of my parents had ever laid a hand on me. My cheek stung to remember it.

"Ned did it?" she asked finally. "But Ross said he was—"

"No one knows for sure who did it," I said quickly. "Ned didn't confess to anything in the letter." I took off my sunglasses and rubbed my eyes. "I think it's likely he did, Mom. I mean, that's what makes the most sense, but Ethan can't believe Ned could have done something like that and the police are looking at every possible suspect. They may want to talk to you. I hope not, but it's possible."

My mother looked toward the vegetable garden, where the tomatoes were ripening and the zucchini vines were quickly getting out of control. I knew she was not truly seeing the garden, though. Her mind was someplace far away.

"I'm sorry, Mom," I said. I wasn't sure what I was apologizing for. Telling her about the letter. Isabel's murder. Everything.

"George Lewis was innocent?" she asked me, as if I knew for sure.

"The letter makes it sound like it," I said.

She stared at me for another moment and I wasn't sure she'd understood what I said. Then she stood up slowly. "I'm going to take a nap," she said, brushing a few small leaves from her overalls.

"Are you okay?" I asked.

She didn't answer and I got to my feet as well and started walking toward her, but she held up her hand to stop me.

"I'm fine," she said. "This all just makes me tired. It's so..." She looked at me then. "You lose a child and they make you lose her all over again. Again and again and again..." Her voice trailed off as she walked away from me. I wasn't sure what to do. Should I follow her into the house? Make sure she was all right? It was clear that she wanted time alone. I would give that to her, at least for the moment. I picked up the pruning shears and headed toward the hydrangeas.

CHAPTER 26

Maria

I couldn't believe what was happening.

All of a sudden, a time I had tried to put to rest more than forty years ago was coming back in a most hideous way. My Isabel. I'd failed her so. If only I had been a better mother. If only I had known how to handle her rebellion.

Was there a day in the past forty-one years that I hadn't imagined what her last moments had been like? This is what I'd been picturing for all those years: Isabel was at the bay, alone on the platform in the darkness, excited that Ned would soon be joining her there. Then the black boy, George Lewis, appeared on the beach and started to swim out to her. Next followed the part I could never understand. Isabel was an excellent swimmer. Why didn't she jump into the water to try to escape him? Why didn't she swim to the beach or the pier or...I don't know. Or maybe she didn't see him. Maybe he'd cut through the water so quietly that she'd been unaware of him until he climbed onto the platform with her. There had been bruises on her arms. Did he try to rape her? Did she jump into the water to escape him? Did she hit her head on the platform or did he knock her out with a weapon? I didn't know. I couldn't know. All I knew was that my baby had to have been terrified. My little girl had been trying to act so much like a woman, trying so hard to be grown up, to make decisions for herself, albeit poor ones. She thought she was so independent, on the road to freedom from me and my rules. I was certain that, at that moment on the platform, she was reduced to the little angel of a child I used to carry around on my hip. The little girl who called me Mommy, who thought the sun rose and set on me.

Whenever I thought of her final moments, I felt her fear, a wringing, wrenching terror, in the center of my chest. It made me want to scream and pound the walls. It once made me strike my little daughter, Julie. It was hard to admit to hating one of my children, but for a few days, I believe I did hate Julie for her part in Isabel's death. It wasn't until much later that I realized it was myself I loathed. But back then, Julie took the brunt of it all. She took the full weight of my grief.

Sometime in the last forty-one years, I'd been able to make a sort of peace with that night. *Peace* might have been the wrong word, but I'd at least been able to live with what happened and with my failings as a mother. I'd forgiven Charles for his permissiveness with Isabel, and I'd taken comfort in knowing that the man responsible for her death and for those last horrible minutes of her life was rotting in prison. I'd felt such hatred for George Lewis, and that hatred extended to every other black man I'd see, before my intellect would take over and I could remind myself that Lewis was one man who acted alone and was not representative of his entire race and gender. Now it seemed that all the hatred I'd expended on him might have been misdirected.

Had it been Ned himself then who murdered Isabel? That was certainly the implication of the letter he'd written to the police. What else could it mean? I believe he loved Isabel as best as an eighteen-year-old boy could love a seventeen-year-old girl, and therefore I had to assume it was an accident for which he never came forward to take responsibility. In a way, that explanation was reassuring to me, because Izzy would have been with someone she loved and trusted, so fear might not have been the last thing in her heart. But if it *had* been Ned, Ross must have fabricated his alibi.

My mind spun as I tried to figure out what had truly happened. Julie said the police might want to talk to me again. How I would tolerate that, I didn't know. I would tell them that I was a bad mother who didn't know how to parent a teenage girl. I'd tell them that I was jealous of how my husband adored her and that maybe that got in the way of how I treated her. And I would long to ask them questions of my own, but I never would. Asking my questions could only invite more of theirs, and I had far too much to hide.

CHAPTER 27

Julie

I'd never felt more like a part of the sandwich generation than I did the day I told my mother about Ned's letter. I was a middle-aged woman caught between the concerns of her aging parent and the challenges of dealing with her child. I worried that I was going to fail both of them—or that I may already have done so long ago.

After bringing armloads of hydrangeas into my mother's house and placing them in vases in the living room and kitchen, I knocked on her bedroom door.

"Mom?" I asked. "Are you all right?"

"I'm okay," she said. "I'm just tired."

I didn't want to leave her alone but was not sure what else to do.

"Would you like me to stay here awhile?" I asked through the door. "I could make you something to eat or—

"There's no need to stay, Julie," she said. "I'm going to sleep. Don't worry about me."

"All right," I said.

I made some tuna salad for her and left a note on the table telling her it was in the refrigerator. I didn't know what else to do. I felt helpless.

I came home and sat down in front of computer. I checked my e-mail; there were many notes from my fans that had accumulated over the past few difficult weeks. I hadn't had the concentration necessary to answer them and I wasn't sure when that would change. I sat staring at them, thinking that I should open Chapter Four and try again, but I knew I wouldn't. Writing a story about Granny Fran, a woman who didn't exist outside my imagination and whose silly life was filled with silly mysteries solved in three hundred silly pages, seemed completely pointless.

I was still staring at the e-mail when I heard the front door open.

"Mom?" Shannon called, and I felt a rush of much-needed joy. I missed having her around so much.

"In here," I called.

She walked into my office and sat down on the love seat. "Sorry to interrupt your work," she said.

"Oh, honey," I said. "You're never an interruption." We both knew that wasn't the truth. I'd had a rule that I was not to be disturbed while I was writing unless it was a dire emergency. Was that one of the many areas where I'd screwed up?

"Well, I have something I need to talk to you about," she said. She was watching me, making good eye contact with those long-lashed dark eyes, but there was no hint of a smile on her face.

"You sound serious," I said. I suddenly understood how my own mother had felt a few hours earlier when I'd said I needed to talk to her.

"I am," she said, and then she looked away from me, down at her hands. She was pressing them together in her lap, hard enough to turn the knuckles white. "I'm really, really sorry about what I'm going to tell you, because I know how much it's going to disappoint you…and everything."

"What is it, Shannon?" I tried to imagine what she was going to say. Did she want to stay with Glen when she came home on holidays? Had she changed her mind about Oberlin and now wanted to go somewhere else? I was unprepared for her next words because they were so far from anything I might have guessed.

"I'm pregnant," she said.

I was dumbfounded. Absolutely dumbfounded. "You...you haven't even been seeing anyone," I said.

"Yes, I have," she said. "I met someone during spring break, although I'd actually known him for months over the Internet."

Oh, no, I thought.

"He's from Colorado and he was here visiting friends and he and I have stayed in touch by phone and e-mail and I'm in love with him." She smiled then and gave a happy little shrug of her shoulders.

I don't know what she made of my silence. I was measuring my response, afraid of driving her away with anything I might say. I moved next to her on the love seat and took her hands in mine. Hers were ice-cold.

"I'm so sorry," I said. "This must be very difficult for you." It was the best I could do. I would make myself support her, no matter what option she chose. I can understand a woman having an abortion early in her pregnancy—in some circumstances. So, I would let this be Shannon's decision, let her be the grown-up. She looked surprised by my reaction.

"Thank you," she said.

"Did you just find out?" I asked. "Do you know how far along you are?"

"Eighteen—almost nineteen—weeks."

"Oh my God," I said, realizing that an early, first-trimester abortion was not even an option. "You're...are you trying to decide..." I was stammering, and she stepped in.

"I'm going to have the baby," she said.

"But what will you do?" I asked. "What about school? What about...you're only seventeen!" I was losing it. I felt the control of my head and my heart and my tongue slipping away from me.

She shook her head and her voice was much calmer than mine. "I'm not going to go to school this fall," she said. "Someday I will, but not right now." She offered me an apologetic smile. "Mom, I'm so in love with him. His name is Tanner. He's an awesome person. He goes to the University of Colorado in Boulder. And...Mom, don't be mad," she pleaded, "but I've decided to move there and start a life with him and our baby."

I let go of her hands and stood up, simply unable to sit there another second. I ran my fingers through my hair. "All of this has taken me by surprise, Shannon," I said. "And I'm going to need some time to absorb it, but the one thing I know right now is that you can't move away."

"Tanner and I have talked about this for hours and hours," she said. "We want to do this right. We want to—"

"You *cannot* go to Colorado with a baby and a total stranger," I said. "I don't know if you've thought through what it's going to be like for you to be a mother at seventeen."

"I'll be eighteen when the baby's born."

"You're still more of a child than a woman," I said, "and the fact that you got pregnant to begin with is proof of that."

"Mother," she said. "Don't start."

"I know you've been having sex," I continued. "And I knew you were on birth control. I've seen your pills around—you've made no secret of it. I haven't said anything to you about it and I've tried to be really…" I frowned at her in bewilderment. "How did you let this happen?" I asked. "Did you do it on purpose? Did you feel like you weren't ready for school? What is going *on* with you, Shannon? I feel as though I don't know you anymore."

She stood up, toe to toe with me but two inches taller. "I am a woman who is going to have the baby of the man she's deeply in love with," she said. "That's who I am, Mother." There were tears in her eyes. "And there's really nothing you can do about it. I just thought I should let you know. And now I'm going back to Dad's."

She turned on her heel and walked out of the room, and I didn't know what to say to stop her. I heard the door slam behind her and I sank numbly to the love seat. I couldn't have said how long I sat there before I finally lifted the phone and dialed Lucy's number.

"Hey, sis," Lucy greeted me.

"Shannon's pregnant," I said.

There was silence on her end of the phone that went on for too long.

"You *knew?*" I asked.

"Yes," she said.

"Lucy, damn it! Why didn't you *tell* me?"

"I haven't known long," she said. "And I was going to tell you but wanted to give her a chance to talk to you herself first."

"Oh, my God," I said. "I just can't believe this. I can't believe my class president, straight-A, musically gifted daughter is pregnant by some guy in Colorado I've never even heard of. This is just insane."

"I know," Lucy said, and it scared me that she agreed, because there was very little that Lucy considered insane. "You know, the only thing that I find completely unbearable is his age," she added.

"Which is…?" I'd figured he was a little older than Shannon, since he was already in college.

Again the silence from my sister.

"Lucy."

"He's twenty-seven," she said. "I assumed she'd told you."

"Oh, my God," I said again. "Oh, Lucy. It's statutory rape."

"No." Lucy sounded so damned calm. "She would have to be under sixteen for that." I heard her sigh. "I just don't know what to say, Julie. I don't get this any more than you do, and I'm upset, too. The thing is, it's happened, and she plans to have this baby. We need to check this guy out, of course, but I think that this is just going to happen and we have to do whatever we can do to be there for her."

"How can we be there if she's in Colorado?" I asked.

"I hope she'll reconsider that," Lucy said.

I thought of all the colleges we'd visited. The nerve-racking auditions. The waiting for acceptances. Her excitement at getting into Oberlin. "All her plans…" I said, my voice trailing off. There was not much to say about those plans. They had little meaning now.

"I know," Lucy said. She hesitated, then finally spoke again. "On another cheery topic," she began. "Did you tell Mom about Ned's letter?"

"Yes," I said. My voice had gone flat. I felt weary to my bones.

"Oh, Lord," Lucy said. "What did she say?"

"She got really quiet. She went into the house and lay down. I was worried about her and I checked on her before I left, but she said she just wanted to sleep." I looked at my watch. "I was going to call her in a few minutes, but I'm a little too shaken up to do it right now."

"I'll call her," Lucy volunteered.

"Thank you," I said. "Shannon could still have a safe abortion at eighteen weeks, couldn't she?"

"Wow, I can't believe I'm hearing you say that," Lucy said. "Everything changes when it's your own kid, doesn't it?"

"Don't lecture me, all right? Could she?"

"Yes," she said. "But that's not what she wants."

"How does she even know what she wants?" I asked. "She's not thinking straight. None of this makes sense. Do you think Glen knows?"

"She told me she'd tell him after she told you, so I guess he will know very soon."

"I suppose he and I should talk."

"Good idea," Lucy said, then added, "I'm going to call Mom now. Will you be okay?"

"I don't know," I said. "I'll talk to you later."

When I got off the phone with Lucy, I started to dial Glen's number, then hung up. I didn't feel like hearing his voice or listening to his controlled and inevitably dispassionate reaction to the fact of Shannon's pregnancy. I also didn't want to tell him the news through my filter. Let him get it from Shannon, the same way I did.

I lifted the receiver again and dialed Ethan's number. His was the one voice I *did* want to hear.

"Shannon is pregnant," I announced when he answered the phone.

"Oh, no," he said.

I told him the whole story, including Tanner's age and the potentially botched college plans and it felt wonderful to vent to someone who simply listened. He didn't speak again until I'd poured out every ounce of it.

"I know exactly how you feel," he said then.

"You do?"

"Uh-huh," he said. "Abby got pregnant when she was sixteen. I don't think she'd mind me telling you that."

"Oh, Ethan." I felt empathy, both for him and from him. "What did she do?" I asked.

"She placed the baby for adoption," he said.

Adoption. Of course. That made the most sense. That was what Shannon should do.

"Maybe Shannon would consider that," I said.

"I bet Abby would be willing to talk to her about it, if you like," he said. "It was an open adoption situation, and I have to say, as terrible as the whole experience was—and it was very hard for all of us—it's turned out well. She has a relationship with her son, who's nearly ten now. I even get to see him once in a while. His parents are great people."

I was thinking about Oberlin. She would still miss the fall starting date if she placed the baby for adoption. I wondered if she could go in the spring or would she have to wait until the following year?

"I'll talk to her about it," I said, knowing the conversation would not be easy or welcome.

"I think you need me to come up there and give you a hug," he said.

He was right. That was exactly what I needed.

"Could you come right now?" I asked, feeling a little brazen. I remembered him holding my hand on his thigh. I wanted him to do that again.

"How about Friday evening?" he asked. "Can you wait that long?"

There was a hint of sexual innuendo in his voice that both surprised and titillated me and, however briefly, made me forget about Shannon's dilemma.

"I'm not sure," I said, "but I'll try."

I got off the phone and sat smiling for a moment. Amazing, I thought, that I could smile after a day like this one. I leaned my head back against the love seat and looked at my ceiling fan, which was spinning lazily. Could I do it? I wondered. Could I make love to Ethan? I rested my hand on my belly and felt my nipples harden at my own touch. *Yes,* I thought, *I could.*

I stood up and left the office, heading for my bedroom, remembering that long-ago priest telling me I must *never* commit the grievous offense of masturbation. I laughed out loud as I walked into my bedroom. *This afternoon,* I thought, *I am going to sin.*

CHAPTER 28

Maria

The day after I received the news about Ned Chapman's letter to the police, Shannon showed up at Micky D's while I was working. I hadn't seen her since her graduation. She waved to me as she walked in the door and got in line. One look at her, and the suspicion that had formed in my mind at her graduation was confirmed: My seventeen-year-old granddaughter was pregnant.

I waited until she had gone through the line and taken a seat at a table before going over to her. I'd needed a few minutes to collect my wits.

"Hi, Nana." She stood up to kiss my cheek and I sat down across from her, observing the Big Mac and milkshake on her tray.

"You know, Shannon," I said. "That food is not good for your baby."

Her eyes flew open wide. "Did Mom tell you?" she asked.

I wondered how long Julie had known and how long she'd planned to keep the news from me. I supposed she'd wanted to drop one bombshell on me at a time.

"I'm old, Shannon, but I'm not stupid," I said. "I know a pregnant woman—a pregnant *girl*—when I see one."

She looked down at her Big Mac, peeking under the bun as though studying the meat for doneness, and I figured she was waiting for me to chew her out. She was afraid, and my heart broke a little for her. I made a quick decision to be a better grandmother than I had been a mother.

"How did your mother take the news?" I asked.

"Like you'd expect," she said, rolling her eyes. "Like my life is over. Ruined forever. She's so—" She cut off her own sentence, looking away from me. "All she cares about is my music career. She doesn't really care about what I want."

She took a bite of her hamburger, looking around the restaurant instead of at me. The way she talked about her mother sometimes, you would think she hated her. Shannon reminded me so much of Isabel in the early sixties, while Julie reminded me of myself during that same time period. I could see my mistakes being played out all over again.

"When did you tell her?" I asked.

She swallowed her bite of hamburger. "Yesterday," she said.

"And your father?"

"I told him last night." She shook her head. "You know Dad," she said. "He said 'Oh, Shannon,' and that was it. At least Mom yelled. Dad just…he can be so totally lame sometimes."

"I bet it wasn't easy telling them, huh?" I asked.

Her eyes filled suddenly, and she went from hardened young woman to scared little girl. I handed her a napkin, but she only clutched it in her hand as a tear fell from her eye and rolled down her cheek.

"Who is the boy?" I asked.

A light came into her eyes, the first glint of joy I'd seen since she walked into the restaurant. She told me his name was Tanner, that he lived in Colorado, and that she planned to move out there with him. That nearly stopped my heart. *Please, no,* I thought. It was bad enough she'd been planning to go away to college. I wanted my granddaughter in my life. I loved when she stopped by McDonald's just to say hello. How many more years did I have? If she moved across the country, when would I ever get to see her? But I quickly got a grip on myself.

"I tell you what, Shannie," I said, using the nickname I'd given her when she was a toddler. "If those plans fall through and you end up staying here, I'll be happy to baby-sit for you."

Her mouth fell open in surprise. Then she smiled.

"Nana," she said. "I love you."

"I love you, too, darling," I said.

She pushed her Big Mac aside. "I think I'm going to get a salad," she said, rising to her feet. I told her to stay put, and then I went behind the counter and got her the healthiest salad we made.

As I drove home later that afternoon, I felt good about how I'd handled things with Shannon. I thought I'd given her what she needed—some loving kindness, free of judgment. That's what Isabel had needed, too, but that was not what she'd received from me.

My good mood ended the moment I got in my door. The phone was ringing, and when I picked it up, there was Ross Chapman once again.

"Maria," he said. Even speaking that one small word seemed to be a great effort for him. The three syllables came out slowly, sadly. "Has your daughter told you what's going on?" he asked.

I closed my eyes. I was angry beyond measure at him. I believed he'd lied for his son, and now he was badgering me for forgiveness he was never going to get.

"You mean, did she tell me about Ned's admission of guilt?" I responded, and then I hung up. I had let that man toy with my mind before. It was not going to happen again.

1942-1944

On the first day of my senior year at the New Jersey College for Women, I arrived in New Brunswick still able to taste Ross's kisses in my mouth and feel his hands on my breasts. We had grown ever bolder during that summer, each of us seeing several other people in order to avoid leading one person on, as I was afraid I may have done with Fred. Many of the young men—Fred included—were fighting in the war at that time, so Ross had quite a few more dating options than I did, but I did my best. Ross had been drafted, but at his physical exam they discovered a minor heart problem and he was classified 4-F. Although I was patriotic when it came to the war and felt everyone should do his or her part, I was relieved he did not have to go.

My parents had made friends with another couple in Bay Head Shores and they often went to their house to play bridge, leaving our bungalow empty. When I knew they would be gone, Ross and I canceled whatever dates we had for that night and we would have the house to ourselves, free to satisfy the hunger we felt for each other. The summer had been filled with cunning, deception, and a fierce physical passion. I could barely tear myself away from him that last night at the shore.

The fraternity down the street from our sorority house had a "welcome back to school" party the night of my arrival. I went with some girlfriends who were anxious to meet some of the Rutgers boys, even if most of them were "4-Fers," but my heart wasn't in it. I was standing in a doorway, missing Ross and already writing a letter to him in my mind, when a young man approached me. He walked with a pronounced limp, and something about his eyes reminded me of Ross. That was the only reason I could think of for the instant, feverish attraction I felt toward him. He introduced himself to me as Charles Bauer.

"A lovely girl like you shouldn't be standing here alone," he said. "Would you like to dance?"

"Sure," I said. I moved easily into his arms. He was an awkward dancer because of his limp, but he didn't seem at all self-conscious about it and I didn't care a bit, because he felt like Ross in my arms. He was the same height, his shoulders the same slender width, and he used Canoe aftershave, the same as Ross. I inhaled as I rested my head in the crook of his neck, near tears with missing my lover.

After a few minutes, he leaned his head away from mine. "Is something the matter?" he asked.

I started to cry. He let go of me, took my hand and led me outside. We sat on the front steps, the sounds of the party behind us.

"What does a beautiful girl like you have to cry about?" he asked.

"I'm sorry," I said, then lied because it was the only way I could possibly explain my sorrow. "I recently broke up with someone."

"And you still care about him," Charles said.

I nodded.

"That happened to me, too," he said, pulling his handkerchief from his pocket and handing it to me.

"Recently?" I asked, pressing the handkerchief to the corners of my eyes. He was very attractive. A gas lamp burned in the front of the yard and I could see that he did not really resemble Ross one bit. He was brown-haired, for pity's sake, while Ross was fair. His eyes were also brown, while Ross's were a smoky gray. But he was handsome, all the same, and sitting there, I still felt drawn to him.

"We broke up a while ago," he said. "When I was stationed in Hawaii."

"Hawaii?" I asked. I thought of his limp. "Were you at Pearl Harbor when…?"

He nodded. "That's where I got this bum leg," he said, patting his right thigh with his palm.

"That must have been terrible," I said.

"Much worse for a lot of other people than it was for me," he said. "I wanted to go back, but they wouldn't let me. I hate feeling useless here at home."

"But you're in school now," I said, admiring his patriotism. "That's not being useless. What are you studying?"

"Medicine," he said.

"Oh!" I was impressed. "You want to be a doctor."

"I always have," he said. "I thought it would have to wait until the war ends—if it ever does—but I guess that was the one bonus of getting injured. Now, my dream's within reach. And how about you?"

"This is my senior year," I said. "I'm going to teach."

"That's wonderful!" he said, as if I'd said that I, too, planned to become a doctor. "Did you always want to be a teacher?"

"Well—" I smiled "—I've actually always wanted to have a family, but I think it's important for a woman to be able to support herself."

He nodded. "You're a very smart girl," he said. "I want to raise a family myself, but I also want to be sure I can provide well for them."

What a remarkable man, I thought. I liked that he didn't denigrate my choice of career. Ross had made light of my studies as though they were inconsequential.

I smoothed my skirt over my legs and wrapped my arms around my knees. "What kind of doctor do you want to be?" I asked.

"A pediatrician," he said. "I was sick when I was a boy and that's when I decided."

"So," I said, "we've both chosen careers that will let us help children."

He looked suddenly excited and turned toward me, reaching for my hand. "Maria," he said, "you need to tell me something right now."

"What?"

"Please tell me you're Catholic."

I laughed. "I am, but why?"

"Because in the thirty minutes since I first spotted you across the living room, I've fallen in love with you," he said. "And you being Catholic will make it so much easier. Is there a chance you might like to go to mass with me tomorrow? Then maybe we could have lunch together afterward."

I liked his impulsiveness. It excited me, and I had to admit that I'd become a girl in need of excitement. A strange little tug-of-war was going on inside me, though. Only two days before, I'd been secretly making love to a man. Now I was being invited to mass as a date. My family was Catholic, that was no lie, but we were holiday Catholics, attending church on Christmas and Easter and only occasionally in between. I felt as though God was intervening in my life at that very moment. He was giving me an opportunity to turn myself around and put an end to my deceitful and immoral behavior. I felt the sorrow over leaving Ross turn into a sort of relief and gratitude. This lovely man, Charles Bauer, who had fought for his country and longed to be a physician and raise a family, might be able to save me from myself.

"I would like that so much," I said.

"Oh, wonderful!" he said, with an enthusiasm I would come to appreciate in him. "Was your boyfriend Catholic?" he asked.

"Yes, but not devout," I said. An understatement if ever there was one.

"It was doomed from the start, then," he said. "The gal I broke up with last year was a Methodist. My parents wouldn't even talk to her. I should have known it wouldn't work. The values are just too different, you know?"

I nodded, although I didn't really know at all.

"She was...fast, if you know what I mean," he said. "I found out she'd had...you know, *relations,* with the boy she'd dated before me, and I felt sick thinking about it."

I knew right then that I would be starting this relationship off with a lie. I would never let Charles know the truth about Ross and me. Only a few of my girlfriends knew about Ross, so it would be a relatively easy secret to keep. I thought, though, that I'd better bring my ancestry out in the open before things went any further.

"I'm half Italian," I said.

"I thought so." He touched my hair. "You have that rich Italian hair and those big, dark eyes." It didn't seem to bother him at all.

Charles and I attended mass the following day and I saw my religion in a new light. I felt the peace that came over him inside the church. The smell of incense, the ritualistic standing and kneeling, the haunting Latin chanting, and the taste of the host on my tongue struck me like never before. I thanked God for giving me what felt like a second chance.

When we left the church and were back in my car, Charles turned to me. "Are you all right?" he asked.

I nodded, wondering how he had known the impact that service had had on me. "I've never been to mass with a..." I started to say boyfriend, but it seemed too soon to give him that label. "With a date before," I finished.

"You never went with your last boyfriend?" he asked.

I shook my head.

"I understand," he said with a smile. "That's why it would never have worked out with my old girlfriend and with your old boyfriend. They would have been twiddling their thumbs in there, anxious to get it over with."

We fell in love quickly. I think I was in love with him that first night outside the fraternity house. My relationship with Ross was becoming clearer to me: It had been based on the physical and the illicit and little more. This was so different. Charles met my parents, who instantly adored him and even attended mass with us the first weekend he visited. Charles and my father were New York Yankee fans, and they occasionally attended games together at Yankee Stadium, while my mother would marvel that I'd found such a wonderful man.

"I've been worried about you," she said, her Italian accent flavoring the words.

"Why?" I'd asked her, surprised.

"You always flit from one boy to the other," she said. "Never settled on any one of them. It worried me."

"You didn't have to worry," I said to her with a smile. "I was waiting for the right one to come along."

My relationship with Charles was entirely chaste. His kisses were passionate, but if his hands wandered toward my breasts or my thighs, he would pull back in apology. I craved more, and I found the craving exciting. I felt guilty for the lie of omission I was engaged in. He thought I was a virgin, and there was no reason to tell him anything different. The lie was so thorough that even I began to think of myself as virginal.

On Easter Sunday, 1943, Charles asked me to marry him. Of course, I accepted, but as summer grew near and my parents spoke of having him stay with us at the shore, I became increasingly nervous. The rule between Ross and I that we would be lovers during the summers was unwritten and even unspoken, but it existed nevertheless, and I feared his reaction when I showed up with Charles. I hoped it would be clear to him that I needed to put an end to our illicit relationship, and I prayed he did nothing that might arouse Charles's suspicions. I was in for a surprise.

Charles and I followed my parents' car as we drove down the shore, and when we pulled into the driveway of the bungalow, I could see that two cars were already present in front of the Chapmans' house. My heart pounded as we unloaded the car and walked into our musty-smelling house. When I opened the French doors leading to the porch with its panoramic view of the canal, Charles gasped.

"It's wonderful!" he said, walking across the porch and unlatching the screen door to step outside.

I could see people in the Chapmans' yard, although I could not tell who they were, and I felt unprepared to walk into the yard with Charles if Ross was there. I'd wanted a chance to talk to Ross alone first. But with Charles already walking outside, I had little choice but to follow him.

"When will your father get the boat?" Charles asked, motioning at the dock as we walked toward the canal. The wooden bulkheads were in place by then, but it would be years before there would be a chain-link fence to mar our view.

"He'll pick it up tomorrow, probably," I said, my eyes on the Chapmans' yard. Two figures stood in the far corner: Ross and a woman. I should have been pleased that he, too, would be preoccupied with a guest, but instead, a breath-stealing jealousy sprang up in my chest.

"Looks like you share your backyard." Charles nodded toward the twosome.

Ross had his arm around the woman, but as he turned and saw us, his arm fell quickly from her shoulders. He was just as uncomfortable as I was, I thought.

"Hello, Maria!" he called. He put his hand on the woman's elbow to turn her toward us. In his other hand, he held a cigar.

"Hi, Ross," I said.

He said something I couldn't hear to the woman, and they began walking in our direction. I felt Charles's hand on my back, lightly pushing me forward until the four of us met in the middle of the yard.

Ross looked wonderful, a little trimmer than the year before. I had trouble meeting his eyes. The delicious, woody scent of his cigar surrounded us.

"This is Joan Rockefeller," he said. "Joan, this is my neighbor, Maria Foley. And this is...?" He raised his eyebrows in Charles's direction.

"Charles Bauer," I volunteered. "This is Ross Chapman."

The two men shook hands while I studied Joan. She was a blond stunner. Huge blue eyes, carefully coiffed hair, a dress that hugged a very slender frame.

"Any relation to the New York Rockefellers?" Charles asked the question I was thinking. How much was this girl worth?

"I'm about a fifty-first cousin, thrice removed." Joan laughed. Then she turned to me. "Ross said that your family and his have been summertime neighbors since you were small." Her high-pitched voice was almost childlike.

"That's right," I said.

"Maria taught me how to dance," Ross said.

"Oh, you did a wonderful job." Joan nodded at me with a smile.

"And Ross taught me how to play tennis," I said.

I thought of all the other things Ross had taught me that had nothing to do with tennis and felt myself blushing furiously. I couldn't get a handle on my feelings. I loved Charles, of that I was certain, so it was ridiculous that my chest ached at seeing Ross with another woman. She would be the sort of girl his parents wanted for him. A Rockefeller, no less. I wondered if he felt jealous at seeing me with Charles. He didn't seem to. He was smiling easily, touching Joan's arm in an intimate way and I knew that *she* was the one receiving his fiery lovemaking these days.

We put Charles in the attic, which now contained two double beds and four twins, ready for the cousins and other company who would arrive during the summer. There was no privacy up there, which was not a problem as long as Charles was the only inhabitant, but the week before my cousins were due to arrive, he made a suggestion.

"What if I hung a system of wires up there," he said over breakfast one morning. He pulled a fountain pen from his shirt pocket and drew on the back of a paper napkin. "Then we could hang curtains from the wires, so that there would be four cubbyholes around the beds, leaving this middle area open."

"That's a fine idea," my father said.

"I can make the curtains," my mother suggested, and I offered to help.

"And one other thing," Charles said. He held his hands up in apology. "I hope I'm not overstepping my boundaries here, but what about adding a toilet and sink up there? I'd be happy to do it. My father taught me carpentry and plumbing."

"Where would it go?" My mother stared at the napkin and its crisscrossed lines.

"I could build it right above the downstairs bathroom to make it easy to do the plumbing. It would be very small, of course, but then your guests wouldn't have to climb down those stairs in the middle of the night. And we wouldn't have to put a door on it. Just hang another curtain for privacy."

I could tell my father was excited by the idea. "Let's go to the hardware store as soon as we finish breakfast," he said to Charles. "And I'll pay you for your time and expertise."

"Oh, my gosh, no," Charles said quickly. "You're giving me room and board all summer. It's the least I can do to repay you."

Both my parents were in love with Charles, as was I. He enjoyed fishing with my father in our motorboat, and in addition to building the upstairs bathroom, he reshingled parts of our roof and painted the trim on the house. He never saw my mother's accent as something to be ashamed of, but rather as part of her heritage to be celebrated, in spite of the fact that he'd nearly lost his life in a war in which the Italians were our enemy. On her birthday in August, he shooed her out of the kitchen while we made her an authentic five-course Northern Italian meal. It was all his doing; I never would have thought of it. Mother cried when Charles presented the cannoli he'd made, completely by hand and with our carefully rationed sugar, for dessert.

We did not socialize with the Chapmans. Aside from Ross's and my "friendship," my family rarely had. We were the sort of neighbors who were there for each other if your car got stuck in the sand, but it was clear we were from different social classes, different worlds. Although our backyards were connected, they were divided by an invisible line drawn in the sand.

Ross and I did not have one single private conversation that entire summer. I was curious to know how he'd met Joan, but she was always standing or sitting right next to him and I never had the opportunity to ask. That was probably just as well.

A few weeks after our arrival at the bungalow, Charles and I were sitting in the backyard enjoying the evening when he suggested we talk to Ross and Joan about double dating with them sometime.

"They're around our age," he said, although Charles was technically six years Ross's senior. "They seem nice. Wouldn't it be fun to have a couple right next door to do things with?"

I hesitated as I tried to think of a response, the idea of getting together socially with Ross and his new love horrifying to me. I settled on telling him a partial truth.

"Charles," I said, "when Ross and I were in high school, he asked me out, but when his parents found out, they told him he was not allowed to date me."

"Why not?" Charles asked.

"Because I'm Italian."

Charles looked stunned. "That's certainly small-minded," he said, making me love him all the more.

"He and his family have never been friendly with us," I said. "So, I really would rather not—"

"Of course," Charles said. He looked over his shoulder toward the Chapmans' house. "Was Ross in the military?" he asked.

"He was 4-F," I said. "A minor heart problem."

"Ah," Charles said, and I knew I had just planted an immutable wall between my boyfriend, recipient of the Purple Heart, and Ross Chapman. A man who didn't serve his country, yet nevertheless appeared to be hale and hearty, was a coward in Charles's eyes.

"If he would just stop smoking," Charles said, "that heart problem would probably go away."

I think Charles was a bit disappointed to discover that my parents were not regular churchgoers, but he said nothing about it. I went to mass with him at St. Peter's every Sunday and we'd stop at Mueller's Bakery afterward and bring home rolls and crumb cake for a late-morning breakfast with my parents. I enjoyed going to church with him, never ceasing to be touched by the way such a strong and intelligent man was able to find peace and comfort there. He also prayed the rosary every night before falling asleep. I prayed, too, although not the rosary. I prayed for my small, jealous feelings about Joan Rockefeller to disappear. I prayed to be able to look at the blueberry lot without longing. I prayed to forget the ways Ross had touched me—*taken* me, really, for he could be rough in a way I'd enjoyed. He'd never hurt me, but he could ride me like I was a bucking bronco. A heart problem, my eye.

Charles was a believer in prayers being answered. I could only conclude that I did not pray quite hard enough.

Charles and I were married in June the following year. I feigned pain when we first made love, and to my great relief, he believed I was a virgin. We took our honeymoon in Niagara Falls, and then joined my parents at the bungalow, this time sharing the small downstairs bedroom that had always been mine. We unpacked our suitcases, then went onto the porch and I stopped dead in my tracks at the sound coming from next door: the cries of a baby.

"Whose baby is that?" I asked.

My mother was sitting at the table. "It's Ross and Joan's," she said. "Sue Clements told me they got married last September and the baby was born just a few weeks ago. Ross's parents retired to Florida, so it's just the three of them in the house there now."

I did the math in my head and felt a wave of disappointment that he had not married her simply because she was pregnant. He must have married her for love, then, the sort of love he and I could never have known because of all the forces against us. Would I ever get over it?

We saw the baby that evening. Joan carried him over to us in the backyard, cooing and showing him off. Although I didn't ask to hold him, she carefully transferred him to my arms and I felt an involuntary pull of my nipples at cradling his beautiful warmth.

"His name is Ned Rosswell Chapman," she said.

Charles leaned over and gently drew the blanket away from the baby's cheek. Ned Rosswell Chapman sucked his fingers in his sleep.

"He's adorable," I said sincerely. I didn't need eyes in the back of my head to know that Ross was approaching us from behind. It was some sort of sixth sense I had, so strong that I was not surprised when he suddenly appeared at Joan's side, slipping an arm around her waist.

"What do you think of him?" he asked me, nodding in the direction of his son.

"He's precious," I said. I looked up at him and saw that he was gazing at me, the look in his eyes raw with desire. For me? For Joan? I didn't know, and I looked quickly away from him, back to the face of his child.

We chatted a while about little Ned and about our honeymoon, and gradually the conversation shifted to the war, as it usually did in those days. Joan and I withdrew into silence as the men's voices grew louder. Ross complained that the government was handing us propaganda about how well the war was going while hiding the truth

about the number of casualties suffered. Charles argued back, showing a side of himself I had not known existed. Both men were stri-
dent and impassioned, and I could see the future mapped out ahead
of us: Ross Chapman and Charles Bauer would never be friends. They
were lawyer and doctor, on opposite teams. That night in our shared
backyard, we forged the cool and contentious relationship with our
neighbors that would remain for the rest of our years—even as our
children became friends.

CHAPTER 29

Julie

I'd like you to see my obstetrician.
Would you like to go to my OB/GYN?
My obstetrician is the best in the area.

I'd practiced every way of saying it, trying to find the words that would offer the path of least resistance when I presented the idea to Shannon. I should have known it wouldn't matter. My daughter had her own plans.

I called her Friday morning, timing the call so that I'd reach her before she had to be to work but late enough that I knew she'd be up.

"Hi, Mom," she said, apparently seeing my number on the caller ID of her cell phone. I took it as a good sign that she'd answered de-spite knowing it was me.

"Hi, honey," I said. I was sitting on my bed, cross-legged, leaning back against the sham. I'd changed the sheets after getting up that morning, just in case: Ethan was coming to Westfield tonight. "How are you feeling?"

"You mean because I'm pregnant?"

No matter what I said to her, she seemed to take it as an attack. "I mean, in general," I said.

"Fine."

"I thought I'd call to see if you'd like me to make an appointment for you with my OB/GYN. I know you'd like her. She's—"

"I've been meaning to talk to you about that," Shannon interrupted me. "I already have a doctor."

"You have?" I asked. My daughter was living a completely secret life. "Where are you…are you going to a clinic?"

"Not a clinic. It's Dr. Myers-Blake in Morristown. She's good. A friend told me about her."

"Myersblick?" I repeated. I'd never heard of her.

"Myers-Blake," she said slowly. "It's hyphenated."

The name was still unfamiliar to me. "But how did you pay?" I asked. "Our insurance—"

"Tanner sent me money," she said, "but she *does* take our insurance. I picked a doctor who did, so that once you knew, I could start having our insurance pay for her."

I was quiet, amazed that she had thought the issue through so carefully and thoroughly when her other recent decisions seemed to have been impulsively made. Through my bedroom window, I could see the massive oak tree Shannon used to climb as a kid. I missed that girl. I missed her so much. But I looked away from the window. The future was here and now.

"I'm proud of you for getting prenatal care on your own," I said. "But please consider going to my doctor."

"No," she said. "I'm in charge of my life from now on."

"Well, listen, honey." It was time for a new tack. "Abby Chapman, Ethan Chapman's daughter who is about twenty-six, is willing to talk to you about how she handled getting pregnant when she was about your age. She—"

"I'm handling it just fine, Mom." Her voice was filled with irritation; I was losing her.

"I know you are," I said. "But, see…what she did…and maybe you haven't considered this option…is that she placed her baby with adoptive parents, and she—"

"Mother, would you please respect my decision?" Shannon asked. "How many times do I have to tell you I'm keeping this baby? I didn't mean to get pregnant. I didn't set out to mess up my college plans. But it happened and now I'll deal with it. And there's something else I need to tell you."

Oh, God. "What?"

"Tanner is coming here next week," she said. "He's staying with his friends in Morristown for two weeks, and then he has to go back to Colorado and I'm going to go with him. So, I'll be going to a doctor there, ultimately, anyway."

"You mean, you'd be going there *now?* To *stay?*"

"In about three weeks," she said. "And I don't know if we'll stay there forever, but we'll be there at least until he finishes his Ph.D. program. Then, who knows where we'll end up."

I felt panicky. "Let's talk this over, Shannon," I said, standing up from my seat on the bed. "Talking something over doesn't make you any less a grown-up. I talk to Lucy about important decisions I have to make, and this decision is certainly important."

She sighed. "I have to get to work, Mom, so maybe we can talk later, okay?"

"All right," I said. What else *could* I say. "But please, Shannon. Please let's talk later."

I called Glen at work the moment I got off the phone with Shannon. I spoke quickly, telling him about her going to a doctor we didn't know and her planned move to Colorado. He listened quietly. He was always quiet. I'd once appreciated his gentle, compliant nature. Now I hated it. "Can you exert any influence over her since she's living with you?" I pleaded.

"I think we need to let her do it her way," he said finally.

"You're afraid to make waves with her," I said. "You're always afraid to make waves. I would probably still not know you were having an affair if what's-her-face hadn't called to tell me."

Glen said nothing. He knew it was the truth.

"Do you *want* her to move away?" I asked, looking for some response. I would take any response at that point.

"I think if she's old enough to get pregnant," he said, "she's old enough to deal with the consequences."

"That's ridiculous," I said. "Eleven-year-olds can get pregnant, Glen. You think an eleven-year-old should deal with the consequences?"

"She's not eleven."

"Don't you care that she's leaving?"

"She would have left for college anyway," he said, most likely with one of his *c'est la vie* shrugs.

I hung up. I couldn't remember ever hanging up on anyone before in my entire life, but I could no longer tolerate his inability to confront difficult situations head-on. That's what had cost us our marriage. I wasn't going to let it cost me my daughter.

I got online to e-mail Lucy regarding Shannon's latest plans and discovered a message from Ethan.

The police found Bruno Walker's sister. She said he's on a solo sailing trip around the world. The cop I spoke with said they'll find him and "cut his trip short."

And they questioned Dad.

See you tonight.

CHAPTER 30

Julie
1962

I loved to ride my bike around Bay Head Shores, but Lucy never felt very steady on hers. She would ride on our end of the dirt road, and that was about it. One day, though, I told her that if she would ride her bike to the corner store with me, I would buy her penny candy. She loved those strips of button candy, and I could tell she was tempted.

"It's too far, though," she whined.

We were sitting on the sand in our front yard, our bikes parked in the driveway.

"How about this," I said, coming up with a way to shorten the trip. "We can *walk* our bikes across the blueberry lot, and that will cut off about a fourth of the distance." It would probably be an even harder trip doing it that way, since we would have to carry our bikes over the deepest sand, but my suggestion seemed to work.

"All right," she said, getting to her feet. She shuffled barefoot toward her bike, afraid of stepping on one of the holly leaves that sometimes blew over from the Chapmans' yard. I had to admit, the points on those leaves *hurt,* but Lucy looked like a spaz walking that way.

We walked our bikes more easily than I'd anticipated across the blueberry lot, but I was perspiring anyway by the time we got to the street on the other side. We mounted our one-speed, low-to-the-ground bikes and began riding in the direction of the store, dense woods on either side of us. Although there were no cars on the road, Lucy still hugged the shoulder, causing her tires to slip off the pavement and into the sand from time to time, but I didn't say a word. When we neared the corner of Rue Lido, she held her left hand up in a turn signal even though there were no cars in sight, and I had to stop myself from laughing. I didn't want to discourage her from making this trip again.

We pulled into the lot next to the little store and parked our bikes. Inside, I bought eggs and milk for our mother, candy buttons and root beer barrels for Lucy, licorice lace and Mary Janes for myself and a pack of teaberry gum for Isabel, because I knew she liked to use it to cover up the fact that she'd been smoking. I put the bag containing our purchases in my bicycle basket and we got back on the road.

We were on the long stretch of Beach Boulevard when I heard the sound of a truck somewhere behind us. I glanced over my shoulder to make sure Lucy was well to the side of the road and saw that she was practically riding in the woods. Then I saw the vehicle that was making the noise: It was the mosquito truck, coming toward us, just ahead of a dense fog of DDT.

The mosquito truck drove through Bay Head Shores every week or so. I liked the smell and I liked the way you could run through the cloud of insecticide with a friend, unable to see one another until you emerged on the other side. We were naive to the perils of DDT back then. If Lucy had not been with me, I would have welcomed the thrill of finding myself smack in the path of the truck, but I knew she would not.

"Hey, Luce!" I called behind me. "The mosquito truck is coming. Let's pretend we're in the sky inside a cloud."

I had barely finished my sentence when the truck drove past us. The driver either didn't see us or didn't care that we were there, and we were instantly engulfed in the chemical fog.

"Help!" Lucy called. "Ack! Help!"

"It's okay," I shouted back to her. I didn't want to stop. It was too exciting. I couldn't see the road ahead of me. It was like riding my bike with my eyes closed, which I did occasionally when I knew I was someplace safe.

"Julie!" Lucy's voice had grown fainter, and I figured she must have stopped and gotten off her bike.

I turned my bike around and rode back the way we had come, but even though the fog was lifting, I couldn't see her on the road.

"Lucy?" I called.

"I'm over *here*," she said. "I went over the handlebars."

Then I spotted her in the woods, half sitting, half lying down. I jumped off my own bike, tossing it to the ground, and ran through the fog to reach her.

"Lucy!" I dropped to my knees next to her. "Are you hurt?"

She was flailing at the fog with her hands, her eyes squeezed shut, and I looked at her legs and arms, afraid I might see bones jutting through the skin. Except for a nasty scrape along the length of her forearm, she looked okay.

"Open your eyes," I said. "C'mon. The fog's almost gone."

She opened her eyes, but she was crying, trying to catch her breath, and I figured she'd been holding it to avoid breathing in the spray. Now she was forced to drink in the odorous air in big gulps. Looking down at her wounded arm, she let out another scream. It *was* ugly, a two-inch-wide band scraped raw along her forearm, dots of blood breaking through here and there.

"It's okay," I said, but she held her arm to her as if it were a fragile thing and let out a wail.

I knew I was not going to be able to persuade her to get back on her bike. The fog was thinning, and I tried to find a landmark to tell me how far we were from the house. There were woods on both sides of the road but I could see the opening to the blueberry lot a distance ahead of us.

"Get up, and we'll walk our bikes home," I said. "We're not that far."

She peered down the street, then shook her head. "I don't want to touch my dumb bike," she said.

Where *was* her bike? I looked around, finally spotting it several yards away from where she'd landed. She must have *flown* over those handlebars, and I felt sorry for her. She was lucky a scraped arm was all she'd suffered.

"Okay," I said, "then we'll leave the bikes here and walk home."

Sniffling, she got slowly to her feet.

"You're an old lady in a girl's body," I told her, helping her up. "Grandma has more energy than you."

"Shut up," she said.

We heard the sound of another vehicle on the road and Lucy gave me a look of alarm before running a few feet into the woods.

I turned around to see a red car heading toward us. "It's only a car," I said. Then I realized *what* car it was: Ned's red Corvette convertible! "Hey!" I called to Lucy. "It's Ned!"

Lucy came out of the woods and stood by my side, still cradling her arm. I waved as Ned stopped the car in front of me. Bruno Walker was in the passenger seat, and the radio poured "Cryin' in the Rain" into the air all around us.

Bruno grinned at me. "Hey, good-lookin'," he said, and I wasn't certain if he was being serious or just teasing me, so I kept a half smile on my face which I figured would work either way.

"What's going on, Jules?" Ned asked. I liked that he used Isabel's nickname for me.

"Lucy crashed into the woods on her bike," I said.

Ned turned off the engine and he and Bruno got out of the car. They were both tan and gorgeous, slender Ned with his soft-looking blond hair and Bruno with his sexy black ducktail and muscular build. I didn't think there were two better-looking, non-movie-star guys in the universe and I wished I was with one of my Westfield girlfriends instead of with my little sister.

"Are you okay, Lucy?" Ned asked.

Still sniffling a bit, she stuck her arm out for him to look at. He held it gently in his hands, studying the injury, and for a moment, I wished it had been me who had fallen off her bike.

"It's not broken, is it?" he asked her, carefully moving her arm this way and that.

Lucy shook her head. "Just bleeding," she said.

"Not much blood," Ned stated the obvious. "Your mom just needs to clean it up and put a bandage on it."

I stood right next to Ned, feigning my own interest in Lucy's arm but really just reveling in the cigarette-and-Coppertone smell of him.

Bruno had found Lucy's bike in the tangle of weeds and vines at the side of the road. He lifted it up over his head as if it were made of feathers and set it down on the road, studying the front wheel as he moved it back and forth. A cigarette hung from one corner of his mouth, and I could see why some of the girls thought he looked like Elvis Presley. His eyes had that hooded look to them, and his lips were thick and pouty.

"You fucked up your bike pretty good," he said to Lucy.

"Hey!" Ned said sharply. "Cool the language."

I was both shocked and thrilled by his use of the forbidden word. I watched as he carried the bike to the back of the car and opened the tiny trunk. It didn't look like either of our bikes would fit in there, but he managed to get them both in partway, cushioning the Vette's shiny red paint with beach towels at Ned's request. The trunk would have to stay wide-open, but we were only going around the corner. He handed me the bag of things we'd bought at the little store.

"Well," Ned looked at his car with its two bucket seats. "Lucy, you sit on Bruno's lap, and Julie, I'll share my seat with you."

I couldn't believe what I was hearing! I couldn't have dreamed up a better scenario. Ned sat far to the left of the driver's seat, and I squeezed in next to him. My body was inescapably pressed against his. My legs were crammed into the passenger side along with Bruno's and Lucy's, but I was *very* comfortable.

Ned drove slowly so the bikes wouldn't bounce around, and I wished we'd had farther to go.

"How's that gorgeous older sister of yours?" Bruno asked me as we turned onto Shore Boulevard.

Why don't you ask Ned? I wanted to say, but figured that wouldn't be appreciated. Every time I saw Bruno at the beach, he said something to me about Izzy. He had a thing for her, that was clear, and I wondered if Ned had figured it out.

"She's fine," I said.

"She's fine, all right." Bruno laughed, holding his hands in front of his chest—as best he could with Lucy on his lap—and I realized he was alluding to Isabel's breasts.

"Knock it off," Ned said to him. Then he spoke to me. "Hey, Jules, I have something for you to give her."

I wasn't surprised when he reached down to the floor of the car and came up with the toy giraffe. He handed it to me, and I cradled it on my lap.

"What's that?" Lucy asked. She reached for the giraffe with her un-injured arm, but I held the toy away from her.

"It's for Isabel," I said, and she withdrew her hand.

"Izzy and I appreciate your tight lips, Jules," Ned said.

I twisted my neck to try to get a look at his face. The sun was a bright star in each lens of his sunglasses. I thought I would treasure that moment forever.

We pulled into the Chapmans' driveway. I saw our car in our own driveway and knew that my mother and Isabel were home.

"You know," I said to Ned, putting on the most grown-up voice I could manage. "If Bruno went with you, I think my mother would allow Isabel to go in your boat. Safety in numbers and all of that." I'd heard my father use that term when he talked about Isabel going out with a crowd.

"Oh, yeah?" Ned exchanged a look with Bruno. Lucy walked across the yard, sliding her feet through the sand, holding her arm, already working up the tears she would show our mother.

I nodded. "Want me to ask?" I asked him.

"Would you?" he said. "If she can, you can send her over. Other-wise, come tell me yourself, okay?"

I nodded and tried not to look like a jerk as I walked carefully be-tween the holly leaves that littered his yard.

In our living room, I found Isabel folding the clean laundry while my mother and grandmother clucked around Lucy and her arm. They painted it with Mercurochrome, which I knew had to sting like the devil, but to Lucy's credit, she held her arm still and squeezed her eyes shut.

"Izzy," I said, handing her the giraffe, which she quickly buried in the pile of clothes in the laundry basket. "Ned wants to know if you could go for a boat ride with him and Bruno."

Isabel gave me a sharp warning look before turning back to the laundry.

"Bruno's going, too," I repeated.

My mother unwound a long piece of gauze from a box in the first-aid kit. She snipped it from the box with scissors, then looked over at us.

"I suppose that would be all right, Isabel," she said. "Just a short ride, though. After you finish the laundry."

"I can fold the laundry," I said.

Isabel looked at me in astonishment. I had somehow, miraculously, won her a ride in the boat with Ned and was offering to take over her task, as well. I knew she wondered what I was up to, but she was so happy at the turn of events that she didn't bother to ask me.

"Thanks," she said, either to me or my mother, I was not sure which. Surreptitiously, she took the giraffe from the laundry basket and walked toward the porch. I knew once she was outside, she would break into a run.

I folded the laundry, burying my face in its clean smell as I tried to imagine what was happening in Ned's yard. Izzy and Bruno and Ned would climb into his boat, and maybe something would change on that ride. Maybe she would notice Bruno's handsomeness. He had certainly noticed her beauty. Maybe she'd realize that, compared to Bruno, Ned was a little dull.

I knew it was wrong to pray for small things, but I couldn't help the prayer that ran through my head. *Let Isabel forget about Ned and fall in love with Bruno.* If that happened, then maybe Ned would realize what a wonderful girl *I* was. I knew he saw me as a kid and that if he were free, he would probably find some other girl his own age to date, but my fantasies ran rampant. I couldn't bear that Isabel had him when I wanted him. He wasn't perfect. He smoked cigarettes and I had the feeling he drank a bit too much when he was out with his friends, but maybe the love of a good woman—even if she was only twelve—could change him.

CHAPTER 31

Julie

There was not a single solitary sexual thought in my mind as I sat at my kitchen table stuffing giant pasta shells for the dinner I would serve Ethan. What had happened to my lusty yearning from the other day? It was gone. A fleeting hormonal aberration. I not only lacked desire, I didn't *care* that I lacked it. It was almost a relief. I wouldn't have to worry how I looked nude. My hips were bigger than they should be from too many days in front of the computer. My breasts seemed to hang a little lower every time I looked in the mirror. I didn't have to worry about all that if I didn't care about sex. But I *was* worried that I might have given Ethan the wrong idea during our last, faintly suggestive phone conversation.

An hour later, though, when I opened the front door to find Ethan standing on my porch, a bunch of flowers in his hand, the blue of his eyes matching the color of the sky behind him and his soft voice telling me how beautiful my neighborhood was, my body suddenly reacted as if it belonged to a twenty-year-old. I wasn't sure how I would make I through dinner without dragging him upstairs to my bedroom.

I gave him a hug, and the press of his body against mine only intensified my feelings. I let go of him with a smile.

"I am really happy to see you," I said.

"Me, too." He leaned over to kiss me gently on the lips. "Do you have a vase I can put these in?" He held the flowers out to me.

I found a vase for the flowers and set them on the table on the porch. It would be cool enough to eat out there this evening.

In the kitchen, he looked at Shannon's framed senior picture resting on the windowsill.

"This has to be your daughter," he said.

"Yes," I said, as I opened the oven door to peek at the pasta shells.

"I see your family in her," he said. "That exotic beauty."

I glanced at him as I closed the oven door. "She looks a lot like Isabel," I said.

"I don't remember Isabel well enough," he said, grinning at me. "I only had eyes for her little sister."

I smiled, handing him a knife and pointing him toward the cutting board. "Would you slice the tomatoes, please?"

We worked together easily in the kitchen. He seemed as comfortable in my house as he had been in his own. His self-confidence was sexy to me. The way he touched my arm when I walked past him was sexy. *Everything* about him was sexy to me tonight.

We didn't talk about anything heavy over dinner. I wanted to know about his father's interview with the police, but that could wait. I didn't want anything to break the mood, and he seemed to feel the same way. We sat at the table on the screened porch, eating in the fading light. I talked about what it was like growing up in Westfield, and he talked about learning carpentry as a teenager. Listening to him talk, I felt relaxed for the first time in weeks. I wanted to stand up, lean across the table and kiss him. I wanted to unbutton the buttons on his blue plaid shirt.

I made it through dinner and was carrying plates to the sink when Ethan came up behind me, put his arms around me and kissed my neck. My insides melted and I barely managed to set the dishes on the counter without dropping them.

"I'm so glad you're back in my life," he said, his lips against my ear.

I briefly remembered my mother's words entreating me to disregard his "overtures." *Sorry, Mom,* I thought, as I leaned back against him. I lifted his hand to my lips, letting his forearm brush against my breast.

"Let's go upstairs," I said.

We made love for what seemed like hours. I'd had no lover other than Glen for the past thirty years, and although the newness of being with Ethan was alluring, so was the familiarity I felt with him, the sense of having known him for a very long time. It wasn't until afterward, when we lay comfortably in each other's arms, that we finally broached the topics that weighed heavily on each of us.

"So," I said, smoothing my hand across his chest, "tell me about your father's talk with the police."

Ethan pressed his lips to the top of my head, and I pulled closer to him. I loved the feeling of being cradled in his arms.

"He didn't seem all that upset, actually," he said. "I was relieved. But you know, he's an amazing guy. He can still turn this switch and get back in his old judge-and-lawyer mode to handle a situation. He said he's sure he satisfied their doubts about Ned's alibi."

"That's good," I said. I would not mar the moment with my own thoughts about Ned's guilt. What mattered most to me right then was that Ethan no longer seemed worried about his father.

"I think they went easy on him," he said. "And they would probably go even easier on your—" He stopped talking, lifting his head from the pillow. "Did you hear something?" he asked.

I raised my own head to listen. There might have been some movement in the hallway outside my room, but I wasn't sure.

"Mom?"

I was up in an instant. "Oh, shit!" I whispered, using a word that rarely passed through my lips. "It's Shannon," I said, uncertain whether to reach for my jeans or run to my closet for my robe. I opted for the jeans, balancing on one foot as I pulled them on.

"Mom?" Shannon knocked on my door.

"Just a minute, Shannon," I said. "I'll be right out."

Ethan was up and dressing, too.

"Stay here, please," I whispered to him as I pulled my T-shirt over my head. I opened the door and walked, braless, into the hallway.

I found Shannon in her own room sorting through her bookshelves, putting some of the books into a cardboard box on her bed.

She looked over at me. "Were you asleep?" she asked. "Your hair's a mess."

"Yes, I took a little nap." I combed my fingers through my hair. I felt winded as I sat down on the corner of her bed. "It's good to see you," I said.

"Did you have friends over for dinner?" she asked. "I smell tomato sauce."

"Yes," I said. "I made stuffed shells and there's plenty left if you want to take some with you."

"Maybe I will, thanks," she said. She looked at the hardcover book in her hand. "I came over to start packing," she said.

"Packing?"

"For my move." She didn't look at me as she returned her attention to the bookshelf. "It's still a few weeks away, but I thought I should start going through my stuff." She pulled out a book, looked at the title and slipped it back onto the shelf again. Her belly seemed to have grown enormously in the past few days.

"Shannon," I said, "have you really thought this move through?"

"It's all I've been thinking about for the past few months, Mother." I hated it when she called me *Mother.*

"Please don't go, honey," I pleaded. "Please. At least stay here until after you've had the baby." I was *not* going to let this happen. I wondered if there was something I could do legally to keep her here.

"I want to be with my baby's father, Mom," she said, pulling out a book and dropping it into the box. "That's the way it should be."

"When can I meet him?" I asked. Maybe I could reason more easily with *him* than I could with my daughter.

"I was thinking about that," she said. "It might be better if you didn't meet him right now, since you're so—"

There was a slight thud from the direction of my bedroom, as if Ethan had bumped his knee on the dresser in the darkness.

"Daddy?" Shannon looked up, her eyes suddenly those of a

hopeful child. She started for the hallway and I quickly grabbed her arm.

"Daddy's not here," I said, shocked that she might think that was a possibility.

"Then who's in your bedroom?"

I thought of lying, of pretending she had imagined the sound, but I knew that was not going to work.

"*Mother,*" she said. "Who is in your bedroom?"

"I have company," I said awkwardly. "Ethan Chapman."

I thought she was going to hit me. The look she gave me was nothing short of murderous.

"How could you *do* that?" she asked. "I leave and you start screwing around? You and Dad haven't even been apart that long. You're not giving getting back together a chance!"

"There is no chance of us getting back together, Shannon," I said. I felt terrible that she'd been nursing that fantasy for the past two years and I hadn't known. "Ethan is an old friend, someone I feel very close—"

"Shut up!" She put her hands over her ears. "Just shut up."

She pushed past me and ran down the hall. I closed my eyes and leaned against the wall as I listened to her race down the stairs and out of the house, and I only jumped a little bit when the front door slammed shut behind her.

CHAPTER 32

Lucy

I was playing the violin in the turret room of my apartment, trying to learn a piece the ZydaChicks hoped to perform next season, when I heard thumping on the stairs. Except for my violin practice, the house I lived in was always quiet. My neighbors were not the type to have friends who would clomp up the stairs, so I stopped playing and listened, knowing that if the thumping continued to the third story, it was someone coming to see me. Sure enough, I heard the footsteps reach my landing, and I pulled the door open before my visitor even had a chance to knock.

Shannon burst into the room, her face red with bottled-up tears that exploded as soon as she threw herself onto my couch. I was frightened by her demeanor. I thought something was wrong with the baby, or that Tanner had broken up with her, or that Julie had been hurt in an accident. I knew that sort of thinking was more like Julie's than mine, but I couldn't help myself. Something traumatic had happened, and Shannon was sobbing so violently that she couldn't get the words out.

"Tell me," I said, sitting down next to her, grasping her hand. "What happened?"

She shook her head, nearly hyperventilating, tears flying from her cheeks. I thought I was going to start crying myself. Anything that could hurt my niece that badly was bound to hurt me, too.

Finally she caught her breath long enough to speak.

"I went home," she said, "to Mom's...to start packing and I heard this noise coming from her bedroom and I thought maybe Dad had come over and they were..." She shut her eyes. "You know, having sex. But it wasn't Dad." She looked at me. "It was that Ethan Chapman guy."

Relief washed over me, followed quickly by a joy I did not allow to show on my face. *All right, Julie!* I thought. *You go, girl!*

"And that's what has you so upset?" I asked.

"I'm *angry.*" She pulled her hand from mine to punch it into my sofa cushion. "I'm furious at her. She was a shitty wife to Dad and then she makes this like, totally major dinner for someone else and then actually has *sex* with him. She never appreciated Daddy, and it pisses me off to see her treating some other man like he's a god or something. Ethan Chapman, Ethan Chapman. She hasn't shut up about him since she saw that letter."

I hurt for Shannon. I knew the divorce had been hard on her—harder, I thought now, than any of us had realized. She loved both her parents—her hardworking, worrywart of a mother and her reserved and gentle father—and as much as the end of the marriage had been a surprise to Julie, it had been a far greater shock to Shannon. She'd cried for a month when Glen moved out, and I knew she'd blamed Julie then, just as she was blaming her now. Julie took on that blame rather than say anything that might tarnish Shannon's feelings about Glen. I was not feeling quite that noble.

"What has your father told you about why he and your mother got divorced?" I asked.

Shannon leaned back against the couch with a groan, looking at the ceiling.

"Not *this* again," she said. "I'm sick of talking about it, and it doesn't matter. He said he still loves her, but she was too wrapped up in her work. Mom never got it...that her marriage was more important than her stupid Granny Fran. If she'd figure that out, they could get back together. "

"Your dad said that?"

"Not exactly, but I think it's obvious," she said. "He never dates. I think he's just waiting for Mom to get her priorities straight and put her stupid career second instead of first all the time."

I was starting to get angry myself and had to work to keep my voice level. "Her stupid career bought you your car, your cello lessons, your summers at music camp, and is going to pay for your college," I said. "Or at least, it *was* going to pay for your college."

She rolled her eyes and looked at the ceiling again. She'd figured out whose side I was on.

"Listen to me, Shannon," I said. "I understand how much you love your parents and want them to get back together, but that's little-girl kind of wishful thinking. It's not going to happen. And although your mother may have spent more time working than was healthy for her marriage, that divorce was in no way her fault. Your mother loved your dad. Try to remember the things she *did* do for him. The surprise trip to France, because she knew how much he loves it there? How she canceled part of her book tour to nurse him through pneumonia that last year? How she stuck little love notes to him all over the house? And who did the cooking, even though she was working all day just like he was?"

Her face was turned away from me, but I saw her swallow hard.

"And she did all of that in addition to making a really beautiful home for him. Yes, she was busy with her work, but so was he. Your mother wasn't a bad wife." I steeled myself, knowing I was coming close to blowing her world apart. "The truth is," I said, "your father had a typical midlife crisis."

She turned her head to look at me then, frowning. "No, he didn't," she said.

"Yes, he did." I was emphatic. I wondered how much I should tell her. "Your mother has let you blame her for everything, but your father was the one who wanted to end the marriage. He wanted to—"

"Are you saying he cheated on her?" She was obviously prepared to argue that point with me. There was a deep furrow between her eyebrows.

I hesitated. "I think that he should be the one to talk to you about that, not me."

"I don't believe it." She folded her arms across her chest, on top of her ever-expanding belly.

"*Yes,* he had an affair," I said. "The woman he was seeing called your mom to fill her in. Do you know what that did to your mother? Do you care? Her heart was torn out. Imagine if someone you loved...imagine if you suddenly found out that Tanner, who you obviously trust and who is your friend, if you suddenly realized he was seeing someone else behind your back. Imagine that pain. Then multiply it by a thousand, because that's what it was like for your mother."

Shannon stared at me, stunned. For a moment, neither of us spoke.

"Why didn't she ever tell me that?" Her voice was quiet, a whisper.

"Why do you think?" I asked.

"So I wouldn't turn against Dad?"

"Of course."

She looked away from me, gnawing at her lower lip. "I can't believe Dad could do something like that," she said.

"He's human, Shannon. It doesn't make him evil." Glen would kill me. Julie might, too. "He was going through a screwed-up time and sometimes people think an affair will solve their problems. But the bottom line is that your mother is not in love with him anymore. She was hurt too badly and that trust is gone, and I think it became clear to both of them that they weren't right for each other any longer. The main thing they still have in common is that they love *you,* and they always will. Your mother's struggled the past couple of years, trying to learn how to be a single woman again when she'd expected to be married to your father for the rest of her life. Finally she's met someone who's both a friend and a...romantic interest. Let her have that, Shannon. She needs that companionship. Please don't be selfish."

The tears were back in her eyes again, but they were soft tears this time, just lying along the base of her thick lower lashes. "Do you think I'm selfish?" she asked.

I hesitated. "I think it's normal for someone your age to be wrapped up in herself," I said. "Which is why it's usually hard for a teenager to be good mother material. You're really going to have to work at it if you keep this baby."

She blinked, and one of the tears trailed slowly down her cheek.

"I told her I didn't want her to meet Tanner," she said.

"Well," I said as I brushed the tear away with my hand, "why don't you fix that?"

CHAPTER 33

Julie

Last night, two amazing things happened. While talking with Ethan on the phone, I complained about my writer's block and how Granny Fran's latest adventure was eluding me. He asked me to tell him about the story, and I found that as I described the problem I was having with Chapter Four, I began to get excited about writing the scene. It was a relief to talk about something unrelated to Isabel's death or Shannon's pregnancy for a change, and I was grateful to him for the inspiration. I knew I had to be cautious, though. Writing had always been my refuge, and I didn't want to use it as my escape any longer. I wanted to find a balance between my life and that of my characters. It was time for me to let reality in.

The second amazing thing was a phone call from Shannon in which she'd apologized for her reaction to discovering that I was seeing—and sleeping with—Ethan.

"It's okay with me if you want to date," she said. "I'm sorry I made a scene."

I wondered where her change of heart had come from but decided to enjoy it rather than analyze it.

"Thank you, hon," I said. "That means a lot to me."

"And I want you to meet Tanner when he gets here," she added.

"And I want to meet him," I managed to say.

We decided to have a barbecue at my house once Tanner arrived so that he could meet my mother and Lucy and me all at once.

"Would that make him uncomfortable, though?" I asked. "I mean, would he be overwhelmed having to meet so many people at one time?"

"No, Mom." A little of her usual testiness was back in her voice and I knew our truce was fragile. "He's very cool about social situations and stuff."

"Okay," I said, and then I ended the conversation, afraid that if I dragged it out too long, we could move into dangerous territory— such as her proposed move to Colorado—and lose the ground we were gaining.

So I felt good as I drove to Bay Head Shores to visit Ethan this morning. Since it was the middle of the day in the middle of the week, the Parkway was not clogged with traffic, but I wouldn't have cared one way or another. I would have made that drive to spend twenty minutes with him, if that's all the time either of us could spare.

Ethan had told me that his father would be visiting him, so I picked up sandwiches at the deli for the three of us, wondering what it would be like to see Mr. Chapman again after all these years and what safe topics we might find to talk about. The day was lovely, if too hot, and the smell of the sandwiches in the bag on the passenger seat was enticing. The only twinge of anxiety I felt was when I turned onto Shore Boulevard and spotted the canal between two of the houses on my right. It was an involuntary reaction, a little twisting of something in my gut, but it had nearly disappeared by the time I reached Ethan's house.

I saw a car behind Ethan's truck in his driveway and assumed it was his father's, so I parked in front of the house on the street. As I got out of my car, I noticed that a plump, dark-haired woman was sweeping sand from the stoop in front of my old bungalow. How many hundreds of times had I performed that same task on that same front step?

"Hi!" I called, waving with a bit too much enthusiasm.

She looked up and returned my wave, an uncertain smile on her face as she resumed her sweeping. She probably thought I was strange.

I started to knock on Ethan's front screen door, but I could see straight through the house to his backyard and spotted him and his father sitting near the fence, facing the canal. I went into the house, dropped the sandwiches on the tiger-maple counter in the kitchen and walked outside. They didn't see me as I approached and my eyes were drawn to the yard next door, where two little boys played noisily in the circular, above-ground pool under the shade of the oak tree. It bothered me that the mother was sweeping out front instead of in the yard watching them. Something could happen to them in a heartbeat.

"Hello!" I called as I neared the men.

Ethan stood when he saw me. Smiling, he moved forward, his hands on my arms as he planted a kiss on my cheek. "Good to see you," he said.

Mr. Chapman was getting to his feet. It appeared to be a struggle for him.

"Don't get up," I said, walking toward him. He was already standing, though, and he took the hand I offered in both of his, his smile warm and kind. His fingers trembled as he held my hand. He seemed so much older than my mother. I understood why Ethan had wanted to protect him from Ned's letter and the resulting investigation.

"Little Julie Bauer," Mr. Chapman said. "How good to see you. You've grown into a handsome woman. Hasn't she, Ethan?"

Ethan grinned at me. "Extremely handsome," he said. He dragged a chair through the sand and set it behind me. "Have a seat," he said.

"It's good to see you, too, Mr. Chapman," I said as I sat down, and the elderly man lowered himself once more onto his chair. "I was very sorry to hear about Ned," I added.

"Thank you," he said with a nod. He was wearing sunglasses in dated, horn-rimmed frames and I wondered how long he had owned them.

"How was the drive?" Ethan asked. He was still standing, leaning against the back of his chair, arms folded across his chest. He had on his jeans and a navy-blue polo shirt, *Chapman Joinery* stitched in red across the pocket. He looked terrific.

"No problem at all," I said. "I brought sandwiches and left them in the kitchen."

"Great," Ethan said. "You hungry, Dad?" He raised his voice a little when he spoke to his father, and I guessed the elderly man was hard-of-hearing.

"Sure." Mr. Chapman nodded.

"Shall I get them?" I started to stand up, but Ethan put his hand on my shoulder.

"Stay here with Dad," he said. He took our drink orders and left me alone with his father.

"Well, Julie." Mr. Chapman folded his hands across his belt buckle. He looked relaxed now that he was not having to exert himself physically. "You've made quite a name for yourself, haven't you?"

"Oh, a bit," I said, smiling. I shifted my chair a few inches in the sand, ostensibly so that I could see Mr. Chapman better, but I really wanted to keep an eye on the two unsupervised boys in the pool next door.

"I see your books at the library and always tell the librarian, 'I knew that author when she was just a little girl,'" he said.

"Thank you."

"I bet you don't know it, but I remember you the best of your siblings," he said.

"Really?" I was surprised. "How come?"

"Because you——" he pointed one long, slightly gnarled finger at me "——you had the most spunk of the three of you," he said.

"You think so?" I asked. I thought that Isabel had had the most spunk of the three of us, but I wasn't prepared to dive into the subject of my older sister.

"Oh, yes," he said. "And you were the smart one, too. You always had a book in your hands and you weren't afraid of anyone or anything. You went over there——" he waved his hand toward the opposite side of the canal "——with the blacks and befriended them. Who else would do something like that? No one living on this side of the canal, that's for sure," he said, answering his own rhetorical question.

"I got in a lot of trouble for it," I said. The boys next door were riding on a big, blow-up alligator, and they yelped with glee as they splashed water out of the pool with the wake they created.

"You tried to figure things out for yourself and I liked that about you," Mr. Chapman said. "I know that was hard to do in your family, but you weren't the sort to simply accept your parents' values without questioning them first."

I'd had no idea he had been observing me so keenly when I was a child, and although I couldn't help but enjoy the compliments, I knew my "spunk" had turned out to be more of a liability than an asset.

"My parents were very conservative," I said. I reached down to slide off my sandals, then dug my toes into the warm sand.

"Especially your father," Mr. Chapman agreed. "And you were willing to buck him, weren't you? You were a lot like your mother that way."

My mother never bucked my father, as far as I knew, but I didn't bother to say that. This conversation was social, and I didn't need to delve into my family's dynamics with him.

"I always forget that you and Mom were friends when you were kids," I said. The sun was hot on my arms. I'd put on sunscreen before leaving the house, but I would have to borrow more from Ethan if we sat out here much longer.

"Yes, we were good buddies, just like you and Ethan were," he said. "It's nice you two are back to being friends again." He looked out at the canal. Not a single boat had passed by us since I'd sat down. "I'd like to be friendly with your mother again," he said, "but she doesn't even want to talk to me."

I hesitated, not sure what to say. "You know, Mr. Chapman," I began, "it's just that anyone from those days reminds her of a very difficult time for our family." Well, there. We were into the subject now, and it was my own doing.

"Yes," he said. "I realize that. Have the police spoken with her yet?"

I shook my head. "I don't think so."

"It must be very hard for your family to have this opened up again," he said.

"Well, and yours, too," I said.

A fishing boat, loaded with men and gear, glided north through the water in front of us, probably headed for the inlet. We watched it in silence for a moment.

"Do you think Ned killed your sister?" Mr. Chapman asked, and I was taken aback by the directness of the question.

I looked toward my old yard again. The boys were quieter now, their heads bobbing below the edge of the pool where I couldn't see them, then popping up again. They were probably playing the "who can hold his breath the longest" game. I hated that game. I'd forbidden Shannon ever to play it, a rule I'm sure she broke many times when I was not around. What kid wouldn't?

"I don't know what to think, Mr. Chapman," I said. "I can't imagine what else he might have meant in that letter to the police."

He licked his dry, chapped lips. His face looked gaunt to me and I wondered if he were ill, although Ethan had denied that.

"I think Ned's letter may be one of those things we'll never be able to figure out," he said.

"Could Ned have slipped away during the time you said you and he were together that night?" I asked, trying not to sound accusatory.

Mr. Chapman looked disappointed that I'd asked the question and didn't respond. He licked his lips again, looking out at the water.

"I'm sorry," I apologized. "I'm just trying to puzzle it out."

"He was with me at midnight," he said. "That I know for certain. And that's when you said...it happened."

"Well, I was never completely sure of the exact time," I said.

"Ned was with me out here," Mr. Chapman said. "We were watching a meteor shower. And then he went to bed. It had to have been long after midnight by that time. Besides, what possible motive did he have? He adored your sister."

I couldn't tell him my suspicions about his son's relationship with Pamela Durant. I would have to trust that the truth would come out in time.

"I guess you're right," I said.

I was relieved to hear the screen door bang shut as Ethan walked into the yard, and I stood quickly to help him. He was balancing three full glasses, stacked plastic plates and the sandwiches on a tray. I handed Mr. Chapman his glass of cream soda.

"I remember how you used to zip around the canal in your little runabout," he said, as Ethan and I sat down and began to eat. "Back and forth, between here and the bay."

"That's as far as I was allowed to go," I said.

"I bet you grew into a hellion of a teenager," Mr. Chapman said. He did not seem to be hungry. He had not touched his sandwich.

"Well," I said, "I really didn't. After Isabel died, I became a lot more afraid of things."

Mr. Chapman looked saddened by that news. "That's a shame," he said.

"She won't even go in the boat," Ethan said.

"No?" Mr. Chapman inquired. "Oh, you should. I'm leaving after lunch and I think the two of you should take a ride. It's a beautiful day, not at all crowded on the water."

"How about it?" Ethan raised his eyebrows at me.

"No, thanks," I said. Next door, the boys climbed out of the pool and ran into the house, and I was relieved to be able to give up my self-imposed lifeguarding.

"You've got yourself labeled again, don't you?" Mr. Chapman said.

"What do you mean?" I asked.

"I mean, you used to call yourself 'the Nancy Drew Girl,'" he said. "'The Adventure Girl.' Now you're 'the Scared Girl.' You don't have to stay that way, you know."

"He has a point," Ethan said.

It was strange the effect Mr. Chapman's few simple words had on me. *You don't have to stay that way.*

"Maybe I'll go," I said, not quite ready to commit to the possibility but suddenly ready to consider it.

Mr. Chapman left right after lunch, and Ethan and I stood in the front yard, watching him drive away.

"You ready for that boat ride?" Ethan asked, putting his arm around me.

I made a face that clearly said *I don't think so.*

"How did you feel when you were a kid and went out in your boat?" he asked.

I thought about it for a minute. "Free," I said. "Until that last night. That changed everything."

He used his arm to turn me around and we headed through his side yard toward the dock. "That was 1962," he said. "It's a new century now. Come on."

I let myself be led to the edge of the dock. Ethan began to untie the boat from the hooks on the bulkhead. I watched, remembering how my runabout's damp, fibrous rope used to feel in my fingers. Grandpop had taught me many different knots. I bet I still remembered them all.

Ethan was on the other side of the dock. "Go ahead and hop in," he said. "I'll be right in after you."

I looked down at the boat's camel-colored interior. It swayed slightly on the wake of a motorboat that had just passed through the canal, and watching the seats move up and down made me light-headed. But I did it. I sat down on the bulkhead, caught the gunwale with my bare feet and slipped in. My heart was pounding as if I were standing on the edge of the Grand Canyon. I lowered myself quickly to the front passenger seat and clutched the side of the boat.

Ethan jumped into the boat with ease and took his seat behind the wheel. The smell of oil and gasoline mixed with the scent of the water. I used to like that smell. I breathed it in, wondering if I could learn to like it again.

"You okay?" Ethan smiled at me.

I nodded.

Putting the boat in Reverse, he backed into the canal, then took off in the direction of the river. I was quiet and anxious, one of my hands still holding on to the side of the boat as we approached the new—to me, anyway—Lovelandtown bridge. This bridge was higher than the old one and the pilings were much farther apart, so that we sailed beneath it with ease. We passed houses that were unfamiliar to me, having been built or remodeled since the last time I'd traveled the length of the canal, and I welcomed that unfamiliarity. We exited the canal and sped into the open water of the Manasquan River. The hot, damp air whipped my hair around my face and a spray of water cooled my eyes, and I found that those sensations brought back not the night I lost my sister, but rather the hours upon hours of fun I'd had in my little boat.

I studied Ethan's face as we cut across the surface of the water. In his profile, I could still see the boy who'd dissected crabs and kept eel guts in alcohol and lay on his stomach in the reeds, examining marine life in the shallows. Who could have guessed I would be here with him now, enjoying him, wanting him, *loving* him?

I swallowed hard, suddenly hoping that Ned would *not* be found responsible for Isabel's murder after all. It was going to hurt Ethan far too much.

He glanced over at me and smiled.

"You're lovin' this, aren't you," he said. It was not a question.

I moved closer to him, putting my arm across the back of the seat.

"I'm lovin' *you,*" I said into his ear, and I leaned my head against his shoulder.

CHAPTER 34

Julie

Two nights later, my mother, sister, Ethan and I gathered at my house for a barbecue, the main purpose of which was to meet Tanner Stroh. I'd told everyone to arrive at six. It was now six thirty-five, and Shannon and the guest of honor had not yet arrived. I felt wound up as the minutes ticked by. If someone touched me in the wrong spot, I was going to unravel.

I carried the bowl of potato salad from the kitchen out to the porch. My mother sat at the head of the long, glass-topped table, slicing a few of the beautiful Jersey tomatoes she'd plucked from her garden and arranging them on a platter next to lettuce leaves and pickle slices. Outside on the patio, Ethan, who was wearing a blue-and-white-striped apron he'd brought with him, turned chicken and burgers on the grill. Lucy stood near him, nursing a glass of beer and chatting. I could tell she liked him—she'd given me a barely concealed thumps-up sign the moment he walked in the door—and I was glad.

My mother had greeted Ethan warmly in spite of the fact that I knew she had not wanted me to nurture a relationship with him. She seemed her usual feisty self tonight, which relieved me after the somber way she'd reacted to the news of Ned's letter the other day.

"Do you think it's too warm to eat outside?" I asked her now. It had seemed cooler earlier, but I was probably in the midst of a hot flash.

"It's fine." She transferred the last tomato slice to the platter and set the knife on the cutting board. "What time did you tell Shannon to come?" she asked.

"Six," I said, lifting the cutting board and knife from the table.

"This young man of hers is going to make a poor impression, strolling in here late." She took a sip of beer from the glass in front of her. She always said she liked to drink a cold beer about once a year, and apparently tonight was the night. "I can't wait to grill him," she said. She actually rubbed her hands together, as if she was talking about devouring some choice morsel of food, and I had to laugh.

"Well, let's try not to be too obvious about it," I said over my shoulder as I carried the cutting board into the house.

I was back on the porch with the hamburger buns when I heard a couple of car doors slam out on the street.

"Maybe that's them now," I said, placing the plate of buns on the table.

I heard voices in the side yard, and then Shannon appeared on the patio holding the hand of a tall, slender man. Mom and I walked outside to greet them. Tanner Stroh looked freshly showered with short, neatly cut dark hair. He wore khaki Dockers and a short-sleeved Hawaiian shirt in a muted blue pattern. There was a preppy look about him that I knew would be a turnoff to Lucy but which offered me some small bit of reassurance.

He held his hand toward me. "Hi, Mrs. Sellers," he said. "I'm so glad to meet you. I'm sorry we're late."

"Not a problem," I said, shaking his hand. "I'm glad to meet you, too."

Until that moment, I hadn't realized that I'd been expecting him to have numerous body piercings, baggy pants and long greasy hair. He did *not* look like the artsy sort of guy Shannon was usually drawn to, but he was an attractive man nonetheless. Way too old for her, though. His hair was actually beginning to recede and I could see creases at the corners of his eyes.

Introductions were made all around, and I caught Shannon giving Ethan the same sort of scrutiny that I was giving Tanner, a fact which, I had to admit, made me smile. Everyone shook hands and uttered greetings in a respectful interchange. Tanner was cordial and courteous, and I thought of Eddie Haskell, the kid on *Leave it to Beaver* who hid his sociopathic tendencies behind impeccable manners.

The food was ready. Ethan brought the platter of burgers and grilled chicken onto the porch and Lucy and I took drink orders. Tanner wanted a beer; Shannon, lemonade. I would be sure to monitor Tanner's alcohol intake. I realized it would be more than three years until Shannon could legally join him in a drink. She hadn't even had her driver's license for a year yet.

Once we were all seated at the table on the porch, it was my mother who got right down to the nitty-gritty.

"So," she said, her attention squarely on Tanner. "How did you let this happen?"

Surprised, Tanner opened his mouth to speak, but Shannon rescued him. Even *I* felt ready to rescue him. My mother could sometimes lack tact.

"It was my fault, Nana," Shannon said. "I forgot a pill."

"It's not the best way to start out a future together, Mrs...." Tanner blanked on my mother's last name.

"Bauer," she said.

Tanner nodded. "Mrs. Bauer," he said. "But I love Shannon and we're going to do our best to have things work out."

"She's my only grandchild," my mother said, "so I'm going to hold you to that."

"I promise," Tanner said, looking uncomfortable for the first time since his arrival.

"Where are you from originally, Tanner?" Ethan tried to shift the conversation to something neutral.

"Southern California," Tanner said. "My family's still there."

"How do they feel about..." I waved my hand through the air, encompassing both him and Shannon. "About everything," I said.

He hesitated. "They're not happy about it," he said, and I respected his honesty, "but they'll accept Shannon. They'll love her once they meet her."

Where would he and Shannon spend their vacations? I wondered. With his family or with hers? East Coast or West? Would I ever get to see my daughter?

"Shannon said you're working on your doctorate," Lucy prompted him.

"Yes." Tanner added a second slice of tomato to his burger. "It's sort of my own independent study program. Part history, part social science."

"Have you started your dissertation?" Lucy asked.

He nodded. "It's on the children of Holocaust survivors meeting the children of Nazi perpetrators. I'm half German and half Jewish, so the subject had a natural fascination for me."

"Wow," Lucy said, with genuine interest. "How cool." She engaged him in one of the intellectual, academic discussions that she adored, and her enthusiasm was matched by Tanner's. Ethan added his own contribution; he'd recently seen something about the children of the Nazis on the History Channel, and my mother talked about a Holocaust survivor who was a regular customer at McDonald's. Shannon piped in from time to time, showing that she knew something about the topic herself and that their relationship was *not* just about sex. Why, oh why, couldn't he be a decade younger or Shannon a decade older? I would have felt so much better about the entire situation.

I seemed to be the only person at the table who could think of nothing to say about Tanner's dissertation. My mind was elsewhere, and when there was a long enough lull in the conversation, I spoke up.

"Tanner," I said, "I think Shannon really needs to stay here at least until the baby is delivered and she has her feet on the ground and gets into the routine of caring for—"

"*Mother.*" Shannon nearly stabbed me with her eyes. "We've already discussed this."

"I've got a doctor lined up for her, Mrs. Sellers," Tanner said, wiping his lips with his napkin. "I have some money put aside that will hold us until I'm out of school and teaching. We'll be okay. I know it's upsetting to you, and I was sort of upset, too, at first. I thought Shannon was a lot older when I met her. She looks older, she acts older. She's so intelligent and..." He looked at my daughter and smiled. "She's amazing."

Shannon smiled back, almost shyly. He was gaga over her, of that I was certain, but I didn't think he had a clue what he was getting himself into.

"Mom said your daughter got pregnant when she was my age, too," Shannon said to Ethan.

I winced, but Ethan seemed undaunted.

"She did," he said. "She was sixteen, and her baby was adopted by a wonderful couple who couldn't have kids."

"I don't think I could do that," Shannon said.

"Well, her situation was different." Ethan took a sip of his beer. "She didn't have a real relationship with the boy. She'd been out with him a couple of times and on this particular occasion, he forced himself on her."

"Date rape?" my mother asked, and I was surprised she even knew the term.

"Exactly," Ethan said. "Abby was afraid to tell us at first, but she did and we helped her press charges against the boy. He had to serve time and do some community service."

"At least we don't have that problem," Shannon said, for my benefit, I thought. *See?* she was saying. *Things could be worse.*

I liked what was happening. Not the topic of conversation, of course, but I liked the fact that we were sitting around like adults, talking. I liked that Shannon was, for the most part, not acting in an openly hostile way toward me. I knew now that I owed that to Lucy, that they'd been talking. I didn't know what Lucy had said to her, but I was grateful to her for saying it, whatever it was. I tried to look at Shannon in a new light, as an adult, but no matter how hard I tried, she still looked like a pregnant child to me.

The conversation continued through dessert, and only when we'd finished eating and everyone was helping me clear the table did I realize that my mother had grown very quiet. She hadn't said a word while we'd eaten our ice cream and cake.

I watched her as she stood at the counter, transferring the left-overs into plastic containers, and I leaned over to speak into her ear, "Are you okay, Mom?" I asked.

She nodded. "Beer makes me tired, though," she said. "I think I'll go home."

She'd walked the two blocks to my house. It was still fairly light out, but I didn't want her walking home alone if she wasn't feeling well. I studied her color, which was her usual healthy olive tone, pink-tinged by her time in her garden.

"Why don't you take a nap here and one of us will drive you home later?" I suggested.

"All right," she said, setting down the lid for the container she'd filled. I was surprised that she gave in to me without a fight.

"Bye, Nana!" Shannon, oblivious to the conversation, plowed between us to give her grandmother a hug. "We've got to go."

"Goodbye, darling," my mother said, hugging Shannon tightly and kissing her cheek.

We all said goodbye to the couple, Lucy the only one able to muster up a sincere hug for Tanner, and once they were gone, I turned to my mother again.

"You can use my room," I said. I was reminded of the other day when I'd told her about Ned's letter. She was behaving the same way now as she had then. "Do you want me to come with you?" I offered.

My mother didn't respond. She stood in the middle of the kitchen, shaking her head slowly back and forth. She was actually scaring me.

"Mom?" I said, with enough concern in my voice that Lucy and Ethan turned to look at us.

"Nobody said one word tonight about Shannon and her cello," my mother said. There were tears in her eyes. "As long as that girl's been able to speak, all she's ever cared about was music. And tonight it was like that part of her didn't exist." She pointed toward the door through which Shannon and Tanner had made their exit. "That boy cares about himself and his own...his Nazi children, or whatever they are," she said, waving a hand through the air. "I bet he's never even asked to hear her play."

Lucy tried to put an arm around her shoulders, but our mother brushed it away.

"I'm tired, Lucy," she said. "I'm going to take a nap. Then maybe later you could drive me home."

"Of course," Lucy said, dropping her arm to her side.

Ethan came to stand next to me, and we watched my mother disappear down the hallway.

"Whoa," Lucy said. "What's with her?"

I remembered Shannon as a little girl. She didn't want to listen to the funny little songs that other kids found entertaining. "I wanna hear YoMaMa!" she'd say, cracking Glen and me up.

"She's right," I said. "No one said a word."

CHAPTER 35

Maria
1944

Date Rape.

I knew many people my age ridiculed that term, believing it was a way of pinning the rap on a boy when a girl later had regrets, but I embraced the concept, because it eased my guilt about what happened toward the end of the summer of 1944.

That was the first summer that Charles spent his weekdays in our new home in Westfield while I remained at the bungalow with my parents. Charles was doing his residency at a veterans' hospital, choosing it over pediatrics because he was passionate about continuing to serve his country in whatever way he could. The war permeated every aspect of our lives, from the constant newscasts on the radio to the rationing that affected our food and our gasoline and nearly everything else we needed to exist.

I'd considered staying in Westfield with Charles, only going to the bungalow during the weekends as he did, but he insisted there was no point in my staying in the heat of the suburbs when he would be able to spend so little time with me there. His hours were long and grueling, but he loved what he was doing and the contribution he was making. I was very proud of him, yet I missed him during the week. I missed sleeping next to his warm body and our long, happy conversations about the future. We'd talk about the children we would have and all the things we wanted to be able to provide for them. And we made love, though not as much as I would have liked. I knew he was tired, but I often wondered if I simply had a stronger sex drive than most women. My friends and I never talked about that sort of thing, so I was not sure if I was normal.

My parents had developed a thriving social life as more people who were tolerant of my mother's heritage moved to Bay Head Shores, so they were often out having fun, and my old girlfriends were either working or busy with new babies. Many of their husbands were enlisted men, some of them fighting in Europe. I knew I was lucky that *my* husband was safe on American soil. But without Charles or my friends around, I was lonely, and loneliness could be a dangerous thing. In the fall, I would begin my second year as a teacher, but that summer was nothing but one lazy day after another. I read a great deal and thought about Charles and had far too much idle time on my hands.

One weekday night when my parents were out, I was on the porch reading *A Bell for Adano* when I spotted Ross sitting alone on the bulkhead in his backyard. Dusk was quickly falling, and I could see the burning tip of his cigar. He'd flick the ashes into the canal from time to time, and I felt mesmerized by the red glow arcing through the darkness.

I watched him smoke for the longest time, my book forgotten. I imagined how his mouth would taste—like wood and leather—and then, as if on automatic pilot, I stood up from the rocker and walked outside. I let the screen door slam behind me so he would not be surprised when I appeared in my own yard.

I walked toward the canal and sat down on the bulkhead, bending my legs and wrapping my arms around them. The water was as smooth as gelatin, and the reflection of the nearly full moon was a brilliant white disk floating on its surface. I was perhaps four yards away from Ross, and although he had put out the cigar, the scent of it was still strong in the air.

"Beautiful night," I said, turning to look at him. I could see him more clearly than I'd expected, the moon was so bright. His eyes were on me, his hand rubbing his jaw lightly as if he were deep in thought.

"It is," he agreed.

"How come you're able to be here during the workweek?" I asked.

"I took the summer off from law school to be with Joan and the baby," he said.

I turned to look back at their darkened bungalow. "Where are they tonight?"

"Joan has some friends in Brielle," he said. "She took Ned over there for a visit."

"Ah," I said. He, too, was alone.

"I imagine it's hard not having Charles here during the week," Ross said.

"Yes," I said. "But it could be worse. He could be overseas." I thought of how, without Charles at the bungalow, I felt like the single girl I used to be, ready to go to Jenkinson's at night with my gang of friends or to the movies with a date.

Ross stood up and stretched, and for a moment, I feared he was going to go into his house. But he walked toward me and my head felt light as he sat down next to me, letting his legs hang over the bulkhead.

"I'm glad you found someone like Charles, Maria," he said. "His politics are screwy, but he'll be able to lift you up. Your social status, I mean. The wife of a doctor."

"That was not why I married him," I said.

"No, of course not," Ross said. "But that's a nice bonus for you."

"I really don't care about that sort of 'bonus,'" I said.

He smiled. "You're still a feisty one, aren't you." He lifted his hand to my chin, turning my head toward him. "I've missed you," he said. "Not just...you know, the physical part of our relationship. I've missed *you*. All of you. The friendship we used to share."

I wasn't certain how to answer. Did I miss him? Yes, I did, but it *was* the physical part of our relationship I missed. Charles met my needs for adult conversation and companionship, but there was a puritanical quality to his infrequent lovemaking that left me wanting more. I longed for the stolen, impassioned sex Ross and I used to enjoy in the blueberry lot.

"I miss..." I gently pushed his hand away. "I miss things I have no right to miss," I said.

Ross glanced toward my house. "Where are your parents?" he asked.

"Out," I said.

He stood up and held out his hand. "Come with me," he said.

I stood up, not stopping to think, and took his hand, which was smoother than Charles's, the skin softer, cooler. I had almost forgotten the feel of it. We walked through my small yard, then along the path between our two houses and past the bedroom window through which I used to escape to meet him. We continued down my short, packed-sand driveway and only then did I admit to myself where we were headed. I felt the cool orange dirt beneath my feet as we crossed the narrow road, and then we were on the white, moonlit sand of the blueberry lot.

"We shouldn't do this, Ross," I said.

He didn't reply, and I didn't let go of his hand. I could feel my heartbeat—or perhaps I was feeling his—where our hands were pressed together. The delicious sense of doing something forbidden and daring propelled us, as it always had, and soon he was pulling me down inside the half circle of blueberry bushes. He plucked a few of the berries from one of the bushes and held them to my lips. I took them in, rolling them around in my mouth before biting into them. I would never again be able to taste blueberries without feeling the rising tide of guilty pleasure.

He lay me back in the sand, then leaned over to kiss me. Briefly I thought of Charles, of how the feral hunger I felt in my body at that moment was something he had never experienced from me. I returned Ross's kisses as I unbuttoned his shirt. He took off my blouse, my shorts, my bra, my panties, leaving me nude and aching with desire for him. I felt the moonlight reflect off my skin as he sat back on his heels to look at me.

"I've missed your beautiful body," he said. He leaned over to run his tongue across my nipple. "Joan has a boy's body," he said. "Even when she was pregnant, she had no breasts to speak of."

The words were his mistake. At the mention of Joan, my body went cold. I could not do this to her. I could not do it to Charles.

Ross pressed his thigh between my legs to spread them apart, and I gripped his thigh with mine to stop him.

"Let's not do this, Ross," I said.

"Don't be crazy," he said. Somehow, he'd managed to get both his legs between mine. I felt the pressure of his penis against my pubic bone.

"Ross, I mean it," I said, trying to squirm out from beneath him. "I don't want to do this."

He drew back slightly, letting his penis find its mark. No matter how desperately I wanted to keep him from entering my body, the earlier hunger I'd felt had left me wet and vulnerable, and he slipped inside me effortlessly. Furious, I pushed down on his shoulders. I bit his collarbone and dug my fingernails into his back. My attempts to stop him only seemed to increase his ardor, and he thrusted harder and deeper, his breath ragged in my ear. I started to cry, my body going limp, my own breath coming out in small gasps.

"*Please,* Ross," I begged. *"Please stop."*

He finished quickly, and for that much I was grateful. He pulled out of me, then rolled onto his back, and I sprang to my knees as I searched the sand for my underwear.

He caught my arm as I picked up my bra. "What are you doing?" he asked. "Don't get dressed yet."

I stared down at him, incredulous. "I told you to *stop,*" I said.

"I didn't think you meant it," he said.

I swatted his chest with my bra. "I *did* mean it. You forced yourself on me."

"Maria," he said. "Come on. You were an animal. Just like you used to be."

"I was trying to fight you *off.*" My voice broke.

"If you really wanted to fight me off, you could have."

"You're a thousand times stronger than I am," I said.

"I don't remember any objections when I kissed you," he said. "Or when I undressed you."

He was right, and I was so filled with shame that I wished I could rewind the night back to the moment I spotted him from my porch. I would have chosen differently if I'd taken two seconds to think about Charles and Joan—and the little baby, Ned.

I put on my brassiere while he watched.

"Let me do that for you," he said, when I struggled with the hooks.

I stood up, nearly leaping away from him as I tossed my blouse on over my unfastened bra.

"Are you really upset?" He sounded perplexed.

"Yes!" I said. "I'm *extremely* upset."

I pulled on my shorts; I could not find my panties.

"I'm sorry," he said, sitting up. He reached for my ankle and missed. "I'm very sorry, Maria," he said. "Honestly."

I ran through the lot, kicking sand behind me, and I didn't stop until I was in the bungalow. I sobbed as I heated water on the stove to bathe in. I wanted to clean any trace of Ross Chapman from my body. I changed into my robe, shook the sand out of my hair, then stood barefoot in the kitchen watching the water slowly warm up. I felt crazy. Insane. And I repeated over and over again, *"I'm sorry, Charles, I'm sorry, Charles."*

I never really got over that night or forgave myself for it. Even at eighty-one years of age and with the knowledge that what happened could well be considered date rape, I would sometimes still wake myself up in the middle of the night, chanting that phrase of apology and guilt.

CHAPTER 36

Julie
1962

I knew the day everything went wrong. It was August fifth, a Sunday. It was also the day Marilyn Monroe died.

That morning after church, all of us except Isabel took our seats at the porch table, ready to dig in to our usual hearty Sunday breakfast.

"Isabel?" My mother leaned back from her chair so she could see into the living room. We would not be allowed to start in on the eggs and bacon and rolls and crumb cake until my older sister was at the table and grace had been said.

We heard Isabel's bare feet skitter across the linoleum in the living room. She zipped onto the porch and sat down in the chair next to me.

"Marilyn Monroe is dead," she announced, just as we all reached for one another's hands to say grace.

"What?" My mother took Lucy's hand in hers. "What are you talking about?"

"I just heard it on the radio," Isabel said. "She killed herself."

"Oh, what a shame," my grandmother said.

My father made a sound of disgust. "It figures that she would die committing a sin, since that's the way she lived," he said.

"How did she kill herself?" I asked, curious.

"I don't want to hear about it!" Lucy plastered her hands over her ears and hummed loudly as my sister started to answer.

"Not now, Isabel," Grandma said. "Lucy doesn't want to hear it."

I knew little about Marilyn Monroe, only that she was blond and beautiful and extremely sexy. Men swooned over her and women envied her. Why would someone like that kill herself?

"Let's say grace," my father said, reaching for my hand on one side of him and my grandmother's on the other. We bowed our heads, reciting the words by rote, and then settled down for some serious eating. My father was the chef on Sunday mornings and his scrambled eggs were always doctored with onions and peppers and tomatoes. Sunday breakfasts were one of my favorite times with my family.

"Tonight," Grandma said as she cut her eggs with the side of her fork, "Grandpop and I want to take you girls to the boardwalk."

I whooped with joy, but I wasn't surprised when Izzy begged out.

"Thanks, Gram," she said, "but I already have plans."

"Will you come, too, Mom?" Lucy asked.

My mother poured herself a second cup of coffee. "No, honey," she said. "I'll stay home and catch up on housework." It would be years before I realized how much my mother probably welcomed an occasional respite from having us all underfoot.

It wasn't until halfway through the meal that the topic of Marilyn Monroe's suicide came up again.

"Girls," my father said, "there's a lesson in Marilyn Monroe's death."

"*Daddy.*" Lucy set down her juice glass and looked at him indignantly. "We're not supposed to talk about it now."

"You're not too young to know these things," he said to her. He looked at me, then at Isabel. "She lived in sin in many, many ways. Not only didn't she care about how she was hurting God, she didn't care about how she hurt other people, either."

"I don't think she was *that* bad, Charles," Grandpop said as he buttered his second hard roll.

"Look at the facts," Daddy said. "She had affairs with married men. Many of them. She broke up marriages. She posed...without clothes on for calendars and magazines."

"They found her nude," Isabel added, and my father shook his head, as if to say *See what I mean?*

"Probably the worst thing she did was have abortions," he said. "Several of them."

I cringed. I'd been taught so well by my father. How could any woman take the life of her unborn child?

"What's an abortion?" Lucy asked.

"You don't need to know that." My mother sent my father a look of exasperation above Lucy's head.

"And many people believe that she's been having an affair with President Kennedy," my father added.

"Oh, that's ridiculous," my grandmother said. "You're filling these girls' heads with rumors."

"I believe it's true," Daddy said, tapping his fingertips on the rim of his coffee cup. "I'm sorry to say it, but I believe Jack Kennedy's capable of breaking his marriage vows, and Marilyn Monroe was certainly capable of tempting him to do so. Nothing good could come of the sort of behavior she was known for."

I thought of my impure thoughts, reassuring myself that they were mild in comparison to the things Marilyn Monroe had done.

"I heard about a girl who cheated on her husband." Isabel had one elbow on the table, her hand holding a piece of crisp bacon that she waved a little in the air as she spoke. "She went off on a vacation with her boyfriend and they were in a helicopter and when they got out of the helicopter, the propeller was spinning around and it cut off her head."

"Oh, Isabel!" my mother said.

"I am *not* listening to another disgusting word!" Lucy got up, lifted her plate from the table and carried it into the house.

But Isabel, as usual, had won my father's affection. He looked across the table at her, nodding.

"Exactly," he said.

My father was so blind. I wished I had the guts to tell him that Isabel and Ned met on the platform in the bay every night. My attempts to push Bruno and Isabel together had failed so far, and on those nights when I snuck out on the boat, there they were—Isabel and Ned, hugging and kissing...and much, much more.

My father left for Westfield later that afternoon and I saw that Wanda and her family were still on the other side of the canal. They usually fished only in the morning, but the weather was cool and I guessed they had simply decided to make a day of it. I thought I would join them.

I got my fishing gear from the garage, then walked around the side of the house to grab a dry towel from the clothesline. Isabel's wonderful giraffe towel hung there among the plain old beach towels. I assumed that Izzy was already at the beach, so as long as I returned the towel to the line before she got home, she would never know that I'd borrowed it. I tossed the towel over my arm, then headed around the house to the backyard.

My fishing line had snapped the last time I'd used it, so I sat on one of the Adirondack chairs to repair it. Next door, Ned, Ethan and Mr. Chapman were in their boat in the dock. I could see the tops of their heads and I could hear conversation, some of it heated, but I could not make out the words.

Suddenly Mr. Chapman's voice rose. "I said *no!*" he shouted.

Ned yelled something back at him, his words unintelligible.

"Go in the house, Ethan," Mr. Chapman said, and I guessed that Ethan was either being punished for something or—more likely, from the sound of it—the conversation was not meant for his ears. I buried my head close to the fishing line, pretending to be engrossed in my task in case one of them glanced in my direction, but I was actually straining to hear what was being said.

Once the door to the Chapmans' porch had slammed shut behind Ethan, Mr. Chapman spoke up again. "You're not going to see her tonight," he said.

Curiosity and hope welled up in me. If *I* couldn't break Ned and Isabel up, maybe Mr. Chapman could. My nose was so close to the fishing line that I could smell the briny scent emanating from it.

"If you've known all this time," Ned said, "why are you cracking down all of a sudden?"

Mr. Chapman lowered his voice, and although I leaned my head a few inches closer to their yard and pushed my hair behind my ear, I could not hear what he said. Their conversation lasted only a few more minutes before Mr. Chapman went into the house. I felt sorry for Ned. I knew what it was like to be chewed out and how powerless and angry it could leave you feeling.

I had long since finished working on my fishing line, so with the excitement over next door, I carried my pole and bucket and the giraffe towel to my own dock. I descended the ladder and was about to jump into the runabout when I heard Ned softly call my name. I peered over the bulkhead to see him walking toward me, and I dropped everything into the boat and rushed up the ladder to the sand.

I started to call hello to him, but he put his finger to his lips.

I nodded. *I understand,* I was saying to him. He didn't want his father to hear.

He waited until he was right next to me before he spoke again, his voice very low. "Is Izzy home?" he whispered. He glanced toward his house as though afraid his father might be watching him. I could just about smell the fear on him.

"No," I said. I looked at his hands expecting to see the toy giraffe, but he didn't have it with him. "She's gone to the beach with Mitzi and Pam, I think." I watched his face to see if the mention of Pam sparked any reaction in him, but he barely seemed to notice. I was one-hundred-percent certain George had either mistaken someone else for Ned that day in the river or else he'd just been teasing me.

"I was wondering if you'd give her a message for me?" Ned asked.

"Sure." *I would do anything for you,* I thought. It was great that he was talking to me on a Sunday. My hair always looked pretty and wavy on Sundays because I washed it and set it for church. I wondered if he noticed how good it looked. I tossed it over my shoulder as we talked, hoping the gesture was as sexy as I thought it was.

"Tell her I can't see her tonight, okay?" he asked.

I nodded. I felt so adult. So proud to be trusted with their secrets. "Don't worry," I reassured him. "I'll tell her."

"Thanks." He reached toward my head and I gritted my teeth, expecting him to tousle my hair as if I were a kid, but instead, he rested his hand on the back of my head and looked into my eyes. "You're the most, Jules," he said.

I wanted to stand on my tiptoes and kiss him. It would have been easy. He was so close, so handsome. But I kept my bare heels glued to the sand and simply smiled at him, acknowledging the compliment. Then I headed for the ladder once again.

I was still elated by the thrill of his touch a short time later, as I cast my line into the water from the other side of the canal. I'd hung Isabel's towel over the fence in front of me so that the giraffe was watching us with his big, long-lashed eyes. Wanda loved the towel so much that I wished I could give it to her.

"You ever seen one of them for real?" she asked me, pointing to the giraffe.

"Sure," I said. "At the zoo in New York. Haven't you?"

"Uh-uh," she said, and as we started fishing, I began hatching a new plan. I could save some money and take Wanda—and maybe George, if he was nice to me—on the train to New York and we could spend the whole day at the zoo. If Wanda had never seen a giraffe, she'd probably never seen an elephant or a rhinoceros or any other wild animals. It would be so much fun to introduce her to that whole new world. I was trying to figure out how I could get away from the house for an entire day when George interrupted my thinking.

"So," he said as he baited his hook, "why's your big sister's boyfriend talkin' to a raggedy little child like you?"

I guessed he had seen Ned and me talking in my yard.

"He happens to think I'm the most," I said, my nose in the air.

"The most *what?*" he asked, laughing.

I ignored him. "What if someday soon, the three of us go to the zoo in New York?" I suggested.

"How you gonna get your daddy to let you do that?" Wanda asked, and George shook his head.

"You two on your own," he said. "I ain't gonna get my ass caught taking some white girl across the state line."

Our banter went on that way for nearly an hour, with me plotting our trip and the two of them telling me why it wouldn't work. Salena and the men were a distance away from us, and I could hear them singing along with the songs on the colored radio station they listened to. Nothing was biting, but none of us minded.

The canal provided plenty of entertainment with the Sunday swarm of boats in all shapes and sizes. A few of the taller ones rocked in place in front of us as they waited for the bridge to open and let them through. More and more of the larger vessels clogged the canal, and finally, the bridge began making its familiar clanking sound as the roadway above the water slowly swung open. I wasn't used to seeing the bridge from that side of the canal, and I was watching in fascination when a speedboat pulled up alongside the bulkhead right in front of me.

"Hi, Julie!"

I looked down, surprised to see Bruno Walker sitting below me in his boat.

"Hi, Bruno," I said. His nearly black ducktail was a bit windblown which made him look even sexier than usual, and he wasn't wearing a shirt. You could see every bulging muscle outlined beneath his tan skin. Even lifting his cigarette to his mouth was enough to turn his arm into a brawny network of hills and valleys.

"What are you doing over here?" He looked at Wanda, then George, then back at me again. He wasn't wearing sunglasses and he could barely mask the surprise in his eyes at finding me fishing with colored people.

"Fishing," I said, not answering the question he was really asking. "These are my friends, Wanda and George. That's Bruno," I said, nodding toward him.

Wanda and George said nothing. They knew my world did not mesh well with theirs.

"I wanted to ask you something," Bruno said. His boat bobbed on the wake of a passing ship, but he held it steady in front of us. "Are you and Isabel real close?"

I shrugged. "Sort of," I said. "Why?"

"How serious do you think she is about Ned?"

Although the boat ride I'd arranged for my sister, Ned and Bruno didn't seem to have sparked the triangle I'd been hoping for, I could see another possibility opening up in front of me. "I think she's losing interest in him," I said.

"You don't say." He barely moved his lips when he spoke, like the words weren't very important to him. But I knew that was just his style, and I grew bolder.

"You should talk to her about it," I suggested.

"I don't know," he said. "I don't think I'm her type."

"Well, maybe she hasn't really figured out her type yet." I sounded like Dear Abby, giving advice to the lovelorn.

"It's hard to get to talk to her, though," he said. "I hardly ever see her without Ned or one of her girlfriends around." He was playing right into my hands.

"I know how you can talk to her alone," I said.

"How?"

"Sometimes around midnight, she swims out to the platform in the bay and just sits there, thinking," I said. "She likes that alone time, you know? Just to think about things." Isabel actually hated being alone. I was really talking about myself, how I relished my time in the runabout on the bay at night. But it didn't matter. This conversation was not about the truth.

"That's weird," he said. I doubted Bruno was the type to appreciate moments of quiet introspection, either. He and Izzy would be perfect for each other.

"She just likes to be alone sometimes," I repeated with a shrug. "You could find her there tonight. Then you'd be able to talk to her without anybody else around."

"I don't know," he said. "Ned's a good buddy." He looked toward the open Lovelandtown bridge, the sun in his gorgeous green eyes as he gnawed his lower lip. It was funny to see such a powerful guy look so unsure of himself. "It's a neat idea, though," he said, nodding as the plan grew on him. "She goes almost every night, you said?"

"Uh-huh. And I'm sure she'll be there tonight."

"Why are you so sure?" he asked.

"It's Sunday night," I said. "Dad goes home to Westfield on Sunday, so she always feels a little freer. You know, like she won't get caught."

"Well, thanks, Julie," he said. "You're okay."

"You're welcome," I said.

He looked behind him to see if it was safe to pull away from the bulkhead, then waved as he took off, heading toward the bridge. When the sound of Bruno's boat could no longer be distinguished from all the other sounds on the canal, George turned to look at me.

"You up to no good, girl," he said.

I never gave Isabel the message from Ned. Lucy and I went to the boardwalk with our grandparents that evening, and Izzy went out with some of her girlfriends. I knew that she would eventually leave them to meet Ned on the platform. Her curfew was eleven-thirty, but I doubted she'd bother coming home first, because she knew Mom would be asleep by then. I was excited about my plan and it was all I could think about as I rode the merry-go-round and Tilt-A-Whirl and ate the cotton candy Grandpop bought us. I thought I was so clever.

After we got home from the boardwalk, I went upstairs with Lucy to wait for her to fall asleep. I lay on my own bed, rereading *The Clue in the Jewel Box* behind the curtain, but I couldn't read more than a sentence before my mind turned to Isabel and what might happen at midnight. I hoped Bruno would come on a little smoother than he usually did. I pictured him pulling the boat up to the platform, saying, "Isabel, is that you?" as though he was surprised to see her. I hoped he *would* act surprised and not say something stupid like, "Julie told me I'd find you here." God, if he did that, I'd kill him.

Then I imagined that Isabel would look over her shoulder toward the beach, wondering why Ned hadn't yet arrived. Maybe it would make her nervous to have Bruno there as she waited. It probably would, because she wouldn't want Ned to catch her with another boy. Maybe she and Bruno would talk for a few minutes, though, and she'd begin to relax. She'd realize that, for some reason, Ned wasn't coming. Something had gone wrong with their usual arrangements. And maybe she would look at Bruno in a different way. There was only a little sliver of a moon out tonight, so it was unlikely she'd be able to see his pretty green eyes, but maybe she'd still be attracted to him. My fantasy did not go so far as to have her invite him onto the platform, but at least they would start talking. At least she would begin to compare him to Ned and, with any luck at all, find Ned lacking.

Lucy fell asleep quickly, as she often did when I was present, and I piled up the bedspread beneath the covers. Then I padded quietly across the attic floor and down the rickety steps.

Grandpop was already in bed—I could hear him snoring as I passed through the living room—and I joined my mother and grandmother on the porch for a game of canasta. I could not concentrate on the cards any better than I'd been able to on my reading.

"What's wrong with you tonight?" my mother said, after I dealt twelve cards to each of us instead of eleven. It was the third or fourth mistake I'd made.

"I'm tired, I guess," I said.

Grandma pressed her palm against my forehead.

"I'm not sick," I said with a laugh.

"The two of you make a fine pair," Grandma said, shaking her head. "Julie's tired and Maria can hardly see."

My mother's eyes were red and teary. She'd told us that she'd shaken out a beach blanket before washing it and sand had blown in her face.

"I can see just fine," she said. She sounded a little annoyed.

Grandma returned her attention to her cards. "I bumped into Libby Wilson at church this morning," she said.

"Yes, I saw you talking to her." My mother drew a card from the stock. "How's she doing?"

"Oh, who knows," Grandma said. "You never hear about how Libby's doing from Libby. You just hear about everybody else's problems, never her own." She was talking fast, and I loved how cute and hard to follow her Italian accent could be when she was on a roll.

"What did you learn about everybody else's problems?" Mom asked. She placed a four of spades onto the discard pile, then pressed a tissue to the corner of her red and watery left eye.

"Betty Sanders is sick again," Grandma said.

"Oh, dear," my mother said. "This is what? The third time. Do they think it's…?" She let her voice trail off. People didn't mention cancer in those days, as though speaking the word aloud might cause you to catch it.

I was trying to see my mother's watch. It looked like it was around ten thirty-five, but I couldn't be sure.

"Probably," My grandmother placed four queens on the table in front of her. "But no one's saying. They took all her female parts this time."

"Ugh," I said, my big contribution to the conversation. My mind was elsewhere and I didn't know who Betty Sanders was, anyway.

"I'll send her a card," Mom said.

"Libby said that, last fall, Madge's boy got arrested and you'll never guess why," Grandma said.

"Why?" my mother asked.

"Rape." Grandma whispered the word.

"Oh, my goodness," my mother said. "Is he in jail?"

"They couldn't pin it on him because the girl was a tramp," Grandma said. Then she nudged me with her elbow. "It's your turn, Julie."

"I think that's terrible," my mother said, as I drew a card from the stock. "Rape is rape, whether the girl is a tramp or not."

I liked that they were talking about something to do with sex in front of me. I felt like I had crossed some kind of threshold when I got my period and was no longer considered a child in their eyes. I knew rape meant sex forced on a woman, but I couldn't understand how that could happen. How did a man do that? How did he pry a woman's legs open? Imagining sex—even mutually desired sex—was so hard for me. I remembered trying to force that tampon inside my-self. It had been impossible. If sex was so difficult to accomplish to begin with, then how could rape occur?

"Well, she *did* have a reputation," Grandma was saying. "Libby said Madge was furious that anyone would think her son would do some-thing like that."

My mother laughed. "And the last thing anyone wants to see is Madge Walker furious," she said. "Remember the time her husband accidentally spilled a drink on her at the clubhouse?"

It took a moment for the name to sink into my distracted mind. Madge *Walker.*

"What's her son's name?" I asked.

"I don't know," Grandma said. "But she only has one."

Oh, my God, I thought. How many Walker families could there be in our tiny community?

"Bruce," my mother said. She looked at Grandma. "That's it, isn't it? Bruce?"

"Maybe," Grandma said with a shrug.

My heartbeat kicked into high gear and I stared at my mother's face. She was concentrating on her cards, not making the connection between the Bruce Walker who was a possible rapist, and Bruno, the boy who hung around with Isabel's crowd of friends. Mom had even allowed Isabel to go for a boat ride with Ned because Bruno was with them!

And now I'd sent him out to visit my sister, who would be alone with him, in the dark.

"So the police decided he really didn't rape that girl, right?" I asked as I discarded a seven of clubs. I didn't care what card I got rid of.

"The girl was...loose," my grandmother said, "so they couldn't prove it one way or another. Even though she had bruises. That's why you always have to keep your reputation clean." She wagged a finger at me.

"Well, even if it wasn't actually rape—" my mother pressed a tissue to her eyes again "—he's doing things he shouldn't be doing."

"It was rape," my grandmother said. "Libby was sure of it."

My grandmother and mother continued talking about the neighborhood gossip, while my mind drifted even farther away. I remembered how unsure of himself Bruno had looked on his boat that afternoon when I suggested he talk to Isabel. He'd seemed intimidated and vulnerable. A rapist wouldn't look so unsure of himself, I thought. He had to be innocent. The girl probably lied just to get him in trouble. But when I went to bed for real at around eleven o'clock, I couldn't sleep. Was there a chance I had set Isabel up to be harmed? Was she still at one of her girlfriends' houses? Should I sneak out and try to find her? I wished I could use the phone, but it was on the living-room wall, too close to my parents' bedroom.

I moved over to the other bed in my curtained cubicle so that I could peer through the window. It was as dark as dark could get; I could barely make out the canal. The water and the woods and the sky were all the same shade of navy-blue. I sat there, listening to the crickets in the woods next door, feeling my options slip away from me as the minutes passed. I suddenly remembered Bruno talking about Isabel in Ned's car, using his hands in a wordless allusion to my sister's breasts. *Oh, God.*

It would be all right, I told myself. Maybe Bruno wouldn't even show up. Then Isabel would come home, angry with Ned. That would be good. Maybe that would be an even better outcome for me—until Ned told her he'd entrusted me with the message that he would not be able to meet her. I hadn't thought about that, about how annoyed Ned would be with me when I said I'd forgotten to give her his message. That would probably mess up any tiny chance I'd had with him to begin with.

The word *rape* kept slipping back into my mind. Was Bruno really a rapist? I thought of the girl who'd accused him. *She had bruises,* Grandma had said.

I got off the bed, unable to stand it anymore. The clock on my night table read eleven forty-five. I'd spent too much time thinking and not enough time acting. I was going to the beach. I quietly descended the pull-down stairs, thinking that if the current was moving in the direction of the bay, I would take the boat. If not, I would run to the beach. I wished I could take my bike, but it was in the garage and if I opened the garage door, I would wake up everyone in the house.

I should get Ned, I thought as I walked onto our porch. I should admit to him what I'd done and have him go with me. This was important enough, serious enough, for me to come clean with him.

I quietly left my house, then raced across the sand to the Chapmans' back door. I lifted my hand to knock, but hesitated. The Chapmans' house was dark, not a light on. I just couldn't do it. I couldn't knock on the door, wake up his parents, and have to explain my stupid scheme to all of them. Certainly they would get my own parents involved and that would just waste time. I turned around, and although the night was very dark, I could see the outline of their Adirondack chairs, four in a row, as I ran back to my own yard and our dock.

The current was lazy, probably on its way to slack tide, but it was still pulling in the direction of the bay, and the water sparkled with phosphorescent jellyfish. I'd seen that glittery display of light before, but not yet this summer, and I decided it was a good sign, for no reason other than that I needed to think positively about what lay ahead. I untethered the boat and climbed down the ladder, then used the oars to push out of the dock.

The current caught the runabout and carried it slowly toward the open water of the bay. I sat near the motor, clutching the tiller handle to keep from being pulled against the bulkhead. How much time had passed since I'd checked the clock? Five minutes? Ten? The second I hit the end of the canal, I would start the motor and head toward the platform. Bruno probably wouldn't be there yet if it was not quite midnight, and I would tell Isabel that I'd forgotten to give her Ned's message. She'd get in the boat. I'd bring her home. And what if Bruno was already there? I'd make up something on the spot. Anything. I just wouldn't let her stay there alone with him.

"Come on. Come on." I urged the boat as it neared the bay. I was certainly far enough from the house to start the motor now. I pulled on the cord but received only a sputtering reply. I yanked again. And again. The motor was behaving as it had the day I took Wanda and George to the river, only this time I didn't have George to get it started for me. I drifted into the bay as I fought with the motor. A slim finger of panic ran up my spine as the dark expanse of water surrounded me, and an unexpectedly stiff breeze pushed me away from the beach that was my destination. I *had* to get the boat started. I yanked several more times, my arm aching with the effort, my fingers burning, probably blistered. For a moment, I stopped pulling the cord. I looked in the direction of our beach, trying to see the platform. Without the sound of my sputtering motor, the air was quiet, blowing lightly and steadily into my face. And then I heard it: a scream.

I stood up, nearly toppling overboard, spinning my arms to stay upright. "Isabel!" I called, but I felt the breeze steal the words from my mouth and carry them behind me.

One more scream cut through the air, this time forming a word: *"Help!"* It was Isabel's voice. I was sure of it.

I cupped my hands around my mouth. "Izzy!" I shouted. "Izzy!"

I dropped to my knees in the boat again, tugging with all my might at the cord to the motor. I was barely aware that I was sobbing—sobbing, shouting, calling for my sister—and all the while fighting with a boat that carried me deeper and deeper into Barnegat Bay.

CHAPTER 37

Lucy
1962

The moment I woke up in the attic, I knew I was alone. The reading light was on in Julie's curtained bedroom, but the silhouette in her bed was a bulbous mountain that could not possibly have been her body unless she'd gained fifty pounds since the evening before. The windows were all open, the night sounds of crickets and lapping water sifting through the screens on a breeze. The curtains had not yet been pulled around Isabel's bed and I could see that the white chenille spread was still tucked neatly beneath the pillows. I stiffened with the panicky feeling that was my companion when I found myself alone in the attic. I held my breath, trying to listen. Was someone behind the chimney that rose up through the middle of the attic? Or maybe in the bathroom, standing behind the curtain?

I tried not to lift my eyes to the ceiling, but I couldn't seem to help myself. And there it was: the man's head. I wouldn't scream like I did that one embarrassing night. I was going to get out of there, but I wouldn't scream like a baby while I was doing it.

I must have lain there for three or four minutes, my body paralyzed by fear, before I was able to sit up. I moved slowly and quietly, so as not to alert anyone who might be hiding behind the chimney or in the bathroom. I tiptoed to the door, but I nearly fell down the stairs in my race to get away from the attic. In the living room, I stood in the darkness, heart pounding. Where was everyone? The whole house was dark. What time was it? Julie was probably sleeping out on the porch, and Isabel must have stayed over at Mitzi's or Pam's house.

I walked down the hall and stood outside my parents' room. Daddy was in Westfield, but I could hear the comforting sound of my mother's even breathing. That was all I needed. I went back to the living room and lay down on the soft cushions of the sofa, inhaling the musty smell of the old upholstery as I drifted off to sleep.

"*Lucy.*" My grandmother's voice woke me up. She stood in the living room with a pile of plates, ready to set the porch table for breakfast. "Did you sleep here all night?"

I opened my eyes, confused for a moment, then sat up on the couch. "Uh-huh," I nodded. "Isabel wasn't home and Julie slept on the porch."

"What are we going to do with you?" she asked, walking out to the porch. I watched her glance in the direction of the bed. "Where's Julie now?" she called back to me as she set the plates on the table.

"I don't know," I said. "She must have gone upstairs."

"Go get her and tell her it's breakfast time," Grandma said. "Are you sure she slept down here? The bed doesn't look like it's been touched."

Still feeling groggy, I climbed the attic stairs. Julie wasn't in her bed. Her night-table lamp was still on and I walked behind her curtained cubicle to turn it off. I could see where she'd sloppily piled her bedspread beneath her sheet to try to fool me. I was not in the least worried. She'd probably slept on the porch, gotten up early and made the bed—which I had to admit *was* unusual for her—and then headed out to go crabbing or fishing.

I put on my bathing suit and pulled my shorts on over it, then went downstairs again. The morning smells of coffee and bacon were already strong in the air and I could see my mother taking her seat.

My grandfather carried a plate of bacon through the living room.

"Good morning, sunshine," he said, tousling my hair with his free hand.

"'Morning, Grandpop," I said, following him out to the porch.

"Where are Julie and Isabel?" My mother looked at me as I took my seat at the table.

"I don't know," I said. "I thought Isabel slept over at one of her friends' houses."

My mother frowned. "Whose house, do you know?" she asked. "I don't remember giving her permission."

I shook my head. "I don't know," I said.

"Is Julie upstairs?" my mother asked.

"Uh-uh. I thought she slept out here."

My mother glanced at the bed, as my grandmother had twenty minutes earlier. I watched her frown deepen. "I made that bed the day before yesterday," she said. "It looks untouched."

Grandpop stood up so suddenly the table shivered as his thighs brushed against it. He was staring toward the dock. "The runabout's gone," he said. We all turned as he pushed open the screen door and walked into the yard. We watched him look right and then left when he reached the fence by the canal. From where I was sitting, I could see two small sailboats heading in the direction of the bay.

Grandpop walked briskly back to the house and onto the porch. "I don't see her," he said. I felt frightened by the worry in his voice, and I dropped my slice of bacon onto my plate, no longer hungry.

Mom stood up. "I'm going to call Mitzi's house," she said. "Although…" She looked puzzled, turning to Grandma. "Why would they both be missing? And the boat? It doesn't make any sense."

"Don't get worked up," Grandma said to her. "There's a logical explanation, I'm sure."

My mother called Mitzi's house, then Pam's. Isabel was not at either one, and the girls claimed not to have seen her since late the night before when she'd left Mitzi's to come home. I watched as my mother hung up the phone after speaking with Pam. She was facing the Chapmans' house, and although there were several walls between her and Ned Chapman, I knew that was who she was seeing in her mind.

She took off her apron and walked quickly out the back door. Grandma and I sat at the table, not touching the food. "We're all getting worked up over nothing," Grandma said.

Grandpop stood at the screen door, his gaze on the canal as he waited for my mother to return. In a moment, I saw her run across the yard toward our porch. I'd never seen my mother run before and I knew something terrible had happened.

Grandpop pushed open the screen door for her and she rushed onto the porch.

"Something's wrong," she said. "Ned hasn't seen her since yesterday morning. And Joan Chapman said she was up at sunrise this morning sitting in their yard, and she noticed that our boat was gone even then. She thought you'd taken it out for an early fishing trip."

I stood up, starting to cry, wringing my hands together like an old woman.

"We should call the Marine Police," Grandpop said.

My mother looked toward the Chapmans' yard, where I could see Ned untying his boat from their dock. "Ned's going to take his boat out to look for them," she said.

Grandpop pushed open the screen door again and stepped outside.

"Where are you going?" Grandma asked.

"With Ned," he called over his shoulder to us.

"I'm calling Daddy." My mother started toward the French doors that led into the house from the porch. "He needs to come here—"

"You're jumping to conclusions," Grandma said. "Don't you think—"

My mother spun around to face Grandma. "Mother!" she said, sounding more like Isabel than herself. "They are both *missing*. The boat is missing. It makes no sense. Something is wrong."

Grandma had gotten to her feet, her arm tight around my shoulders. "You're upsetting Lucy," she said.

"Well, maybe she *should* be upset." My mother walked past us into the living room.

My grandmother let go of me, muttering something in Italian as she began clearing the forgotten food from the table. I walked to the screen door until my nose was right up against the wire mesh. It smelled like dust and metal, a smell I would always equate with that moment, as I watched my grandfather and Ned in the Chapmans' boat, speeding toward the bay.

CHAPTER 38

Julie
1962

Sometime during that horrible night, my boat hit land. I'd hoped I'd run aground on one of the small shrubby islands in the head of the bay, but I was so disoriented by darkness and anxiety that I wasn't sure. The water barely made a sound as it lapped against my boat, and crickets and frogs created a steady barrage of white noise behind me. The mosquitoes were invisible and insatiable, buzzing in my ears and dive-bombing my arms and legs and face. I was so rarely afraid of anything in those days, but I was filled with fear that night.

I cried over what Bruno might have done to Isabel, and I prayed that she'd managed to escape from him before he could hurt or rape her. I pictured her running home, barefoot and possibly naked, never stopping to catch her breath until she'd reached the safety of the bungalow. If she was unharmed, I promised God, I would never have another impure thought, never tell another lie, never again disobey my parents. I needed to change my ways. I was a terrible girl.

I sat in my boat, afraid to get out of it because I did not know what

I might step on in my bare feet. Suddenly my world was not safe. For the first time, I thought I knew how Lucy felt in the dark attic. I would not make fun of her again. I would treasure my sisters. *Please, please, God, let Isabel be all right!*

When it was apparent I was going nowhere, I lay down on the bottom of my boat. I wished I had a towel to cushion the hard and unyielding floor, and that's when I remembered that I'd left Isabel's towel on the other side of the canal. I cursed myself; I'd made one mistake after another that day. I tried to get as comfortable as I could with the mosquitoes trying to eat me alive. Above me, a few stars shot across the dark bowl of the sky, but I could take no pleasure in being a witness to them, and I drifted into a fitful sleep, the sound of my sister's scream echoing in my head.

I awakened beneath a pink sky, the rising sun just beginning to heat the air above the bay. I jerked up suddenly, remembering where I was and why, and yelped with the pain in my neck from sleeping on the hard surface of the boat. I had to turn my whole body to look around me, to see that I was indeed on one of the small islands in the head of the bay, so far from our beach that I could not even see the platform in the water. If my boat had missed this island, who knew where I might have ended up?

There were a few other boaters in the water. I could see a couple of sailboats in the distance and a runabout like mine with two men in it, probably fishing. I stood up, balancing carefully, and waved my arms.

"Help!" I called. "Please help me!"

The fishermen didn't seem to hear me, and the sailboats never changed direction.

I heard the sound of a motor and turned around to see a ski boat shoot past my little island. I waved my arms frantically, screaming "Hey! Over here!" as I tried to get the attention of the four people in the boat. I thought I'd failed, but then the boat circled around and headed toward me.

The young man at the wheel stopped the boat about ten yards from the island, obviously afraid he'd run aground if he came any closer.

"You stuck?" he called to me. There was another guy in the boat with him, along with two girls. A pair of skis jutted up from the floor.

"Yes," I said. "I couldn't get the motor…I mean, I stalled and can't get it started again." I didn't see the need to tell him how long I'd been out there. I was itching all over from the mosquito bites. God, I wanted to go home! I would gladly take whatever punishment was meted out. I just wanted away from the mess I'd gotten myself—and my sister—into. I wondered if she'd had to go to the hospital. Did you go to the hospital if you were raped?

The guy in the boat pulled off his T-shirt, jumped into the waist-high water and waded over to me. He came on shore, then climbed into the runabout. He was much younger than I'd thought, probably only sixteen or seventeen. He worked at the motor, yanking the cord over and over again, but with even less luck than I'd had.

"It's dead," he said. He stood up, looking down at my motor, shaking his head. "Get in our boat and I'll take you to…where do you want to go?"

"I live on the canal," I said. I wanted to be home in the worst way.

He grunted as though he wasn't crazy about my answer. "Okay," he said. "Your boat's not going anywhere. Come on."

I waded back to his boat with him, and as his fellow sailors were helping me in, I spotted the Chapmans' Boston whaler not more than fifty yards away. I saw my grandfather in the boat with Ned, and I was so exhausted and confused that it didn't even register as odd to me that the two of them would be together.

"Hey!" I yelled, startling the people in the boat. "That's my grandfather," I said to them. "Hey," I yelled again, and the guy who had tried to help me start my boat laid on his horn.

My grandfather looked toward us and I waved my arms over my head again. Instantly, Ned's whaler changed direction and headed for me. When the boats were side-by-side, I thanked my rescuers and transferred to the whaler, my grandfather holding my arm. I sank down onto one of the seats, so relieved to have my ordeal over that I wanted to cry, but I wouldn't do that in front of Ned.

"Where's Isabel?" Ned said as the other boat pulled away from us.

"What do you mean?" I asked. A slow horror began to fill my chest.

"We woke up this morning and you were both gone," Grandpop said.

I froze. Instinctively I started thinking of lies to protect myself.

"I...I forgot to tell her you couldn't meet her last night," I said to Ned. "And I..." I remembered my prayer of the night before. *Keep Isabel safe and I'll stop lying.* "I didn't forget," I admitted. "I didn't tell her because Bruno wanted to talk to her, so I told him she'd be on the platform at midnight."

Ned stared at me. It was so early that he didn't yet have his sunglasses on, and for the first time I could remember, I saw anger in his blue eyes.

"You set her up with *Bruno?*" He looked at me with disbelief.

"What's this about a platform?" my grandfather asked.

Ned took a step toward me. He put his hands on my waist, lifted me up and threw me overboard.

I shot through the water like a stone, then sputtered to the surface. Ned leaned over the edge of the boat. "You little bitch," he said.

"Hey, hey," my grandfather said. He held his hand in the air to stop Ned's words, then he leaned over to help me climb back into the boat. I was shivering, although the air had to be eighty degrees and the water was not much colder. My stiff neck sent shards of pain up the back of my head. "All right, you two," my grandfather said, taking charge. "Whatever differences there are between you, put an end to them now. This is serious and I want the truth." A larger boat sailed by and the wake lifted us up and then let us fall. I felt sick. Ned and I looked at each other. We both had things to hide, and I could tell that he knew as well as I did we could hide them no longer.

"Isabel and I meet on the platform at the beach sometimes," Ned said. "At midnight."

I could see my grandfather struggle with his anger, not letting it show on his face. "All right," he said. "And what happened last night?"

"I asked Julie to tell Isabel that I couldn't meet her last night."

"And Bruno stopped by and asked where he could find Isabel and I said I didn't know right then but I knew he could find her on the platform at midnight. And I was out here then, and I..." I was afraid to say the words out loud.

"You what?" Ned asked.

"I heard her scream. I heard her call for—"

"Hit your horn!" Grandpop said to Ned, but he stepped past him and blew the horn himself, waving with his other hand. Ned and I turned to see the Marine Police clipper he was trying to flag down.

We were quiet as the clipper came beside us. "We've got the twelve-year-old—Julie," Grandpop said to them, and only then did I realize they'd had the Marine Police out looking for me. "But the older girl's still missing."

"They weren't together?" one of the officers asked.

Grandpop shook his head. "Check the platform at the Bay Head Shores beach," he said. "This one heard a scream there around midnight last night."

We followed the clipper in the direction of the beach. Grandpop stood next to Ned, holding on to the windshield, staring straight ahead.

"Grandpop," I said, "I'm sorry."

He didn't reply. Maybe he hadn't heard me over the deafening sound of the engine as we sped toward the beach. Ned slowed his boat when we reached the water near the empty platform. The only person on the beach was a woman walking a large brown dog.

The Marine Police clipper pulled alongside the platform, but Ned was staring toward a clump of sea grass at the edge of the beach. Suddenly he stood up.

"Oh, God," he said. He pulled off his T-shirt and dove from the boat. I grabbed Grandpop's arm as we watched him swim toward the reeds and cattails, and it took me a long time to realize that there, among the low grass and seaweed, was the body of my sister.

My strongest memory from the rest of that day was of a dull pain in my chest and throat. I thought I was having a heart attack. It was the day I learned what the word *keening* meant. And the day my mother hit me. She'd never before laid a hand on me, but she slapped me hard across my face when she learned about my part in my sister's death.

"How could you do such a terrible thing to her?" she asked me.

My cheek stung and tears flowed freely down my cheeks.

"You sat on the porch with your grandmother and me last night," my mother said. "You heard us talk about the Walker boy being a rapist, and you said *nothing!* How could you do that? Why didn't you tell us?" She tried to strike me again, but Grandpop had moved next to me and he raised his arm to catch the blow.

"Maria, don't," he said to my mother.

"Why didn't you tell an adult what was going on?" my mother screamed at me. Grandpop put his arm protectively around my shoulders, but my mother could not stop yelling. "How could you *do* this?" she cried. *"How?"*

I had no answers and the words *I'm sorry* would be so weak, so useless, that instead, I said nothing. I hung my head, trying to lean into my grandfather's chest, but even he seemed distant from me in spite of his arm around my shoulders. I felt my insides coiling up like a snake ready to squeeze the life out of me.

"I'm going to throw up," I said, and pulling away from my grandfather, I ran to the bathroom.

I did not throw up; I had nothing inside me to come up. I sat hunched over on the closed toilet, sobbing, listening to the wailing of my mother and grandmother in the living room. No one came to comfort me. I must have sat there for forty minutes, afraid to leave the room, afraid to face my family.

I heard my father arrive, heard him with my mother in the hallway outside the bathroom. I pictured them embracing. His sobs were as loud as hers, and I cried harder, hugging my arms, rocking back and forth, knowing that I had stolen his favorite daughter from him. I heard car doors slamming and leaned forward to look out the window. A police car was parked on the dirt road in front of our house, and two men in uniform were walking up the sidewalk.

I closed my eyes, listening to the voices in the hallway. There was a knock on the bathroom door.

"Julie?" It was my grandfather. "Are you all right?"

"Yes." My voice squeaked.

"You need to come out," he said. "The police want to talk to you."

I wanted to stay in the small, safe room, but I stood up and opened the door. I looked at my grandfather's basset-hound face. His eyes were red. "Grandpop," I said. I wanted to say that I never meant for this to happen, but that was an excuse for what I'd done, and there were no excuses big enough to cover this particular multifaceted sin. He put his arm around me again and led me down the hallway. I could see all the way through the living room and porch to our yard, where the police were talking to my father. And I could hear voices coming from my parents' bedroom. My mother and grandmother and Lucy were in there, hushed voices cut with sobs. I heard my sister hiccup.

I wiped my face with the back of my hand as we walked across the porch. Grandpop opened the screen door and I nearly tripped down the two steps to the yard, my legs felt so wobbly. My father and the policemen looked up as the screen door slammed closed behind us. I recognized one of the policemen as Officer Davis, who had lauded me when I'd found the little boy. I felt humiliated now, the fallen heroine.

Ned and his father were there as well. All at once, I realized what a fool I'd been: Ned was a man, standing there with four other men. I was a skinny-legged idiot for thinking he could ever be romantically interested in me. I'd been playing a twelve-year-old's game with grown-up consequences.

My father limped forward to hug me, and the gesture caught me off guard. "I know you didn't mean to hurt her," he said into my ear, his voice cracking on the last word. I would never forget the gift he gave me with those words. He pulled away from me, turning back to the police.

"And you were supposed to meet her last night?" Officer Davis was asking Ned.

Ned looked as though he was already tired of answering questions. "Originally," he said. "But I couldn't..." He glanced at his father, and I remembered the argument that had led to him telling me he could not see Isabel last night. "I wasn't allowed to go out last night. So, I asked Julie if she'd give Izzy that message."

"Why weren't you allowed to go out?" the other office asked.

"He hasn't been helping out much around the house this summer," Mr. Chapman said. "Always on the go. My wife and I decided he needed to stay in for a change. Help the family out."

"And did you?" Officer Davis asked. "Did you help the family out last night?"

Ned nodded slowly. "Yeah," he said. The word came out in two syllables.

"What exactly did you do?"

"I didn't kill her," he said. "Why aren't you talking to Bruno Walker?"

"I'm not saying you did kill her, and we're in the process of looking for Mr. Walker," Officer Davis said. "Right now, I'm trying to put together a complete picture of last night. What did you do around the house?"

"I swept the whole house," Ned said. "I washed the dishes. My brother dried. I folded laundry. I fixed a radio. Is that enough?"

"Shh, Ned," Mr. Chapman said. "That attitude isn't going to help."

"And where were you around midnight last night?" Officer Davis asked.

"I thought you weren't looking at him as a suspect," Mr. Chapman said. "He's not answering any more questions until we contact his lawyer." I remembered suddenly that Mr. Chapman was a lawyer himself, as well as chief justice on the New Jersey Supreme Court. He would know how to advise his son and I was relieved. I didn't like how Ned was being questioned. Officer Davis had been so nice to me when I found Donnie Jakes. This was a different, no-nonsense side of him.

"Answer the question, Ned," my father said. "Where were you last night?" I noticed the other cop had his hand around my father's arm as if holding him back from punching Ned in the face, and I wondered what had transpired before Grandpop and I had gotten out there. I could imagine how Daddy'd reacted to the news that Ned and Isabel met on the platform nearly every night.

"He worked like a dog around the house," Mr. Chapman said. "I was proud of him for finally helping out. So then he and I sat out in the yard for an hour or so looking for shooting stars. The meteor shower." He looked at Ned. "We were eating bowls of ice cream. I think it was about twelve-thirty when we went inside. Wouldn't you say it was about twelve-thirty?" He asked his son, who dropped his eyes under his father's steady regard.

"I didn't look at the clock," Ned said.

"All right." Officer Davis flipped his notepad closed, then nodded in my direction. "I'd like some time with Julie, here," he said, then looked at Ned and his father. "You two can go. We'll be in touch."

Ned walked ahead of his father toward their house, and Daddy led me over to the double Adirondack chair. I sat down next to him and my grandfather took a seat near us, while Officer Davis and the other policeman leaned against the chain-link fence.

"Why don't you start at the beginning, Julie," Officer Davis said to me, kindly.

I told him everything and I tried not to cry so that I would be a good witness. I told him how I'd set up the meeting between Bruno and my sister when I was fishing with Wanda.

"I told you not to go over there," my father said, as if fishing with the Lewis family was the cause of all that had happened.

I admitted that I used to sneak out in my boat to watch Ned and Isabel on the platform. "This whole thing is my fault," I said. My voice had grown hoarse and it came out in a whisper. "I was jealous of her. I didn't want her to have Ned. I didn't mean for her to get killed, though." I felt my father's hand on my back and I wasn't sure if he meant the touch as a comfort or if he was telling me to stop talking, that I was saying too much.

I was sorry when the policemen left, because I was suddenly alone with my family again and I no longer knew how I fit in. There was an air of helplessness in the bungalow. My mother and grandmother worked in the kitchen, their silence broken by sudden bouts of sobbing. My grandfather and father sat on the glider near the bed on the porch, deep in conversation. Lucy was curled up at one end of the couch in the living room, her eyes closed, thumb in her mouth, her nose still red from crying. I did not know where to go. I thought of reading, but felt sick again when I thought of the childish, made-up mysteries in my Nancy Drew books.

I sat on the couch with Lucy for a while, staring into space, wishing she would wake up and talk to me, but she slept as though she'd been drugged. Maybe she had been. Maybe someone had given her something to let her sleep through the grief.

Finally I got up and walked into the kitchen.

"Can I help?" I asked, my voice small as I tried to tiptoe my way back into my family.

My mother looked at me, surprise on her face as though she'd forgotten I existed. She turned back to the frying pan where she was searing a roast.

"I'm sorry I hit you, Julie," she said, her attention on the roast instead of on me.

"That's okay," I said.

"Here." My grandmother handed me the potato peeler and pointed to the pile of potatoes on the counter. "You can peel."

We worked in a silence that was rare in my family, but I welcomed it because the only things that could be said would be full of pain and anger. I peeled every potato perfectly, leaving no hint of skin and carving out every eye. I wanted the task to last all afternoon because I wasn't sure what I would do once I had finished.

The phone rang, and my mother jumped but made no move to walk into the living room to answer it. She stood at the sink, a half-washed spatula frozen in her hand, as we listened to my father's footsteps in the other room, then his Hello? into the receiver. The three of us listened hard, but could not hear much of his conversation. Finally he walked into the kitchen.

He stood in the doorway, the color of his face so ashen I felt afraid for him. He might die, I thought. This might kill him. I would be responsible for both their deaths.

"She wasn't...there was no rape," he said. "Thank God for that."

"What do they think happened?" I had never heard my mother sound so tentative and weak, as if she was afraid of the answer.

"They said she drowned, but that she'd been...manhandled first. She had a bruise on her shoulder and her arm and a lump on her head. They guess she fought the Walker boy off and then fell or maybe jumped into the water and hit her head on the edge of the platform."

My mother suddenly threw the spatula against the wall, then buried her face in her hands. My father was quickly next to her, pulling her into his arms. My grandmother moved to them, wrapping her arms around them both. I stood alone in the middle of the kitchen floor, the peeler in my hand, tears no one noticed running down my cheeks.

Officer Davis returned to our house just as we were sitting down to a dinner we had no interest in eating. My father answered the door, then walked with him back to the porch.

"Sorry to disturb you folks," Officer Davis said, "but I need to talk with Julie again."

My father nodded to me without saying a word.

I stood up, scraping my chair away from the table, then walked outside with my father and the policeman. Daddy and I sat on the double Adirondack chair again, and this time, Officer Davis took a seat as well. He pulled his chair in front of me and leaned forward, his elbows on his knees and his hands clasped together loosely in front of him.

"We found Bruno Walker," he said.

I was filled with hatred for Bruno. I remembered how he'd looked toward the bridge the day before, how I'd hoped my sister could be drawn in by his lovely eyes.

"Where'd you find him?" my father asked.

"In Ortley Beach," the officer said.

"Did he confess?"

The officer shook his head. "He said he was with some friends at one of their rental cottages and that he left them around one in the morning and went home to bed. We talked with several of his friends separately, and they all confirmed his story."

"What crap," my father said.

Officer Davis locked his eyes onto mine. "Tell me again about informing Bruno that your sister would be on the platform at midnight," he said. "Where were you when you told him?"

"The other side of the canal," I said.

"With your friend." The officer nodded. "What's her name?" he asked.

"Wanda Lewis."

"They're not really friends," my father said, and I knew it was not the time to argue with him.

"Who else was there?" the officer asked. "Was there anyone else who might have heard your conversation with Mr. Walker?"

You up to no good, girl.

"George was there," I said. "Wanda's brother. Her other relatives were there, too, but they were down——" I pointed across the canal to the area where Salena and the men had been fishing. "They weren't close enough to hear."

"But this George was," the officer said.

I nodded. Suddenly I realized where this was going.

"George wouldn't hurt anybody," I said.

"Why are you asking her about this...George?" My father said his name as though he was talking about an object and not a person.

"Mr. Walker claims that Mr. Lewis looked very interested when he heard Julie say that Isabel would be alone on the platform."

"Bruno's just trying to pin the blame on someone else," I said, but I could feel my heart sinking. I remembered George's occasional appreciative comments about my sister and the scary way he'd cut his eyes at my father the day he came over to drag me home.

"Well, that may be so," Officer Davis said. "Just the same, we need to talk to Mr. Lewis. Do you know how we can reach him?"

I shook my head. "I don't have a phone number or address or anything," I said. "But I think they live on South Street. And they'll be back across the canal in the morning, probably, if it's a nice day. But I know he didn't do it."

"You don't know that, Julie," my father scoffed. "You don't really know those people. You don't know what that boy's capable of doing."

"He's nice to me," I said, but that only enraged my father more.

"This is what happens when you disobey me," he said, and I supposed he was right.

I couldn't sleep at all that night. I went up to the attic early with Lucy, who was weepy and withdrawn, and I didn't bother going down again. I kept crying—we all did. I would think I was okay, that I'd gotten a grip on my emotions, and then all of a sudden, I'd be sobbing again.

I replayed the night before in my mind over and over again, examining my actions to see if I could have done something different and thus prevented my sister's death. I remembered looking out the attic window at the dark canal. If only I'd left the house earlier. Would that have made a difference? And what if I'd gone through with my idea of getting Ned to go with me? Then we would have been in his boat and been able to reach the platform safely, although we might have been too late.

Suddenly, I sat bolt upright in my bed. I remembered running over to the Chapmans' house, getting ready to knock on the screen door only to realize their entire house was dark. I remembered looking toward the canal and seeing the empty Adirondack chairs. And then I remembered the policemen questioning Ned that afternoon, and the way he had looked down at the sand when his father said they'd been watching a meteor shower together in the backyard. Had Mr. Chapman fabricated an alibi to save his son?

I pressed my hand to my mouth, a shiver running through my body. *Oh, Ned,* I thought to myself. *Why?*

CHAPTER 39

Julie
1962

I awakened the next morning with new resolve and a plan: I needed to do my own investigation. The facts I knew did not fit together. I would tell the police my suspicions about Ned, but not until I'd seen what other evidence I could gather. As heartsick as I was at the thought of George being my sister's killer, I was triply distressed to think it might have been Ned. I would be objective, though, as detached as I could possibly be from the outcome as I gathered my clues.

I was relieved to have something to do that would both ease my sense of helplessness and also allow me to avoid my family. I left the house early and started walking toward the beach. What made no sense, I thought as I walked, was that Ned had told me to tell Isabel he couldn't meet her that night. Then why would he have thought he could find her on the platform? My question was answered only minutes later.

I was nearly to Mitzi's house when I noticed she was in her front yard washing her parents' car. She tried to hide from me on the other side of the car, but she knew I'd already seen her. I saw her shoulders sag with resignation as she watched me approach.

"Hi, Mitzi," I said, walking up her short driveway.

"Hi, Julie." She stopped scrubbing the car with her soapy sponge. I almost felt sorry for her, she looked so uncomfortable. "Are you all right?" she asked. "How's your mother and grandmother?"

"Messed up," I said. "Did the police talk to you?"

"They called, but they just asked me what time Izzy left my house the night…the other night."

"What time did she leave?"

"Eleven-thirty." She wrung suds out of the sponge onto the driveway. Her hands were pudgy, like the rest of her. "She was going to…I know you know she always met Ned at midnight."

"Yeah," I said.

"He was so peeved at you for not giving Izzy that message that he couldn't come. Even though he could. Although he actually couldn't." She laughed, then sobered, remembering the seriousness of the conversation.

"What do you mean?" I asked. "What do you mean that he could, but then he couldn't?"

"He called her here at my house to tell her he might be able to meet her after all," Mitzi said. "That's when he found out you hadn't told her he couldn't. Izzy was peeved at you, too. Anyway, he said he might be able to, but he wasn't sure, but he'd try. He couldn't get away, though. Isn't it unreal? The one night he couldn't get out that colored boy was there? What crappy luck. You must just be—" She shook her head. "I bet you could just kill that guy if you could get your hands on him."

"Right," I said. It was easiest to agree with her, but my head was spinning. I had to think through all of this new information.

"They caught him, though," she said. "Well, I guess you know that."

"Caught who? George?"

"The colored boy. Right. I heard it on the radio before I came outside."

"What did they say?" I asked.

"Just that they found him and he says he's not guilty," Mitzi said.

"Maybe he's not," I said.

"Who else could have done it?" She tried to smooth her frizzy dark hair away from her face, but it sprang back again into a curly mess. I felt sorry for her having to deal with hair like that. "What I can't get over is that I was the third to the last person to see Izzy alive," she said, as though she had practiced the statement.

"What do you mean, the third to the last?" I asked.

"The...you know, the person who did it was number one," she said. "And Pam. Pam left here with her, like she always did, so she was number two."

Pam's house was between Mitzi's and the beach. That made sense.

"Ned'll probably start going with Pam now," Mitzi said.

It was years before I realized how tactless Mitzi Caruso had been with that statement. The boorishness of her words went right over my head. At that moment, I was only thinking about their content.

I left Mitzi's and continued walking to the beach, cataloging the clues I had so far in my mind. First, Ned's alibi appeared to be a lie, since I had not seen him with his father in their backyard. Second, Ned had told Isabel he might be able to meet her after all—something he had not mentioned to the police, as far as I knew. Third, his motive might have had something to do with his interest in Pam, but murdering Izzy to get her out of the way seemed extreme.

I walked past Pam Durant's house on the lagoon, thinking I would talk with her after I explored the beach. She would be less suspicious of me than she would be the police, so maybe she would open up to me more than she would to them.

The beach was completely empty. I thought there might still be policemen in the area, but maybe they had finished searching for clues. Most likely, they thought they had their killer now. I was growing more certain by the minute that they were wrong.

I headed for the patch of sea grass where my sister had been found. I looked for things washed onto the shore by the small, gentle waves. I found a Popsicle stick and a plastic cup, but I seemed to have lost interest in collecting any old thing I came across, and I didn't bother to pick them up.

Tears welled up in my eyes as I walked through the creepy tangles of seaweed. I sat down in the place where Isabel had been found, letting the water wash over my legs. I ran my hands through the tendrils of eel grass. There was nothing here. What had I been expecting?

I left the beach empty-handed and empty hearted and walked along the road leading to Pam's house. A dog barked when I knocked on the Durants' door. I could see through their house to the lagoon behind, just as I could see through my house to the canal.

Pam herself answered the door, her Doberman pinscher, the only dog I've ever been afraid of, at her side.

"Oh, Julie!" she said, pushing open the door. "I'm so sorry. Come in." She hugged me, but I felt stiff inside and I kept one eye on her dog.

"I just wanted to talk to you," I said. The dog sniffed at the back of my hand.

Pam drew away from me, studying my face, but I studied hers harder. The whites of her eyes had the bluish tint of skim milk. No trace of red. No trace of tears.

"Let's go out back," she said.

"Are your parents here?" I asked, as we walked through the small living room.

"No one's here except me," she said.

She stopped at the door to the kitchen. "Can I get you some soda?" she asked.

I shook my head.

"I almost died myself when I heard," she said, pushing open the screen door and stepping into her yard, which was covered with smooth, blond stones. I was glad she left the dog in the house. "I was the last person to see her alive," she said. At least Mitzi had been modest enough to say she was third to the last. Pam put herself right at the top.

We sat on the bulkhead, our feet dangling above the still lagoon water. Pam was so pretty. Her nearly white ponytail fell in a long spiral over her shoulder.

"I just can't believe she's gone," she said. "I've never known anyone who died before. It's so tragic."

"Do you know where Ned was the night Isabel was killed?" I asked, point-blank.

"He was home," she said, as though she knew this for a fact.

"He says he was watching a meteor shower with his father in their backyard," I said.

"That's probably what he was doing, then." Pam shrugged. "He wasn't allowed out, right? And you were supposed to tell that to Izzy, but you didn't."

"But then he called her at Mitzi's to say he could."

"He said he *might* be able to. Not that he could for sure." She tilted her head to look at me. "You know Ned would never hurt Isabel, don't you?"

"I'm just trying to figure some things out," I said.

"He was over here yesterday." Pam straightened her legs to look at her painted toes. "He's all torn up," she said. "He was really scared the cops thought it was him."

And you comforted him, I guess, I wanted to say. "Maybe it was," I said, instead.

"*What?*" She lowered her legs again, frowning at me. "Oh Julie, don't be crazy," she said. "Ned was a *lifesaver.* He would never kill anyone."

I wasn't sure what else to ask. I was doing a poor job of keeping my misgivings about Ned to myself; Nancy Drew would have been far more clever at questioning Pam than I was being. We talked a while longer, and then I left her house with nothing to prove my hunch other than my own suspicions.

There was one more person that I needed to interview, and I was quite sure where I could find him. I walked to the shallows at the end of Shore Boulevard and along the path cut through the tall grass.

"Who's there?" Ethan asked as I rustled through the cattails. I heard the anxiety in his voice. I guessed we were all a little on edge.

"Me," I said.

I found him sitting at the water's edge, where he had set up a little marine research laboratory, complete with a small fish net and microscope and a booklet on sea creatures.

"What do you want?" he asked.

I sat down next to him, the damp sand cool beneath my thighs.

"Was Ned really home all night the night Isabel was killed?" I asked.

"How would I know?" He shook his head at me. "You really think you're Nancy Drew, don't you?"

"And you really think you're some sort of scientist." I reached out and knocked over his microscope with my hand and then felt instantly remorseful. With the exception of Lucy, he was the only person in the world weaker than me, and I guessed I just needed to take out my frustration on someone.

"Hey!" He lifted the microscope from the wet sand. "This is a precision instrument," he said, cradling it in his hands. "You might have ruined it. What's the matter with you?"

"I think your brother might have killed my sister," I said.

"You're full of soup," he said, pushing his glasses higher up his nose. I hated when he did that. "The police already got that—" he nodded in the general direction of the opposite side of the canal "—that colored boy. If anybody's responsible for killing your sister, it's *you,* for letting him know Isabel was going to be alone on the beach that night."

"I didn't kill her," I said, my eyes burning.

"Well, my brother sure didn't, either. He was grounded."

"Ned probably just snuck out anyhow," I said. "That's what he usually did."

"You don't know what you're talking about." With tender care, Ethan set the microscope upright in the sand again. "How do you know what my brother usually does?"

"I know plenty," I said.

"If Ned did it, why would he be such a wreck right now? He's sitting around crying about your sister."

"Yeah, well, maybe he's crying 'cause he killed her and he—"

"Shut *up!*" In a flash, Ethan was on top of me, his skinny arms pinning mine above my head in the sand. His knee dug into my belly, making me gasp for air. I mustered up all my strength and pushed him off me, rolling him over until I was on top of him. I punched his cheek as hard as I could. He yelped and I saw a little blood coming from his nose. I didn't care. I punched him one more time. His head was in a few inches of water, and I could easily have turned his face until the water covered his nose and mouth. The realization that I could have such a thought shocked the sense back into me. I let go of him and scrambled to my feet, choking on my own sobs. I ran back through the tall grass, blinded by tears and confused by a rush of emotions. My heart was in a vise; my hands formed fists so tight I would later find blood on my palms from my fingernails. I wanted to kill someone. I just didn't know who it was that I should want to kill.

I called the police myself. My parents and I were not talking easily with one another and I could hardly ask them to do it for me. I told Officer Davis my suspicions. He listened carefully. Then he told me that George Lewis had no verifiable alibi. George had told the police he'd been on the Seaside Heights boardwalk waiting for some friends who never showed up. He had scratches on his face and arms, and said that he'd gotten into a fight on the beach that night with a white boy he'd never seen before, but the police had been unable to find any witnesses to a fight. At the Lewises' house, they found George's wet trunks, and—most incriminating—a towel belonging to Isabel.

"But *I* took that towel across the canal and accidentally left it there!" I said, almost shouting into the phone.

"There was blood on it, Julie," Officer Davis said. "Mr. Lewis claims he used the towel after the fight he was in, and both he and your sister have the same blood type, so it's not possible to know if it was his or hers, but it's clear he was in an altercation."

"The chairs in the Chapmans' backyard were *empty* that night," I said, repeating a fact I'd already told him.

"We'll reinterview them about that," Officer Davis said. "I know you're troubled and need to feel sure we have the right suspect in custody, and I'm grateful that you called. But you let us do our job now, all right?"

When they were questioned again, Ned and Mr. Chapman said that they'd been lying on a blanket in their backyard the night Isabel was killed and that's why I didn't notice them when I ran to their house. I still thought I would have seen them, and it seemed odd that they didn't notice *me* running through their yard, even though I'd been a distance behind them. Surely they'd heard me get into the runabout, but no one else seemed troubled by their story.

Bruno's father hired a lawyer—the same one who had gotten him off on the previous year's rape charge. George didn't even know who his father was, much less have the money for a lawyer. He was charged and eventually convicted of voluntary manslaughter.

Ned was not even considered a suspect. The son of the chief justice of the New Jersey Supreme Court was presumed innocent—by everyone except me.

CHAPTER 40

Julie
1962

Within a matter of days, we had packed our belongings and left the bungalow for the last time, and that put an end to my sleuthing. Isabel's funeral took place the day after we returned to Westfield. I didn't go because I woke up that morning with what, in retrospect, was surely a psychosomatic stomachache. Simply lifting my head from the pillow caused the room to spin and my stomach to churn. Lucy was sent to a neighbor's house, while I stayed home alone with my aching belly and my troubled conscience. I wondered if I had cancer. I was terribly afraid of dying with such an enormous mortal sin on my soul.

The following Saturday, I waited for my turn in the confessional. I sat between my mother and Lucy in the pew at Holy Trinity, trying to figure out what I would say to the priest. I was always so mechanical in the confessional with my carefully rehearsed list of sins. This sin did not fit neatly into my usual categories, and although I'd tried to think of a way to confess many times since it had happened, I still walked into the tiny dark cubicle with no idea how to begin.

It didn't matter. The second the priest drew back his little window, I started to cry. I recognized my confessor as Father Fagan, the oldest priest in our parish. He was white haired and walked with a limp, like my father, and he had big hands that had rested gently on my head more than once over the years. I let out huge, gulping sobs that could probably have been heard throughout the church. I thought my mother might open the door to the confessional to see that I was all right. Maybe she would hold me as she had not held me since Isabel's death, but that didn't happen.

Father Fagan managed to find a break in my weeping to say, "Tell me what's troubling you, my child."

"I..." I gulped down a fresh set of tears. "I did something that got my sister killed," I said.

"Ah," he said. His voice was very calm, not at all incensed or shocked, and I wondered if he knew about Isabel's death and my role in it. I would later learn that he had been the priest at her funeral. "I think it would be good if you and I met together in the rectory tomorrow after church," he said. "Could you do that?"

I was surprised. I couldn't imagine confessing my sins face-to-face with a priest, but I knew I could not decline the invitation.

"Yes, Father," I said.

"Good. Come see me at one o'clock and we'll chat."

I started to stand up, but dropped to my knees again. "What if I die between now and then?" I asked. "I have a mortal sin on my soul."

"You're forgiven that sin, child."

"But...I haven't even told you what I did. It's...I think it's unforgivable."

"Nothing's unforgivable, Julie," he said, stunning me by using my name. "Right now, go to the altar and say three Hail Marys and make a good act of contrition. And then I'll see you tomorrow."

"Okay," I said, standing up again. But I didn't feel forgiven. I felt as though he didn't quite understand how terrible I'd been.

The next day, my father took me to the rectory and waited in the parlor while I spoke with Father Fagan. We sat in a small room furnished with fancy chairs and a chandelier hanging from the center of the ceiling. I told him everything I'd done, and he listened, nodding slightly every once in a while.

"Your sin was envy." He sat in a large chair that made me think of something a king might sit in. He held the fingertips of his hands together as though he might start to pray at any moment. "And lust for your sister's boyfriend," he continued. "And lying to your parents, as well as to a number of other people. And also, disobedience."

I nodded as he catalogued all the things I'd done wrong.

"But," he said, "your sin is not murder."

"It wouldn't have happened if I didn't——"

"You did not mean for her to die."

I lowered my head and watched as a tear fell from my eyelashes to form a dark stain on my blue skirt. "No," I said.

"You did not mean for her to die," he repeated, as if he wanted me to truly believe it.

I shook my head. "I loved her," I said.

He nodded. "I know," he said. Then the tone of his voice changed, and I knew we were coming to the end of our session together. That disappointed me. I could talk about everything here. I couldn't talk about any of it at home. "Julie," he said, in his new voice. "I want you to feel you can come to me any time you need to. Any time. You can call me in the middle of the night if you need to. The Lord and I will always be here for you. Now, let us pray for your sister's soul."

That's what we did. For a few minutes, I sat with my head bowed as he asked God to watch over Isabel. I felt the tiniest molecule of peace work its way into my heart as he spoke.

When we had finished praying and I was on my way out of the office, it suddenly occurred to me that he had not given me a real penance. The Hail Marys from the day before surely didn't count; they were far less than I would have received from the priest in Point Pleasant for one single impure thought.

"You forgot to give me my penance," I said, my hand on the doorknob.

"You need no penance from me," Father Fagan said. "Your true

penance is that you will have to live with what you did for the rest
of your life," he said.

He could not have been more right.

My grandparents put our bungalow on the market, and it sold
quickly. That, too, was my fault. The house had meant so much to
all of us and had been part of my family's history for nearly forty
years. We would never again go down the shore in the summer. That
chapter of our lives was over.

No one ever said, *Julie, you are to blame for this, you are a horrible
person,* but no one needed to. Everyone knew that was the truth. It
was weeks before my mother could talk to me without asking me,
"*Why? Why? Why?*" For a while, I felt cut off from the warm family life
I had always known. That improved over time, although except for
my father's initial compassionate response to me, no one ever said,
It's all right, Julie. We know you didn't mean for Isabel to die. Only Father
Fagan provided that sort of comfort in the weeks and months that
followed Izzy's death, but I really needed to hear those words from
someone in my family. And I never did.

CHAPTER 41

Lucy

"Do you recognize that little building?" Julie asked me, as we turned the corner into Bay Head Shores. She pointed to our left, where a tiny antique shop was tucked beneath the on-ramp of the Loveland-town Bridge.

I shook my head. "Not even a little bit," I said.

"Well, it looks completely different, of course," Julie said. "And the big bridge was just a little one back then, but the antique store used to be the corner store. Or at least that's what we used to call it. You loved the penny candy."

"I remember the penny candy," I said, picturing long strips of colorful candy buttons.

"One time we rode our bikes here and got sprayed by the mosquito truck on the way home," Julie said.

"I remember that, too," I said. "I fell off my bike and cut my arm." I looked at my arm as though expecting to see a scar, but I wasn't even sure which arm I'd injured. "We'll probably die premature deaths because of that DDT or whatever it was," I added.

Julie turned the next corner. "Do you want to drive by the bay and our old beach before we go to Ethan's?" she asked.

I shook my head. "Later," I said. I had a urinary-tract infection, which seemed terribly unjust since I hadn't had sex in months. At that moment, all I could think about was using the bathroom at Ethan's house.

It was early on Friday afternoon and Ethan had invited Julie, Shannon, Tanner and me to his house for the weekend. Shannon and Tanner had begged out, but I'd accepted. Something was pulling me down to the shore. I wanted to see what I remembered.

For a number of reasons, I wished that Shannon and Tanner were with us. I wanted my niece to see an important part of her mother's childhood, but more than that, I thought that both Julie and I needed more time with Shannon and Tanner. I liked the little I knew of Tanner. I'd only gotten to spend time with him at the barbecue, but he'd impressed me and I thought Shannon could do far worse than a bright, socially conscious—not to mention handsome—young man. Not nearly young enough; I agreed with Julie on that point. Still, that was not our choice to make. The thing that wrenched my heart and that I knew was killing Julie, was that Shannon wanted to move so far away from us. I remembered what it was like to be young and in love and yearning for my independence, and visiting home had been one of the last things on my mind.

"You know," I said now to Julie, "we'll just have to go to Colorado ourselves a couple of times a year. We'll take Mom with us."

"What?" She glanced at me in confusion, then laughed. "Oh, you're back on that topic again." We'd talked about Shannon and Tanner for most of the ride down the shore, but I could see that Julie had now shifted gears to our old neighborhood and Ethan. "I don't plan to go to Colorado a couple of times a year," she said, "because I don't intend to let Shannon go."

"She's pregnant," I said. "She can become legally emancipated and do whatever she likes if she wants to."

"Can we talk about this later?" she asked, as we turned yet another corner.

"Sure," I said. We'd recently gotten into this dance of Julie denying the reality of Shannon's leaving and me trying to force it down her throat. "Sorry to be a pain," I added.

To our right, between some houses, I saw the canal.

"Oh!" I said. "Is this our old street?"

"Uh-huh."

"Wow. I'd never recognize it," I said. Then I asked rhetorically, "Where did all these houses come from?"

Julie stopped the car in front of a sunny yellow-and-white Cape Cod.

"Do you recognize this one?" she asked.

I didn't. "Is that ours?" The house meant nothing to me.

She nodded.

I looked at the mailbox, painted to resemble the sea and topped by a sailboat. "Somebody loves this house," I said.

"And this is Ethan's house," Julie said as she pulled into the next-door driveway. She opened the car door before even turning off the ignition. The recent change in her was dramatic. I knew she was upset about Shannon, and I knew the past was weighing heavily on her in a way it had not for many years, but there was also a joy in her I couldn't remember ever seeing before, not even when she was falling in love with Glen as a young woman. And the cause of that joy walked out the front door of his house and over to us, giving Julie an embrace that lasted several seconds as he planted a kiss on her neck. The scene made me smile.

"Welcome, Lucy!" he said to me, giving me the much shorter and more perfunctory version of the hug he'd laid on my sister.

"Hi, Ethan," I said. "I'm desperate for a bathroom."

He laughed, pointing behind him to the house. "Halfway down the hall on the right," he said. "We'll meet you in the yard."

When I left Ethan's bathroom, I headed for the back of his house. Through the open jalousies on the sun porch, I could see the canal clearly and suddenly everything seemed familiar. I walked outside to where he and Julie were leaning against the chain-link fence watching the beginning-of-the-weekend array of boats on the water. I felt almost dizzy with déjà vu. The current was so fast, and I remembered my fear of it. I'd have nightmares of falling into the canal and being swept away by the water as I struggled unsuccessfully to swim into one of the docks.

I shivered as I leaned against the fence next to my sister.

"Whew," I said. "I remember how scared I was of the water."

Julie put her arm around me. "You were," she said. "Poor little kid." She nodded in the direction of the yard next door. I had not even thought to look over there. "Do you remember it?" she asked.

I looked across a short metal fence to see a little boy playing in a swimming pool. He was riding—and falling off—a huge plastic alligator, while a heavyset, dark-haired woman relaxed with a book on a lounge chair nearby. I could see the top of a boat in the fenced-in dock, but the long, dark, deep-green screened porch was the most familiar part of the scene to me.

"I'd love to see the house inside," I said. "See how it's changed."

"It's totally different," Ethan said. "I'll give them a call later and we can go over." He glanced at Julie. "You don't have to go with us, if you don't want to."

Julie bit her lip. "I think I can do it," she said. It was clear they'd had a conversation about this before.

We spent the rest of the afternoon on Ethan's boat on the canal and the river. It was my first voyage ever in those waters, since I'd been too chicken to go out on our boat when I was a kid. I loved it now, but what was most amazing to me—*thrilling* to me—was seeing Julie in a boat again. She laughed when the wake of a much larger boat sent a wall of water crashing over us, making us look like two women in a middle-age wet T-shirt contest. She was not only finding love in Ethan, I thought, but also a rekindling of the courage and vitality she'd lost many years ago. Watching her laugh put a lump in my throat.

After dinner, as the sky turned fuchsia from the setting sun, we strolled barefoot across our old front yard and knocked on the frame of the screen door. The young dark-haired woman I'd seen in the backyard pushed the door open for us.

"Hello!" she said, as we entered. "I'm Ruth Klein. And you guys must be the former residents of our house."

"Hi, Ruth," Ethan said to her. "This is Julie Sellers." He rested his hand on Julie's back. "And her sister, Lucy Bauer." We stood packed into the hallway near the front door.

"When did you live here?" Ruth asked. She was beautiful in spite of the fact that she was quite overweight. Her pink skin was flawless, her blue eyes a vibrant contrast to her dark hair.

"Our grandfather built the house in 1926," Julie said. "Lucy and I lived here during the summer in the fifties and early sixties."

"Oh, wow," said Ruth. "I bet it's totally different by now. Where do you want to start your tour?"

"Well," Julie looked at the partly open door on our left. "This used to be our grandparents' room."

"Go ahead in." Ruth leaned forward to push the door open. It was a small room with a queen-size platform bed and sleek-lined dresser and armoire. "This is the master bedroom, as you can probably tell," she said.

Julie nodded. "And across the hall was the bathroom."

"Still is," Ruth said, and we followed her across the hall, taking turns peering into the tiny bathroom. The toilet and pedestal sink looked new. In the corner was a small triangular tub.

"We just had a shower there," Julie said.

"I think the people before us put the tub in," Ruth said.

We walked a short distance down the hall. "Here's our son's room." Ruth pointed to her left. Inside, the room was just barely wide enough to fit a twin bed and a tiny dresser.

"This was Mom and Dad's room, right?" I looked to Julie for confirmation.

"Yes." She smiled. "They didn't have much space, did they?"

Across the hall was the kitchen, and it was unrecognizable as any room we'd ever lived in, with white glass-fronted cabinetry and granite countertops. Julie laughed.

"Well," she said, running her hand across the blue-gray granite. "I can tell you our kitchen looked nothing like this. This is beautiful."

"This—and being on the water, of course—were what sold us on the house," Ruth said.

We walked the last few steps of the hallway into the living room, which was painted a soft yellow and furnished with chairs and love seats upholstered in a variety of blue-and-yellow prints. Gauzy white curtains hung at the windows.

"This room seems much more open than it did before," I said.

"You're right," Julie said. "I think it was a darker color or something. I love it like this."

"We used to play Uncle Wiggly in here," Ethan said.

"I beg your pardon?" Ruth asked with a laugh.

"It was a board game," Julie explained.

I looked down at the oak-colored laminate beneath my bare feet. "This used to be linoleum," I said. Then my eyes were drawn to the staircase at the side of the room. "Look!" I said. "Real stairs!"

Julie laughed. "We had pull-down stairs when we were kids," she said. "Lucy was terrified of them."

"Would you like to see up there?" Ruth asked.

"Would you mind?" Julie lifted her hair off her neck, as she often did when she was having a hot flash. "It was an open attic when we were kids," she continued. "Just a bunch of beds divided by curtains."

"Like a dormitory?" Ruth asked.

"Sort of."

The three of us followed Ruth up the stairs, where we discovered the attic had been completely transformed. Now it contained an office with three skylights, a large playroom, two small bedrooms and a bathroom with a shower. Everything looked scrubbed and neat and well loved. You would have to work really hard to feel any bad memories in this house, I thought. There was nothing from the past left to trigger them.

I thought of asking to use the bathroom. I was okay for the moment, but I knew that my infected urinary tract could and would act up at any minute. Julie, Ruth and Ethan, though, were already heading back toward the stairs. I could wait.

Once we were downstairs again, Julie turned to Ruth. "It makes me happy to see how nice the whole house looks," she said, touching our hostess's arm. "I can tell you love living here."

"We do," she said, guiding us through the open French doors onto the porch. "Was the porch screened when you lived here?" she asked.

"Uh-huh," Julie said, looking from one end of the porch to the other. "This is where we spent most of our time."

I remembered the porch. Of all the house, it had changed the least, perhaps because the view was still of the small sandy backyard and the water. A long farm table and six ladder-back chairs stood where our old table used to be, and white faux wicker rockers and love seats and coffee tables filled the rest of the space.

The little boy I'd seen in the pool was sitting in the backyard, sharing a lounge chair with a man who appeared to be reading to him in the fading light. Nothing made me happier than seeing a parent sharing a book with a child.

Ruth must have seen me watching them. "Come meet my family," she said.

We walked outside. The sand in the backyard was already cooling down, and it felt good beneath my feet. The man spotted us and he and the boy stood up.

"Hi, Ethan," the man said. "And these must be the former owners."

Ethan introduced us to Ruth's husband, Jim, and their seven-year-old son, Carter. We chatted about the house and the area for a few minutes, swatting mosquitoes as darkness began to close in on us.

Julie's gaze shifted to the part of the yard nearest the corner of the house. "When I was a kid," she said, pointing, "I buried a box of treasures right over there."

"A treasure box?" Carter asked, looking interested in our conversation for the first time.

Julie nodded.

"Could it still be there?" Ruth asked.

Julie shrugged. "I don't know," she said. "Maybe someone found it during the last forty years, or they had some work done to the house foundation and it got disturbed."

"Or maybe it *is* still there," Ethan said. He nudged Julie. "Do you want to see?"

Julie looked at our hosts. "It wasn't buried very deep," she said, and I knew she was reassuring them that we wouldn't be digging up their entire yard. "Just a few inches, really."

Ruth looked at her husband, whose expression said, *Why the heck not?* "I'll get a shovel and flashlight," he said, and he headed toward the garage.

Carter looked up at Julie. Even in the dim light, I could see he had his mother's pretty blue eyes. "What did you put in the box?" he asked.

"Things I found," she said, as we started walking toward the corner of the house. "Just silly things."

Jim returned with a garden shovel and a strong halogen lantern.

"You know," Ruth said, looking at the small shovel her husband had provided, "people have brought in fresh sand over the years. We had a couple of truckloads come in when we moved here. It might be down pretty far by now, if it's still there at all."

Julie took the shovel and knelt in the sand, glancing at the corner of the house, taking some measurement with her eyes. I could tell that, even after all this time, she knew exactly where the box should be. With the shovel, she smoothed away a couple of inches of sand from the surface of the ground. Then she set the blade of the shovel into the sand at a ninety-degree angle, and we heard it hit something solid.

"Oh, my God," Julie said. "It's still here."

We all sat down on the ground, and Carter and I helped sweep the sand away with our hands, while Julie worked with the shovel and Jim held the lantern balanced on his knee. Soon the top of the box was completely exposed, and Julie dug her fingers around the lid on one side while I did the same on the other.

Julie looked at me across the box. "One, two, three," she said, and we lifted the lid together, sending a fine dusting of sand onto the objects below.

Carter reached into the bread box, and I wanted to stop him. This was Julie's box of treasures. I wanted her to be able to do this herself.

Ruth seemed to read my mind. "Wait, Carter," she said. "Let Julie do it, since it's really her box. Then maybe she'll let you use it for some of your own toys and things in the future."

Julie nodded her thanks to Ruth. "Of course, I'll let you use it," she said to Carter. "After tonight, it will be yours."

"Oh, good!" Carter folded his hands in his lap. What a nice kid.

I could see how hungry Julie was to dig through the old remnants of her life, but I had to go to the bathroom and that was all I could think about. I wished the antibiotics would kick in and knock the infection on its rear. I was about to tell everyone I needed to leave, when Julie suddenly let out a squeal. She reached into the box and pulled out a tiny leather baby shoe. It had probably been white at one time; in the lantern light it took on a yellowish-orange glow.

"Omigosh," Julie said. "I found this in the shallow water where Grandpop used to keep his killie trap." She looked across the open box at Ethan and smiled. "And where Ethan kept his marine laboratory."

Ethan laughed. "Oh, yeah," he said. "I forgot about that."

"Did your microscope still work after I...you know?" she asked him, and I could tell the question had an esoteric meaning known only to the two of them.

"It was fine," Ethan said.

Julie reached into the box again. "And look at this!" she said, pulling out an old record, a forty-five. She held it under the splash of light from the lantern and laughed. "Neil Sedaka. 'Happy Birthday Sweet Sixteen,'" she said. "I don't know where I picked that up."

I had to interrupt. "I'm afraid I need to use the bathroom," I said, getting to my feet. "I'll go over to Ethan's and be back in a min—"

"Use ours," Ruth said, nodding toward the house. "Go ahead."

"Thanks," I said. I walked up the two steps to the porch, pushed open the screen door, then raced down the hallway toward the bathroom, leaving my sister's yelps of discovery behind me.

CHAPTER 42

Julie

Sifting through that box was the strangest thing. I was glad for the poor lighting in the backyard, because my eyes were misty and I didn't want anyone to notice. I felt sympathy for the lonely girl who'd tucked meaningless objects away, longing for a mystery to solve. She'd never imagined the real, unwanted mystery that would await her midway through that summer. Picking out the scraps of old cloth, the dented Ping-Pong ball, the baby shoe, I became aware as never before that I had indeed been a mere child, a twelve-year-old with little concept of real danger. The only scary things I'd known about were from my Nancy Drew books, where the heroine always prevailed in the end.

Something caught my eye in the bottom corner of the bread box, tucked beneath another record and a piece of cloth. It couldn't possibly be what I thought it was.

"Could you move the lantern a little closer, please, Jim?" I asked.

The circle of light fell into the box, and there it was. Red and purple, as I remembered it. I reached into the corner and pulled out the small plastic giraffe.

"I never put this in here," I said, quite certain that was the truth.

"What is it?" Ethan asked, leaning closer. I could feel his breath against my bare shoulder.

"A toy," I said. "A giraffe. Isabel and Ned used to—"

"That was Ned's," Ethan interrupted me. "Our uncle gave it to him. He gave us both one. Mine was an elephant. It's a puzzle." He reached for it.

"A puzzle?" I was confused. "I thought it was just a token they used to pass between each other."

"Who did?" Ethan examined the giraffe. "Ned and your sister?"

I nodded.

"I'm not sure how this one works," he said. He was manipulating the giraffe's tail and neck; I had never even realized the toy had moving parts. Suddenly the red and purple halves of the giraffe sprung apart, and I laughed out loud.

"They must have sent *notes* to each other in the giraffe!" I said. "I never guessed."

Ethan held the halves of the giraffe beneath the lamplight.

"It looks like there's a note in here right now," he said.

CHAPTER 43

Lucy

I finished in the bathroom and walked into the dimly lit hallway. I was standing next to the screened front door when I heard laughter out on the road. I turned to look, but it had grown so dark that I could barely make out the group of small, giggling children as they ran down the street. I couldn't have said how many there were or if they were boys or girls, but watching them, I began once again to remember the night Isabel died, and for a moment, Julie and her Nancy Drew box were forgotten.

I remembered waking up alone in the attic that night, determined not to scream. I remembered my frantic race down the pull-down stairs and the way they'd shivered under my light weight. But I had not gone immediately to my parents' room and then to the couch to sleep, as I'd previously recalled. First, I'd gone to the back porch to find Julie. I'd looked in the direction of the bed at the end of the long porch, but it had been too dark to see if anyone was there.

"Julie?" I'd called.

There'd been no answer and the darkness had felt suffocating to me. I could hear the water lapping against the bulkhead, and the croaking of a frog joined the nighttime music of the crickets. I was aware of the woods outside the screens to my right, but I couldn't see the trees for the darkness, and the thought of what might be lurking out there made me turn and run back into the living room and then down the hall.

That's when I stood outside my parents' door, listening to my mother's breathing. I'd thought of pulling the cushions from the sofa, setting them on the floor outside her room to sleep there, as close as I could get to her. But before I could act on that idea, I realized I needed to use the bathroom. I walked quietly down the short hallway, comforted by the sound of my grandfather's snoring from the front bedroom he shared with Grandma. The screen door leading to the front yard was in front of me, the main door held open by a heavy iron doorstop shaped like a Scottie dog. It was as dark on the other side of that door as it was in the hallway. I hated that we never locked the doors at night. Oh, the screen door was secured by one of those flimsy hook-and-eye locks, but that had offered me little peace of mind once I realized how easily it could be foiled.

I turned on the light in the small bathroom, glad to finally be able to see everything. I urinated, not bothering to flush because I didn't want to awaken anyone and have to explain what I was doing downstairs at that hour. I turned off the light and quietly left the room. To my right, the hallway leading back to the living room looked dark and foreboding, so I stood by the screen door as I waited for my eyes to adjust again to the darkness.

Outside, I saw a flicker of light through the woods, somewhere near the road. I thought at first it was a firefly, but the tiny light burned bright orange and I quickly realized it was a cigarette. I watched the light arc and sway as the shadowy person carrying the cigarette walked along the dirt road in the direction of our house. I smiled in relief. *Isabel*. She was probably walking home from Pam's or Mitzi's, enjoying one last smoke before she had to come in. But how did she expect to get in with the lock on the door? I thought it was her good fortune that I happened to be there.

I lifted the lock with my finger and was about to push the door open when the shadowy image and its cigarette continued down the road, past our sidewalk, past our driveway. I slipped the lock back into the eye. It was not Isabel after all. I lost sight of the person, but the light of the cigarette continued to burn, making a sharp angle in the air as the smoker turned to walk up the Chapmans' driveway.

CHAPTER 44

Julie

"It's too dark to read it out here," I said, carefully unfolding the small sheet of paper I'd removed from the front half of the giraffe. "I'm not even certain there's any writing on it."

Jim moved the lantern closer to my hands, but Ethan touched my shoulder.

"Let's take it back to my house," he said. "We've taken up enough of the Kleins' time."

I sensed his concern. He knew that a note written by my dead sister or his dead brother was sure to elicit emotions he didn't want to share with his neighbors.

"Oh, but this is fun," Ruth said, obviously curious about what we'd found.

"Probably just a love note from my brother to Julie's sister," Ethan said. "Not fit for the PG-13 crowd." He got to his feet.

I tucked the paper back into the giraffe, holding the red and purple halves of the toy together as Ethan helped me up. Jim and Ruth stood, as well, but Carter remained seated next to the buried bread box, still peering inside it, although without the lantern light I was certain he could see little. I guessed he was thinking about the wonderful treasures he could bury there himself.

The screen door squeaked open as Lucy left the porch and rejoined us in the yard.

"Thank you so much for the tour," I said to the Kleins. "And Carter, the treasure box is all yours now."

"Awesome!" he said, getting to his feet.

"Thank Julie," Ruth instructed him.

"Thank you," he said.

"You're very welcome." I looked at Ruth and Jim. "And thanks for letting us dig up your yard."

"Sure." Jim grinned, his face ghostly in the lantern light.

"Please feel free to come over anytime," Ruth said.

We walked between the two houses to get to Ethan's front yard. I held on to Lucy's arm.

"We found this old plastic giraffe in the Nancy Drew box," I told her. "There's a piece of paper in it. Ned and Isabel used to use it to send notes to each other. But the weird thing is, I am ninety-nine point nine-percent sure I never put it in the box."

Lucy was quiet. As Ethan pushed open his front door, she whispered in my ear, "I remembered something about the night Isabel was killed," she said.

"What?" I whispered back, uncertain why we were being stealthy. She didn't answer me.

"What?" I asked again, and she shook her head quickly.

"Later," she whispered, and I knew better than to push her; she must have had her reasons for keeping her memory from Ethan.

We followed Ethan out to his porch, where he turned on the floor lamp, flooding the table with light.

"Let's take a look at that paper," he said, as the three of us sat down.

I opened the giraffe and the folded piece of paper fell out. Carefully I flattened it on the tabletop. It was a note, written on what looked to be half a sheet of pale pink stationery, its one edge ragged, torn on an angle. The writing had faded to a bleached bluish purple, but I recognized it instantly.

"It's Izzy's writing," I said. Isabel had had a distinctive, rounded handwriting that had gotten her into trouble with the nuns in catechism class.

I read the note aloud.

"You are a decietful pig and I hate you," I read. *"I can't wait to tell my father everything. He adores me and you can bet he will kill you."*

The three of us were quiet, letting the words sink in.

Ethan was first to speak, his voice a tired whisper. "Damn," he said. "She and Ned must have been on the outs."

I thought of telling him my suspicion about Ned's involvement with Pam, but before I could speak, I realized that Lucy was crying.

"Oh, honey." I put my arm around her, guessing that she was moved and shaken by seeing a note from our sister. But that was not it.

"I remembered something," she said, to both of us now.

Ethan pulled a handkerchief from his pocket and handed it to her, and she pressed it to her eyes.

"The night Isabel died," she said, "I woke up alone in the attic. I was afraid and came downstairs, looking for you—" she spoke to me "—but of course, I couldn't find you, since you'd gone out in the boat. I went to the bathroom, and when I came out, I happened to look toward the road and I saw someone out there. I saw the burning tip of a cigarette. I thought it was Isabel at first, walking home from one of her girlfriends' houses. But then the person walked right past our house and up your driveway." She looked at Ethan.

Ethan closed his eyes and leaned back in his chair. We were all quiet for a moment.

"I feel sick," he said finally.

"Did Ned smoke?" Lucy asked.

Ethan nodded without opening his eyes. "Like a chimney."

"I'm sorry, Ethan," I said.

"It still doesn't make sense, though." Ethan opened his eyes and looked at the note again as if he might be able to read between the lines. "What does this mean? How did he deceive her?" He shook his head with a stubborn resolve. "I still refuse to think that Ned was capable of killing anyone."

"I think he was seeing Pam Durant on the side," I said.

"Why do you say that?" he asked.

I told him the reasons for my suspicions—George possibly spotting Ned and Pam together on the boat, Mitzi's suggestion that they would start dating after Isabel's death, and how Ned had turned to Pam for comfort.

"Isabel probably found out," I suggested. "She wrote him this note. He met her on the platform at the bay and they argued and he…"

"Maybe it was an accident," Lucy said kindly. "He didn't mean to kill her."

"Things don't add up," Ethan said. "I mean, to begin with, Ned told you to tell Isabel he couldn't meet her that night."

"But remember, he called her at Mitzi's to say he might be able to."

Ethan looked surprised. "I don't think I ever knew that," he said.

"How did the note end up in your Nancy Drew box, of all places?" Lucy asked.

"I have no idea," I said. "They used me as a messenger, giving me the giraffe to pass between them, but I never realized it was a puzzle. Something they could hide notes in. And maybe I…I have no memory of this at all…but maybe I *did* stick it in the box and don't remember doing it."

"Or maybe Ned put it in there thinking you'd find it and realize what had happened and turn him in," Lucy said. "Maybe he felt guilty but couldn't bring himself to admit what he'd done."

"Wait a minute," Ethan said. "He had an *alibi.* He was in our yard with my father."

"Ethan." I rested my hand on his forearm. "Did it ever occur to you that your father was just trying to protect him? That he made up the alibi for him?"

Ethan shook his head. "He wouldn't do that," he said, but I thought he was only saying what he longed to believe.

I don't think any of us slept that night. Next to me, Ethan tossed and turned. I was haunted, not so much by what Isabel had written or by the realization that Ned was probably responsible for her death, because this was not a surprise to me, but by seeing Izzy's handwriting. By seeing that part of her, still so alive all these years later. Seeing the rounded *a*'s and the misspelling of *deceitful*. The misspelling made me want to cry. It humanized my big sister and made her seem so young and guileless.

Over breakfast the next morning, Lucy suggested we leave the shore early, drive home and pay a visit to our mother to tell her about the note before giving it to the police.

"I don't think we need to tell her," I argued. "You know she hasn't been herself lately, and this would only upset her more." I knew I was protecting myself, as well. I didn't want to talk to my mother about Isabel any more than I had to.

"I know it'll upset her," Lucy said, "but that's inevitable, and I want to keep her abreast of things. The less she learns from the police instead of from us, the better."

"I think Lucy's right," Ethan said. "And as soon as the cops see this note, they're going to want to talk to my father again. I can't believe, though, that he would have lied about where Ned was that night."

"Maybe he wasn't lying," Lucy offered. "Maybe he was just off on his timing. Give him a chance to explain."

Ethan looked toward the canal and the heavy Saturday-morning boat traffic. "Damn," he said, more to himself than to us. "I wish Ned were here to tell us what really happened."

"Me, too," I said.

I dropped Lucy off at her house in Plainfield, and we agreed to meet at Mom's that afternoon when she got home from McDonald's. By the time I turned onto my street in Westfield, I felt a mixture of deep sorrow and vindication. I had been right about Ned all this time. I wished George Lewis were alive. I wished I could hug him, tell him how sorry I was that I had not been more capable of proving Ned's guilt when I was twelve years old.

I slowed down as I neared my house, surprised to see cars crowding my driveway, spilling out into the street. One of them was Shannon's car. The rest were unfamiliar to me, and with a sense of betrayal and disappointment, I realized that Shannon had taken advantage of my weekend away to use the house for a party, one that had apparently continued overnight and late into the next morning. Perhaps she planned for it to run the entire weekend.

I had to park in front of my neighbors' house, since there was no room in front of my own. I walked into the house, greeted by the overwhelming stench of stale beer and possibly marijuana, although that might have been my imagination. Teenagers were sleeping on my living room furniture as well as on the floor. One girl lifted her head from the sofa when I walked in.

"Where's Shannon?" I asked, barely able to control my anger. I could feel my face and neck redden with it.

"Shannon who?" the girl asked. "Oh, the girl who lives here?"

"Yes," I said through my gritted teeth.

"I think she's upstairs."

I marched upstairs and into Shannon's room, where I found two blond girls sleeping together, one of them nude, their arms wrapped around each other. My fury mounted as I walked toward my own bedroom. I threw open the door to find my daughter and Tanner in my bed. Tanner was asleep, but the noise of my entry apparently awakened Shannon. She sat up quickly, pulling the sheet against her chest, her long hair tangled over her bare shoulders.

"Mom!" she said.

I threw my pocketbook down on my dresser. "What the hell do you think you're doing?" I asked.

"I'm sorry, Mom," she said, clutching the sheet tighter to her chest. She was speaking softly, as though she didn't want to disturb Tanner. "People just kept showing up," she said. "I'm really sorry. We were going to clean everything up before you got home. Change the sheets and everything. And vacuum."

I stared at her. Who *was* this child?

"I feel like I don't know you," I said. "What happened to the responsible girl I raised?"

"I *am* responsible," she argued. "I planned to tell you what happened. About the party and everything. I didn't expect you to come home yet."

"That's obvious," I said. "You know what, Shannon? You are absolutely *not* moving to Colorado. I'm still your mother and I'm not going to let you live like this." I waved my hand in Tanner's direction. "And what kind of a man would sleep with you in your mother's bed?" I asked. I couldn't believe Tanner was actually sleeping through my tirade. He was probably awake and listening, but had decided it was best if he pretended otherwise.

"I am too going," Shannon said.

"No, you're not."

She shook her head, an ugly expression on her otherwise beautiful face. "Sometimes I really hate you," she said. I hadn't heard those words from her since she was a four-year-old begging in vain for candy in the grocery store, but I didn't flinch.

"I don't care," I said. "I'll lock you in your room if I have to. I have to protect you."

My voice broke on the word *protect,* and I began to cry. I sank onto the chair in front of my vanity dresser, burying my face in my hands. I could hear her getting out of my bed, pulling on her clothes, but all I could think about was Isabel's angry note hidden in the giraffe. Her fury in that note had not been directed at our mother, but it often had been in those days. I could remember her telling Mom that she hated her, and I wondered if my mother had felt as hurt and helpless as I did right now.

Shannon came to my side, wrapping her arms around me, and I leaned against her, aware—so aware—of her swollen belly beneath my cheek.

"I'm sorry, Mom," she said. "I know I screwed up."

I couldn't speak. I sat there with Shannon's arms around me. I remembered how hard my mother had tried to rein Isabel in and how spectacularly she'd failed. She must have been so scared to see her daughter slipping out of her control. Just as I was scared now.

CHAPTER 45

Maria

Julie and Lucy were waiting for me in my living room when I got home from Micky D's. I'd planned to change my clothes and head to the hospital to do my volunteer work, but they said they needed to talk to me and I knew by their serious faces that I'd better cancel my plans.

"What's wrong?" I asked them. There was way too much going on in my family for my comfort level. My best guess was that the police were finally ready to question me about Isabel and that made me nervous, but I tried not to let it show.

"We just want to talk to you," Julie said.

Bullfeathers, I thought, but I didn't push her for the truth. I would find out soon enough.

Lucy called the volunteer coordinator at the hospital to cancel my shift, while I changed out of my uniform in my bedroom. When I returned to the living room, the two of them were sitting in the armchairs near the sofa looking so grim that my heart began to pound. I sat down on the sofa, folding my hands in my lap.

"Now," I began, "what is going on?"

"We need to talk to you about Isabel's death," Lucy said.

"Are the police ready to interview me?" I asked.

"No," Julie said, "but Lucy and I made a discovery we thought you should know about. We wanted you to hear about it from us first, rather than from the police."

I was quiet and calm on the outside, but my hands began working at one another in my lap.

Julie reached into her pocketbook and pulled out some kind of toy.

"What's that?" I leaned forward, and Julie held the toy in the air so I could see it better. "Is it a giraffe?" I asked.

"Yes." Julie lowered the red and purple toy to her knees. "Lucy and I stayed at Ethan's house last night, and we talked to the people who now live in our bungalow."

I felt a sharp blow to my solar plexus at the mention of our old summer home.

"Do you remember my Nancy Drew box?" Julie asked. "The bread box where I used to put any clues I found?"

Bread box? I didn't know what she was talking about.

"I remember you used to collect clues," I said. "You did that when we lived here in Westfield. Did you collect them down the shore, too?"

"Yes," Julie said. "Grandpop found an old bread box for me to keep the clues in, and he buried it for me in the yard."

"I don't remember that," I said.

"Well, it was something I kept secret," Julie said. "But anyway, when we visited the people who live in the house now, I asked if I could dig up the bread box. When I did, we found this giraffe inside it. But I don't think I ever put it there myself."

I felt as though I was struggling to make sense of a riddle. "So?" I asked.

"Well, this comes apart." Julie did something with the giraffe's tail and the toy broke into two pieces. "Ned and Isabel used to pass it back and forth, with notes inside it."

"Oh," I said, more to myself than to them. I had tried so hard to keep those two children apart, and until the very end, I'd thought I'd succeeded.

"We found a note inside it," Julie said. She removed a folded piece of paper from inside the back end of the giraffe. "Should I read it to you or do you want to see it for yourself?" she asked me.

I reached out a hand. "I want to see it," I said.

She looked reluctant to turn the piece of paper over to me, but after a moment's hesitation, she stood up and dropped it into my hand. I unfolded it and flattened it on my lap, adjusting my glasses so that I could read the faded writing.

"*Oh,*" I said again, this time with some distress as I saw Isabel's girlish handwriting. Then I read the words and was filled with horror. *Oh, my God.*

"I'm sorry, Mom," Julie said. "I know it's painful to read."

"Our best guess is that this was Isabel's last note to Ned," Lucy said. "Maybe Ned put the note in Julie's Nancy Drew box, expecting her to look in there before we left the shore. He had to know she'd take it to the police, who would then realize that Isabel had been angry at him, and that he probably did meet her on the—"

"Hush," I said, shutting my eyes.

The room grew so still I could hear my own breathing.

"Would you rather not talk about this, Mom?" Julie asked softly. Neither she nor Lucy could possibly understand the reason for my distress. I was going to have to tell them things I'd never wanted known.

I opened my eyes again and looked first at Julie, then Lucy.

"I am as certain as I can be that this note was not meant for Ned Chapman," I said.

"Oh, Mom," Julie said, "I'm sure it was. I'm sure—"

I held up my hand to stop her. "I have to tell you girls something. It's...I'd hoped I'd never have to tell anyone about it. It's something I regret. But it needs to come out. You need to know."

"What are you talking about?" Lucy asked.

I looked down at the note in my lap, touching the paper my Isabel had once touched, and I knew my eyes were glassy when I raised my eyes to my daughters again.

"I wasn't just friends with Mr....with Ross Chapman when we were kids," I said. "We dated as teenagers, as well."

"You did?" Julie asked.

"We did," I said. "But his family didn't approve of me because I was half Italian, so we had to see each other on the sly for years."

"Like Ned and Isabel," Lucy said.

"Were you in love with him?" Julie asked.

I nodded. "For a while, yes. And I was always...I was attracted to him." I felt uncomfortable. I'd never talked to Julie or Lucy about this sort of thing before. "But I knew he was shallow because he let his parents dictate who he could or could not see," I said. For a moment, I got lost in my memory, and the girls were patient as they waited for me to come back.

"I married your father in 1944," I said, "but that summer, I...I had relations with Ross."

"Oh, Mom," Lucy said, and I heard sympathy rather than condemnation in her voice.

"It might have been what they call date rape today," I said. "Like what happened to Ethan's daughter. I don't know." I shrugged. "I went along with him at first and then realized what I was doing...what we were doing...and told him to stop, but he didn't. I'm so ashamed to tell you this," I said, unable to look either of them in the eye.

"Oh, Mommy." Julie moved to the sofa, sitting close to me, and I was touched that she had called me "mommy," that the endearment just spilled out of her that way. She rested her hand on my shoulder, a little awkwardly, but I loved the touch. "You were young," she said. "Things like that happen. Don't be ashamed."

"I am, though," I said. "The terrible thing is that, a few months later, when I realized I was pregnant, I wasn't sure if the baby was your father's or Ross's."

I saw my daughters look at each other as the meaning of my words dawned on them.

"Isabel might have been Mr. Chapman's daughter?" Lucy asked.

"I don't know," I said. "I never knew for sure. Your father and I...well, we made love nearly every weekend during that time and I'd only been with Ross once, but I still was never sure whose child I was carrying."

Isabel had been born in April. She'd been fair, like Ross, but Charles had thought nothing of it. To him, she was his little angel, while I feared she was proof of my sin. When we took her to Bay

Head Shores in late June, Ross took one look at her, did a little math in his head and figured she was his. I could see it in his eyes.

"Her hair was light when she was born," I continued, "but you know how dark it got as she grew older, and she had your father's straight nose. Still, I was never completely certain."

"No wonder you wanted to keep Ned and Izzy apart!" Julie exclaimed. "You poor thing. That must have been terrible for you." Her hand was on my shoulder again, this time rubbing me gently through the sleeve of my jersey. It felt so comforting.

"Could you talk to anyone about it, Mom?" Lucy asked. "Any of your girlfriends?"

I shook my head. I knew Lucy would find such a lack of confidantes unbearable. She *had* to talk to people about whatever was going on with her. If she got a pimple, she would find herself a pimple support group. But all I cared about back then was *not* talking about it. I desperately needed to keep my indiscretion to myself.

Lucy moved to the couch, sitting next to me on the opposite side from Julie. "I'm so glad you're telling us now," she said.

I could smell each of them—Lucy and her lemony shampoo, Julie and her subtle floral cologne. I had never before felt the way I did at that moment—comforted, supported and understood by my daughters. I knew they were shocked by what I had told them, but I felt no blame from them. I loved my girls.

I took one of their hands in each of mine and raised them both to my lips.

"Thank you, dears," I said. "But there's more you need to know."

1962

The summer Isabel died was, for obvious reasons, the worst summer of my life. Even before her death, though, I was deeply troubled. Isabel had grown difficult over the previous year. It was normal adolescent behavior, I knew, but still challenging to deal with and I was not good at it. I was so worried about her that I clamped down too hard and she fought back like a caged animal. I was particularly concerned that she was getting too close to Ned. I prayed every night that they were not brother and sister, and in my heart of hearts, I felt certain they were not. Yet I knew the chance existed and felt it was my duty to keep them apart. The more I tried, though, the more Izzy fought me.

The evening before Isabel's death, my parents took Julie and Lucy to the boardwalk and Charles had already left for Westfield. I thought I heard a knock on the screen door of the porch. I was washing dishes in the kitchen, and I turned off the tap to listen.

"Maria?"

I knew the voice. I only heard it those days when Ross was in his yard with his sons or his wife, but I knew it all the same.

I dried my hands on a dish towel, then walked through the living room to the porch. Ross stood outside, his face close to the screen, his hand over his forehead so that he could see into our bungalow.

"Hello, Ross," I said, standing a distance from the door.

"Can I come in?" he asked. "I need to talk to you."

I pushed the screen door open, and he stepped onto the porch. In retrospect, I should have gone into the yard with him. Everything might have turned out differently, if only I'd not let him in.

Ross looked nervous, or at least as nervous as a State Supreme Court chief justice was capable of looking.

"I saw your parents leave with the girls," he said.

"They've gone to the boardwalk."

"Did Isabel go with them?" He looked behind me as if he might see her standing there.

"No," I said. "She's out with her girlfriends."

He looked relieved. "Good. I need to talk to you."

"Yes, you mentioned that." I was standing with my arms folded across my chest, conveying, I was certain, a tired sort of impatience.

He glanced toward the end of the porch that faced his bungalow. "Can we go inside?" he asked quietly.

I followed his gaze in the direction of his house. I could see no movement on his back porch, but it was apparent that whatever Ross wanted to say to me, he wanted to say in private. I gave in.

"Come into the living room," I said.

He followed me inside the house, then sat down on the wicker rocker and rubbed his chin. I leaned against the side of one of the upholstered chairs rather than sit down myself. I didn't want this conversation to be long.

"Listen," he said. "I'm certain that Ned and Isabel are involved...romantically."

Did he mean they were having sex? "I don't think so," I said.

"You've got your head in the sand," he said. "She and Ned are together more than you know. More than *I* knew. Ethan told me they sneak around to be together."

My heart gave a great *thump.* "Maybe Ethan is trying to get his big brother in trouble," I suggested. "I always know where she's going and who she's with and she's good about keeping to her curfew." That was nonsense, but I wasn't going to let him know I'd lost control of my daughter.

Ross smiled at me. "Your parents and mine would have said the same thing about us when we were Isabel and Ned's ages, don't you think?"

I looked away from him. He was right.

"Humor me for a moment," he said. "Pretend that I'm right about Isabel and Ned being involved. Then you and I would need to find a way to put an end to their relationship, wouldn't you agree?"

I had spent the early part of the summer making sure Izzy and Ned were *not* involved, and until this discussion, I'd thought I had succeeded. But now I was faced with a different problem: I was unwilling to admit to Ross that Isabel actually might be his. I was ninety-percent certain she was Charles's child, but that ten percent haunted me.

"I do agree," I said, "because of the very, *very* slight possibility that...you know. But it's moot, because I'm certain she's not seeing him. I would know. I would—"

"Would you *wake up,* Maria?" He stood up, his voice loud, his hands moving through the air. "She doesn't look a thing like Charles."

"She doesn't look like you, either," I said. "She looks like me."

"She has my mother's chin and cheekbones," Ross said.

"Oh, stop it." I covered my uneasiness with a laugh. "Why don't you go home and—"

"I am *not* allowing my son to screw his sister!" he shouted, his face red.

I was furious. "Get out," I said. I walked across the porch toward the door. "Get out right now."

He stared at me a moment, then walked past me onto the porch. "You better hope she doesn't turn up pregnant," he said.

Once he was gone, I let out my breath and was rubbing my hands over my eyes when I suddenly heard a sound coming from the attic. I froze. Footsteps skittered across the attic floor and I turned to see Isabel on the stairs. They swayed and creaked beneath her as she rushed to get down them, and I pressed my hand to my mouth.

"What were you *talking* about?" she shouted as she jumped the last few steps to the floor.

"*Izzy,*" I said, struggling to make my voice light, as if anything she'd overheard could be explained away with a chuckle. "I thought you were out with Mitzi and Pam."

"I had a headache, not that it's any of your business," she said. There was fire in her dark eyes. She looked *nothing* like Ross. *Nothing.* "What did Mr. Chapman mean about me being Ned's sister?" she asked.

I tried to look surprised. "What?" I said. "I think you must have misunderstood him, honey."

"How could I possibly be his sister?" she asked.

I couldn't find my voice. Isabel shook her head at me as understanding dawned on her. "You tramp," she said. "You were married to Daddy and you slept with Mr. Chapman?" She put her hand over her own mouth as though she might get sick. "Oh, God," she said. "You're disgusting."

I had no words left in me to deny it or explain it. "I made a mistake, Isabel," I said. "But I am as certain as I can be that you are Daddy's child. You don't need to worry about that."

"Is this why you've tried so hard to keep Ned and me apart?" Her eyes were brimming with tears now. I wanted to hold her, but I knew she would never allow it.

"You and Ned are too young to get serious with anyone," I said.

She looked at me with something like hatred in her eyes. "I cannot *wait* to tell Daddy about this," she said. "You're nothing but a slut, Mother. And you give me all these rules I'm supposed to obey. What a joke you are." She turned and ran down the hallway toward the front door and out of the house.

I stood still in the electrified silence, pressing my hands together in front of me. It would destroy Charles if she told him, and in turn, it would destroy me. Charles would never divorce me, but our marriage would be ruined forever. I had to put those thoughts aside, though. Right now, my main concern had to be the emotional state of my child.

I went outside and spotted Isabel across the street sitting among the blueberry bushes, not far from the very place she might have been conceived. She was crying her heart out. I walked across the street and sat down next to her, trying to pull her into my arms, but she stiffened at my touch.

"Tell me it's not true," she pleaded. "Tell me Ned's not my brother."

"I don't think he is," I said. "But it is true that he could be."

"Oh, God." She stood up, her body heaving with her sobs. Then she leaned over, picked up a fistful of sand, and threw it directly into my face. I blinked quickly. The sand seared my eyes and I covered them with my hands, trying not to cry out from the pain.

"I mean it, Mother," she said, her voice somewhere above me. "When Daddy comes this weekend, I'm going to tell him every single thing. I'm going to tell him he has a whore for a wife. I can't wait. I hope he divorces you."

It was minutes before I could open my eyes well enough to make my way back to the bungalow and I spent half an hour in the bathroom trying to wash out the sand. I knew I would have to tell Charles the truth before Isabel was able to, but as it turned out, neither of us ever got the chance.

"Izzy wrote that note to Mr. Chapman," Julie said, when I'd finished my story.

I nodded. "That makes the most sense," I said. "I don't know how or why it ended up in your...your bread box, but this—" I lifted the piece of paper. "I'm sure this note was meant for Ross."

CHAPTER 46

Julie

I waited for Ethan in the parking lot of his father's independent-living residence in Lakewood. I'd arrived as the sun was setting and I lowered my windows, letting a light, hot breeze fill my car. I kept my eyes trained on the entrance to the lot as I watched for Ethan's truck.

It had been a long and difficult day, starting with my discovery of the remnants of Shannon's party in my house. While I was at my mother's, Shannon and Tanner worked like dogs to clean everything up. Tanner had been contrite, but my opinion of him had taken a nosedive from which he would have a hard time recovering.

When I got home from Mom's, the house was immaculate and Shannon and Tanner were out. I was glad of that, because I was still reeling from my mother's revelation about her relationship with Ross Chapman. I wasn't sure who had killed my sister, but I knew now that I'd had little, if anything, to do with it. Listening to my mother speak had lifted forty-one years' worth of guilt from my shoulders. Isabel had not died because of me. I had been little more than a blind alley in a complex maze of a story. My guilt was replaced by a deep sympathy for my mother, who had lived with her own demons for most of her life.

I'd sat in my spotless living room, the phone in my lap, for many minutes before getting the courage to call Ethan. Once I did, I told him about our conversation with my mother, being careful how I couched it. I made her one-time, extramarital lovemaking with Ross Chapman sound consensual. Maybe it was. Who knew what sort of twist my mother had given the event in the past sixty years to ease her conscience? I didn't want to hurt Ethan more than I had to.

He grew so quiet on the phone, I thought he'd hung up.

"My parents had such a good marriage, though," he said finally.

"That's probably true," I reassured him. I hated that I was shaking his world. "So did my parents. What happened between your father and my mother was very early in both their marriages. They were young and…maybe they were still adjusting to being married."

"So," Ethan said slowly, "if the note was written to my father, that still doesn't explain how it got in your bread box."

"I know," Julie said.

"Are you thinking he…that he was the one who…" He couldn't seem to finish the sentence.

"I don't know, Ethan," I said. "I don't know what to think."

"I need to talk to him," he said. "In person. How do you feel about going with me?"

I thought of how I had Lucy to share the burden of the past with me. Ethan had no one. I didn't want him to go through this alone. "Of course I'll go with you," I said.

So here I sat, while my mixed-up daughter was out somewhere with her baby's father and Lucy comforted our distraught mother.

I saw Ethan's truck turn into the lot, and I got out of my car as he pulled up next to me.

Once out of his truck, he drew me into a hug. "Thanks for agreeing to meet me here," he said into my ear. He held on to me for a minute and I pressed my palms flat against his back.

"You okay?" I whispered.

He let go of me. "Not really," he said. I could see the frown lines between his eyebrows and the tight set of his jaw.

"Does he know we're coming?" I asked.

He nodded, taking my hand as we walked toward the entrance to the large brick building. "I called him and ended up telling him nearly everything because he kept asking questions. I said that your mother told you about her relationship with him and the possibility that he had been Isabel's father," he said. "And I told him about the note in the giraffe."

"What did he say?"

"Nothing for a minute. Then I could hear him crying." Ethan shuddered, squeezing my hand tightly. "I've never seen my father cry," he said. "I've never even seen him near tears, not when my mother or Ned died. He couldn't speak, and I told him that I was coming over and not to worry. That we'd work everything out." We were in the lobby now and Ethan pushed the button for the elevator. "He said 'all right.' I swear, Julie, he sounded like a scared little kid."

A couple of the residents—two elderly women using walkers—got on the elevator with us, so we said nothing as we rode to the fifth floor. We got off the elevator, and Ethan led me down the hall at a quick pace. He knocked on a door bearing a small, faux-ivy wreath. We could hear noise inside. A thud. A squeak. But no one answered Ethan's knock.

Ethan leaned close to the door. "Dad?" he called. Still no response.

He looked down at his key chain and sorted through the keys until he found the right one. Slipping it into the lock, he pushed open the door.

We were in a small, neat living/dining room combination, with heavy, dark cherry furniture and rich leather wingback chairs befitting a former chief justice.

"Dad?" Ethan called toward what must have been the bedroom. He took a step in that direction, but froze at the sound of a scream coming from somewhere outside the building. We looked toward the living-room windows. One of them was open, the screen missing.

"God, no!" Ethan rushed toward the window.

I followed him and rested my hand on his back as he leaned out the window to look at the ground below.

"No," he wailed. "Oh, my God, Dad! No."

Now there was a chorus of screams coming from the ground far below us and I started to tremble. I did not want to see what he was seeing. Ethan pulled away from the window and dropped to the floor, his hands covering his face. I sat down next to him and wrapped my arms around him, and I rocked him, as we waited for the sound of sirens.

Mr. Chapman had used the second bedroom in his apartment as an office, and it was there, on an otherwise empty desktop, that one of the police officers found the letter addressed to Ethan.

Dearest Son,

On August 5, 1962, Isabel Bauer approached me in our backyard and slipped a note to me. That was the note you found, in which she threatened to tell her father about my indiscretion with her mother. I suppose all these years later, it's hard for you to understand how threatening that was to me. Charles Bauer could do irreparable damage to my career. He had power and plenty of friends in high places. He could easily have ruined me and my political aspirations.

I knew that Ned was in the habit of meeting Isabel on the beach at midnight. I forbade him to meet her that night, but I overheard him talking to her on the phone, telling her he might be able to sneak out after all. I saw that as my opportunity to talk to her alone. I lit into Ned, telling him he could not go out. Then I went to meet her myself. Please understand, I had no intention of killing Isabel. I merely wanted to talk to her in private so that I could dissuade her from speaking to her father about me. I found her on the platform. It was dark and I think as I swam out to her, she may have thought I was Ned. She was furious when she discovered I had come to speak with her. She tried to jump in the water to get away from me, but I grabbed her arm and we struggled. I guess that's when her sister heard her scream and yell for help, although I don't remember everything that happened. All I know is we argued and she fell into the water. I did not push her. I had no idea that she'd hit her head or that she'd drowned. I thought she was simply swimming underwater to get away from me. I didn't know she'd died until the next morning. I told the police I'd spent the night stargazing with Ned in our yard, knowing that Ned would think my lie was meant to protect him, but it had really been to protect myself and my career.

I've struggled with my guilt all these years, not only over Isabel Bauer's death but over Ned's descent into depression and alcoholism as well. I am quite certain that Ned found the note from Isabel, as it disappeared from the cigarette box in which I'd placed it, though he never said a word to me about it. I'm sure that he put two and two together and realized my role in Isabel's death. I feel as though I killed them both.

Don't grieve for me, Ethan. I've had far more joy in my life than I've deserved and much of that has come from watching you become the skilled carpenter, wonderful father and honorable man you are today. I love you.

Dad

CHAPTER 47

Maria

Lucy left about eight last night, once I'd convinced her I was fine—which I most certainly was not. Then Julie called at ten-thirty, just to check up on me, she said, but her voice was strange. A little too falsely chipper. She told me she wouldn't make it to church this morning, but she asked me to come over to her house after mass for brunch with her and Lucy and Ethan. I accepted the invitation. I kept trying to still my mind, telling myself the truth would come out in time and that I couldn't change it by thinking about it, but despite my efforts, my thoughts raced and I barely slept a wink all night long. I knew something was up. I was not an idiot. I suspected Julie was going to tell me what I'd already guessed: Ross Chapman murdered my child.

The sermon at church this morning was about repentance. *Aha,* I thought, *this sermon is custom designed for me.* I was prepared to give the priest all my attention, and yet my mind still wandered. I was glad when mass was over, and I actually ran a yellow light in my rush to get to Julie's.

I arrived before Lucy and Ethan and let myself in the front door. I heard shouting coming from the kitchen. Shannon's voice, then Julie's. I was about to walk into the middle of an argument. Shannon screamed an expletive at her mother, and I cringed. Not an argument, I thought. A down-and-dirty *fight*.

Julie was yelling about cutting Shannon off from her health insurance if she moved to Colorado with her young man.

"And forget about me paying for college if you ever decide to go," she yelled. Julie was not a yeller, and I knew she had reached the point of desperation with my granddaughter. "Forget about any monetary support from me, period!" she shouted.

Shannon gave as good as she got, calling her mother manipulative, conniving and cruel before I'd even taken six steps across the living-room floor. She was crying, though. I could hear the tears in her voice. I walked toward the kitchen and quietly observed from the doorway. Julie was at the granite counter using a melon baller on a ripe cantaloupe, going at it as though she was cutting out her daughter's heart. Shannon paced around the island punching numbers into her cell phone as she hollered ugly words at her mother. I watched the two of them perform the dance I remembered all too well.

Shannon was first to notice me. She closed her phone, dropped her gaze to the floor, then walked past me out of the room.

"Bye, Nana," she muttered beneath her breath, and I heard the front door open, then slam shut.

Julie set down the melon baller and raised her hand to her forehead. Her eyes were closed and she looked as if she had a headache. I wasn't sure what to say. What words would have helped me when I was in her position? What words would have gotten through my thick skull?

"What's going on?" I asked.

Julie wiped her hands on a paper towel, then leaned against the counter, arms folded across her chest. "She insists she's leaving in a week with Tanner," she said. "They had a big party here while I was out of town, Mom. Dozens of kids. Alcohol and who knows what else. She and Tanner slept in my bed."

Petty little things in the big picture, I thought. I felt tired. I thought of Isabel on the bay at midnight with Ned. Of me out in the blue-berry lot with Ross. "It's a never-ending circle," I said, "and Shannon is doomed to face it with her own child in another seventeen years or so."

Julie looked at me as though she didn't understand a word I'd spoken.

We heard the front door open, and in a moment, Lucy and Ethan came into the kitchen. Ethan didn't even acknowledge me as he walked over to Julie for an embrace. Julie shut her eyes tightly as she held him. Then she backed away, her hands on either side of his face.

"How are you?" She looked into his eyes, and I knew there was something strong growing between the two of them. I'd suspected it at the barbecue, but now I knew it for sure.

Lucy put her arm around my waist. "Did you tell her?" she asked Julie, who shook her head.

"Tell me what?" I asked. "What's going on?"

Ethan looked at me. "My father killed himself last night," he said.

My God. I wasn't sure if I'd said those words out loud or to my-self. That was not what I'd expected to hear. I felt light-headed, and Ethan grabbed a chair from beneath the kitchen table and slipped it under me. I held his arm as I sat down, then I looked into his red-rimmed eyes. "I'm so sorry, Ethan," I said.

He nodded.

"You sit, too," Julie said to him, and he didn't argue as she led him to a chair. He looked as numb as I felt.

"He confessed, Mom," Julie said. "You were right. Isabel had writ-ten that note to him. After he read it, he told Ned not to meet her on the platform that night so that he could meet her himself to try to convince her not to tell Daddy about...about you and Mr. Chap-man. He said it was an accident, that Izzy lost her balance and he tried to grab her arm to keep her from falling. He didn't realize that she'd hit her head. He didn't know until the next day that she drowned."

"At least that's what he claimed," Ethan said, rubbing his eyes.

"Poor old soul," I said. If I'd agreed to see Ross, might I have prevented his suicide? That was something I could never know. I looked at Ethan. I wanted to lift a bit of his sorrow. "Your father was as flawed as any human that ever walked the earth," I said, "but I believe him. I don't think he was capable of premeditated murder, especially not of a girl he believed was his daughter." The thought of Isabel's last minutes came to me again, as it did too often, and I brushed it away. I would deal with that later. Not here. Not now. "The person I feel the worst about is poor George Lewis," I added.

Julie suddenly started to cry. Ethan got to his feet and pulled her gently into his arms again, and I felt grateful to him for coming back into her life the way he had. Despite my earlier misgivings about the two of them getting together, I liked seeing the comfortable intimacy between them and I was glad something good had come out of this mess. But although Ethan was sweet in his attempt to comfort her, Julie was inconsolable. She couldn't seem to stop crying. Ethan looked past her at me. "She's always felt as though everyone blamed her for Isabel's death," he explained.

Oh no, I thought. Was that my fault? I stood up and moved next to the two of them.

"Sweetheart," I said, rubbing Julie's back. "I never blamed you." That wasn't precisely the truth. In the beginning, I *did* blame her, but it was a short-lived anger. I knew in my heart she'd never meant to hurt her sister. My anger toward her had evolved into a grief that had consumed me for a long time. It never occurred to me to take back the cruel things I'd said to Julie in the hours and days after we lost Isabel. Julie had seemed fine to my grief-blinded eyes. I saw now how she'd suffered, and I also saw my opportunity to address the mother-daughter strife that seemed to plague our family.

"Julie," I said, "if anyone besides Ross is to blame for Isabel's death, it's me."

Julie was quick to shake her head. Pulling away from Ethan, she brushed the tears from her face with her hands. "No, Mom," she said. "Don't even think that."

"It's the truth," I said. "I pushed Isabel away from me by trying to hold on to her too tightly." I looked hard into my daughter's face. "Do you hear me, Julie?" I asked. "Do you? I don't want to see you make that same mistake with Shannon."

CHAPTER 48

Julie

I had prepared plenty of food—melon and strawberries, bagels and cream cheese, scrambled eggs and sausage—but none of us ate more than a bite. We sat in the dining room, since it was too hot to eat on the porch. The eggs and sausage grew cold as we talked, as we washed the air clear of things never before said. If I'd only had the courage to talk to my mother decades ago about Isabel, my suffering—and I am sure hers, as well—would have been far less. Instead, I grew into adulthood nursing my guilt, still holding on to a twelve-year-old's version of all that had happened. Why had we spent forty years tiptoeing around the elephant in the room? Did we think it would go away, that if we starved it by ignoring it, it would shrink until it was skinny enough to slip out the door? I vowed to never again make that mistake. Bringing things out in the open when they happened could be painful, but it was like a getting a vaccination: the needle stung, but that was nothing compared to getting the disease.

After brunch, Ethan went upstairs to my room for a nap. His

daughter, Abby, and her husband and baby were coming over later and together, we would make the arrangements for Ethan's father.

Lucy left after helping Mom and me clean up a bit; she had a ZydaChicks rehearsal to go to. My mother stayed with me a while longer, though. Once the kitchen was clean, she sat with me on the sofa in the living room, holding my hand. Or maybe I was holding hers. Either way, I liked the way it felt.

"There's one other thing we never talk about," I said to her after we'd sat that way for a few minutes. "Something I never tell you."

"What's that, Julie?" she asked.

"How much I love you," I said. "I always told you that when I was a kid, and then somewhere along the line, I got out of the habit. You're going to hear it from me a lot from now on."

"I knew it even when you didn't say it," she said. "But it *would* be wonderful to hear."

"Also," I was on a roll, "I think you're smart and beautiful and vibrant. And I feel lucky to have you as my mother." I couldn't believe how good it felt to get those words out! "I hope I'm just like you when I'm your age."

She chuckled. "I'll ask Micky D's to hold a job open for you," she said, but then she sobered. She gave my hand a squeeze. "I…I made light of what you just said, didn't I?" she said, shaking her head with a sigh. "That's what we do in this family. When we get too close to the honest truth, we start squirming and back away." She turned to face me. "I heard every word you said, Julie, and I'll treasure them always. I love you, dear."

We hugged, and I could have sat with her arms around me for hours. I felt blessed, my happiness at that moment marred only by my thoughts about the man sleeping in my bed upstairs. He would never have the chance I was having to heal his own family with truth and forgiveness.

When my mother left, I sat in my office—it seemed like months since I'd actually *written* in that room—and began making phone calls to funeral homes in the Lakewood area. I wanted to gather information to give Ethan when he woke up. I didn't really know what I was doing. This was the first time I'd ever been in the position of handling such arrangements. For Ethan, it would be the third time in less than two years.

I was hanging up the phone when I heard Shannon's car in the driveway. She came into the house through the front door and headed up the stairs, probably to do some more packing.

"Shannon?" I called.

Her footsteps stopped.

"What?"

"Could you come here, please?"

She didn't budge. I could picture her standing there, debating whether to continue to her room or come to my office. I heard her sigh. In a moment, she was standing in my office doorway. She didn't look at me directly. I guessed that she expected me to continue our argument from earlier in the day.

"Sit down, honey," I said, trying with my tone of voice to let her know I had no intention of fighting.

She hesitated, then walked over to the love seat and sat down. I rolled my chair closer to her.

"I've been doing a lot of thinking this morning," I said. "I love you very much. You know I don't want you to go to Colorado, but if you want to go, I won't stand in your way." The words nearly choked me, but I got them out.

Shannon looked puzzled for a moment, as though she wondered if she'd stumbled into the right house.

"Are you kidding?" she asked.

I shook my head. "I won't lie to you, Shannon. I'm sick about you leaving. I want to lock you in your room and keep you here. I'll be so worried about you, because you are the most important thing in the world to me." My voice broke ever so slightly. I doubted she'd even noticed. "But you can go if that's what you want," I said. "Just remember that you're always—*always*—welcome to come home, with no recriminations. Okay?"

She'd broken into a slow smile as I spoke. Now she stood up, leaning over to kiss my cheek. "Thanks, Mom," she said. "That is totally cool."

She left the room, heading up the stairs again, and I could hear the little beeps as she dialed her cell phone, calling Tanner to tell him the good news.

EPILOGUE

Lucy

"She's never going to fall," Ethan said, glancing over his shoulder at Abby, who was balanced on one ski behind the boat. She looked relaxed, almost bored, as she cut across the water, and Ethan might have *sounded* like he was griping, but he was smiling with pride. He'd told me that he'd taught his daughter to ski when she was ten. Now, at twenty-seven, skiing was as easy to her as walking.

I was holding Abby's daughter, eighteen-month-old Clare, on my lap. "See Mommy?" I leaned down to say in her ear.

"Mommy ski!" Clare said, pointing at her mother.

"Yes, she sure is," I said.

"We'll get her down." Ethan's tone was malevolent, and he turned the steering wheel so that Abby would have to cross the wake of a much larger boat. I could hear her laughter over the sound of the motor as she realized what her father was doing.

"Your grandpop's a meanie," I said to Clare.

"Pop Pop's a meanie!" Clare said.

Ethan was anything but mean. He'd been my brother-in-law since

January when he and Julie got married, and he was a doll. I was staying with the two of them for a few weeks this summer, and he and Abby and I had gone skiing nearly every day since my arrival.

As for *me* and men, though, I thought I was finished with them. My life was too full to add a man to the mix. Between my students, the ZydaChicks, my women's support group and my ever-expanding family, I really had no room for anything or anyone else.

Abby rode the wake of the larger boat like a champion mogul skier, elegantly rising and falling over the rolling water. But then she raised her hand and waved at us, letting us know that she was willing to give Ethan or me a turn.

Ethan slowed the boat and Abby dropped smoothly into the water as we circled around to pick her up. She climbed the ladder into the boat, her body long limbed and tan, and she gently shook her short wet hair in front of Clare's face, tickling the little girl's nose and making her giggle.

"You go, Luce," Ethan said to me.

I handed Clare to her mother, climbed over the side of the boat and jumped into the water. Abby tossed the skis down to me and, as usual, I struggled to put them on. I was pitiful at every aspect of skiing: putting on the skis, getting back into the boat, and most significantly, staying up for longer than a few seconds. All the stops and starts probably drove Ethan and Abby crazy, but they never complained and I loved every minute of the adventure—especially knowing that I was in water that was way over my head, and I was one-hundred-percent certain that I was not going to drown.

Maria

Something I figured out long ago was that life rarely turns out the way you expect it to. How could I have predicted that, at eighty-two years of age, I would find myself planting geraniums in the Chapmans' window boxes? For that matter, how could I have predicted that my daughter, Julie, would one day be a Chapman?

By the time Julie and Ethan were married, I think we'd all gotten over the astonishing fact that we were embracing the son of Isabel's killer, and we welcomed him into the family. No one had suffered more than Ethan during the past couple of years. He'd lost his entire nuclear family and learned a terrible truth about the father he'd idolized. I came to admire his life-embracing attitude and his resiliency. He was one of us—a survivor.

Julie and Ethan divided their time between Julie's house in Westfield and this old bungalow in Bay Head Shores. I hadn't wanted to come here at first. The thought turned my stomach, but I didn't keep my discomfort to myself. I'd discovered that you can still learn things when you're an old lady. Maybe you couldn't change the core of your personality—that ingrained identity deep inside you—but you *could* change how you dealt with the world. The way I'd changed was that I didn't keep things to myself anymore. If I had a gripe or a sorrow or a joy, I would call one of my girls and share it with her. That's why, when Julie first suggested I spend time with them at Ethan's house, I told her how hard that would be for me. Julie listened to everything I had to say on the subject and then said they would love to have me, but she understood my concerns and the decision was ultimately mine to make. Given the choice between staying home in Westfield while my family built new summertime traditions without me, or facing my fears and becoming a contributing part of their future, I chose the latter. It hadn't been as hard as I'd expected. The world looked different from Ethan's backyard than it did from ours. I spent as much time with them as I could—when I could get away from Micky D's, of course.

Julie

It was so peaceful on the sunporch. I had my computer on my lap and a cup of coffee on the table next to me. I could hear the snipping of the pruning shears as my mother worked on the window boxes and planters in the front yard. I was writing what I expected to be the last book in the Granny Fran series. Fran Gallagher was eighty-four now, and it was time for her to retire. I planned to leave the impression that she'd be called in occasionally to help her younger, greener colleagues solve their crimes, but really, it was time for her to move to Florida, find a nice old fellow to pal around with and rest on her laurels.

My fans wouldn't be happy with me for ending my series, but I was ready to move on to something new and different. I longed to write a story with a little more meat on its bones. I wanted to delve into life's experiences, both the good and the bad. I wanted to write books filled with heartache and love, evil and goodness, death and rebirth—all those highs and lows that made up reality. Some of my readers would follow me along that path; others would mourn the loss of the lighthearted escape reading I'd given them for so many years. But I would be writing what felt right for me now, and I couldn't wait to get started.

I looked up from my work as I pondered the scene in which Fran realizes she is tired of solving other people's mysteries. The canal was calm, the tide slack as a sailboat made its quiet way toward the river. Across the water from where I sat, a handful of African-American men were fishing. Were any of them related to the Lewises? I would never know.

I went to see Wanda Lewis in the fall. She was Wanda Jackson now, and she had four sons and countless grandchildren, but no amount of family could make up for the loss of her brother. She had not welcomed me, and I didn't stay long. I didn't blame her for the chilly reception, but one thing I'd come to understand was that I couldn't undo the past. I could only try to learn from it.

The sound of a motor disturbed the quiet morning, and I looked up to see Ethan steering his boat toward the dock from the direction of the bay. Ethan, Lucy, Abby and baby Clare went out nearly every morning while I wrote. Once they came inside, I would put my work away. I was trying to learn to balance my time between work and play. I was not very good at it yet, but I was improving.

Everyone got out of the boat, but only Ethan walked toward the house. Abby and Lucy took Clare into the open side of the dock, holding her hands as they walked with her down the slope into the water that had once held such fear for my younger sister.

Ethan opened the door to the porch and came inside, taking off his sunglasses.

"How's Granny Fran doing?" he asked. His hair and his bathing suit were wet. I knew he'd had fun this morning.

"She's on her last legs," I told him.

He bent over to kiss me and I could smell the saltwater on his skin. "And how's Granny Julie?" he asked.

As if on cue, Kira Sellers Stroh, who'd been sleeping peacefully in her Portacrib on the other side of the porch, began to whimper.

"Granny Julie couldn't be any happier," I said.

This year had certainly been full of surprises. Shannon *did* go to Colorado with Tanner, but she was there less than twenty-four hours when she called to tell me she was coming home.

"We got to his house and all his friends were there waiting to meet me," she said, when I picked her up at the airport. "They were really nice, Mom, but the youngest one was *twenty-five,* and I thought, 'What am I doing here? What am I doing with this old guy I barely know?'"

Ethan walked over to the Portacrib and lifted Kira into his arms. He kissed her temple and rocked her a little, cooing to her.

"Is Shannon napping?" he asked.

"Uh-huh." Shannon had been up with the Kira most of the night. The baby had been born at exactly midnight on the twenty-first of December and she'd been a night owl ever since.

I moved my laptop to the floor and Ethan lowered Kira into my arms, then sat down next to me. I snuggled the baby against my chest. I liked it when she was half-awake like this, in that gurgling, not-quite-ready-to-eat state, easily placated by a little cuddling. I pressed my lips to her thick hair and inhaled the scent of baby shampoo. She was a beautiful child, with her mother's—and her great-aunt Isabel's—dark eyes, dark hair, and double rows of jet-black eyelashes. She and Shannon lived with us, and although Tanner sent money every month, I contributed as well. Shannon still gave cello lessons at the music store and would be entering the music program at Drew University in the fall, commuting from home. She had a hard road ahead of her. I'd given up analyzing whether I was helping her too much or too little. I was just trying to follow my heart.

Ethan leaned his head against my shoulder, rubbing Kira's back as we watched Abby, Lucy and Clare splashing and laughing in the dock. Then Lucy hoisted Clare onto her shoulders for the walk up the slope. From upstairs, I could hear the sound of water running and knew that Shannon was up, and the front screen door squeaked open as my mother came inside. In a moment, everyone would be on the porch.

I covered Ethan's hand where it rested on Kira's back. "Is this how you thought your life would turn out?" I asked him.

"Are you kidding?" he said. "I couldn't have dreamed up anything this good."

I laughed, then returned my attention to the granddaughter in my arms. I wondered what sort of challenge Kira would present to Shannon when *she* became a teenager. I could imagine Shannon struggling to hold on to her child, trying to rein her in to keep her safe.

And I would be there to help her let go.